PRAISE [FOR]

Queen of the Night

"The novel is infused with an operatic sensibility . . . *The Queen of the Night* is a celebration of these women of creativity, ingenuity, endurance, mastery, and grace—a gala in their honor."
—Kelly Gardiner, *New York Times*

"Epic . . . Brilliantly extravagant in its twists and turns and its wide-rang[ing . . .] [cast of characters.]"
—Julia Felsenthal, *Vogue*

"[A] . . . [C]hee's writing . . . icts is dazzling . . . glittering, luxur[iant] . . . ntion, from its c[. . .]
[. . . Wall Street Journal]

"A[. . .] [you]ng woman's tur[ns . . .] [sop]rano at the Par[. . .] [Hubba]rd, *People*

"A[. . .] identity, betra[. . .] ns and roses, ma[. . .] [w]ill keep the rea[. . .] Begley, *Time*

"Gorgeous prose . . . Extraordinarily beautiful and dramatic, a brilliant performance."
—Wendy Smith, *Washington Post*

"[A] postmodern bodice ripper . . . It just sounds terrific. It sounds like opera . . . It offers a rare, intriguing psychology: the heart as a buried place, where someone is hiding, singing—words you can't quite hear."
—Joan Acocella, *The New Yorker*

"[A] wild opera of a novel . . . Swift, smart, immersive, and gorgeous."
—Garth Greenwell, *Guardian*

"A lush, imaginative novel, one that you'll hope never ends."
—Claire Luchette, *Travel + Leisure*

"A multi-stranded, thoroughly researched epic."
—Joe Fassler, *Atlantic*

"*The Queen of the Night* is an astonishing universe into which its lucky readers can dissolve completely, metamorphosing alongside its shape-shifting protagonist. Lilliet Berne steals her name from a gravestone and launches into a life of full-throated song; her voice is an intoxicant, and this book is a glorious performance. Chee's enveloping, seductive prose is perfectly matched to the circus world of the opera."
—Karen Russell

"A luminous tale of power and passion. Chee gives us an unforgettable heroine and a rich cast of characters—many of them real historical figures. The story dazzles and surprises right up until the final page."
—J. Courtney Sullivan

"One doesn't so much read Alexander Chee's *The Queen of the Night* as one is bewitched by it. Beneath its epic sweep, gorgeous language, and haunting details is the most elemental, and eternal, of narratives: that of the necessities and perils of self-reinvention, and the sorrow and giddiness of aspiring to a life of artistic transcendence."
—Hanya Yanagihara

"Alexander Chee packs his extraordinary second novel, *The Queen of the Night*, to the seams with music, love, misery, and secrets. The kind of book—world—characters—you could live inside, happily, for days and days and never once want to come up for air."
—Kelly Link

"A night at an opera you'll wish never-ending." —Helen Oyeyemi

"*Queen* is as operatic as its shape-shifting narrator . . . This is classical, full-throated melodrama, not so much a meditation as an aria on fate."
—Boris Kachka, *New York*

"Triumphant . . . Chock-full of romance, intrigue, and sprinklings of real history, *The Queen of the Night* is the first truly epic novel of the year."
—Jeva Lange, *The Week*

"Sweeping, historical, and baroque . . . Glittering."
—Constance Grady, *Vox*

"While the book does owe much to the extravagant spirit of mid-nineteenth-century novels and operas, it pays its debt with grace. It is wonderfully free of the faintly smirking self-consciousness and knowingness that so often attends such ventures. It works on its own terms, boldly."
—Katherine A. Powers, *Newsday*

"*Queen* joins ranks with the best historical novels and made me think, not infrequently as I read, of one of my all-time favorites—E. L. Doctorow's *Ragtime*."
—Sonya Chung, *The Millions*

"A fantasia set in a world of opera, dance halls, and the court intrigues of Second Empire Paris." —Trisha Collopy, *Minneapolis Star Tribune*

"The urgency with which Chee has Lilliet telling her tales . . . keeps the reader off balance, racing through the pages without any possibility of stopping for fear of falling flat. It is that kind of novel, the kind one devours in a weekend or stays up too late reading."
—Ilana Masad, *Electric Literature*

"Impossibly deep and lyrical . . . You'll be hard-pressed to find a more complete reading experience this year."
—Jonathon Sturgeon, *Flavorwire*

"Epic and gorgeous . . . It's a tale of glamour, glitter, secrets, and intrigue."
—Lincoln Michel, *Men's Journal*

"A sprawling and operatic novel." —Jane Hu, *The Awl*

"Remarkable . . . Reading this book is deeply pleasurable, and its incorporation of historical detail feels seamless . . . It has all the trappings of the period: the artifice, the meticulously researched details, but at its heart is the story of a woman, lost, in love, and singing in the dark." —Natalie Bakopoulos, *San Francisco Chronicle*

"Sprawling and dramatic . . . Plotted with baroque intricacy."
—Nicholas Mancusi, *Bomb*

"A brilliant bright star of a book . . . A dizzying, delightful carousel ride through traveling circus troupes, harrowing prison escapes, the pleasure dens of courtesans, and an empress's palace wardrobe that would make Lady Gaga's look basic . . . *The Queen of the Night* is a soaring falcon." —Tabitha Blankenbiller, *Bustle*

"A fabulous saga of an indomitable woman . . . Its like going to a grand opera; or reading Proust. Take your pick."
—Thomas Urquhart, *Portland Press Herald*

"A singular and powerful novel . . . Its plot is gripping . . . but it's also a fascinating look at art, isolation, and acclaim."
—Tobias Carroll, *Vol. 1 Brooklyn*

"A grand, impeccably researched rollercoaster of a picaresque . . . *The Queen of the Night* unleashes the kind of thrill found only when you hear the voiceless sing." —John H. Maher, *Entropy*

"*The Queen of the Night* is a radical act of art-making . . . Quite simply, it's a very intricate devotion to character and story, to believing in what an act of language can become."
—Carrie Lorig, *ArtsATL*

BOOKS BY ALEXANDER CHEE

Edinburgh

The Queen of the Night

The
QUEEN
of the
NIGHT

ALEXANDER CHEE

Mariner Books
Houghton Mifflin Harcourt
BOSTON · NEW YORK

This novel is for D. S., who likes to write his initials in his books.

———————————

First Mariner Books edition 2016
Copyright © 2016 by Alexander Chee

For information about permission to reproduce selections from
this book, write to trade.permissions@hmhco.com or to Permissions,
Houghton Mifflin Harcourt Publishing Company, 3 Park Avenue,
19th Floor, New York, New York 10016.

www.hmhco.com

Library of Congress Cataloging-in-Publication Data is available.
ISBN 978-0-618-66302-6 (hardcover)   ISBN 978-0-544-92547-2 (pbk)

Book design by Melissa Lotfy

Printed in the United States of America
DOC 10 9 8 7 6 5 4 3 2 1

Act I

The Curse

One

WHEN IT BEGAN, it began as an opera would begin, in a palace, at a ball, in an encounter with a stranger who, you discover, has your fate in his hands. He is perhaps a demon or a god in disguise, offering you a chance at either the fulfillment of a dream or a trap for the soul. A comic element—the soprano arrives in the wrong dress —and it decides her fate.

The year was 1882. The palace was the Luxembourg Palace; the ball, the Sénat Bal, held at the beginning of autumn. It was still warm, and so the garden was used as well. I was the soprano.

I was Lilliet Berne.

The dress was a Worth creation of pink taffeta and gold silk, three pink flounces that belled out from a bodice embroidered in a pattern of gold wings. A net of gold-ribbon bows covered the skirt and held the flounces up at the hem. The fichu seemed to clasp me from behind as if alive—how had I not noticed? At home it had not seemed so garish. I nearly tore it off and threw it to the floor.

I'd paid little attention as I'd dressed that evening, unusual for me, and so I now paused as I entered, for the mirror at the entrance showed to me a woman I knew well, but in a hideous dress. As if it had changed as I'd sat in the carriage, transforming from what I had thought I'd put on into this.

In the light of my apartment I had thought the pink was darker; the gold more bronze; the bows smaller, softer; the effect more Italian. It was not, though, and here in the ancient mirrors of the Luxembourg Palace, under the blazing chandeliers, I saw the truth.

There were a few of us who had our own dressmaker's forms at Worth's for fitting us when we were not in Paris, and I was one, but perhaps he had forgotten me, confused me with someone else or her daughter. It would have been a very beautiful dress, say, for a very young girl from the Loire. Golden hair and rosy cheeks, pink lipped and fair. Come to Paris and I will get you a dress, her Parisian uncle might have said. And then we will go to a ball. It was that sort of dress.

Everything not of the dress was correct. The woman in the mirror was youthful but not a girl, dark hair parted and combed close to the head, figure good, posture straight, and waist slim. My skin had become very pale during the Siege of Paris some years before and never changed back, but this had become chic somehow, and I always tried to be grateful for it.

My carriage had already driven off to wait for me, the next guests arriving. If I called for my driver, the wait to leave would be as long as the wait to arrive, perhaps longer, and I would be there at the entrance, compelled to greet everyone arriving, which would be an agony. A footman by the door saw my hesitation at the mirror and tilted his head toward me, as if to ask after my trouble. I decided the better, quicker escape for now was to enter and hide in the garden until I could leave, and so I only smiled at him and made my way into the hall as he nodded proudly and shouted my name to announce me.

Lilliet Berne, La Générale!

Cheers rang out and all across the room heads turned; the music stopped and then began again, the orchestra now performing the refrain from the Jewel Song aria from *Faust* to honor my recent performances in the role of Marguerite. I looked over to see the director salute to me, bowing deeply before turning back to continue. The crowd began to applaud, and so I paused and curtsied to them even as I hoped to move on out of the circle of their agonizing scrutiny.

At any other time, I would have welcomed this. Instead, I nearly groaned into my awful dress.

The applause deepened, and as they began to cheer again, I stayed a moment longer. For I was their creature, Lilliet Berne, La Générale. Newly returned to Paris after a year spent away, the Falcon soprano whose voice was so delicate it was rumored she endangered it even by speaking, her silences as famous as her performances. This voice was said to turn arias into spells, hymns into love songs, simple requests into commands, my suitors driven to despair in every country I visited, but perhaps especially here.

In the Paris press, they wrote stories of me constantly. I was receiving and rejecting gifts of incomprehensible splendor; men were leaving their wives to follow me; princes were arriving bearing ancient family jewels, keys to secret apartments, secret estates. I was unbearably kind or unbelievably cruel, more beautiful than a woman could be or secretly hideous, supernaturally pale or secretly mulatto, or both, the truth hidden under a plaster of powder. I was innocent or I was the devil unleashed, I had nearly caused wars, I had kept them from happening. I was never in love, I had never loved, I was always in love. Each performance could be my last, each performance had been my last, the voice was true, the voice was a fraud.

The voice, at least, was true.

In my year away, the theaters that had once thrilled me — La Scala in Milan, La Monnaie in Brussels, the Mariinsky in Saint Petersburg — no longer excited me as they once did. I stayed always in the apartments given over to the company singers, and soon it seemed as if the rooms were a single place that stretched the length of Europe and opened onto its various capitals.

The details of my roles had become the only details of my life. Onstage, I was the druidic priestess, the Hebrew slave in Egypt, the Parisian courtesan dying of consumption, the beautiful orphan who sang as she walked in her sleep, falling into and out of trouble and never waking up until the end. Offstage, I felt dim, shuttered, a prop, the stick under the puppet. I seemed a stranger to myself, a changeling placed here in my life at some point I couldn't remember, and the glass of the mirror at the entrance to the palace seemed made from the same amber of the dream that surrounded me, a life that was not life, and which I could not seem to escape no matter where I went or what I sang.

And so their celebration of me that night at the ball, sincere as it was, felt as if it were happening in the life neighboring mine, visible through a glass.

I tell you I was distracted, but it was much more than that. For I was also focused intensely, waiting for one thing and one thing only, my attention turned toward something I couldn't quite see but was sure was there, coming for me through the days ahead. I'd had a premonition in accepting the role of Marguerite that, in returning to Paris this time, I would be here for a meeting with my destiny. Here I would find what would transform me, what would return me to life and make this life the paradise I was so sure it should be.

I had been back in Paris for a little more than a month now, though, and my hopes for this had not yet come true, and so I waited with an increasingly dull vigilance, still sure my appointed hour was ahead of me, and yet I did not know what it was or where it would be.

It was here, of course.

I rose finally from a third curtsy and was halfway to the doors to the terrace when I noticed a man crossing the floor quickly, dressed in a beautiful new evening suit. He was ruddy against the white of his shirt and tie, if handsomely so. His hair was neatly swept back from his face, his blond moustache and whiskers clean and trim, his eyes clear. I nodded as he came to stand before me. He bowed gravely, even ostentatiously.

Forgive me this intrusion! he said, as he stood upright. The diva who throws her suitors' diamonds in the trash. The beggars of Paris must salute as you walk by before they carry your garbage shoulder high.

I made to walk past him, though I smiled to think of his greeting. I had, in fact, thrown diamonds in the garbage twice, a feint each time. My maid knew to retrieve them. I did it once to make sure the story would be told in the press, the second time for the story to be believed. I was trying to teach my princes to buy me dresses instead of jewels—jewels had become ostentatious in the new Paris, with many reformed libertines now critical of the Empire's extravagance, and there was little point to a jewel you couldn't wear.

I enjoyed your magnificent performance in *Faust* last night—it was tremendously subtle, very moving, he said.

He waited to see if his flattery would affect me. It did. I also believed that last night's performance had been my finest night as Marguerite. And as he was very awkward, like someone who had never done what he was about to do, I stopped for him, thinking to be kind.

I made to curtsy to him for the compliment, as I had just previously, and he laughed. No! Please. Let me bend to you, and with that, he knelt as he took my hand. I am Frédéric Simonet, a writer. I've longed to meet you, he said, but never more than tonight. I have a proposition for you, if you'll allow me a moment of your time. There are no loathsome diamonds involved, I promise, unless you insist. Will you hear me out?

I held my hands out and smiled by way of invitation.

Last year I was at a dinner in Rome, recounting a favorite memory, of a girl singer at the Exposition Universelle in 1867. Did you see her? They called her the Settler's Daughter, and she was said to have been rescued from the savages and able to sing only a single song her mother had taught her—and was entirely unable to speak otherwise. She was performing in a show from the colonies, Canada, I think. Her song moved the Emperor to give her a token of his right there in the hall. A tiny ruby brooch of a rose. Shortly after, the papers reported she'd vanished, escaped into the Paris surroundings. I never saw any sign of her again. In the months after, I wondered what had become of her and eventually even checked with the Conservatoire, as I wanted to see if perhaps she had come to them, perhaps to be made over into one of their mediocre sopranos. They said they had no knowledge of a singer of this kind. Incredible, yes?

I nodded, and he continued.

I then thought nothing of it for years until I bought a property in the Marais, a beautiful *hôtel,* and as it was prepared for me to occupy, the workers made an extraordinary find. The young singer's possessions, even the ruby brooch! And what seems to be her diary of her life here in Paris. It is quite plainly hers. She taught herself to speak French—it even contains her practice lessons. She abandoned it and her things, having lived, it would seem, in that *hôtel* in the Marais. And it was when I saw the brooch that I remembered my search for her. It was all found in what had been the noble family's chapel, as if she had held some private ceremony there. As if she meant to return for it all and never did—it was there the novel truly came to me. I should think they will fetch a fair price at auction, should I ever sell them. It was such incredible luck. I was completely under her spell that day, and here were her things! Everything but her. It felt like an order from the gods to undertake this work.

Of course, I'm sure she's some maudlin chimney sweep now, raking out stoves for a living. But a chimney-sweep ending would sell few books, he added. So I wrote my own. The novel is called *Le Cirque du Monde Déchu*. We follow her into a life of degradation as a *fille en carte* and her subsequent redemption through love. Like Zola's *Nana*, but as an *opéra-bouffe-féerie*, of sorts. Or it will be.

He paused here dramatically. Which is why I have come to speak with you. Some of the other guests at that now-fateful dinner in Rome recalled her as well, and among them was a composer, recently a winner of the Prix de Rome and something of a protégé of Verdi's. I believe he is planning to be here tonight. He was likewise moved by her and vowed that evening if I were to write the libretto, he would make an opera of it.

Here he paused again, summoning his courage.

It is our desire to have you originate the role of the singer. It would be a stupendous coup, we feel, and would ensure the opera's success. And you, well, who better for the Settler's Daughter than the singer who does not speak?

Yes, came the thought at last. Who better?

For I had also seen the young singer he spoke of. I had been her. I knew all about her.

The brooch was an imperial trifle, a tiny thing to an emperor, I think, but for me at the time, so much more. Made of rubies, several to each petal, set in either platinum or white gold—I had it before I knew the difference—the stem inlaid with jade. There was even a thorn. At his mention of it, the flower had glowed in the air between us, a tiny phantom, and then was gone.

Here it was, the source of my premonition, the meeting with my destiny.

My little game of not speaking in public came from when I was her. A circus ruse, theatrics done for the audience. Not one of us in that little act had been as we said we were. "Lilliet Berne" was in every way my greatest performance, but almost no one knew this to be true.

The various shocks of this conversation—that it seemed my life had been the basis for this man's new novel, that it was to be an opera in which they wanted me to create the role, that he had in all likelihood effects I'd long believed lost—all had the result of casting the life I led now as a disguise, assembled in haste, to cover over the one he described. I struggled to consider a reaction, but I felt as if I were misremembering halfway through a performance the role I was playing—on the verge of singing an aria from *Norma,* say, but within *Don Giovanni.*

In an opera this moment would be the signal the story had begun, that the heroine's past had come for her, intent on a review of her sins decreed by the gods. This writer perhaps a god in disguise, like Athena, or a demon, say, as in *Faust.* If he were either, though, his disguise as a mortal was impeccable. He was for now the picture of a nervous if handsome man, waiting for me to answer, and still I could not move, I found.

When I did not so much as nod to him, he smiled and said nervously, Perhaps . . . you can sing me your answer, yes? Would you at least be interested? He leaned in as he said this.

I managed to offer him my arm, for I still meant to enter the garden. I intended to speak to him, and given my reputation, this also required privacy. He accepted, and I made a gesture toward the ter-

race. He led me that way. We passed through the doors and down
the lawn, and then I released his arm and turned so that I would be
in shadow and his face, lit by the chandeliers inside, behind me. I
wanted to see him clearly as I spoke to him. I needed to see his reaction in his eyes.

If this was a joke, perhaps, or some strange, unforeseen malice.

He looked at me expectantly, even with fear, as I set a finger on
his mouth before he could respond or interrupt. Yes, I said. I will
speak to you of this.

His eyes were sincere, I noted, as I began.

The faith you have in my abilities is wonderful, I said. And the
origination of a role is the one honor that has eluded me thus far.
Thank you. I do admit to being intrigued. I am committed for now
to *Faust* this season, and then Verdi's *Un Ballo in Maschera* next, in
London, but I will look into my schedule to see what room there
could be in the year ahead. Do you know how far the music has
come or what schedule you intend?

Forgive me my earlier impudence, he said, gesturing back inside.
I . . . Thank you! You honor me. I do not have these answers. We
have neither music nor schedule as yet. Perhaps you will come and
meet my new friend? I believe he's arriving with the Dumas set.
When we pass through to dinner, I can bring you to him.

I can see them by the light of their cigars. There, he said. Do you
see them, on the balcony above? Come, let's see if we can find our
way.

He gestured to a crowd of gentlemen shadowed by the gaslights
of the courtyard, who waved back.

I waved as well.

I return to this moment frequently, for it was when everything
that came next in my life was decided. Meeting the composer in
this dress was out of the question, though I could not say this. I was
eager, also, to leave, or at least be alone, even for a moment, for this
offer no longer felt like fate but something disguised as fate, a dangerous ruse meant to draw me into a trap.

The fit of a dress determines the stride of a woman—whether

she can bend at the waist, sit, or ride—and so for a woman to change her dress was to change even the way she walked and the speed at which she ran to her fate.

If I had stayed in the terrible dress, or if a better dress had been made and sent over, if I had gone up the stairs, had dinner with the writer and composer, all would have been different.

But I did not stay.

He extended his arm and made to lead me back in through the crowd.

He saw I had not accepted the invitation to walk in and let his arm drop again with a questioning smile.

Yes, I said. How incredible. The gods indeed.

It's no use, we'll never make it through the crowd right now, he said, looking at the stairs. We shall wait a moment. But what a pleasure it is to hear you express interest.

Thank you, I said.

I can see it right now, he said. If I can ever find a store willing to stock the book between their piles of Zola and Daudet, I think it will be quite a success. But an opera with you in it, well, *Ceci tuera cela,* he said.

This will kill that.

I know this, I said of his quote. What is it from?

It's Hugo, the writer said.

Of course, I said.

I now remembered what I knew of him. I had even heard him at a salon at least once, carrying on about this very quote. He was very mortal after all, then, known for writing novels based almost entirely on the scandals of his friends. While he typically hid their identities, his most recent subjects could be guessed at by whoever dropped him for the season following his most recent book. He knew everyone, though, and was otherwise everywhere.

He nodded, pleased. It's the complaint from a priest character of his, that the written word would destroy cathedrals. The novel would separate us from God. He smiled as he said this.

I should warn you, he said.

I waited as he tried to think of what he would say. My novels . . . it would seem they have a way of coming true. He looked away as he said this, as if ashamed.

It came to me this was perhaps how he explained the way he stole from his friends' lives. Not theft then, but magic.

So if I accept, I said, then . . . for you have not told me of the ending.

She rejoins her circus. You would become an equestrienne in a circus, in love with an angel. He would give up his wings for you, and you . . . well, your voice.

So be it, I said.

He laughed, surprised. Very well then, he said. *Caveat cantante.*

He presented his card, and there, indeed, was the address. I had not seen it in years.

I set his card in the wallet at my wrist and made the excuse of feeling too poorly to stay for dinner, but I promised to read the novel and await the music.

Oh, but you really must at least meet the composer . . . He gestured at the balcony.

Perhaps we will set an appointment, I said. I would like very much to see the brooch.

His face brightened at this. Yes! You must come; I will show you everything.

I offered my hand to say good night and watched his back vanish into the crowd.

I stayed there until I could move again. It had taken all I had just to stand. I then recalled I'd not asked the composer's name, but I couldn't shout to Simonet without a scene. I was to dine with the Verdis the next day, though, and resolved instead to ask after this composer then.

I turned and walked farther into the dark back of the garden, full of fear. Yet once there, my feelings had changed. I was no longer sure I could wait contentedly for my dinner with the Verdis before meeting this composer. I had the impulse to strip this dress off and walk back through the *bal* in just the corset, for the corset, at least, was beautiful. I'd had one other dress ready at another dressmaker's, Félix, the man I relied on besides Worth, and thought sadly of having chosen this dress over that.

The *bal* was full now and wheeled in the night, monstrous, the picture of the fifth act ballet in *Faust,* in the Cave of Queens and Courtesans. The demon Mephistopheles, having rejuvenated Faust and aided him in the seduction of the virtuous young Marguerite, finds him desperate, preoccupied by her imprisonment, as she awaits execution for the crime of killing the child he fathered on her out of wedlock. He has driven her mad. Mephistopheles convenes a ballet orgy with the most famous beauties in history — Cleopatra, Helen, Astarte, Josephine — all to cheer his sad philosopher, who will not be cheered. The queens and courtesans frolic around him with madcap ballerinos and ballerinas, all while Faust thinks only of his doomed beloved.

My cue to enter is when the dancing ends, when I, as Marguerite, appear before Faust, an apparition only he can see. He demands Mephistopheles help him rescue me, the scenery shifts, and Faust is then magically in my prison cell, exhorting me to leave. I refuse him — I refuse to be saved by devils — and beg for forgiveness instead from God and His angels, who descend finally as I die redeemed.

Standing here now, it was as if I'd escaped from the jail into the fifth act ballet, arriving before my cue, a prisoner to this dress.

I withdrew a cigar to console myself, and as I clipped the end, a man I hadn't noticed held out a flame for me. I drew carefully, and as the tip glowed, I saw him and his companion more clearly. They smiled and nodded, and I smiled as well and began to turn away.

Mademoiselle, said the man who had offered his light to me.

My madcap ballerinos, then.

They introduced themselves, but I knew very well who they were. Brother dukes, known to most for their handsome profiles, philanthropic works, enormous wealth, and, most important to me on this evening, their reputation for returning women from an evening in their company with their dresses cut to pieces by sabers — and for supplying those women afterward with more dresses in return, presumably to meet the same fate. Their sabers were said to be quite sharp, and the women never harmed. Many had spoken of this preference but none had ever admitted to submitting to it, except to say, *And if you were never going to wear the dress again . . .* This was usually punctuated with a laugh.

This perhaps my destiny also, then. My luck changing from bad to good in a single trip through the garden.

Ceci tuera cela.

I drew the first saber myself, holding my first new friend's gaze as I plunged it into the taffeta flounces and cut all the way to the hem. He uttered a soft cry of happiness and fell to his knees to press the dress to his face before he lay back in ecstasy, groaning.

When he and his brother were done, the taffeta resembled an enormous flower torn to petals in the grass. Only the gold wings of the bodice remained, the skirt now like a very short tutu, as if I'd been transformed into one of *Faust*'s ballerinas.

I shivered, pleased with the result. I'd learned long ago, for men with pleasures this specific, the rest was of no consequence to them. There was no mark on me as I stood there, free at last of the evening's first mistake, and they were well satisfied.

Fantastic, said the one.

You are our goddess, said the other.

Whatever you ask of us, whatever we can provide, we are at your disposal, the first said.

As we made our way out through the back of the garden to their carriage, the jacket of one of them on my shoulders, the jacket of the other at my waist, I knew what they could provide and handed them my other dressmaker's card.

Félix was in his evening suit when I arrived. He was about to set off for the ball himself—he'd been busy dressing clients and was only just now ready. He threw open the door and pulled us in.

My dears, what possible errand could you be on? he asked, smiling in greeting first at me and then at the young dukes.

Yes, it seemed, the dressmakers of Paris would know them quite well. I walked to Félix's ledger, took his pen from his stand, and wrote:

These good gentlemen have said they will do anything I ask of them tonight. Let us help them keep their word.

I had Félix's assistants box up the ruined dress and send it back to Worth, including a note that said only *Pas comme ça*.

I made my second entrance to the ball in a beaded black silk satin gown, the train behind me like the glittering tail of a serpent. The dukes were on each arm. As we were announced together, the crowd turned and, at the sight of us, roared with delight. The dinner had been served, so many stood on their chairs to see us as I descended again to the garden to enter under a roof of crossed swords made for us by officers who had served in the army with the dukes. As we made our way off the terrace again, I looked to the balcony the writer had indicated to see the men there watching me, their faces changing as they took in what had happened, and then I heard the cheers in the garden and the laughing as the men saluted me.

This was the entrance I deserved. This was what I wanted this composer to see. I had returned for this.

I took a breath. *O Dieu! Que de bijoux!* The opening words to the Jewel Song aria from *Faust* rang out across the garden. There was a shocked silence, and then the orchestra quickly joined in.

This was the song Marguerite sang after being presented with the demon's gift of jewels meant to seduce her into a life of sin. The chaste girl is transformed at once into a woman in love with her beauty, a beauty the jewels reveal to her. It begins and ends in classic soprano entrance style, on long, clear, high notes, as if Gounod knew it should be sung in a palace garden at a Paris ball at night.

I sang it as a gift to the audience, to the composer, to me. I sang it as a taunt to the Fates, too. I was weary of my fears as well as my desires, and so I sang it in simple defiance of all of it, even defying myself. I covered the night and its secrets and regrets in coloratura cavatina, until all that could be remembered was me.

La Générale! the crowd shouted as I finished and came down the stairs, and I lifted both my hands into the air to the crowd, smiling. I could feel the applause beat against my skin as it echoed and grew. A woman screamed as her dress swept the candles on her table and caught fire as she stood on her chair to see me. She was rushed to the fountain, where it was put out, and even this was cheered. The group of officers who had roofed my entrance with their swords then knelt, offering them to me, and the crowd changed from shouting my name to laughter as I took one and mock-knighted them all. *La Générale! La Générale!*

The fear, the feeling of the mad scene, the sense of a trap in wait, even the feeling of destiny, all faded into the applause. I looked afterward for the writer to see if I might finally meet the composer, but as in a fairy tale, he was gone.

~

My maid Doro waited until the afternoon and then came and pulled the shutters in my bedroom open.

I had lain awake in my bed for some time, which was unlike me. I had not slept well. The strange amber twilight I'd lived with was gone, and in its place was some terrible new brightness. I'd gone from feeling lost in a dream to lost in wakefulness, as if I might never sleep again.

No more gaslights as I dress, candles only, I said to Doro.

Of course, she said, and tied back my drapes.

Gaslight is a liar, I said. She smiled as she stepped back. On second thought, gaslight and then a last check by candlelight, I said. My dresses must look good in both. Last night's dress was a foul betrayer. Candles would have caught it out.

Perhaps it only gave its life to make room for the ones to come, she said, and hung the new gown away with a faint smile.

As she walked past, I saw the morning's papers on my tray with my coffee. Between them and the new dress she had not put on me, she likely knew the story. She asked no questions, though, as ever.

I stood; she put on my dressing robe and left me to my coffee by my window. The alley was unchanged. But here, within the robe, I felt myself to be an imposter in my own life.

I was unnerved after I'd been unable to find my new friend and his composer, and had even withdrawn his card again to prove to myself the conversation had been real. I went again to my wallet and withdrew it once more. *Frédéric Simonet*, it read, and with that address, the letters like a fracture, the faintest of cracks along this life of mine.

He had not lied. The Marais house was indeed his.

Of all the accolades heaped at my feet, the one I lacked for was the honor of originating a role, a part written precisely for my voice. This was the opportunity with the power still to entrance me. I could not turn away lightly. For a singer, this was your only immortality. All the rest would pass.

But this story was somehow of my life — and to immortalize it, this was not in me to do.

I went to my closet and touched the new dress, hung there just now.

A singer learned her roles for life — your repertoire was a library of fates held close, like the gowns in this closet, yours until your voice failed. Though when you put them on, it was then you were the something worn — these old tragedies took you over.

Here was my old tragedy, then. Waiting, held open, as if the writer had come to me with my old costume, asking me to put it on.

Had there been even one poster left somewhere, still on the side of a wall, peeling away? The Settler's Daughter had been my first role. I did not know how to be her again, the girl who sang her way over the sea with a single hope in her heart, abandoned here — abandoned, in fact, the morning after she took the Emperor's favor from his hand. To be her again or, really, perform as this odd shadow of her? This was too much.

The life I led now I'd made so I would never be her again. I'd never wanted to be reminded of her and her struggles again. And yet I knew I had always been her; I still was her. I had come back to

Paris once again with one hope in my heart, sure of my moment of destiny, and had been given this, the past I'd hoped to forget, asking to be my future.

An earlier suspicion returned then, renewed, something odd in Simonet's story I could not forget. He had mentioned a chapel, and there was no chapel that I remembered. The other details he'd mentioned were so close to my life, this alone of all of it seemed a lie, even a clue. Less like the work of Fate, then, and more like an imitation of Fate. A plot.

That little ruby flower, I knew the reason I had left that flower behind. I knew just where I had left it, the exact room of the house. It was no chapel. To be recognized from my song that day at the Exposition Universelle, this alone did not bother me. The one secret that mattered to me could be said to be there in the Marais with Simonet.

Whatever this was, it had come from that room.

Two

THE NEXT EVENING, after my performance, I washed the maquillage from my face, exchanged my Marguerite prisoner cap for the wig I wore as a disguise, and easily passed by the men waiting outside the theater, fogging the streets with their hundred kinds of tobacco smoke. I arrived to my dinner with the Verdis that night determined to get an answer on the question of the protégé.

Verdi's verdict on his talent, character, and prospects would make my decision final, I had decided.

Verdi had cooked, as was his custom when circumstances allowed, and Giuseppina usually made sure this was so. The maestro insisted on eating only his favorite foods, even when working abroad, and always only in the ways he could make them. He was as proud of his risotto as he was of *Aida*, perhaps the more so. Whatever problems he encountered as he worked, with publishers, theater owners, or sopranos, his wife knew the recipes to these various foods were the recipe to him. To eat something else would literally unmake him. So he traveled crated down with dry risotto, *maccheroni*, and tagliatelle; anything that could not be brought would be arranged for by Giuseppina at whatever the cost. To dine with him was to dine on food prepared either by him personally or by his chef, who usually came with him, nearly as dear to him as his wife. We did not go much to restaurants.

When I entered their hotel suite, I was greeted by Giuseppina, who took my hand in hers, and led me to the dining room while poking at my wig and laughing.

Who is this woman of mystery? And where is our Lilliet? she said, her voice deepening as if she were onstage. From somewhere out of sight, Verdi laughed in answer as he finished some final preparation.

Giuseppe and Giuseppina were slim, gray in the same ways, oddly twinned, her profile more Roman than his. Her eyes were darker and intent, his filmed over, as if by ghosts; they were like sentinels of a kind, one who watched for the living, the other, the dead.

Verdi had lost his first wife and children when he was a young man, and was rumored to have fathered a secret daughter on Giuseppina, born to them from before their marriage. Giuseppina herself was said to have two other children, back from when she was the imperious soprano lover of Donizetti, but I had never met any of them. When I came to see them, I liked to pretend I was the secret daughter, abandoned and then found again. I wanted to belong to them forever. No one could fit easily between them, though a few had tried.

I sat with them at the small elegant table laid out in their suite, relieved by the familiar smell of his *maccheroni*. Giuseppina asked me about the ball of the night previous — had I really returned in a new gown? And why?

For the Jewel Song, of course, I said. A costume change. And I winked. I was inspired by the way the ball resembled the fifth act ballet.

Verdi looked to her gently before he poured champagne for us all and made a toast.

To Gounod, Faust, and . . . and the fifth act ballet, he said.

We laughed, raised our glasses, and drank.

A ballet is nothing to add lightly, he said. *Un Ballo in Maschera*, did you know it was not always set in America? I was forced to set it in America so as not to offend a prince. An American masked ball! I'd never heard of such a thing.

I did not, I said, amused. I was to perform this next for him in

Milan, to open the season at La Scala in December with it. Where was it set previously? I asked.

Sweden! But the offended parties were Napolitanos! And Napoléon III, also, strangely. He usually only minded if an opera was overlong.

We laughed.

A few courses were served and then he asked me if I might agree to another opera altogether. This as he set the plates full of risotto in front of us.

I Masnadieri, he said.

I smiled and looked down to my risotto. This offer surprised me. When he'd asked me to dinner that night, I'd thought it was to discuss some further detail of the Milan production. I knew this other opera a little—I would be killed by bandits instead of dying in my cell this time—and I was about to say yes, as I usually would to such an offer, and then did not.

Speak freely, my dear, he said. Something bothers you.

How to say it? I was tired of dying this season, tired of playing so long at death and madness. My initial hesitation began there and was joined by the irony of his granting an old wish—acting as if I did belong to him—even as a new one had appeared. The idea of originating a role written by a protégé of his had taken root in me over the course of the day and had even grown into a romantic fable, the more plausible to me as I sat here. Giuseppina had met Verdi when he was a struggling young composer beginning his career with *Nabucco.* She had created both the lead soprano role and her life with him, leaving behind the more famous Donizetti for the handsome young composer. Composers often courted singers with original roles in operas, as they both knew well.

I thought of myself as a Giuseppina then, waiting for my own Giuseppe to appear and hoping, perhaps, that he had.

But I had not yet met this new Giuseppe. They, it seemed, had; they knew who he was. I couldn't say no to Verdi, though, especially for an opera without a score, written by the protégé I had meant to ask after next. He would eventually find out, and this would insult him. And so I could not say yes, and I could not say no, and I could not ask my question, not right then. I could lie, the thought came, but as quickly came the thought that to lie to him was a grave sin against our friendship. For he would know.

What's more, I had no lie prepared.

This is a surprise. We were so sure you'd be pleased, Giuseppina said. She raised an eyebrow, and they sat back in their chairs again. Verdi held his glass to the side near the candle flame, and along the tablecloth a deep red shadow pooled.

My novels, I heard the writer say, in my memory of the night before. *They all come true.* And I knew what I would say.

As you can tell, I said, I am afraid to consent.

The lie was still forming on my tongue when a feeling came, like that premonitory trill of the string section in an opera, the warning of danger.

I feel it brings a curse, I said.

Verdi squinted and looked up. The red light from his glass flashed along the pressed white linen tablecloth.

I fear the roles I take come true, I said. Condemn me to repeat the fates of my characters in life. This I worded as a suspicion, for I already regretted this lie, which had seemed small and ridiculous just a moment before, but still useful somehow, and now was an explosion, the words still in the air around me like smoke, a smoke that could grow to cover my entire life. And Verdi's face was now so grave, so solemn, I was about to contradict myself, or laugh, or agree to take the role if only to please him when Giuseppina reached for my hand. She glanced at her husband, who did not meet her eyes, and then she leaned very close to me.

Of course they do, my dear, she said. This is why I have sung nothing since marrying.

Verdi put his glass down. Cursed? I wonder. What have you dared? He stroked his beard as he met my eyes, a faint smile on his face.

The great tragedies are told of the families who'd caught the attention of the gods with their hubris, struck down but known forever to us. The House of Atreus, for example, he said. But perhaps you are cursed. Perhaps when we do as we do, he said, the gods learn something. Certainly we do not. He pulled my free hand to him and kissed it, as if I had bid him good night. Take very good care, he said. Our prayers are with you. I do understand. And if this means you must withdraw from the other production, please, tell me.

I sat silent before them, humiliated, unable to answer until I remembered the matter of my other mission and decided to proceed as plainly as possible.

What is this I hear of a protégé? I asked. A young composer, a recent winner of the Prix de Rome?

Verdi said nothing but stood and removed our plates and then returned to the table with grappa, which I took.

It's nothing to speak of, he said. I'm sure I just made the mistake of doing someone a favor, and now he is telling people he is my protégé.

He exchanged the briefest look with Giuseppina before turning back to me.

If I had as many protégés as I am said to have, I would command an army, he said.

There was no avoiding any longer that the evening, and perhaps more, was spoilt, and the only rescue for it began with my exit.

I excused myself, they brought my cape, we exchanged muted kisses good night, and I hired a driver home.

As the little *calèche* made its way to my home through the dark, past the Tuileries, the Palais-Royal, on its way to the avenue de l'Opèra, I pushed back into the seat, and the wood and hide creaked. In the wind, I could smell the mushroom whiff of dead leaves and earth.

He had lied to me, you see. That was clear from the look he'd exchanged with Giuseppina—he had lied to me and was warning her not to contradict him. But this had the effect of telling me the protégé was real. The new mystery as I left was as to why he'd lied.

And as to what I had dared that might offend the gods, well, I had lied to Verdi. And he knew.

The Paris I'd met when I first arrived during the last days of the Second Empire and Napoléon III was a series of ascents that looked at first like descents; going down brought you up—*succès de scandale*. The women I met then dressed as if choosing weapons; their balls, parties, and dinners were a series of duels and mêlées, and the salons and ateliers of the city, outfitters for a vast assassins' guild too decorated by half. A girl could enter this world as a *grisette*, taking in laundry, and in a week or two, be at Worth for a gown; two weeks more, leave at dawn in the carriage of an Austrian industrialist, having been stolen from the bed of the Emperor just to be protected from the Empress. She'd be returned within the month if the industrialist were either assassinated for presumptuousness or titled for his rescue of the Emperor's happiness. Everyone I met had the look of seeing a story repeated in front of them, actors in a rehearsal on a marked stage: the laundress, the couturier, the industrialist, the Emperor, the Empress. As I passed each, I soon saw that this world was new only to me; and when I was done with my turn, I had found my place and learned to listen for the wooden shoes of the next girl as she came through.

Napoléon III was now dead, in his mausoleum in England, the Second Empire replaced by the Third Republic, but I could still make out the shapes of the new *grisettes* in the dark, walking and waiting for their lovers, careful of the police, studying me and my *calèche* carefully as they shifted from foot to foot, as I once had, and wondering how to become one such as me. I nearly saluted from where I sat.

By one unhappy thought, the chorus sings in *Lucia di Lammermoor*, a thousand joys are lost. Perhaps, I told myself, I could write to Verdi in the morning and accept. I could tell him it was foolishness and beg his forgiveness. But each time I thought it, there stood Madame Verdi, with her blithe assurance that my lie was the truth, greeting me at what I did not know would be this next station in my journey.

Her quick acknowledgment of my little lie as some long-standing secret truth among singers did not reassure me, though. Instead, it made the lie seem like a spell I'd been tricked into casting on myself, one that made it so. As if I had cursed myself.

The music for *Un Ballo in Maschera* as well as *I Masnadieri* waited on my tray at home, no doubt sent over before or during our dinner —he had been so certain! There was a note, a short *Brava!* And his looping signature below.

I prepared to send the one back and then could not—not just yet.

In *Un Ballo in Maschera,* my character, Amelia, was dishonored but would live. The orphan Amalia in *I Masnadieri* was murdered. They were like so many of the roles I'd played, roles close to my life, a procession of orphans, *grisettes*, courtesans, wronged lovers, the disgraced ones. But Amelia, the American, Amalia, the orphan, they were very close, like some strange duo that was really the same girl leading the way. The letter *e* in Amelia changing to an *a,* like a tiny mask just for me, all of them, perhaps, leading to this next role, if I agreed to it, as the Settler's Daughter in *Le Cirque du Monde Déchu.*

Me, as I once had been.

What was her fate? Was her ending happy or sad? The writer had said something about an angel and love, and Hell, of course.

Why was there never an opera that ended with a soprano who was free?

The first thing determined in the career of a singer is her *Fach.* The word is German and sounded like *Fate* to me the first time I heard it. It is a singer's fate, for it describes the singer's range and the type of roles the singer will sing. Some soprano tones are associated with virtue, others with seduction, others with grief. If your voice is a collection of the highest notes, you are to play the good girl. If your voice reaches only to the near heights, you are the spurned one or the dishonored. A bit lower and you are the rival or the seductress, and still lower, the maid or matron. To move from the confines of your *Fach* was to risk sounding suddenly as if there had been no education in singing at all. The voice loses all its qualities.

Mine was a voice that sounded at first as if it did not have the capacity for high notes, until they emerged, surprising, with great force. A voice for expressing sorrow, fear, and despair. The tragic soprano is what I was called, also known as a Falcon.

Nothing to fear from a fate that was already yours, then, except, perhaps, that it would never leave you.

Three

THE PIONEER EQUESTRIENNE remembered by Simonet and his composer friend took her first steps out onto the streets of Paris when she was sixteen years old, as a member of the Cajun Maidens and the Wonders of the Canadian Frontier, a small traveling *cirque*. The Emperor Napoléon III had emptied out the world's pockets for the audiences at the Exposition Universelle of 1867. And as France was especially mad for stories of America and Canada, settlers and Indians, horses and beasts from the woods, we came to supply them.

We came to Paris for the pleasure of the Emperor. Him, his appetites, his reign, all controlling me even then.

We were three palomino horses, and Mela, the roan, with an actual Iroquois for our Indian Chief, a Russian Jewess from Saint Petersburg for the Indian Princess, and a troupe of five clowns — four brothers from Minsk and a woman from Portugal who was certainly not their sister — as their tribe. The magician was from Palermo and got himself up as the Medicine Man, and there were three trapeze artists for the Spirits of the North, two women and one man, who all hailed from Poland and were, I think, lovers, all three. A Swedish giant, a complete gentleman, wore a suit of fur and a false monster head, and was called the Wendigo, summoned forth by the Medicine Man. The show's stars were the Cajun Maidens, five powerfully built sisters, all truly from Quebec, who began their routine as if doing ordinary household chores but with extraordinary tools — sweeping a broom the size of a husband, balancing firewood on their head — and then led up to ax juggling, knife throwing, somersaults on and off of horses.

Together they were my family for five months.

The show told the story of a young woman's escape from captivity—mine. I played the Settler's Daughter, adopted by the Cajun Maidens after having been "captured by the Indians and raised in their wild ways." It was said I could fire a bow and arrow or a rifle, track an animal through the woods, and while I'd lost my English living among the Indians, I could still sing one song, a song my mother taught me, which I came out and sang in a round at the end.

By appearance, I am often thought to be Bohemian or Italian, though sometimes French, English, or Scandinavian. As a girl, I was slender, small, but with a large head and features—large brown eyes, dark red hair nearly brown. Any kind of beauty I had seemed to me to be in my hair, and when I wore it bound close to my head in braids, it was like a secret.

The Settler's Daughter was a part invented by the show boss —he'd gone looking for one to replace the girl who'd left. I never knew her, and no one ever spoke of her. The story he invented he'd adapted for me because there was no other way to explain that this girl he'd found in New York could sing but not speak.

I was silent because I believed I was damned. I was sure I was a foul liar before God, a girl who'd tried to invent a miracle, and He'd taken my whole family except me to show me what He thought of me.

The one song I sang, I believed, was all that the Lord had left me. It was the song my mother had loved to hear, the one noise I thought He'd let me make and live. As for why I joined, it was because I could do this and, I swore, only this until I had been safely returned to my mother's people, her family in Lucerne.

When I arrived in Paris, I thought I'd nearly made it there.

The girl I was when I arrived in Paris, she came believing herself cursed as well. If my voice really was cursed, I was sure it was that one, somehow still with me all these years.

She is coming for me out of the dark, the girl I once was. She hasn't spoken in years past remembering. I can't tell you her name and she won't, either. Not for shame at my family's modest origins

—I became something they couldn't imagine, something they would have kept me from becoming, and that, it seems to me, was always in my nature to become. They would not be proud of me.

I never belonged to them, though they tried.

To truly tell you my story, we start not with the Settler's Daughter, then, but the one before her, the one who hid inside her, who walked down to the pier, where she found a tent full of horses and music that took her in.

∼

My invented miracle began as a prank. It was only to punish my mother for punishing me.

I was the child of a Scottish father and a Swiss mother who'd met when they came to settle America for God, Methodist settlers, farming the new state of Minnesota. My father received his plot in 1862, given land in the Homestead Act, and we moved from Ohio, even as the Dakota War began that summer, and the Civil War burned the lands farther east.

It could have been my fate to have lived out the story I would later perform, but instead, we passed these conflicts strangely unharmed, so much so that my mother and father said we were blessed, and so I was allowed to grow up to be a girl approaching the age of my Confirmation and First Communion in the summer of 1866.

I was a tomboy, to the despair of my mother, whom I loved. While the singers I knew were studying in convent schools, I was chasing storms on our horses and drinking the rain. To prepare me, and to tame me, my mother tested me on my Bible subjects, the names of the apostles, the trials of Jesus, the story of creation, and when she was done, said, Well, I'm glad you at least know the name Jesus.

No other God before me, my mother quoted to me. Do you think when your time comes and you appear before the Lord, He'll want you to sing? That He'll forgive all the rest?

It was, in fact, what I was sure was true.

I loved to go to church with her, but it was only to sing the hymns. This little church was my first theater. When the time came to sing, I was the very picture of an eager Christian, standing first out of the whole congregation, hymnal open, waiting impatiently for the pastor's wife to pick out the refrain on the church's piano. But when the singing was over, I'd sit numb for the rest of the service until my mother pulled my sleeve to show we were leaving. As we left, the congregation would come to say to her what a voice I had and wasn't she so proud of me. And I would glow beside her, beaming at her, waiting for her to be proud of me. She would sometimes reach out and tuck my hair behind my ears if it had come loose.

I loved my mother but I did not love God. For reasons unknown to me still, I'd never quite taken to the idea of God. At this age I could only imagine the words we said in church going off into the empty air. In the presence of my mother's assertions about the Lord, I tried to assume the same gravity that everyone around me had, but whenever I said *Lord my God,* I never believed it and knew myself to be a liar.

I did it only because I loved her, but I was not sincere, and she could tell, and so it dismayed her, and she punished me as proud.

The next Sunday, after my failure at my Bible test, she met me at the door with a piece of black ribbon and velvet, and she tied them in place over my mouth.

You'll wear this today and think of how, when you know what you should know as a proper Christian, you can sing in church again, she said, and pushed my hair back into place around the collar of my coat. Your voice is a gift from God, and it deserves to be treated with respect—as does the Lord.

As we climbed down from our buggy in the yard by the church, the other members stared, but my mother had told her friends of her plan, and they quickly murmured the story to those who didn't know, so that no one asked me about it, not even the pastor when I shook his hand at the door. I noticed he threw occasional anxious glances my way, but my mother's stern regard seemed to quiet him.

I've made a mistake in telling you it's a gift, this voice of yours, my mother said to me, as she removed the ribbon gag at home and folded it into her sewing kit. But it's a test as well. There's no gift like yours without a test.

The weeks leading up to the ceremony drifted by with a terrible slowness. Each Sunday I made my way past the staring children and sat out the service; each week I sat at the table with the prayer book at home and recited the prayers to my mother as she cooked dinner, as if I were praying to her. As if she were the angry and vengeful God, her back to me while she tended to the fry pan.

Unlike God's, her replies to my prayers were straightforward. Very good, she'd say. Again.

And then, mercifully, the long-awaited day came. I dressed in a new dress; I appeared in the church as I once had, my mouth uncovered. I stood before the pastor and repeated the prayers in a steady voice. And then he said, *Body and blood of Christ,* and he dipped the bread in the wine and put it on my tongue.

And then it was done.

I went back to my seat next to my family, as the pastor's wife made her unsteady way through the introit. I turned to see my mother, her head bent low but her eyes on me, and my father smiling. But my brothers, they stared at me as if my troubles might come for them.

I took the hymnal, flipped it open, and began to sing. I hadn't sung in so long, the noise of my voice startled me, but it was there, not only undiminished, but perhaps even changed into something more powerful than before. I wanted more than anything to use it, but instead I held it back, tightening my throat slightly. I made a deliberately thin, weak noise that blended quietly, like the noise of another girl.

I could tell, for all I was trying to blend my voice, that my mother heard my every effort. I stood out even now. But as the second chorus began, she looked over at me and nodded her head, pleased at last again.

. . .

A few days later, I took one of our horses and rode to the farthest edge of our property, past the long fields of new rye and hay, until I reached a long hill that sloped down sharply and hid everything below. I tied the horse carefully to a tree and walked down until I was sure I was out of sight.

This was my favorite place.

I wanted to hear my new voice. I was angry at being punished for what I was sure was God's only gift to me, and yet I was ashamed still to sing in front of my mother, afraid the pleasure I took would be seen as pride. And as I often sang when I was sad as well, I could not even console myself as I once had, not in the house.

So here I was.

The song I chose for my test was a song my father sang often, a sea chantey. I later learned there was more to it than this, but this was the fragment he sang over and over.

> What will you do, love,
> when I am going,
> with white sails blowing,
> the seas beyond?

I liked to imagine my young father, pacing the deck at night on his crossing, singing this song. I sang it to myself there and then sang it again, falling into it, wandering into the woods as I did so. I imagined leaving my family, leaving the town, leaving it all and never returning. I saw their sad, empty days without me. When they missed me, they'd be sorry for how they'd treated me. My mother would cry for having made me wear that gag.

When I came out of the woods, I began to head back to the horse when I heard it whicker and looked to see my mother at the top of the hill.

Is it to make a fool of me, then? she said.

No, mother, I said, as unhappy to have been caught as I was to have made her sad. For she looked as though I'd insulted her.

I can't have you running off like this, she said. You're not a child anymore. You have responsibilities. We're to be making your trousseau, in case you forgot.

I protested, but she would have none of it.

After that, as punishment, I was to wear the gag for another week.

All the time? my father asked of my mother that night back at the house. We were eating dinner.

All the time, she said, except at meals. Her voice has gone to her head, and that will be trouble.

Ah.

The other children say she's possessed, my little brother said; Frank was his name. That if we hear her sing we'll all be possessed as well.

Is it true, then? Thomas, the older one, asked.

It's just foolishness and gossip, my mother said. Don't repeat it. Or I'll make a gag for you as well.

My parents left then to speak with each other out of our hearing.

Is it true? Thomas repeated to me.

I glared. And then nodded. The boys leapt up and cleared the table.

Now, if I wanted to scare them, I had only to make as if I were going to pull down the gag and look at them meaningfully. And while I hated not being able to speak, I enjoyed their fear. I liked how at church the other families stared at me, liked that the boys who once chased me now stayed back, afraid. But this was also pride. My mother noted it, and then said, One more week.

I don't like it, my father said to me the following week as we washed our hands for dinner. It's not right. I'm working on your mother. But she has it in her head that this will cure you, though I'm not sure how we're to know you're cured.

I started to cry when he said this.

Can you take it off at night? he asked me.

I nodded.

Well, then, I suppose that's a blessing at least.

That night I heard him argue with her. I sat hidden on the stairs and listened. It's you ought to wear it, he said. She's a girl, not a freak, but now she's being said to be possessed. Is that what you want for her? How are we to get her a husband if the men think she's cursed?

You haven't seen the wicked pride in her, my mother said.

You haven't seen the wicked pride in you.

My mother began to cry, which startled me.

It's not right, what you're doing, he said. It's not right at all. Nothing good will come of it.

Despite my fantasies of running away, I loved them too much to do it. I made another plan.

That night as they slept I went to where my mother kept a kettle on the stove. The water in it was still warm. I walked with it to my bed and soaked my sheets, careful not to wake my brothers asleep together in the bed across from me.

Careful not to wake them until my nightgown was wet and my hair as well, I lay down in the bed and then, with great purpose, rolled onto the floor, landing heavily with a crash. My brother Frank woke, sat up, and then got down from the bed to investigate me where I lay, very still, my eyes closed. He touched my forehead, rubbing my wet hair with his little fingers.

Thomas, he said. Wake up. Wake up and get Mom and Dad. Tell them she's got the fever.

Soon I heard my parents come in. Get her downstairs, my mother ordered my father. Good Lord, her bed is soaked. I'll have to hang the bedding out to dry. I'll wash it in the morning.

I kept my eyes closed as my father carried me, not wanting to let on. If he was to look me in the eye, he'd know, I was certain.

When the doctor came the next day, I pretended my voice was gone, and he determined me to have been rendered mute, at least temporarily, perhaps permanently. There's nothing wrong with her now, he said.

Well, my mother said. This was God's will. She surprised me then for she began to weep.

I prayed for the Good Lord to take away your pride, she said. I suppose he has taken away mine also.

Whatever shame I'd felt before was nothing compared to this. As she wept next to my bed, she asked me to forgive her. I could not decide which was worse, to continue to pretend or to reveal the pretense. I decided to take my time, to act as if the voice had returned slowly—having planned this miracle, I would plan another.

My parents, in the meantime, returned to being loving with each other; the children stopped staring; my brothers no longer feared me and played with me again. Everyone was kind and told me how much they missed my voice at church. All returned to how it had been before except for me.

Then the real fever came and took them from me, every one.

My family died the fall of that year, my mother the last to pass. Her death left me alone on our farm, far from the town and the one road that ran to it. I decided it was more trouble for me to find someone to bury her than it was for me to bury her myself, and as I'd helped her bury my father and brothers, I felt I knew what had to be done and began.

I went to what was now the family graveyard, selected a spot for her to lie in, and when I found the dirt too frozen to move with a spade, paced out a fire the length of her to thaw the ground. I tended that fire for a week, sometimes cooking and reading there through the night, the three graves a short fence against the wind. There wasn't much wood left for fires, so I pulled boards from the house and the barn. At the end of the week I was able to dig a narrow trench through the warm dirt, but I found the ground three feet down still frozen, so I set my fire again and waited.

I didn't want my mother washing out of the ground with the first floods of the next spring, as I had seen once, coffins swept down a river as the current left its course and ate the bank.

I took more boards from the smooth wood of the doors to her bedroom and the kitchen, and made her coffin as I had seen her do for my father and brothers. I never thought to spare the farmhouse.

I knew I could not stay. The farm settlement would return to the animals and the Minnesota storms, which had always appeared better suited to it.

I could have cremated her, but my mother had been a devout Christian woman and cremation would have disappointed her as pagan, a refutation of the Last Days and the Glory. She'd want to take my hand then and she'd need a hand to do it with, would be her argument. The fires I lit never touched her.

The second fire was enough to finish the hole. The earth turned easily again under the spade, the ash blew around me as I worked and found its way into my clothes so that when I was done and took a bath dead cinders shook loose from my skirts as I undressed and the water turned as gray as the sky. The work had been cold and hard, but I was glad to have taken my time. I took note of the snow on the ground outside the window, Minnesota's winter gathering to the north of the farm across the lake, and hurried through my cooling bath. I was not its equal.

The next morning the pail at the well knocked on ice. I left it out to collect the new-falling snow while I hurried to finish. I knew I had a day before the snow would be too deep to get to town.

The coffin I made was shabby and uneven, but sealed tight. I ran my hand through it as I imagined my mother at her final rest. It wasn't right; I hadn't the skills for more than a rough box. And yet this was all I knew how to do.

I set it beside her bed and climbed in to get a good hold on her. Under the shroud I'd sewn of her sheets and blankets she lay, arms crossed, dressed in her best dress by me the morning she'd gone. I lit a candle on her bedside table, sang a short blessing above her, and prayed that He welcome her into His arms, and then added, in the silence made deep by the new winter, a request for the strength to get her into her grave.

And then I began.

The cold had kept her but she was heavy to the touch as she had never been in life; Death seemed to have left something with her, some new weight to help her keep her place under the earth. It startled me as I pulled against her, and the composure I'd felt since her illness had begun left me. I became frantic to move her and finish. She slid from my grip and fell to the floor. I tipped the coffin on its side, rolled her into it, and nailed it shut.

Getting her to the grave took the remainder of the day. I would move her, rest, move her, and then rest. Halfway to the hill I fell and the coffin slid back down on the new snow. The old snow's edges were like glass where my steps broke it, and when I went back to the house for a lunch, I saw I'd cut my shins; my blood had soaked to the edges of my skirt and, when I returned to finish, lay in frozen stripes along the path.

When we reached the grave's edge, I saw I'd forgotten the dirt would freeze again and the mound mocked me, shining.

I sat down on it and hid my head from the sight. I heard from the barn the sound of the horses, forgotten by me until now, complaining, and I remembered how we had used them for the lowering of the other coffins; they were to take me to town when this was done and needed feed and water. I shut my eyes until my breath grew calm, and then I left the hill, took the bucket by the well, melted the snow in it on the stove, and took that to the barn. I returned to the house, took another bath to wash the blood from my legs, and slept that last night on the kitchen floor, my back against the wood stove, my mother by her grave, the night for her mausoleum.

Whatever you think the sacrifice will be, it is not enough. It isn't for us to decide. God wants from us what He wants and nothing else.

I still needed a fire large enough to bury my mother.

From the barn, beside the horses blindfolded against the fire, I watched my home burn.

The fire went slowly and then all at once rose up around the house, the house unchanged until the very last moment when it charred to a shadow and fell in on itself. The windows shattered, pinging out over the frozen fields.

I raked the dirt for coals and took them in the wheelbarrow to her grave.

I had packed a small bag for myself that morning and dressed in my mother's raccoon coat made for her by my father, his pistols belted at my waist. Her grave I staked with a cross made from pieces of the barn door.

I saddled the one horse and led the other and rode the miles into town to sell them and be on my way. I rode and did not look back except to check my direction against what I could see of the sun. None of them had thought the farm was to be mine, my brothers having gotten good with even the sewing. I was to find a man who didn't mind my cooking and loved a song, and this was the way my mother and I lived right to the end, as if in the spring I would marry and he would come to do what the men had done before.

I hummed to my horse the whole way as I rode. When I dismounted, a patch of ice from my breath striped his brown neck.

~

In town at the general store I walked in and set the pistol and the reins on the counter. The store owner picked them up and looked outside to where the horses stood. He began to open his mouth to ask about my mother, as he had the last time I'd been in when she was healthy.

Whatever is the fair price, I said, is all I'd ask of you. Mine was not the first family lost to this fever. He went out to look at the horses then came back in. I counted what he gave to me.

Where to? he asked me.

Of my father's family I knew little; of my mother's, a little more. She was from a well-to-do family in Lucerne—she'd received mail sometimes from her sister there, and some money, which she always took regretfully. On the day she died, I found one of her sister's letters in her hand, and I'd kept it. It seemed to me she had meant to speak to me of it next, as if she were pointing me there.

On my girl's map of the world, it seemed like I could get to Switzerland as easily as anywhere else, and I knew there was only one place to start.

New York, I said, thinking of the oceans that began there and the cities beyond them.

He told me the fare, and I paid and sat near the stove to wait.

~

On that first trip to New York I didn't speak. I watched snowflakes blow in and melt against my clothes, how they shone like tears in the soft winter light. I thought I must have smelled of death, the air around me like match smoke. But no fellow passenger let on.

As we'd buried my brothers and father, my mother had said, This is God's will for us; pray, pray for mercy. Pray. She said this even as she lay dying; she had kept her faith to the end that this was the work of the Lord. When I did not fall sick, she saw that as a prayer answered. But I had prayed not to be left behind, and I was.

The other passengers smiled and chatted with one another as we rode and smiled at me from time to time. I wanted the relief of conversation also, and a few times I nearly joined in, but instead I could only think of how they would ask me where I was traveling to and why. But to speak would have been to burst, to let out all the anger and grief—anger that I was left behind to roam this world without them.

Here, I knew from my parents, this world, here was where we were tested. The next world was Paradise. To live when they had all died told me I'd failed.

I could have sold the farm that day, could have ridden for help, could have asked my mother, before she died, more questions about her kin, of whom she rarely spoke. If I'd been better at all of what I was to have done in the years before then—but I was not; I did as I did instead. I always knew somehow that I would live apart from them and the farm, and then I was, and I had not prepared.

I was that terrible girl, too stupid to get help, who made a bonfire of her house to undo a patch of winter and filled her mother's grave with her own hands.

Why is it so loud when you cry from grief? Because it must be loud enough for the missing one to hear, though it never can be. Loud enough to scale the sky and the backs of angels, or to fall through the earth to where they rest. And so it is sometimes when I sing that the notes come from me as if I believed I could reach them where they rest, they sure of a reunion I still cannot imagine or believe in except, sometimes, in song.

Four

I ARRIVED IN NEW YORK'S Union Square in a coach that was little more than a wood drum dragged by horses through the winter dark. As I stepped down, I found a city as strange to me as if I'd been brought all the way to Mars, like in a novel from Jules Verne.

There were at least a hundred girls like me arriving on just that day. The fever had taken more than my family, and the survivors had fled. New beggars angered the old ones, and while I wished there was more to my purse than there was, I did not want to beg, and so I left quickly, as if I knew where I was going, though I did not. The mute doors I passed, their purposes unknown to me, mocked me. The men and women in the street walked, confident and dour, and I was little noticed by them except in occasional stares.

What I had thought was a fine way to dress for leaving looked to the citizens of New York that day, I'm sure, like a farmer fantasy. I was clean, at the least, and my hair braided, coiled under a rabbit-fur bonnet made by my father.

I could see there was water to either side. Water meant boats; boats meant leaving. I put my head into my collar and walked against the wind until I found one of the rivers. The Hudson.

I was directed to the ship lines, where a ticket clerk confirmed I had nothing like the money required to purchase a passage to Europe, by sail or steam. As I walked away from the counter, my life fit in my hand, only as big as the coins in my purse, and it was not large enough. I could pay for a meal or a room, but not both. If I ate, I would have nowhere to sleep. If I chose a place to sleep, I would have nothing to eat.

As I walked the city of New York, not knowing now where to go,
I cursed it silently, and my eyes felt like the judgment of angels, as if
they could light my way in the gathering dark.

I still did not know where to go or what to do.

My family had been the borders of my world before then, and
with them gone, the world had revealed itself to me.

The trees were the wrong trees; the buildings, the wrong buildings; the people, the wrong people. The reek of the streets, of the
horse manure, the garbage, the spilled beer, and the drunken piss, it
all seemed to say to me, *Your mother is dead, your father is dead, your
brothers are dead, and no one can help you.*

And so I cursed these things. I cursed these wrong trees; the carriages; the low, sooty buildings; the high ones. It was warmer here,
the ground not quite frozen, but cold all the same—I cursed that
as well. The mud under my feet. I cursed the fine clothes and the
poor, the buggies, the trains, the men, the women, the beggars, the
horses, and the birds, all of it—I wished it all to burn, to become
a fire that would lay waste to the city, for me to turn from ember
to inferno under the breath of whatever it was that would listen to
my prayer and answer it. And while I'd not cried once for the entire journey, I began to as I began my curses. I wept continuously,
though I did not sob or shake.

~

By nightfall I remained more ash than ember. My face burned from
where the tears had glazed my face and I had brushed them away. I
sank against a stone wall. Nothing had answered my prayers, again.
And so, having cursed everything that came near me, I cursed myself.

I was dazed from hunger—I'd never eaten away from home in
my entire life. I looked at the window of a tavern full of people
laughing and drinking, and saw no clear way to feed myself, no way
to join them. I remember I was afraid that it was their house and
they would not let me in.

The confidence that came with cursing the people in the street left me, and they frightened me now. They seemed to me like a swarm, indistinct from one another, foreign and of a piece with one another in a way I would never be. And while I was unsure how they fed themselves, what they would eat and drink, they were not unsure at all and this terrified me. I watched for signs of how it was done, in a furious despair. Not for wanting to die, but to live.

Girl, said a voice behind me, and I turned.

Are you lost? he asked.

I shook my head. This, at least, was true.

You look quite cold, more than half froze, he said. He smiled faintly, and a whisper of charm came through the air.

He was pale, somber, very tall. He had dark hair and whiskers, the whiskers a bit frozen from his breath and the wind, and he looked as if even speaking to me grieved him.

Come join me inside, he said, and indicated the saloon. Let me buy you a bit of something and get you out of the cold.

I went in. He bought me soup and a bit of beer, and I knew I might live.

~

Do you need a position? he asked.

I supposed I did.

He needed someone for help with the washing and the cooking, he said. His wife had just died. Was I handy? For it looked like I was. He was a new widower.

I was no good for it, but I nodded all the same, for I wanted at least another meal and a bed. I hoped desperation might make me better at chores.

Can you not speak? he asked, for thus far I'd said nothing.

I decided I could not and nodded yes. It would be easier this way.

Well, okay then, he said.

It was a very short charade we managed. His house that night was cold and clean, the farm large, familiar and unfamiliar both.

My parents had never used hired men and women so I was unused to them and greeted them warily with a wave. He showed me to a small room off the kitchen he said was to be mine. When I came back through the kitchen and found him asleep by his bottle, a little whiskey was still in the glass.

I was still cold, and though I had come into the kitchen to be close to the fire, I thought to try this—he had said it warmed one, but had not offered it to me. The taste burned, but the warmth was there and ran through me, consoling.

I sipped again.

I roused him, for he should be in his bed, it seemed to me, and helped him up the stairs.

~

By the end of the next day, it was quite clear I was as bad as I ever had been at the cooking and the wash. He was nice enough, but as I cleaned the table and took his plate, he made a face.

I had found him asleep at the table again. He'd stayed late, drinking by the kitchen fire. I woke him to go to bed, and as I did, he looked at me and I saw his eyes.

I slowly understood; I was close to a lesson, one I had long understood would come. I could tell what he wanted from me.

I'd had to break the ice on the East River to wash clothes that froze before they dried. His eyes reminded me of that ice. I wondered if it would be worse than that and decided perhaps it was not.

I guided him to his room. I laid him out on his bed, helping him off with his clothes, pausing before also draping mine. I stood cold, naked, at the edge of this moment. I told myself I could still leave, though I knew I could not, and climbed into the bed on top of him.

He did the rest. There was pain that surprised me, and I was so cold, it burned as he entered me, the heat of him, but this also its own strange pleasure. I pulled his quilt up around me like a cape, pushing it against my face so he could not see me cry, my eyes starting at the shock of it. Soon there was only the terrible cold around us in the room and the new warmth of him, and beneath that, a surprise: the beat of his heart, strange to me, there in the veins.

It wasn't his heart there, though, pushing in me.

He was tough and hard all over except here, with a wiry fur to his chest and belly. A tremor came over him like fear and his head rolled back, eyes shut. He was not a pretty man. Was he falling asleep? He was very drunk. I hoped he was. I reached down and put my hand along his beard, touched his lip to check. He pulled back.

It wasn't to be tender then, I saw. He chose that moment to sit up and made to kiss me. I pushed him back down and held his arms in place until we were done. The kissing I could not bear.

The kissing would be worse than the ice.

Afterward, when he was done, he threw back his blankets and swore. Eh. I've ruined you, have I? he said, for there was blood on him and on me. He went to his basin and washed himself before telling me to do the same.

Men always said it that way — *I've ruined you.* I couldn't explain, but, no, I did not feel ruined. I wasn't sure what I felt at first, besides being shocked by the blood — I felt like I'd slain something else, though the blood was mine.

He let me stay the night in his bed, which was warmer than the room off the kitchen. It was a strange vigil, for he snored so loudly I couldn't sleep. Instead, I felt my body warm.

I could feel how easy it would be to stay, and it was almost tempting, for being easy. I, with only ash for my trousseau, the new girl for the widower. I think he felt this also. But that was not what I wanted. It wasn't why I'd come all this way.

What I felt, by morning, was how it was as if I were someone new. Or, perhaps, more: There was someone I had become, and she had made this decision by way of introduction.

You should leave, this new girl I was said to me. Before he wakes.

I slunk from the bed and stood again in the cold. As I dressed myself in that dim kitchen light, I felt the opposite of ruined. I felt strong again, ready to try to cross the ocean again.

I was sore, that was all. And so this felt like a triumph over death, as if I had been dealt a murderous blow and lived.

~

There was still one member of my family left to bury.

I paused on the hill above his farm, having found graves much like the ones my mother and I had made, though these were made with stones well carved.

He was like me, then, also the last of his family left among the living.

The name I took was from a smaller stone, farther back, older. She had died three years before these new ones, at the age of three. Her last name was different from the rest. She could have been a sister's child. I said it aloud in the air, a whisper.

Lilliet Berne.

I suppose I knew even then what Verdi later told me about the great tragedies, those great families who'd caught the attention of the gods for their hubris and were struck down, known to us now as the subjects of operas. My family was not, to my knowledge, a great family, but they were dearly good—any greatness they had was in their goodness. But I sensed even then, before I knew the word, the hubris was mine. And the gods did not kill for hubris—for hubris, they let you live long enough to learn.

It is only to be for a little while, I told myself, for however long it would take me to get to my aunt. I would go back to my old name then. This one would keep me safe as I traveled. In its disguise, I could hide all my sins, like this one.

Instead, it would be this name I would return to, the name I chose that day, this name that would stay with me when almost nothing else had.

My hubris was hidden from me, as it always is, until it is too late, and it began with this stolen name. I believed I could hide from my Maker and start again. My hubris, then, something I've not yet been punished for, the real punishment still ahead of me.

～

There is a novel all French schoolchildren are made to read in the new Republic of France, written to outline the nation's history. I would read it to teach myself both the language and country while at the Conservatoire in Paris. *Le Tour de la France par Deux Enfants* is the story of two orphaned brothers who travel the entire country in search of their uncle, helped at each turn by the good people of France. When the brothers leave home there is a description of the sky. *Pas une étoile au ciel.* In my clumsy translations I mistook *étoile* for toil, star for work. By a work of the sky, I thought it meant. By a work of the sky, the orphans left. Not a star in the sky, as the orphans left, was what the phrase meant in that sentence. But still I thought, This I understand. Orphans made for stories.

If I was making for you a book for children, the page opposite this one would be an engraving of the girl as she stands on a street in New York, with a girl's map of the world, in which she imagines she can go back the distance her mother traveled from Lucerne in Switzerland to Minnesota and find her kin there. A dotted line would connect the two places, drawn by the author. For the final X, the cemetery near the farm in Brooklyn, where she takes the name of a girl, *Lilliet Berne, 1860–1863,* dead at age three, which she gives the next time anyone asks it of her.

With a dead girl's name, Death would go looking somewhere else, I was sure. No funeral, no prayers said for her, no stone to mark her rest except this name, the heaviness of it on my tongue each time I say the name all these years, until now, when it has nearly worn away.

Her book closes there and this other one opens. In the first picture, she is standing on the back of a horse, waving to a crowd.

I will try and name, by the end of this, the country this tells the story of.

Five

I WENT BACK TO the river and wandered the shipyards.

I had the memory of a story from my father of stowaways, people who managed to hide on a boat and cross the sea, but I couldn't figure out how one went about it. The boats all seemed forbidding, silent, impermeable, and the looks the men gave me warned me to stay back. These men were not the kind I'd known before. The way they looked at me, like I was a lamb. I would soon know how lucky I'd been with my widower.

I found a tent pitched near the water, and it glowed and shook with the noise of singing and horses, gunfire and laughter. As I approached, a flap opened, and a dejected-looking woman stumped out.

It was the strangest thing I'd found, perhaps, in all of my short life, this noisy tent near the water, and I waited to see how I could go in. I walked closer. It did not seem open to the public—there was no audience.

The day grew dark. I watched as more and more women left. I knew I would have to leave soon, to work, and yet I waited.

I noticed a man paying attention to me. He came and stood right in front of me finally, tried to press a piece of paper into my hand, saying something to me and gesturing at the tent door, but he hadn't tried to introduce himself so I ignored him. And after my episode with the farmer, I feared strange men but also myself, a little.

Fine, he said finally, exasperated. Be that way if you must. If we can't get Muhammad to the mountain, we will bring the mountain to Muhammad.

I remembered my mother would say this when I was stubborn. I looked down at the paper, where it lay on the ground, and read it dully.

Female Equestrienne Rider Needed — Audition Today!
Skill with Firearms and Singing Important! Get Ready to See Paris!

He went into the tent, to my surprise.

The flap flew open again, and this time standing there was a small group looking at me.

A light glowed high above the others, separated from them, and moved steadily toward me. As I watched, it twinkled, broke into limbs of a kind, so that it seemed for a brief moment a dancing figure of fire, something small and capable of lighting, say, a cigar. It danced, moving as if it could beckon me somewhere. Then I saw it was coming for me.

It was a tiny oil lamp, set high up into the curly wig of a strange, enormous, and terrifyingly beautiful woman. A few more lamps lit the back of her head, so that she was curtained in light. Thick red curls rose for several feet above her face. She was accompanied by a giant looking at me over the top of her hair, his face shadowed by the light and by what I first thought was another man, but was instead a woman dressed in pants walking with a soldier's powerful stride. I looked away, thinking they'd be on their way, but then looked back when from behind them suddenly appeared the man who'd tried to force the paper into my hand. This one! he said. See? Am I right?

They came to a stop in front of me.

Well, he didn't lie, the woman of fire said to the others, before turning to me and saying, My dear, my name is Flambeau. She gave a curtsy, and the warmth of her fire reached my cheeks and eyelashes. My colleagues and I, it seems to me, have been searching for a girl just such as you.

I stared at her as if she hadn't spoken at all and then opened my mouth to say, *What is it you think I am?* and a strange whispery noise came from my throat instead.

I looked around at them and tried again. The sound was ghostly. It terrified me.

My audience looked on, curious and concerned. Cat got your tongue? she said.

The voice was gone, as gone as if it had slunk away in the night and left this in its place.

How do you be? the giant asked. He bowed deeply.

Here, my dear, whisper in my ear, Flambeau said, and so I did.

What do you think I am? I asked, whispering.

What do we think she is? Flambeau said, repeating my question with a slight smile.

Whatever she is, she's the last one we'll speak to before going home, said the gentlemanly woman. She shifted her legs and then, like my father used to, cracked her knuckles with a swift flex of her clasped hands, and I had a pang of remembering him.

The giant met my eyes, asking, Did you just arrive here?

I nodded yes.

Flambeau smiled and asked, How's your aim with a rifle? Are you a good shot? Can you ride a horse?

I again nodded yes to both.

Then you are the one we seek, Flambeau said. The fine lady there is Priscilla of the Cajun Maidens, and this is Ernesto the Giant. We are colleagues together in a traveling show. We are seeking a Pioneer Girl to join us for our European tour, and you, as you look to be a raccoon in boots in that coat, fit the bill. Will you audition for us?

I pulled the coat closer about me, unsure of how to display my offense at these people who, it seemed, could help me.

Priscilla explained the show was leaving in a few days, as soon as the weather turned, for a tour of Italy, Spain, and France, where there was to be a very important performance in Paris. Auditions had turned up too many women trying to get to Paris for the wrong reasons. All were transparently bad with horses, terrified of guns, and unable to sing.

There's plenty of whores in Paris, Priscilla said. And some of them are a damn good shot. We don't need to bring any more of those.

Ernesto cast his eyes down, caught my eye, and winked. I can't believe there's whores that's bad with horses, he said, and laughed.

At this, Priscilla rolled her eyes, and Flambeau coughed, laughing.

I only smiled as if I understood, which I would, soon enough.

The circus tent shook with the terrible winds coming in off the sea near the shipyards, as if it were undergoing a violent transformation. I felt the same. I wanted desperately to leave with them. Ernesto gave a courtly, exaggerated bow, as did Priscilla, and they gestured toward the tent in unison, as if we were already performing in a show together. I stepped between them, and we walked to the door.

If she can't speak, she can't sing, can she? Ernesto asked Flambeau and Priscilla over the top of my head, as if he thought I couldn't hear him. I don't think himself will go for it, he said. He'll want one that sings. If only she could sing.

And with that, he flung back the tent flap.

The lights from Flambeau's hair threw sharp shadows against the roof of the tent as we entered. She took my arm and walked me to a very exasperated older man leading a roan gelding that also seemed quite tired. The man rubbed his forehead as he chewed the end of a cigar and gave me a long look.

Et voilà la fille, Flambeau said. She was right outside. I think she was just about to enter.

She winked at me.

Is it me, then, or is she perfect? the circus boss asked, inspecting me as he circled me. He plucked at my coat, and I plucked it back into place.

She's nearly perfect, Ernesto said. I don't think she can sing. Or speak, either, for that matter. But she may be as good as we'll get.

He reached a long arm out to prod me. I stepped forward, toward the manager.

The circus boss pouted as his left eyebrow rose up and stayed there. We can't teach her a song?

She can't speak, said Priscilla. She can whisper a bit.

Good heavens, he said, and reached for my coat again. Real coonskins. He held up the coat's hem. We'll use it. Come on, he said to me, looking at me sternly. You can't even sing a little?

I nodded yes. I was sure it was only a moment of the voice being caught at by the cold air.

The boss waved his hands in the air in front of him, as if his own smoke were blowing on him. Fine, fine, if she can ride well, we'll figure it out. This is the horse, he said. Did they tell you?

I nodded yes.

His name is Mela, he yelled. Though I suppose you can't say his name. It's because of how much he likes an apple, though it may be he's had too many—he hasn't taken one from any of our applicants yet. Here, he said, and I looked up in time to catch an apple he threw my way. Perhaps you'll be the one.

The horse was exhausted and a little scared. I went up to him from his right side, tilted my head. He whickered as he saw the apple, and his huge teeth closed over it right as I held it out. He was young and ruddy, the long pale mane and tail beautifully brushed. We liked each other right away. His eyes closed as I ran my hand along his brow and tickled the soft hair at the crest of his neck up behind his ears. I waited until he was done chewing and then blew softly down his nose.

As he chewed at the apple, he started a little under my hands, but with happiness, pushing his nose against my face. I slid my hand down his long neck and then climbed into the saddle. I held out my arms and mimed firing a rifle, and the ringmaster laughed and brought me one in a scabbard I could wear on my back.

The tent had filled with more of the performers, tired, hard faced, waiting to be impressed.

When my brothers and I were lost, we took to standing in the saddle to check the horizon to see where we were. But it was so much fun to do, we were always checking. One time our old bay became impatient and began walking while my brother was still standing, and as we laughed, he stayed standing up and gradually got the horse to a canter. This became our new favorite trick, and so, of course, we soon learned to race at it, our mother usually catching us and screaming in fear.

I gave my new audience a long look as they watched expectantly and then reined Mela back so he reared as I swung him into the track of the ring. We started off at a run. My audience screamed with laughter and I felt it please the horse.

After three laps to get him warm to me and to figure out his timing, I swung in the saddle, rolling onto my back, my legs up as I did a half circle, sitting down again backward.

I heard a cheer and waved to the crowd.

He was a good circus horse and kept steady on his pace. I would later miss him, but for now, I rolled myself back around to face front again. I did it once more and then prepared for the real trick, the one I was sure they'd like.

I did not know how to understand the way life was lived here, but this much I knew.

My eyes moved to Ernesto, who was nodding with pride as if we were already friends.

I took one foot and lifted it slightly up Mela's reddish sides, then the other, until my feet balanced, knees bent, on either side of the center of the horse's back. My audience cheered. I lifted one hand in the air in a salute and then whipped off my hat, shaking my hair loose. Then I pulled the reins in and drew the horse to a stop in a sawdust cloud. From my place on his back I turned to face them.

They were silent as they watched me, except Flambeau, who still clapped sharp, barking claps.

I steadied myself and raised my arm in a salute. I needed them to feed me, to take me with them. I needed to get to Europe. If they did not take me, I was not sure what there was for me.

I cleared my throat and found my voice then, like a coin suddenly in your pocket that'd been missing when last you looked for it. Ernesto's eyes went wide with surprise, almost as wide as mine.

The song was, in fact, the one song my mother had taught me that wasn't a hymn. This was true. I chose it that night as I was homesick and missing her, so it seemed right to sing it now.

> Rose, Rose, Rose, Red.
> When will I see thee wed?
> I will wed at thy will, sire,
> At thy will.
>
> Rose, Rose, Rose, Red.
> When will I see thee wed?
> I will wed as I will, sire,
> As I will.

I'd fiddled with the lyrics, and I guess they knew, for they laughed at my second verse.

I sang it slowly and clearly, steadily stronger, thrilling to the moment. I then sang it again, continuing, repeating it until the other performers joined in the round. Soon they were dancing with each other, and I held my hand out to Ernesto, who came to where I stood on the back of the horse, finally taking my hand and holding it up in the air. Standing on that horse, I was only a little taller than he was. As I finished the lyric that time, he lifted me off and held me there.

Can't speak but you can sing, then, is it? he asked.

The rest of the circus sang around us.

I looked at him, all the terror I'd felt close but not as close, while he held me, and I enjoyed the sensation, new and thrilling, to be up in the air in his arms.

It's nothin' to me, he said. We're none of us made right for this world. But we're still here, aren't we? And then he set me down.

~

Any relations, then? the boss asked, as we sat with my contract and he named my terms.

I shook my head no, the grief again, like a low bell knocking. I bit my lip.

None at all? I shook my head again. Well, every circus story begins by someone's grave. Welcome, he said. You're a natural. Sign here.

Even if you weren't an orphan, Ernesto said to me, as he led me to the food tent, you'd probably pretend to be one anyway.

When you joined, you were always asked if you had family. If you said yes and the family wasn't a circus family, they usually didn't take you. And if it was a family that had rivalries or blood vengeance with another circus family, the answer would be no also.

If the boss still has it somewhere, the contract reads, in careful script, *Lilliet Berne.*

~

Later that night, after I'd been fed and shown to a cot in Priscilla's tent, I lay awake, unable to sleep. I took my hands out and touched my throat, as if that could tell me what had happened.

My throat felt the same. But as I lay there, I tried to speak again and could not.

There was only the same low sound, a scratchy whisper.

It was as if I had two voices now, the one strong and clear, the other turned to ash. As if the voice that could speak had been punished for the pride of the one that could sing.

The gift and the test.

I couldn't tell if this meant I'd been forgiven. I only felt haunted, right down in my throat. No ghostly hands there but perhaps a single phantom finger, pressing in.

A warning.

If my voice had a curse, I was sure it was this one.

Of course, the one I did not believe in is the one that came true.

Six

THE SETTLER'S DAUGHTER, then.

I rode into the ring dressed in their buckskin cowgirl costume with my raccoon coat and rabbit hat, all while the Iroquois made the war calls of several tribes, his own included. I circled twice, firing gunpowder blanks from the rifle, then stopped and stood. While I balanced on the horse's haunches, I directed the audience like a conductor, singing my round. This done, I dismounted with a backflip and chose a young man from the crowd, handing him a paper rose and leading him to the center of the circus tent, where clowns dressed as parents and priests waited and married us in front of the singing audience.

By the time I reached Paris, I'd been married this way a hundred times, in Italy, Spain, and Portugal.

In the first month, whenever the announcer told the story of the girl "captured by the Indians as a child and raised in their wild ways," who spoke no English except a song she'd learned from her mother, I felt as though each time I sang, my mother was listening, watching.

There was no name I could take that would hide me from her, I knew. But as I sang this more, it soon became the song I sang for the show, and it reminded me of her less and less.

My speaking voice had not returned, and the singing voice stayed, which felt like a truce or a sacrifice, depending on the day. I feared that one day it might switch, and I'd wake and find a normal girl's voice there, the singing voice gone — and find that I was done. While the circus became like a family to me very quickly, I always knew it was a family I'd auditioned for, and I could see that if I was to be injured or the crowd tired of the act I could be left behind. You might get to repair costumes, or take tickets, or cook, but only if there was an opening.

No one ever mentioned the previous girl in my spot. No one ever told stories of her, or why she'd left, or said if she was even alive. I thought of her sometimes, as I had her tent and her gun, after all, and her horse. If Mela missed her, he had no way to show me that I could see. He, like the rest, gamely trotted out his paces.

For all I knew, it was her ghostly hands at my throat.

So it was I sought to make Flambeau my teacher. She, or he, as I was to discover, was our barker and stood by the entrance, blowing gouts of fire into the air and then exhorting the fascinated crowds to come inside.

The first few times I watched him practice, I didn't recognize him and wondered who the young man was breathing fire in the yard. He didn't wear the enormous wig for all his rehearsals. He wasn't young anymore, but the fire had made his face as smooth as a woman's—all the hair burned off, so he never had to shave, though he could never grow a beard. I thought he was new, like I was, and didn't mind that he ignored me at first, as I was too fascinated by the fire, and for that alone, I wanted us to be friends. He didn't acknowledge me until after several days he said, very suddenly, You want to do this? And I recognized his voice.

He held out the jar of *pétrole* he used. I nodded my head. It was all I wanted.

You don't want to do this, he then replied, laughing, putting out his palm to stop me. Don't want to ruin that pretty face! You need your eyelashes to bat at the men in the audience!

It seemed like the most beautiful thing in the world, though, much more beautiful than my eyelashes. To tip your head back, hold the torch to your lips, and let out a stream of fire. I could close my eyes and see it, the bright yellow tongue in the dark, blue right near my lips. The very best trick, my favorite, was the ring of fire.

I hoped to use it in my act. I hoped I could learn to blow a ring I could leap through from the horse's back. Horses hated fire, after all, and if I did it this way, they'd never see it, I told myself. It was a stupid idea, but I loved it all the same.

You don't want to do this, he would say again and again the first month. But still I came.

It was Flambeau, then, who taught me to smoke cigars. They were my practice. Smoking a cigar required you to keep the smoke from your lungs. Breathing in the fire was the death of the fire-breather, a terrible, painful death as you choked on smoke and your own blood. The ring of cigar smoke was to be a ring of fire someday. And so I kept at it as practice and learned how to blow smoke rings, practicing for my ridiculous, impossible act, but also to someday join him if my voice ever vanished and left the circus before I did.

Until my departure from the show, I never left the confines of the tent village wherever we were. Some days it was as if the world shifted around us in the night, the foreign cities each time nearly as nameless to me as the men I picked from the ring to meet me beside the clowns.

The Cajun Maidens adopted me and taught me my falls and tumbles, how to walk on my hands, how to understand their mixture of French, Russian, Spanish, and English. They gave me a knife to wear on my thigh, a dagger. They called it a circus dowry, and they never took theirs off except when bathing, and even then they set them on the edge of the tub, and soon I was the same.

I pulled it out of its sheath at night, testing the edge.

The knife came with lessons on how to use it. If a man was attacking me, I was to cut for the places they'd have to hold shut — the underside of a wrist, the throat — not to try to stab for the heart first, they said.

The heart is a difficult target, Priscilla said with a smile. Laughter came from her sisters as she said it. But everyone forgets to protect their hands. This is a mistake. A grim satisfaction crossed her face. Also, you may not want to kill them, she said. But only teach a lesson. And then she paused. But it may be you want to kill them, and there was more laughter.

For your future husband, said the circus matron. To give to him however you might choose. She winked and patted her own.

~

While at first I was frightened of trying to speak, I soon took to trying once each day. For who could say when would be the day I was forgiven? What if the voice was only to be gone three years, or ten, and not forever? This was the way to know. The first times I tried, I felt as though I were sneaking up to God to see if He was still angry, but soon I was at ease trying.

Soon the voice began to whisper back.

That first morning I made a sound; the sound of my voice felt like I had fallen down a well in my own throat. But I took it as the beginning I had waited for.

Understand, I had no love for Paris when I chose to leave that day—it was only another place to pass through, a station on a train. It was enough for me that I could speak again, enough to ask questions. The voice sounded odd but could be understood. The morning I could say "a ticket please" clearly and loudly in English and French was our third morning in Paris, and with that, I hatched my plan.

Seven

THAT DAY I first stepped out onto the streets of Paris was the day
I was to perform for the Emperor, and it began with my sneaking
out to buy a train ticket dressed in a ridiculous costume borrowed
from the costume mistress.

If I had succeeded, I can't imagine the tale I'd tell here now.

I had told the costume mistress I wanted to go out to see some
sights but didn't want to wear my buckskin. She found me the costume for the clown who we hid in the audience, playing at being the
kind of wife never allowed anywhere but brought out to the circus
for a bit of fun. The other clowns typically carried her off screaming, and the performer who played her later returned to the ring
wearing the same dress, complete with clown makeup, and an enormous clown kiss painted along her cheek.

Don't tell a soul, the costume mistress had said to me, to which I
gave an exasperated sigh. Of course I would tell no one. They won't
mistake you for a Parisienne, she smirked. It might do you good to
spend a coin or two on some Paris fashion while you're there.

I greeted this suggestion with bewilderment until I stood almost
in the street.

I was dressed in a dun-colored day dress, the skirt full of crinolines; leather boots laced to just below the knee; a gray bonnet. I
don't know that the average citizen of Paris had ever seen a colonial
farm wife before, but I'd hoped that day, because of the Expo and
the many other more strangely dressed people, that I blended in.
Once I stood in the glassed entrance to the Expo, unable to enter
the crowd, I knew I did not.

A strange pressure was crawling on my skin. What I wanted to do seemed as likely to happen as turning to the wall and passing through the solid stone.

The costume mistress had told me the omnibus would have a flag. Look for the signs for the Gare de l'Est, she'd said.

In the distance I saw the omnibus flag she mentioned above the horizon line created by the tops of the heads in the crowd. Above that still, I saw the street and the strange machines and carriages flying back and forth. Young men mounted on *vélocifères,* phaetons, landaus, fiacres, victorias, all moving at terrific speeds and not, somehow, running into each other.

The omnibus was a beast all its own when it finally came, an enormous viewing stand set on wheels and drawn by three horses with metal sides and windows enclosing the lower levels. The men sat on top, the women inside, forbidden from the upper level, I suppose, to prevent them from showing to the entire street what was under their skirts. Each omnibus was thus typically crowned with two rows of top hats, the men sitting back to back.

As I stood in the line for the omnibus, I became anxious. I knew my costume stood out enough that any member of the circus who saw me might know it was me dressed as the clown bride. But I soon forgot this particular ensemble when I did first see with my own eyes the woman I would come to know as the Comtesse de Castiglione.

She was unlike any woman I'd ever seen. She had just exited the *bateau mouche* of some foreign royal, and as she walked through the gaudy international crowd of the Expo, they pulled back. Even the incredible machines all came to a stop to let her cross, all startled into a silence. She was dressed in mourning, a black veil over her eyes that still allowed you to see their green flash, a hat of black ostrich feathers with a single sapphire glinting at the top. A velvet cape covered her black silk gown, floating behind her with a train held aloft by crinolines, the like of which I'd never seen. Jet beads flashed along her jet shoes, answered by jet beads flashing along the edge of her veil. Another sapphire, this one with diamonds along the rim of its setting, held the cape at her neck.

This, I understood at once, was what the costume mistress had referred to—a woman who, in a single toilette, had silenced the street with awe—and from her dress, silk enough to cover an opera stage hung from her waist.

As she crossed the street, she stopped, picked her train up gently —in a gesture I would one day imitate exactly—and continued.

She walked with a steady stride and did not meet the eyes of a single onlooker, looking past us all—a dark bird of myth, her wings having fallen from her back, these feathers at her neck and brow some last remnant, her transformation into a mortal woman nearly complete.

I knew I would remember this sight forever. For all of us who ever saw the Comtesse in her glory, we all remembered our first time. She was one of the great beauties of Paris.

If I had known everything that was to come, I might have fled, run back to the show, and continued on, away from Paris, never to return. But it is too soon to speak more of this.

Instead, I will tell you of how the omnibus arrived with its flag for the station, just as the costume mistress had said. I stepped up, feeling I had learned a lesson about how women dress in Paris, and paid my fare, dreaming of how one day I'd be as fine a lady as the one I'd just seen once I had been reunited with my mother's family in Lucerne.

～

My first mission to the Gare de l'Est was both easy and unfruitful. I could not read many of the signs at the terminal. Finally, I went to the window of the ticket counter. I was told to go to the Gare du Nord.

At the Gare du Nord I looked for and found the ticket counter and checked the cost of passage to the city of Lucerne. I had nearly enough. I closed my glove over the slip of paper on which the ticket clerk had written the amount and moved through the station, the doves adrift in the beams of light falling in through the windows and the rush of the crowds around me. By the time I returned to the street, I felt as if a wind were slowly lifting me and soon I would be in that far city in the mountains.

The owner liked to boast of how I didn't own a stitch of clothing that wasn't one of his costumes, and it was nearly true for most, but not for me. Only the buckskin was his. He'd forgotten the rest of the clothes were my own. He always showed a thick set of teeth when he laughed at this joke, and he enjoyed this joke many times, in as many ways as he could find, reminding me constantly how I belonged to him. I soon hated the sight of those teeth. When I returned to the tent city with my plan nearly complete, he saw me in my borrowed attire. He was soon laughing again at me.

Where did you steal that? he asked.

I ran past him without stopping.

It should be buffalo skin, he said. Settler's Daughter, not the farm wife. Go and get ready, the show is in an hour.

Paris was lit by gaslights at night, turning the night skies purple, like a bruise—the nights there didn't feel like night to me, but instead like some permanent dusk, as if the sun had caught on something just after setting and wouldn't go all the way down. This evening, I knew, was the special presentation for the Emperor and the visiting royalty of the collected nations, perhaps the most important show I would ever sing, but this meant little to me. Thoughts of the trip to come distracted me. The trains for Lucerne were new and crowded, and gleamed with fresh paint.

I wondered if my family would know me.

As I waited in the center of the ring, the chalk on my hands fresh, the lights down low, the arcade was lit partly by the city outside, light coming through the glass windows of the Exposition building. I could make out the figures of the Emperor and the Empress, still see the glow of leather, the flash of gems.

I considered choosing the Emperor to be the one married to me by the clowns.

Tonight I was to launch into the air and sing from a trapeze as the horses ran the edge of the ring below. I heard the crank of the winch above me and reached for the bar of the swing, which I found with ease.

Mesdames et messeurs . . .

The crowd cheered as I rose into the air in my buckskin, the trapeze pulling me up until I could see as I sang the far edges of the city, enough to imagine myself in the train pulling away into this night the color of a wound.

When I returned to the ground, the crowd was unusually still. No one was singing along. An eerie quiet edged the rise and fall of my voice as I wandered, looking for a young man to choose, and the clowns, when I found one at last, watched me with terrified eyes. The crowd still roared at the end, but I stood through it with a thudding heart. The roaring quieted then, and young men in uniform entered the ring, as formal as if they were there to arrest me.

The circus master nodded, however, in a gesture to me to indicate I was not in danger.

I was brought in front of the Emperor and the Empress, the light disguise of their dominoes no disguise at all—these masks were like crowns. I curtsied as best I could. He withdrew from his pocket that rose brooch and, to my surprise, placed it in my hand.

I knew what they were despite never having seen one— *So these are rubies,* I remember thinking—so much more expensive than anything I'd ever owned in my life.

I looked down, afraid to meet his eyes, whispering only a quick *Merci, mon Empereur,* and as I backed away, my hand closed over the astonishing gift. The audience laughed at how I had spoken to him —I was not yet his subject. He smiled, seeming not at all angry that I had not used the formalities.

I rubbed the flower in my hand. There was nowhere it would be safe from thieves in the circus, but it was more than enough to sell for my fare. I sprinted back to the ring to continue the show, sure of my departure at last.

~

The next morning, from the edge of our tents, I could see clothes hanging to dry in the distance. One was a red silk satin gown. It whipped in the wind like the flag of some other, better country.

Here, clearly, were the clothes of a grand lady. But more important, here was the dress of Rose Red, the dress she would wear as she refused to marry, the dress I had been singing my way to all that time.

I was sure I'd sung the dress into existence, like the brooch. I was sure this all belonged to me.

It was perfect, I decided, for me to wear to Lucerne.

I rolled up my bedroll and tied my money and brooch inside it. I kissed the circus matron as she slept, threw my parcel over ahead of me, and leapt the fence. I left my costumes there, the pistols in their holsters, with a note, saying, *You were right. So long and thanks.*

I walked toward the clothes as if in a dream, dressed in just a pinafore and my mother's old raccoon coat, my stiletto strapped to the outside of my knee. The colored silks, dresses, petticoats, and corsets moved on their lines as if in separate winds. I felt like I had when I was a girl and wore my mother's coat in her room when she was out in the field. Like this was a game and I was pretending at being a grand lady somewhere far away.

The laundry that day belonged to a courtesan, I'm sure. Her silks and satins were hypnotic even when left out to dry. I ran my hands over the one gown I'd followed all this way, made from red silk satin. I slid it off the line, held it to my waist, and then stepped into it and left for the Gare du Nord.

~

This was where Simonet's novel began.

The package had arrived the day after my dinner with the Verdis. I opened it to find he had inscribed it.

To Lilliet Berne,

It's amazing to think of, isn't it? Where she went after she left. Where did she go? May we conjure it together!

I am yours,
Frédéric Simonet

Act II

The Cave of Queens
and Courtesans

One

WHERE DID SHE GO?

Here she is in the Bois, then, in the red dress she stole to go to Lucerne.

She is rubbing her foot. She looks to be a *grisette* with a stone in her shoe, rubbing her foot. Or she is in her Tuileries uniform, the cheap-looking dark dress, the wooden shoes. She is working at the Tuileries, taking the air. Or the dress is something she bought from a junk dealer, a dead woman's dress most likely, it is all she has right now. But soon, so many more.

Soon a gentleman will draw up in a carriage. This is often why she rubs her feet here by the road. It feels good: she is tired from walking. But the bare foot is also her little flag.

The foot is soft and pale, and clean. It has to be clean.

Sometimes, as she rubs it, she is cleaning it. The gentlemen who love her feet, they often do not touch the rest of her, and this is a mercy. One day she will wander the Bois, stripping the bark from the trees to eat. But for now, she is here.

In *The Aeneid,* we find a forest grove in the underworld devoted to those who died from love. Aeneas enters and walks past Dido, and in this way learns she killed herself when he left her to continue the quest that had led him there; the smoke he saw when he looked back was her pyre.

I couldn't remember if she knew he would travel there to see his father again, if she knew this was the one way she could be there, to see him once more. But I think she did.

The underworld is not a place for the living, and those who try to enter are, until they leave, in terrible peril. They are asked to have a very pure heart. The only living girl to ever leave was made to return half the year for eternity, married off to the King of Hell, as she had eaten something there before she left.

I would joke that the entrance was in Paris, in the Bois, until I was nearly sure of it, and then I never made the joke again. But let us say it is there, for the sake of argument, or the story, or what have you. Say it is there and now come in.

Two

IN MY ROLE as Marguerite, I was much closer to the girl I'd been when I left the Cajun Maidens than in any role I'd played previously.

It was not angels who'd saved me then, however, but the Cave of Queens and Courtesans.

Each night of *Faust* was a reminder.

As I put on my prison bonnet for Marguerite's Act V mad scene, I remembered, like a low hum, the sound of Saint-Lazare. Tick-tick-tick-tick-tick-tick-tick-*tick*, tick-tick-tick-tick-tick-tick-tick-*tick*. Again and again, on and on, the sound of women and girls in the cells, tapping our bare fingers, a machine made of women and iron bars, and misery, of course. Sometimes the guards would come and tell us all to be silent, threatening to break our fingers, especially if at some point we all began to tap together as one; mostly they allowed it, for if they did not, some other, worse sound, say, like wailing, would come.

If we kept the tapping soft, just soft enough, it was there, we could hear it, and they didn't mind.

Often, there was still wailing.

There was nothing to do, no occupation to keep us busy other than keeping the mice, lice, and spiders at bay as best we could. The food was repulsive to consider and ended hunger bowl by disgusting bowl. And yet its arrival was still welcome; it relieved the tedium.

There was the spoon, the bowl, the terrible porridge or stew to scrape out.

Was it worse to starve or to eat it, always this was the question.

Was it worse to stay or to leave and return to the street?

Was it worse to stay or be bought? And leave to submit to the hands of the purchaser and his wants, the little favors and would-you-pleases and do-this-nows, which you were sure you could do forever instead of this, but your willingness would not matter: you would do it until the one who'd bought you was done with you, when you would return here, no matter your vows, to the bars and the bowl and the spoon, with the memory of who you'd been when you left, when you'd thought the bowl and spoon were never to be seen again. How foolish you were, how silly and small you were: you, you'd thought you were done.

But the bowl, the spoon, they knew they would see you again.

There's a story told of my voice that says it was bought from a witch, the result of an occult surgery. I am said to treat it nightly with arcane oils and ointments, my real voice in a box on the witch's mantel.

If you lift the lid, apparently, you can hear it saying everything I can't say with this voice, the voice that sings. The witch's bargain is that I cannot perform normal speech.

I never corrected this.

I like to imagine myself returning to the witch to bargain again. Pulling aside my scarf, a door there cut along my throat opening like a clock. I raise the box to my throat, and out comes something small and fierce. It hops in my hand like a little bird.

What would it say?

The real answer to where my voice came from is as ordinary as all of life. In Paris, in the winter, the chestnut trees in the Bois drop their nuts and the poorest gather them and roast them in fires on the street corners. The smell of them to me is the smell of the Paris winter coming. Wrapped in old newspapers, the corners folded back, the chestnuts steam in a neat pile, their split backs curling open.

I wanted to eat and so I learned to sing. I the same as the woman who on a winter afternoon roasts chestnuts from the Bois de Boulogne and sells them so she can buy her dinner. It took more than a witch to make a singer out of me. And if it was a gift from God that made me this way, it was the gift He gave us all, called hunger.

Three

THE NOVEL STAYED on my desk, some strange new artifact. I kept opening it and reading the first page of the chapter on my arrival in Paris and then closing it, unable to read further.

Instead, I would lie down, so as not to run through the bookshops with a torch, burning them all.

I needed to read it, to see what was in it, and yet I could not go past the first page without my thoughts running to who it could be behind this. Simonet still seemed innocent. I still believed he did not know I was the girl singer who so enchanted him. But that did not mean the situation was innocent, only him.

And if the curse was true, I feared that even reading the novel might somehow make her invented fate my own.

It was not much bigger than my thumb, this little ruby rose pin. I could still see it, the jewels so deeply red, my hand closing around it as the Emperor gave it to me. Almost more than I feared anyone who would tell of its secrets, I feared it itself—it had always been bad luck for me. It glowed now, rising in the Paris night from where it still lived, apparently, at the center of my life again, like a tiny midnight sun, tiny and yet enormous, and in its light, a story only I could see.

Or, at least, so I had hoped until now.

There were only three people in Paris who knew of the rose's time with me and the secrets I'd want to keep. It had taken me to each of them in turn, once I had accepted it from the Emperor's hand. The first still loved me but had betrayed me, the second had once owned me. The third, I would say, never thought of me at all. Or so I hoped.

She was the most dangerous of them all.

There was once a fourth, but he was dead. I had watched him die; he had given his life for me. And until the day Simonet approached me at the *bal,* I believed the flower, if not the story, was still with him.

I had left that ruby flower with him.

Not one of the living had any reason to tell this story, and the dead man never would. We had reached our various accommodations and agreements. But if the story had been told, this could only mean something had changed, a mistake had been made or a balance of power shifted. If so, this novel was then either a sign or a signal. And, sign or signal, it was a threat.

When I went down to the bookstalls along the Seine at last, I bought three copies, wrapped one for each of my old friends, determined to give them one and see just what they said.

I began my search with the one who loved me.

You should always begin there, I think. The secret hurt, long nurtured, never brought to light, until it has grown lethal in the dark and the smile of friendship is all that is left to hang there like a lure.

～

She was my one sincere friend in Paris. Euphrosyne, known to most as the Marquise de Lambert now. She ran a salon on Mondays that she named Les Petits Lundis, after the Empress Eugénie's salon evening of the same name—she was obsessed with the Empress. Her husband, who almost never attended, she referred to as *l'Empereur.* She'd had herself painted as the Empress dressed as Marie Antoinette—just as the Empress had. I knew almost nothing about her husband except that he was exceedingly rich and he kept her in style, devotedly, in a beautiful *hôtel* in the sixth arrondissement by the Luxembourg Gardens.

I had sung there on occasion, and it was one of my few diversions, one of the few salons I ever consented to attend.

When I say I suspected Euphrosyne, I mean it was quite possible she knew Simonet well and that the salon I'd heard him at was hers. I expected no treachery from her, except that perhaps Simonet had been her lover and she had said too much. I could imagine him in her bed, writing down everything she said of me, the story not quite her story of me, but his crude drawing of what she knew of me embellished.

The next available Monday, I went and presented myself, was admitted, and waited to be received by her in her reception hall. All seemed to be as it had always been. The hall was still made of white marble and sparely decorated with classical sculptures. When she ran to me, embracing me and kissing me, dressed in some new beautiful lilac chiffon gown, her shoulders bare except for a collar of diamonds, she was a vision, as beautiful as she had always been. I said as much, and complimented her on the gown. She winked at me and said, You. You'll need your compliments. Come with me, you terrible girl, you have something to tell me, and she then pulled me from the gathering crowd into her empty library.

I have heard you are getting married! she said, as she shut the door. I cannot believe you, that I had to hear it this way from someone else. Who is it? Is it really the tenor at the Paris Opera?

I only laughed, stunned. And then after a pause, during which I said nothing from shock, she said, Ah. I cannot believe I was tricked like this. Of course, you would have written at once.

At once, I said. I would have run to your side. No letter at all. And I would have asked you to tell me it was madness. Where did you hear this? I asked.

In the press! She called out for her maid to bring her the day's paper and then showed me a column by an opera reviewer who said he had heard I was rejecting roles out of the fear that my voice was cursed. His column in *Le Figaro* was mockingly referred to as Mon Vieux because all of his sources for gossip were simply called *mon vieux. I have this on good word from my old friend, who says he* believes she may not really be cursed but is, in fact, leaving the stage to marry, and he suspects it is, at last, her longtime costar, a tenor of the Paris Opera.

Absurd, I said. Even ridiculous. Not a word of this is true.

And who could marry you? Euphrosyne said. It would be like trying to marry the wind.

You'll forgive me if I cannot stay, I said. Of course, I knew exactly what was meant by the rumor, though I couldn't say so — to do so would be to spread it again even, or perhaps especially, to Euphrosyne.

You cannot let this rumor of your marriage put you into hiding, Euphrosyne said, grabbing my hand and holding me, laughing. It's not as if it's a shameful thing to marry . . . and she became distracted for a moment by her own thoughts. Her eyes lit and she looked around the music room. Come, she said, and she walked me to her garden.

I cannot stay, love. I must go home and write to him at once, I said.

I will throw a ball in your honor, she said, and you will sing and publicly denounce the rumor at the evening's end. Including the curse. Or is the curse real?

No, it's too much, I said. I will simply take Mon Vieux up on one of his many offers to dine with him, I said. And correct him in person.

I will. I will, she said, not listening to me at all. I could never stop her.

I was thinking the ball should be in honor of your appearance in *Faust* and your return to Paris — I have missed you! In fact, the Cave of Queens and Courtesans will be our theme, the fifth act ballet, which I adore. I will be Eugénie, you can be the Queen of the Night. And you can perform her song, "The Vengeance of Hell Boils in My Heart," she said. She looked ecstatic. I was about to explain to her that Astarte in *Faust* was not the Queen of the Night, but I hesitated — I knew the news would disappoint her. And yet, the Queen of the Night, this was not in my *Fach*.

The curse is not real, my dear, yes? This is also a rumor?

Of course, I said. And, of course, the ball will be perfect. You are too good to me. Thank you. Here, a present for you.

I had almost forgotten my little mission. I handed her the book wrapped in paper. She giggled as she held it aloft. How wonderful, she said, as she unwrapped it. I do not know it! Her eyes showed real surprise, real delight. She was innocent.

I kissed her on her cheeks, and then she held my hand as we walked toward the door. I will make excuses for you, she said, gesturing to the room. It will be incredible. Worth will make all of our costumes, she said. Incredible.

I rushed home.

I was sure I could still undo what I had done.

The newspaper column told me a story of the last few days. I was chagrined to think of Verdi and his wife dining with Mon Vieux and telling tales while I had been lost in my fears and memories. I wrote a note to the Verdis.

> Please excuse me a moment's foolishness at dinner. I am too superstitious. I have found a saint's bone charm and will defy my curse, and am happy to make room in my schedule for *I Masnadieri*.

A moment's foolishness, but I knew only too well what that foolishness could cost me.

The opera world pardoned a soprano's excesses so often that she could imagine all would be pardoned, but once she did, she would find herself lost. Not all could be or would be forgiven, at least not by opera house managers and composers, much less audiences. I feared the news of the curse would render me a pariah, and all my work would vanish.

All I had wanted was the time to consider this offer, and if I rejected it, a way to find some peace with it, and so I had made my little lie. Perhaps you can imagine the despair I felt then, to find this lie of mine racing on ahead of me, and my arriving just after it had moved on, undoing the latches of my life.

~

We had an old oath, Euphrosyne and I. Sworn to each other in the first days of our friendship, solemn as a betrothal. She was the closest thing I'd had to a husband.

I met her fifteen years previous, as we waited together for the omnibus. I had seen her a few times at this stop but had never found a way to speak to her despite my fascination. I remember this day was like all the other nights and days I'd seen her except it was even darker, and as there was only a little light from a street lamp, I was glad I was not alone.

She looked spent, her eyes shadowy, sooty, and so still that at first I thought she was asleep, perhaps from too much drink. When she did move her eyes, it startled me, and her glance made me look at whatever drew her attention.

Her skin was slightly sallow, and she was not pretty, but she exerted a nearly violent need for your attention. Her cloud of hair was like smoke. She was wearing an enormous cancan skirt, the biggest I'd ever seen, filling the seats to either side of her on the bench as she slumped rakishly, her half-lidded eyes watching something directly ahead of her, something only she could see.

Euphrosyne's skirts were hiked up over her knees—she was cooling herself in the night air after a night of dancing. I took in her shoes, the dark leather and bright red laces, the toes of the shoes like smirks and the high heels like stems or talons. They were cancan shoes. I'd never seen them before and so I stared at them. I'd never seen anything for women before that looked so beautiful and dangerous and ordinary at the same time, and so I wanted them immediately.

I tried to think of how to speak with her, how to ask her about her shoes.

The police are so lazy, she said then, surprising me.

Are they? I asked.

Yes, she said. Here they are. They do nothing. I don't know what they do. The Berlin police, now, *they* are not so lazy.

This seemed very sophisticated. Your shoes, I said, now that I had my opening.

She laughed and extended a leg out, pointing her toe. Yes, I love them.

They're so strange, I said. Are they for something?

She laughed again and shook her head. Child, she said. These are for *dancing*. You mean to tell me you don't know about dancing? Cancan?

She held out her hand to me. Euphrosyne Courrèges, she said. At the Bal Mabille you know me only as La Frénésie. She twirled her other hand in the air as she said it. She let go of my hand and then, smiling, got to her feet and stomped her shoes on the stones, holding up her skirt as she did and looking down on them as if to be sure they did their work. Then she looked at me, a wild grin on her face.

We will get you some, child. And then I will show you what they are for. And with that, she stomped them again against the stones.

Are you a registered girl? she asked. She said it *fille en carte*, drawing each of the words out mockingly. Which house do you work for?

I did not know what this meant yet and struggled with the idea. No, I said finally. I'm . . . I'm an equestrienne. I ride horses at Cirque Napoléon, a hippodrome rider.

She struck her forehead theatrically and pressed my hand again. *Fantastique!* she yelled. That is the only thing better than dancing. I laughed. She exuded the tough confidence of the young soldiers who came to my shows and smoked in the front, yelling compliments that felt like insults.

I don't know what this is, I said, *fille en carte*, though I could guess.

It means . . . you are in danger! *Right now!* She laughed. Perhaps I will be arrested for corrupting you. Except for those lazy police. But you, I think it will be worth it.

The omnibus arrived. We got on together, paid our fare, and sat on the lower level with the other women and the men who could not climb to the roof. I will have my new gentleman take me to your show, she said confidingly, and tapped my arm as she said it. I have a new gentleman. We will call on you there. She clapped her hands at the thought. And then from her bag on her wrist she withdrew her card.

You may call on me there, she said, and we looked at the address together. And then, after a moment, she asked, No card for you?

I shook my head, knocking my feet together like a schoolgirl. No, I said. No card for me.

~

On the day I did not go to Lucerne, I sat down in the grass of the Bois and stared at the Emperor's token in my cupped hand, sheltered so no one but me could see it. The coins I'd made thus far surrounded it, minus my most recent pay, left behind in my rush. The feeling of possessing great riches had passed, and now I did not know either how to sell it or how to protect it. Offering it for sale to people on the street seemed a quick way to lose it, but if I did not sell it, it seemed to me I could not go on.

My feet were tired, and I had taken off my shoe to look for a stone. A carriage pulled up. The man in it looked at me beckoningly. I shook my head and he drove off, shocked.

Another came by and it was the same.

Another. I thought of walking up to him to ask him how much he would pay for the pin and then closed my hand over it.

I put my shoe back on and left, annoyed. I had only wanted to sit and think in the grass, but this did not seem possible.

I didn't know how to do anything else, other than try to get my ticket to the town where they lived. Everything since my family's death had led me to this train ride and what was waiting past the station there.

Once I was in the station, a hunger like nausea crept over me. I took a cup of tea at a counter and waited by the gate, watching the travelers.

The cup of tea cost money, of course, and so as I waited I had a little less even than before. Soon I would need to eat. And if I did not get on the train, I would need a place to sleep.

The policemen of the station eyed me warily. I sat with my tea, opening and closing my hand over the flower as I thought of what to do. How to go to Lucerne and also keep this pin.

I stayed until I decided to stay, find more work, and return the dress.

The rose did seem to bring me luck at first. Even my bad luck turned to good.

When I sneaked back to the clothesline to return the dress, the laundress caught me, and while she was angry at first, she soon ridiculed me in French, saying I was a clown, if a pretty one, and asked me why I had no clothes.

I could see the tents of the Cajun Maidens still in the distance behind her as she spoke.

When I didn't answer right away, she told me I was clearly stupid but that she would take pity on me. If I would work for her to repay her for her trouble, she would not call the police. And with that, she led me from the field. By that afternoon, I had from her the plain smock of a *grisette*, not so nice but good enough, and a place to hide from my old circus boss, who I was sure was looking for me. By evening, I was helping to deliver clothes to the room of the courtesan whose dress I'd stolen there at the hotel where the laundry was. She did not receive me, but I saw her small slippered foot from the door.

I did not tell the laundress where I was from. She never mentioned, when the papers the next day announced the disappearance of one of the circus stars, how she had found me. Even if she had connected the girl found near the circus in her mistress's laundry with the one said to have escaped, she would have been incredulous to think the girl who fumbled mending knew how to jump from a running horse and then back on again. I smiled in the first month when, on errands, I saw the circus poster still advertising me standing on the back of the horse, waving my hat in the air. And then soon the other posters covered it and the little cowgirl was gone.

The laundress repaired costumes for the Cirque Napoléon. After I had made a delivery for her, the owner caught me riding on one of the horses, having charmed one of the grooms. Again my bad luck turned good when he was, despite his anger, greatly impressed by my way with horses and insisted I come work for him.

The Cirque Napoléon was like putting a circus in a theater, as if someone had cast a spell on a circus tent and turned it to stone, filling it with gaslight chandeliers and columns. There was a circular track down in the center where we performed, ringed by rows of seats climbing in circles. The audience was larger than any I'd seen at the Cajun Maidens, and we performed with an orchestra, mostly Conservatoire boys, made elegant by their white shirts and frock coats, who played for beer or wine. The patrons came in and out as they pleased with their drinks and cigarettes, down red carpets lining the stairs to the ring.

I rode a horse bareback, tumbling across its back before leaping through flaming hoops, landing back on the horse as it rode on. The act was my idea, born from my dreams of fire-breathing. The hoops were enormous and the flames ringed the top half. They had paper centers that would shatter with a sound like a drum and catch fire, the burning bits fluttering down into the dirt floor of the ring and winking out.

I did not sing, not yet. I still worried that my old *cirque* was still in Paris or nearby and that if I sang they might find me, though I feared this less each week. Most nights the ring exerted a certain magic, and in it, I could feel as if I were powerful, possessed of a grace I never felt when I was off the horse. And never more so than when my new friend Euphrosyne was in the audience. For this felt lucky, too.

～

Euphrosyne came to see me the very next day after our meeting, as she said she would, with her new gentleman. He was a handsome young man, and he *was* new, perhaps just eighteen, barely shaving, a prince with a hero's name. They sat in the front row and clapped wildly with laughter, cheering as I exploded through the flaming paper hoop and landed again on the horse. I'd never enjoyed it so much as then. Afterward, I sat with them at their table and he poured some champagne for me, my first.

She came regularly to see me, and I soon would leave a ticket for her if she had no young man, though this was rare. She took me to her cobbler and bought me my first pair of cancan heels one morning after a visit from the princeling, pulling the franc notes from her bag with a smile and laying them on the table as if we were going to play baccarat. The cobbler folded the notes into his register quickly before motioning me to sit, and then he tenderly took my foot in his hand to measure.

Fille en carte means "prostitute." When I tried to understand what this meant, I asked Euphrosyne, Where is the card?

The police station, she said, squinting as if everyone should know.

In her entry in the *Gentleman's Guide to Paris,* a guidebook listing some of the more well-known *maisons closes* and the women in them, Euphrosyne was noted for her passionate abandon. Of her *prix d'amour,* it said she was neither the most expensive nor the cheapest, but that the client should prepare to pay extra for champagne. Which made me smile.

I would first see the guide a few months later when a man I knew held it out to me and laughingly asked if I was inside. He meant this as an insult, but I had the sense not to give myself away by looking. If I *was* ever in there, I would have been listed after her. By then we were regulars at the Bal Mabille and Euphrosyne had introduced me to everyone with the ridiculous name Jou-jou Courrèges, saying we were sisters. And she did feel like the sister I'd never had.

I still thrill to think of the Bal Mabille. A city garden at night unlike any other, strung with lanterns and full of music, people laughing and dancing, heading off into the groves for more private entertainments.

Here Euphrosyne had earned her name, La Frénésie. This was her *cirque*, her burning ring, and the role of her horse was played by nearly every man there.

Her princeling, we came to know, had something of a pattern, seeing her every night soon after some monthly sum was deposited with him, vanishing as it was spent, and returning again the next month. We began to call him La Lune for the way he waxed and waned. On our nights without him, we would command a table and she would sit with her second- or third-favorite young man of the evening and whoever was mine, ordering bottles, usually of champagne, and we would dance until morning.

I knew I was beautiful to men; I had guessed that by now. But because of my own severity toward myself, toward others, I had none of her sultry grace — my appeal was something of a cooler thing, starker. But this was fine; it made us perfect friends. The men who pursued her would be friendly to me, and those who pursued me friendly to her, but we never competed, never fought for the same man except one.

There was only one she was ever jealous of. And, to be sure, I would have preferred in some ways it had been her he'd chosen, that she'd prevailed. But, unfortunately, I won.

But it is too soon to speak of that as well. For now, we are still concerned with shoes for dancing.

~

Euphrosyne had a quality I felt I also had, but I had feared it was hidden until now. I wanted for her to see me and recognize me as one of her kind, whatever she was. Now that she came and cheered me on in the arena, I became bolder, just as she did at the Bal Mabille with me, I think. In any case, however it came to be, there was a night when, enraged, she cracked an empty bottle on the head of a man who was impatient with her rejection of him.

Without hesitation, I lunged to my feet and pulled my knife as she stood screaming at his friends. They drew back in terror. The offending gentleman groaned from the floor by the table, and in the dark I could see the wetness that I knew to be blood.

Euphrosyne giggled and grabbed me, and we ran from the Bal as the man's friends behind us called for the police.

I'd never pulled the knife, not like that. In my hand it burned, as if aflame. With one swift motion, I threw up my skirt as we ran, and it was back in its sheath.

Every girl in the hippodrome had one.

I had learned the knife was not just for men. The secret to being a rider in the hippodrome wasn't that you must be agile, or that you must be good with horses, or that you must be strong and steady as the horse careens to the far end of the arena and back with you riding on its back. It was that you must hide inside your costume a little of a killer's heart.

The animal will be tender with you, and you with it, but the animal never forgets that when what it wants for survival requires your death, it will become unafraid to kill you. And so you cannot forget this, either.

It is, on reflection, good training to be a courtesan. A woman of any kind.

～

Euphrosyne brought me back her apartment, and we fell through the door into the entrance hall, gasping. Inside, looking very stern in her chaise, was a woman I first assumed was the concierge. At the sight of her, Euphrosyne began laughing, her hand over her mouth at first, which then only made her laugh the harder.

Shit, my friend. That knife. I never saw a man look like that, ever. I could get used to that.

You've quite an arm yourself, I said. I began to laugh as well.

The woman by the door was not amused. Who is this? she asked Euphrosyne. You're not allowed this sort of guest.

It's only for a few minutes, Odile, I promise, Euphrosyne said.

There'll be a fine for this, Odile said ominously, as we passed by her.

In her kitchen Euphrosyne held out her hand for my knife, and when I gave it to her, she stabbed it into the cork of a bottle of wine and twisted it out. She drank from the neck thirstily and handed it to me, and I did the same. This calls for a proper smoke, she said, and fumbled in her skirts, extracting two cigars. She cut the tips and struck a match against the stone of her counter, and soon the fragrant smoke lifted between us. She waved me to her balcony and handed me one.

I held it in my hand, happy.

Pull it into your mouth, not your throat, she said, as if I did not know. And she winked. It's good practice, and then she giggled.

Now I can't, I said, and made a face as I blew the smoke out in a gust.

She laughed openly now, and I smiled and held it to my mouth again.

So it is that I can, I said.

Under the soft light coming off the city in the dark, we smoked and watched the street below, passing the bottle between us until we grew quiet.

She reached out and took my hand and began to sing, loudly down into the street,

> *De préférence chaque soir,*
> *L'amateur contemple*
> *Les belles d'nuit qui s'font voir*
> *Au boulevard du Temple!*

In the street, a pair of drunken men roared their approval. Again, she said to me, and hit me on the arm, Sing with me!

We sang it again, and as we reached *les belles*, she sang instead *les reines*, overemphasizing it, and I laughed at her doing this until I was choking a little on the wine and smoke, and then she laughed at me, also until choking.

Again! she shouted at me. Everyone must hear us!

We sang it again, over and over, until the street complained loudly. At this, Euphrosyne pouted and threw her now-empty bottle into the street, where it made a satisfying crash. The concert is over, she yelled down. We clambered back into her apartment.

Les reines d'nuit, she said, toasting, as she stabbed another bottle open and drank.

Les reines d'nuit, I said, and drank after her.

Do you imagine the police are still searching for us?

I shrugged. I honestly could not say. I was still unused to the world, unused to the idea of police. In my life until then, every time I'd left, I'd left, and no one remembered me, and no one cared. Or, at least, not that I ever knew. As I stood in her kitchen, a glass of wine in my hand, as drunk as I ever had been, it seemed, yes, unlikely that anyone knew me except her.

I would think they are, she said. I am so tired of them, though. Are you?

I was about to shrug again and then she said, Yes, I can tell you are also.

It is dreary, this life, she said, and her head hung down for a moment. When she looked up at me, she said, But there are moments it is very bright. Do you *love* me? she asked.

I nodded.

Yes, I love you, too, she said. She stood and walked over to me. When I watch you in the ring, as you leap through the fire, it's like you're the only beautiful thing in all the world.

No one had ever given me this kind of compliment before, and it lit the air around us. I saw myself briefly as she must have seen me.

All this time I'd admired her, I did not know she also admired me. I had never thought very much of what I did until then.

All the world, she said again. And then, Did I kill him, do you think? she asked. I think I might have killed him.

I said nothing to this, afraid she might have gone mad. I loved her, it was true. But I barely knew her.

I hope he is stronger than that, I managed. She laughed.

We'll need a disguise, she said. Come.

I had never seen an apartment like hers—I did not yet know what it was or where I was. The front rooms were decorated like a theater's lobby, with red velvet and gold braid, as if her bedroom were a theater box. Dark cherrywood furniture and thick rugs. I stopped myself from lying down on the one in her foyer. The door to her bedchamber had been made to resemble a box door exactly, papered in pale pink silk, which matched the fabric of the chairs, the bed, and her tufted vanity seat. All felt vaguely obscene, and yet magical, so different it was from the outside. I wanted to go back out to the foyer and enter again and again, to feel it again.

She went to her closet. They must be very good disguises, she said. For we are now murderesses. She gestured at her bed. Please, she said. Make yourself at home.

Where will we go? I asked.

Oh, she said. Maybe to Biarritz? Do you have any money saved?

I . . . Yes, I said quickly. I do. I thought of the money I'd saved, still there, for Lucerne.

It's only for a little while, she said. I'm sure he's not dead. I'm sure he's just now with his friends, alive and already on to some café for a *digestif.*

On the bed, I nodded. She held out a beautiful tweed traveling costume. This, perhaps, she said. It's so modest, no one will recognize me in this. She smiled at me. Unless they see the shoes.

I wondered how far to go with this. I was expected at the *cirque* the next day.

Now for you, she said. Have you been to Biarritz?

I struggled to think if I had. It wouldn't matter, in a sense. So much of my time with the circus, the towns we'd been in, it had never mattered. Perhaps, I said. If I could just smell the air, I would know. How will we get there?

The train, she said. I've always longed to go. We will dress and find a café near the Gare de l'Est, and have *caffè corretti* until we can leave.

What are those? I asked.

Espresso and an Italian spirit called grappa, she said. It's delightful. Here we are. You will wear black; we'll say you're in mourning. We both will! We will be a cancan funeral. We will wear veils. I'll dress you up like a proper young lady in mourning, and we'll say you've lost your fiancé if anyone is to ask. I'll pretend to be your lady's maid.

I did as she asked. She loved me, and I loved her despite our being nearly strangers. What else was there to do? I took off my night's costume.

Will we really wear the shoes? I asked her. Won't that give it away?

I suppose you're right, she said. And yet I cannot bear to leave them.

I couldn't, either. We left them on. It was as if without them, we might walk anywhere, but most especially, away from each other.

When she was done, I was otherwise entirely disguised. I laughed at the sight of my eyes peering through the veil. How do you walk with this? I asked, and batted at it.

Try to appear lost in sorrow, she said. Someone has, after all, died.

This was meant as a joke, but instead there was then a quiet, as if the ghost of her tormentor had passed through the room.

You are never lost in sorrow, it seems to me, ever. You do know the way. In fact, you don't think there's any other. Sorrow seemed to me to be more like a road wound through life, through the days of your life, like the old Roman ruins near the Tuileries or the rue d'Enfer—underneath this life, but never really apart from it.

Here I was standing on it, with her.

We descended the stairs, singing the refrain of our song again, this time softly, she with a single gloved finger on her mouth for us to be quiet, and then laughing, we threw open the door to the street.

The sky was the color of a blue serge, the edge of it by the horizon beginning to glow red.

We began the singing again, swinging our arms as we walked, singing softly, sometimes loudly, making our way to the omnibus, singing as we walked when no bus came, all the way to the little café across from the train station, where we sat and drank those sharp, hot coffees with grappa. The waiter who served us was a beautiful gentleman, and he delivered each round with perfect solemnness, as if he were doing something grave, all while we chirped and gossiped. It was only after his third visit that I understood he might be observing a solemn tone with me because of my veil. When I said as much to Euphrosyne, we became very quiet, and then we laughed the harder until we were crying and shaking. And yet he was the same when we paid and left.

We could not shame him.

Not until we stood in line at the window did I understand she was entirely serious. As she returned with my *billet* and pressed it into my hand, I asked, What of my show?

She shrugged. Her eyes went dark. I must go, she said. Can you stay? When you go back, they will take you in, they will ask after me. The police will question you; they will want to know about that knife.

You can stay, she said, when I said nothing to this. She kissed my cheek and then turned and left me, walking quickly.

I stood still, as if turned to stone. As I watched her leave, the feeling that the only thing I had in this life was heading down the platform for the train away from me overwhelmed me. I would likely go to jail alone if I stayed. But if I did not show at the *cirque*, I would be sacked and replaced.

As I shifted and I felt the knife at my thigh, I understood I'd made my choice when I drew the knife.

I ran down the platform after her, and when I pulled even with her, I saw her smile.

What does one do in Biarritz? I asked.

We take the air, she said loftily, even a little sadly. She took my ticket from me and handed them both to the agent, who waved us aboard.

When we found our seats, she leaned her head against the window, watching as the landscape passed outside.

She asked, Will you watch me sleep? And then, when I wake, you can sleep. It is the only safe way.

Of course, I said.

I leaned onto her shoulder. I watched her and the land moving outside her window, the speed like nothing I'd ever seen. Somehow monstrous, as if we were moving faster than we should. The enormity of the night's events was becoming clear. My trip to my mother's family was truly abandoned, and yet I was not afraid. With Euphrosyne, a loneliness I had felt even when my own family had been alive was gone. Behind me was the world I'd once lived in and here ahead of me now was something else altogether.

Who would we be? I wondered. Or, rather, *Who were we now?* For it seemed to me the night had wrought a transformation. I pulled my knife out again and held it up in the dark.

She squeezed my hand when she awoke. Good girl, she said. And then I fell asleep, waking only when the porter knocked to ask after our plans for dinner.

~

We found rooms easily enough. Afterward, we counted our money and decided we had enough to last us for two weeks and that, we decided, was enough time for us to discover if we were wanted women. I dictated a letter to Euphrosyne for the *cirque* owner, saying I had to leave suddenly to visit a sick aunt and that I hoped he would understand.

Is he kind? she asked me.

I think he may be, I said. I knew he'd be angry, but I was sure my little rose would bring me luck with him again.

Each day Euphrosyne read the newspapers from Paris for some report of the death of the man she'd attacked, but after the first few days, when we saw no sign of the crime, we relaxed into the idea that he was alive and would be satisfied if she apologized. We decided we would act as if we were on a holiday. I'd need my job once I returned, but, for now, I was still inside the dream born once I'd pulled that knife.

I was unaccustomed to this kind of bathing. It amused me. Little tents covered the beach and from the distance resembled a parade of giant gowns. I imagined enormous women climbing down from them, as if from fantastic machines. The beachgoers made their camps underneath them.

The other apartments here were full of stylish women looking sadly out at the ocean from their windows, the cafés, the boardwalk, anxiously asking after letters. At first we laughed to find so many women here, and then we did not laugh. It seemed many had been promised money or a visit, and sometimes the man or the money came. More often, it seemed, this was where a man sent a mistress when he needed her to be away from Paris and away from the attention of others. A town for the end of an affair.

On our first walk on the promenade, as we drew near the Empress Eugénie's palace there, Euphrosyne became excited. I wonder if we can see her, Euphrosyne said. She looked into the imperial resort with real determination, as if she were about to march up to the front door and ring the bell.

It's like a dream for me, to meet her. Have you ever seen her?

Yes, I said, nodding at the vague memory of the woman in a domino mask. And it was then I told Euphrosyne the story of singing for the Empress and the ruby rose.

I kept it pinned into my bodice, and so I took it out to show her.

She gasped. Her fondness for the Emperor and Empress, her worship of them, this was one of the first things I learned about her, and this was when I did.

He gave this to you? You performed for her? Can you see her, do you think? she asked me. Could you go and call on her?

I shook my head no before saying anything. The idea made me recoil.

You could, you could. I don't understand you, she said. If the Empress herself has seen you, you could be a real singer, and instead you're out with the likes of me! She laughed at this, enough to begin coughing. I don't understand.

You should be a singer, she said. This is what that means.

As we turned to go back, she said, When you do become a famous singer, when you're a grande dame, you remember me, all right? You remember your Euphrosyne. We walked back to our hotel among the legions of waiting mistresses. We should get you back to Paris, she said. Now that it seems we're not murderesses. Get you back to your glorious career.

I laughed.

I want you to swear something to me, she said then, drawing up short as she waited for me to stop laughing. Here, right now. We'll swear it together.

I looked cautiously at her as she summoned what she was going to say.

We're not to be like these, she said, gesturing at the stylish women around us. This is our *vow*. We'll not come here again, ever, if it means waiting for some man to eventually stop paying our bills.

Some of the women near us heard and moved quickly away, indignant or sad, or both. She and I hadn't discussed them once, and I understood why now.

Raise your right hand and place it on your heart, she said. Swear on that heart of yours, never.

Never, I said.

Never, she said.

We returned. We were happy, proud. We were sure we'd succeeded. And we were arrested the night we returned to the Bal Mabille.

~

The man Euphrosyne had attacked was not dead. As a result, he insisted on justice. We had humiliated him and his friends, and he insisted he wanted only an apology from her and it would all go away. At the women's detention center, he appeared with the police to accuse her. His head had an elaborate bandage that contrasted intensely with the conservative black suit he wore.

I didn't recognize him. He was not, at the least, a regular, or hadn't been. I wondered what it was he could have done to offend Euphrosyne enough that she would do this. Either way, she refused him an apology after all.

She's a filthy wretch of a whore, isn't she? the policeman said to the accuser. He shook her by the arm. Come on, you don't want to go to the magistrate now, do you? Apologize and we'll let you go.

There's things you can pay me to do, Euphrosyne said quietly, but that's not one of them. The policeman laughed.

You're a wit, I'll give you that. We'll see if the magistrate likes it.

The magistrate we saw the next day. He eyed her tiredly as he detailed the case. You are the one called La Frénésie, also called Euphrosyne?

She nodded her head yes, defiant.

In the end, he charged her with not just the assault but also with the corruption of an unregistered woman, me. He sentenced her to six months and to pay fines, and she screamed before being led away. Then it was my turn to take the stand. I was surprised to learn I was to be charged with my own corruption—for being unregistered in the company of a *fille en carte*.

Do you understand the charges against you? he asked.

I shook my head no—they seemed spiteful.

He ran through it again.

Is she to have no friends, then? I asked.

This interested the judge. She may have friends, he said. You may be one of them. Though you may not be in her company.

Her friend but never to be with her? I asked.

That is correct, he said. A woman of virtue is a precious thing. Rare as she is, he added.

If I am unregistered and caught with her again, then I will be brought here again, charged again with my own corruption?

Yes, he said drily. Charged with solicitation and forcibly registered, I might add.

This is impossible, I said. But you will never catch me again.

I assure you we will, mademoiselle. How else can we protect you?

I laughed at this, which annoyed him.

Then let it be done, I said, suddenly very tired.

The officer behind me chuckled as the judge looked up at me very intensely.

My dear, you realize you are still . . . you are still a maiden? You have your virtue intact. You could marry.

I will never marry, I said. And she is my only friend. If it is a crime, with me unregistered and her not, if I am to be registered the next time we are caught together, then I can see I have no choice, I must register.

All around me, the other women in the court gasped. Previously muttering on or giggling at my attempt to reason with the judge, they grew still, everyone holding their breath.

I will ask you to consider one more time.

I must, I said.

You *must*, he said. Very well, then. You are a fool. I look forward to your next visit when you beg to be let off the registry and I will refuse. Let the court record the voluntary registration of one . . . And here he peered into the record. Jou-jou Courrèges. He sat back at this.

I do not think you understand what it is you do. This is the end to your life as a virtuous woman, he added.

I shrugged. It was as if he had said I would never be a butterfly or any other impossible thing. And besides, that name was nothing to me. They would be registering a joke.

Very well, he said. Since it is your wish to be registered, follow this officer, and he will undertake it.

It was such a hard thing, this virtue, it seemed to me. Keeping it was like having to grip the knife by the blade and defend yourself with the hilt. Ever since I'd been old enough to know about virtue in a woman, it had seemed like a bull's-eye painted on my head in rouge. I was sure, as I was led away, I would be better off without it. It was better to be done with it and be gone.

~

Euphrosyne and I had different cells; we could not see each other but we could hear each other, and sometimes she would sing our song, and I would pick up with it until the other girls yelled for us to be quiet and the guards came to threaten us with beatings, shouting into the hay-strewn cells.

This place, Saint-Lazare, was my real hell, this woman's prison. I discovered myself with lice; I had food served to me too foul to eat, with maggots at times, the others laughing the first few times I retched. The other girls were uninterested in me except mostly as a figure of fun. A week went by, an eon, and then I heard my name at the door from the guard.

Euphrosyne stood there, dressed again as she had been. A brief hope filled me until I saw the caution in her expression.

La Lune, I guessed, her little boy prince, and said so. She nodded, a hint of a smile. Yes, she said. I had his card; they called for him and, on orders from his father, released me at once.

She set her hand on the bars and touched mine, gripping it.

Sweet, kind Jou-jou! Her beautiful eyes, the fierce eyes, they were weeping. You are next, I swear. No one ever gave me so much as you. I wish I could have kept you from this. I should have warned you more, or better. Now I fear you must stay because you have no house and so there is no one to send for you except me, and I have less than nothing here. I have truly corrupted you.

I will come to visit you and bring you presents, she said. And be sure, be very sure, that nothing happens to your shoes.

I laughed at this, unexpected and sharp, and leaned in to kiss her quickly. And then she left, and the depth of what I had done was finally clear.

Four

THERE WAS NO La Lune to help me. Instead, there was Odile.

First came a basket from her, sent to the prison, with a fine piece of sausage and bread and, to my surprise, a beautiful new dress, complete with stockings, shoes, gloves, a hat. The gloves were stitched with roses. The hat was a bonnet meant to be worn at a rakish tilt. The other girls made a fuss as it was delivered. The note read, *Something to keep you alive until you leave, something for you to wear to come see me when you are free. Your friend, Odile.*

There was her card also, with the address. This surprised me. The only Odile I remembered was the angry concierge in Euphrosyne's foyer. The one who had said to her, *You aren't allowed guests like that.* The one who had threatened Euphrosyne with a fine. Why had her concierge concerned herself with me?

I did need work, however, and resolved to go to see her, thank her, and repay her, and then ask about a job.

On the last morning of my sentence, I dressed in her gifts. Outside, Odile's carriage waited for me—a kindness and a luxury. I blinked back tears I hated as I climbed inside and tried to act on the ride as if I took this trip every day.

~

Odile was certainly no concierge. She was a procuress, a former danseuse in the Paris Opera Ballet corps, and had taken on dancers, actresses, and singers who sought to make arrangements of this kind but lacked for either rooms or liaisons, using the spare rooms of a deaf aunt of hers, who owned a simple, clean house near the Opera. A share went to the aunt, of course, whose idea it was, worried about the prospects of her beautiful niece. Odile's first *théâtre du désir*, then, as she called them, had a view of her aunt Virginie's kitchen garden.

She learned quickly that she could charge more if men had a specific fantasy and that they would be loyal if the fantasy could be fulfilled with brio. When one of her admirers told her Baron Haussmann was set to order her aunt's neighborhood to be condemned for Paris's renovation, Odile took her aunt in hand, sold the house to the city at a high price, and built the current establishment on roughly the same spot with the help of investors—all clients. A portrait of Virginie presided over the salon, where her girls lingered in talk with their gentlemen; and every so often Odile would solemnly toast or bless her, even leaving a glass of claret for her on the mantel.

Odile's new establishment was called l'Hôtel des Majeurs-Plaisirs, a pun on the Menus-Plaisirs, the school of the arts. Each of the rooms was the set to a different fantasy. The room I'd gone into with Euphrosyne on the night of our adventure had not been hers—it was for gentlemen who had a fantasy of seducing a woman while at the opera, something Euphrosyne often provided. The clothes she had taken for us were props for the room. Odile had hired the same craftsmen who'd made the Paris Opera's boxes to make this one.

And despite my role in the trouble Euphrosyne had made for her, and for her unhappy client, once Odile learned of my registration, she had sent her basket right away. There were many men who wanted the attentions of a hippodrome rider. She explained all of this to me once I stood in her office in the clothes she'd sent me. Which she then asked me to remove.

I did so at once. I did not like the dress or the now-visible obligations it represented.

You have the arms of an acrobat, of course. Very strong, if too slim. We will have you eat more for these, she said, and gestured at my smallish breasts. At least they do not sag. Pastries for you. You are no virgin, yes? And at least age sixteen?

I nodded twice.

Virgins fare badly; they know so little. I would have to pay someone to teach you and charge you for it. I may still need to. My doctor will be here shortly to inspect you. She flicked her finger at my arm. So strong, she said. But your face, you look innocent. People think you are good no matter what you do, yes? She walked over to the wall, where an array of cruel instruments hung, whips, crops, paddles. She withdrew a simple crop and handed it to me. I grasped it.

Perhaps we will make use of this. The strong arm and the innocent face. Please, she said, indicating the empty dress. We will discuss your duties.

After I'd dressed again, she took me to a door in her office at the back and unlocked it.

She turned to me, put a finger on her lips to shush me, and led me into a dark passage consisting of a series of viewing stations with peepholes. Today, to begin, you observe, she whispered. She set an hourglass down. When the sand is gone, go to the next one, and the next. Make not a single sound. I will retrieve you when the doctor is here.

At other houses, they throw you to the men, and you are forced to take what wisdom you can. This way, she said of it later, as she brought me to the doctor, you can see even what my girls would forget to tell you.

You will have a week to decide, as will we, Odile said, after I had received my tour. I hope you will make us proud.

At the end of the week I was free to go if, that is, I could repay her. And I could only stay if I pleased her.

When I only smiled weakly at this, she grew sharp. She sat back and raised one perfectly drawn eyebrow.

We entertain some of the world's most important men here. Do not be mistaken, she said. This is a profession; you are performers.

These men, they entrust us with their most secret fantasies, and we, we keep that trust—they rule the day, we rule the night.

She stood and came around her desk, leaning against it to lift my chin with her own hand, and brought her face down before mine.

Do not be sad, then. Be proud. The night is a wonderful country to rule. Welcome to the Majeurs-Plaisirs.

~

Afterward, as I sat in that dark hall, moving from peephole to peephole, turning the hourglass as I did, I felt as if I were a ghost hidden in the walls. The peepholes were either scratched into the silver at the back of a mirror, or looked out through mantels, or were an "eye" set so as to resemble the eye in a painting, or one of a series of glass beads along the base of a lamp.

In the first, I saw a stout soldier, naked, his face firmly between one woman's buttocks as another smacked him from behind and he cried out without lifting his face or running away or striking her. In the second, a woman I soon realized as Euphrosyne in performance as a young girl, waiting for the return of her chaperone at the opera and surprised by her visitor. She was enacting a melodrama, during which he called her by another name, that culminated in her being ravished by him—at which point Odile, playing the chaperone, returned to catch and punish him. In the third, a woman held out her delicate bare foot, and a man spread across the floor kissed it, murmuring her name, begging to do more than that.

She refused until he perfected his kisses to her content.

Anytime you wonder, Odile said later, as to a lover's devotion to another, anytime it seems ridiculous, there is only ever one reason.

What reason? I asked, for I knew it was a prompt. We were seated in one of the theaters as a man waited on us, naked, his eyes downcast in obsequious submission. We were toasting my agreement, signed on the table between us.

He paid me for the privilege of serving us, she said, as the man finished his pours. I am charging him more for you. What is the reason they are loyal? Why would he pay for such a thing? They have found someone to do the one thing they've always longed for, and they are afraid they will never find someone to do it again.

I laughed, and she said, Don't laugh. It's a loyalty greater than love.

She stroked her champagne glass and looked off into the distance over the rim. She did not meet the eyes of the man trembling now by the wall.

It may be the only loyalty there is, she said, and held out her glass to be refilled.

~

Did you get them? I asked Euphrosyne, once we were alone in the dormitory, the long attic hall of beds I now knew was where she slept. I had written to her, asking her to go to my room at the Cirque Napoléon and take my things before they were sold or thrown away.

She nodded her head. Yes . . . except your little rose, it was gone.
Gone?

She laid out my little kit on the bed we were to share—no girl in the house slept alone. Yes, gone, she said. That and your money. But these remained, and she gestured at the contents now on her bed.

I had feared the rose lost already when it was not with clothes returned to me at Saint-Lazare. The coat seemed still quite good as did the rabbit-fur bonnet; and the sight of my little route book, my cancan shoes, and the dagger all cheered me. But I had hoped to sell the brooch to Odile to raise what I owed.

I'm so sorry, my friend, Euphrosyne said. I went as fast as I could.

She then showed me the dresser where I could keep my things, and the *salle de bain*, and as I bathed, she told me of her ordeal after jail, how she had returned to discover she owed fantastically huge fines to Odile for our escapade. When I offered to help her pay them, she refused. You already have, she said, somewhat sadly; and then she told me she would receive a generous recruitment fee once it was determined that I would stay.

My lucky charm was gone, and with it, it seemed, my luck. I survived the first week and was allowed to stay.

If I had felt, back with my widower farmer, like the victor in a battle, here I came to feel like a fighter, a soldier even. Euphrosyne taught me everything she knew I could not learn through a peephole: that a man could be fooled into thinking he'd entered you; that the finger, well placed, could hasten his release; that if you learned to know when he was to release, you could slip him free and guide his emission onto the floor, sparing both bedding and clothes.

All of this, then, as well the names for whatever a customer might request, the etiquettes as well. All of the words for *cunt*, for example, and in several languages. There was only one I liked, *minou*—to me it sounded like something innocent, though this was not the connotation in French.

Euphrosyne taught me a great deal in the care and use of it. The method of a douche, for example, very important, as if it was to be sold, it had to be clean and beautiful. And if it was clean and beautiful, business was good. But here there were also salves for making it easier for the man to enter you, to help you heal after he was done. One to make him hard, and one to make him soft, if that was needed. And if you became with child, you were to speak to Odile, and there were her tisanes, and if that did not work, her doctor.

To keep the child, well, this was expensive. But this, I eventually understood, was how Euphrosyne had come to be here. Her mother was Odile.

This was why everything here was funny to her; it was her childhood home.

There was even a method for rouging your cunt, though you never did that if you knew the client wanted to put his face down there, Euphrosyne explained.

I asked why.

I did once, and he surprised me and went down there, she said.

When he left, he said he didn't want to wash his face, but his whole face had all the color. It was terrible! And I could not stop laughing! Now I charge for it in advance, and then I know.

∼

Each night there was like a long, strange dream of many parts, different each night and also the same. You washed once before the evening began and then after each client, usually a splash of cologne between the thighs, which sometimes stung, a wet cloth to the rest of you, a cold glass held to the face to reduce any redness before you fixed your makeup—to do more was to have to redo the face. Between men, I ran the back stairs to clean myself and return, sometimes two stairs at a time. I returned via the front stairs, stately, renewed, descending again to the salon.

My uniform: fine leather riding boots, stockings held up with leather garters, a man's riding jacket, and, at times, a top hat. I was a horse act with no horse now, dressing each night as a hippodrome rider, satisfying the fantasies of usually three gentlemen, often with a cropping and beginning first in the actual stables and then soon in a room outfitted as a stable stall, much as the other fantasy rooms were.

There was a Moorish palace room, a Tuileries bedroom, a peasant's room, a formal dining room, even a train car.

A *prix d'amour* was agreed on beforehand, but men always tried to have more than what they had agreed to, especially if you were new. It was best if you knew how to do sums in your head. Odile watched over us via her trick mirrors and peepholes, though such surveillance was mostly done on new girls like me, to criticize them, and then on troubling clients and, of course, any important visitors.

Afterward, you returned to the salon, where you were to display yourself at leisure to the men gathered there. But as I had a specialty, I was never much there—the men who sought what I offered soon knew of me, and I was busy at once.

I discovered this specialty quite by accident—the new boots

made my feet sore, and so I took them off in front of a client, who then stared as if I had presented him with feet made of gold.

And I suppose I had. This is why those carriages stopped, I thought.

Soon, I knew to do it at once, and it relieved me of my other tasks, much to my delight.

∼

This long dream ended just before sleep as Odile sat in her chair and ran the numbers in her ledger.

I was making handsome sums, but my debts were also considerable. As Odile had paid my fines, I owed her for that. Also for the clothes she'd sent to me, and though she did not charge me for that sausage and bread, she did charge for each bar of soap, each meal, even a glass of champagne I might enjoy with a guest, and all came at a cost that soon overwhelmed my earnings. When I complained of it to Euphrosyne, she said only, It is like this for all of us, any house in the city. I checked myself, convinced it could be better elsewhere. At least here the food is not bad, and Odile, she likes her pipe, she does not beat us, only fines us. Her prices are only unreasonable, not absurdly so.

I was stunned to learn Odile charged even her daughter. She reached out and brushed my hair back behind my ears, smoothing it, and then leaned in and kissed my brow. We should be called *filles en compte*, not *filles en carte*.

The night ended always with us in bed, dressed in slips, our hair long on our pillows like wraiths. We lay together like the sisters we said we were, talking quietly to each other until we slept. Odile kept the dormitory dark with thick velvet drapes that also shut out drafts, a false night to keep us from waking until the afternoon when she opened them to prepare us to begin again.

∼

I soon had my own tricks to get by. The less I told men, the better they thought they knew me. Silence was a mask of a kind; it let me be whatever or whomever they needed me to be in our hours together, a little cabaret of their loneliness, really.

Of theirs and ours.

To survive, much less succeed, I learned I could not give myself over to either pleasure or misery in excess. Whatever you felt was not important. To feel either enjoyment or self-pity meant you might allow them too much time, and this meant possibly missing your next monsieur. I soon found the pleasure I could sneak, which I preferred, enjoyed like something I'd picked from their pockets. But I somehow knew without ever being told that to really give myself to one of them was to begin to fray, to make in myself a weakness I could never undo, and so whenever some were able to pleasure me, here or there, I tried to bring the hour to its quickest end.

At Odile's direction, I would make notes of habits, gifts received, preferences, and displeasures. I reviewed this before they arrived, and this made each client believe they were so important to you that you remembered everything they liked, every little gesture, each time they visited—an impossible act of memory, really, but one they never questioned, for it suited them to think it was so. This was, of course, part of what they paid for, perhaps more than any of the acts themselves—to be so *remembered*.

A great scandal appeared in the press shortly after I joined the house—all of the girls talked of it—a disappointed lover had rifled a famous courtesan's books, hoping to find the truth as to whether she loved him, only to see she was not kind to him, at least there. She was made to seem insincere in the press, and this angered us. It was like charging backstage, shocked to discover Phèdre had been played by an actress when you knew all along you were in a theater.

Odile joked of hiring someone to write a diary for all of us in which each client was described only in the most flattering terms—and to leave them where they might be found easily, our real journals hidden elsewhere.

To keep ourselves safe, the system was simple enough. We named clients by their jobs, like minor characters in a play. I wanted it to be clear to myself as well as to whatever future spy might see it that I never really thought of him except like this. What's more, names would have made a gentleman into someone I could feel affection for—love, perhaps, or hate. It was better, easier, to feel nothing—if you loved him, he could disappoint you; if he disappointed you, you might hate him; if you might hate him, you would still have to see him for as long as he had funds to pay. It was enough to remember them all; that was all that was needed, nothing more. But this lesson, to feel nothing for them, was one I seemed always to be tested on, never more so than by what happened next.

One night, after I had been there for several months, I returned to the salon to find it consumed with dancing. A man was playing a cancan on the piano, and the room had exploded with it. Even Odile, whom I rarely saw move more than her counting hand, had her skirts over her hips. The dancing spilled out into the hall and from there into the garden, not usually used. The night was warm, and the windows into the garden were thrown open so we could hear the music there as well.

We had been visited by a regiment. Odile didn't usually let her doors open to enlisted men, for soldiers normally used women too brutally.

The piano music finished as I entered. I found Euphrosyne in the arms of one of the soldiers, a beauty. He was Prussian, had arrived that day from Morocco; the sun there had turned his skin bronze, his sleek blond hair bright.

This is her, Euphrosyne said, as she reached out and drew me closer, turning to face him again. She's my friend who can sing, she said.

He's not really a soldier, she said to me. He's a singer.

A tenor, he said.

~

Here then is the one who owned me.

He was the only man Euphrosyne had ever competed with me for, the only one who ever came between us. She introduced us.

Of those I feared had betrayed me to this writer, he was the one I knew was not over me. He was the Prussian tenor at the Paris Opera, rumored to be marrying me, said to be the real reason I was leaving the stage—and the first man to insist I get on one.

Five

IF WE WERE called to perform in a fantasy, we had to do so and do it with all our might. Most times the fantasy held. And so when Euphrosyne's tenor friend suggested to Odile that I sing for him as he took Euphrosyne in the seats of the little theater, she sent me to change into a formal gown at once and put me on the illusion stage there in front of the boxes where no one had ever stood and sung before.

Odile prided herself on the education we received at her hands in preparation for these fantasies. She regularly took us to attend the opera, the ballet, and the symphony, each trip narrated by her, making points as to appropriate conduct, the way to gossip in an entertaining fashion, and then the occasional sharp remark for whichever of us had misbehaved. She had seen too many girls embarrass clients, themselves, and their houses in public with ill manners or ignorance; educating us this way was good for business, and then the sight of us, our little parade in our new dresses and jewels, meant she educated us even as she advertised us to the gentlemen in the room who would see her and then us, and know instantly we were the Majeurs-Plaisirs. Their friends might ask after us; their friends would explain.

I was new and had been to the opera exactly once. The opera was *Lucia di Lammermoor,* the story of a young woman who falls in love with a man her family despises. They love in secret, marry in secret in the woods, and when he becomes a fugitive, are then separated. While he is away, her brother forges a letter to tell her this lover has betrayed her and forgotten her, and urges her to marry the man they have chosen for her instead. Lucia does, reluctantly, and then murders her new husband on her wedding night, at which point her lover returns to find her mad and singing of how they can be together again as she drifts down the stairs in her gown covered in blood. She dies, and her lover, in order to be with her again, takes his own life as well.

Her first aria, *"Regnava nel silenzio,"* or "Reign of silence," is her telling her maid she has seen a ghost in the woods, the ghost of a girl killed by a man from the family of her lover. This is what she sings before she goes to marry her lover in secret.

Whenever I thought of it, I could still hear the oboes murmuring as Lucia enters. The night we went, Adelina Patti sang, one of the very best Lucias in history.

Odile was moved enough by my attachment to this aria that she had urged some of the various musicians who came to the house to help me learn to sing it—so I could prepare, perhaps, for a concert in the salon. She often had us enact salon dramas and *tableaux vivants* as a way to begin the night; some nights we began as be-gowned princesses; others, as harem girls; still others, as goddesses. One composer even promised a salon opera. She had decided I would go from being the girl with a crop to being her opera siren. A baritone client, on hearing of my love for the aria and the opera, had even written out the lyrics for me one night and left them for me as a love note.

I had suspected this meant Odile was somehow moving Euphro-syne out. Which I could not imagine. But if a circus was a family you had to audition for, a *maison close* was a family that would sell you as a compliment.

Regardless, this was truly all the training I had in this kind of singing at the time, and while I was reluctant to sing for anyone with so little by way of preparation, I sang my best rendition of *"Regnava nel silenzio,"* accompanied on the piano by the tenor's friend who had played the cancan in the salon, even though I knew it was all crude improvisation and the illusion stage was so close to them I could see Euphrosyne's legs shake in the air—I still cannot imagine it gave him any pleasure, and yet it did not matter what I could imagine, what matters is what happened next.

It seems to me that when I am near him, heaven opens itself to me, Lucia sings at the end, telling her maid of why she will go to marry in the woods.

When I reached this and the diminuendo of the piano, the scene above came into view: Euphrosyne's tenor leaning over the box, staring at me with fierce ardor. Euphrosyne behind him, her face lit by the ember of a cigarette.

Incredible, he said. And then he began to clap, finally turning to Euphrosyne, who clapped at last as well.

~

What training do you have? he asked me. We were downstairs in the salon again, drinking Odile's champagne, seated on a crimson velvet chaise. Euphrosyne had left for her ablutions.

I gestured to the men around me.

Truly, no training in voice at all?

I shook my head and laughed. His interest seemed preposterous.

How . . .

I sang as a girl, I said. And I have seen one opera. Adelina Patti singing in *Lucia.* I was imitating her.

One opera! You must see more. And with me. I will arrange it with Odile.

Odile, at the mention of her name, appeared at his shoulder.

Chérie, what you have hidden here I cannot begin to explain, he said.

Don't explain, she said, it's too boring. Tell me what you want with her instead.

She must go to the opera, he said. She must sing opera. I will see her on that stage if I must set her down there myself. We start this week. She must see Cora Pearl! I have tickets.

She will be delighted to join you, Odile said, and smiled at me approvingly.

Six

AND SO IT WAS I went to see the legendary courtesan Cora Pearl perform during her infamous two-week run as Cupid in Offenbach's *Orphée aux Enfers*. And began my education as a singer.

We arrived that night to join a long line of carriages for the theater, each disembarking guests who practically bounded up the steps of the Gaîté. The tenor had boasted of having these tickets, for the evening had sold out, as had the entire run. This meant little to me. I arrived largely ignorant as to Cora's legend, the scarcity of tickets, or sold-out runs. Nothing in the *cirque* had prepared me. This was my introduction.

As I sat in the box with my new friend, I could not help but be fascinated by the fevered anticipation in the crowd. To the audience that night, the opera had a single star, despite her slight role. She did not appear until the second act. The opera began, but the murmurs continued — they would remain until Cora appeared.

I had exited the carriage self-consciously, dressed dutifully in what Odile and I could muster for my opera finery, which, I knew from the scene around me, was not quite fine enough, but there had been no time to order better — it was a navy velvet, and the opera bodice had a white lace collar at the neck and machine-embroidered white roses spreading across the front that I hoped made it look better than it was. It was the finest dress I had ever owned, and yet I was not quite proud of it.

I had no jewelry then except a new choker I liked, a pale gray-green enamel perfume locket worn on a black ribbon. I liked it as it looked like something from the sea, almost a natural pearl, and I knew these ribbon chokers were very chic then—the Empress Eugénie wore them, sometimes as many as ten or more, each with a different locket, though she would never have worn them to the opera.

The locket carried a few drops of Eau de Lubin, a gift from this man—he liked it very much and I knew to reapply it at least once before the evening ended. The scent was rose, musk, and oranges; and the richness of it at my throat was, to me, a little like wearing a gem, if secretly—like a ring turned toward your palm. In the short time I'd worn it, I'd learned to recognize it on others and to notice when it acted as a signal as you passed by someone on the stairs of the opera house or as you handed your cloak to the cloakroom; if you wore it, the person encountering you simply understood you to belong.

It was the atmosphere of wealth and security I did not know I had longed for, not just to surround me, but to belong to me; and I enjoyed it, too.

Orphée aux Enfers, the opera we saw that evening, is an *opéra-bouffe-féerie,* a comic farce on the myth of Orpheus—the bereft singer of myth enters the underworld to retrieve his wife only out of a sense of obligation. He finds she has fallen in love with the King of Death. She does not want to return. Gradually, despite the lack of interest in the other performers, the jokes won over the audience, and I nearly forgot, as the first act closed, why we were there.

The roar began from below and above before I could see her. Her hair was a mass of blond curls; her legs at first looked bare in their stockings, shapely, almost stark in their erotic intensity. She carried a bow and wore the most incredible high-heeled boots; as she walked, you could see the soles were made from diamonds. Pearls and diamonds covered her neck, in a sort of ridiculous collar, and the rest of her was a figure made of diamonds also. She glowed and flashed in the gaslight. As she turned so the audience could see all of her and walked toward the back of the stage, little wings, I noticed as she turned, dangled from her back comically. A bow rested against her thigh.

She glanced up into the boxes, as if to take attendance; and noticing my companion, she offered him a sly wink and a wave that made the audience laugh. He smiled back at her and blew her a kiss. And then she sang her song, looking directly at him for the first bars and notching her bow before turning to regard the crowd.

The crowd was silent as she sang, as if speaking might obstruct the view; and her plaintive, off-key voice struggled through its few bars.

She was dreadful, but not one of them laughed. She was the most powerful woman in Paris in that instant.

Paris, which, when I looked close, was a vast *opéra-bouffe-féerie* —and you did not know your role, I think, until it was too late, and the crowd was laughing at the joke you had uttered in all innocence. Which is to say there was another part of the evening I remembered for a very long time, and it began like this.

We will go to pay a visit to her after, the tenor said, as we stood. She is receiving friends.

~

She threw open her own door and kissed me twice as I entered, smirking as if I had told her a joke. Even without her diamond suit, she dazzled. She wore an evening gown of a loose pink silk toile and her golden stage curls were gone—a shocking red mass of hair had replaced them. Up close, I could see she had the pale eyebrows of a blond, painted over to match her hair.

Eau de Lubin, I bathe in it! she shouted past my shoulder, as she drew her head back and looked me over. She had a loud Cockney accent and spoke English and French mixed together. *Un plaisir!* She took my hand and began to pull me up her grand staircase, littered as it was with celebrants. Our mutual friend dragged along behind. *Chérie,* she said to me then, dropping her voice, tell me, how much do you charge? You can tell me, whisper it here, and she pointed to her delicate ear.

Our audience on the stairs smiled drunkenly from below. You

can't afford her! she shouted down at one as he reached up. You still owe me! Look down! Look away from us. He looked down.

Again she asked, How much?

I lied to her, and said, Two thousand francs.

Chérie, it's good that you are that price. Because then he can afford us both, and we can be friends! With that, she pulled me into her dining room.

I turned to see my friend behind me following along, a somewhat hurt expression on his face. Cora turned back with a grin. You see? You bring her here to flaunt her to me and now she's more expensive, just like that. I do believe it's all your fault. Cora pulled me back to her side. You're so pretty, not in the ordinary way at all. You must allow nothing, and I mean nothing, to happen with our friend here until he can bring you to the opera with better than an enamel locket. He can afford it. Come with me. You! There! Give this *petit ange* something; are we still in champagne?

She did this constantly, turning to people you weren't sure were there or in her sight, and she would yell to them directly as if she'd been speaking to them all along.

A cool glass of champagne came into my hand.

This way! she shouted, I understood, at me.

So, we will be like sisters, or first wife and second wife, or who knows? Who knows how many he has? she said airily, as she continued our procession. Three, five, a thousand.

Her dressing room was sumptuous with gowns thrown this way and that, as if it had been the scene of a fight. I dressed quickly, I always do, she said. She reached down to the floor. Here! This is what I wanted. Something for *you*, she shouted as she raised a small bag from Boucheron into the air. The gentleman who gave me this was unworthy, she said. I threw it at him and it landed here, but my maid still has not picked up. I must beat her. But you are a *jeune fille* still, you can wear this, it will look beautiful and it will be a sign of our good friendship, yes?

I pulled the velvet back until the box came into view and opened it.

Inside was a small emerald pendant, perfectly beautiful, but something of a pebble, it was easy to see, a poor companion to the dazzling collar, bracelets, and earrings she wore. I held my hand to my mouth and laughed. You didn't give this to someone who had diamonds on the soles of her boots. You gave it to a woman who said her prayers before bed.

This was meant for his wife, I said finally.

Good eye, she said. Never trust a man who gives you something he was going to give his wife, she said. And with that, she pulled the necklace from the box and draped it around my neck and turned us to look into her mirrors.

The sight of her against my neck, like some terrifying devil come to tempt me, the beautiful small matrimonial emerald glinting in the candlelight. I knew it was more than I'd ever had. She smiled. He's very handsome, isn't he? she said. I nodded.

I will warn you of two things, she said then. He will try to make you a singer. Do you have a good voice?

I do, I said.

Good, she said. I didn't, and I never will. See where I am now! If I had a voice, I could conquer. Now. Do you love him?

No, I said. I wasn't sure, so it was easier to say no. Too easy, and I saw her catch it.

Never love, she said. Do you understand? Not him, not any of them. That is the secret to all of this around me.

Outside in her halls, the party in celebration of her debut raged. I waited silently, finally reaching up to touch the little gem at my throat.

Never love, she said. For if you do, *that* is all you'll get, if you're lucky. And nothing else.

I returned to the party in my necklace, Cora now behind me. My tenor friend smiled up at me and I knew instantly from his expression as he looked to my throat, while Cora's laughter caroled against my neck, that he had given it to her.

～

He did come to love me, and perhaps it began that night, as our Cupid manqué, the woman he really loved, tossed me down the stairs to him wearing his rejected love gift to her.

Years later, when I learned she had died a pauper and subscriptions were being sold to pay for her grave, I took this necklace and sold it and sent the sum and two thousand francs toward the cost.

I did not take her warnings to heart. Such was her vanity, she thought I sought to replace her, and such was mine, I found her warnings of little use. Our mutual friend was already trying to make a singer of me, or to make me into her—it was hard to know which that night. I left suspicious that I was only like a little doll of her to him. It seemed his preferences with me all came from her—Eau de Lubin would not mean the same thing ever. But unlike her, I had a voice, and with it, I knew, a real chance.

This was my consolation then.

As for loving him, how could I not at least imagine what I felt for him, which was perhaps more gratitude and fear than anything else, how could I, ignorant as I was, not imagine it was love?

She wanted only to be feared. I wanted to be feared and loved. I didn't want everything she had as she stood onstage that night. I wanted more.

For years after that night, she haunted me. I would be assembling my toilette and see her face over my shoulder, just as I had that night. The confident way she warned me off.

The word for her in Paris, a courtesan who had made it to the stage, was *grue*—it happened so often there was a word for it. I never wanted anyone to use this word for me. I even wore my hair dark and close to my head so as to be as unlike her as I could imagine.

And then I became a singer, and the night of my eventual debut was nothing like hers, and I was sure I had won my way free.

Seven

IN ALL THE YEARS I'd known the tenor, I had rarely ever visited him at his apartments; he was more often at mine in the years when I belonged to him. His apartment was where he went to be apart from women—near me, on the rue de Richelieu, close to the Place Vendôme and decorated in a German style; to enter was to feel one might have left Paris. The furniture was mostly Bavarian, very dark and carved with German motifs and animals or trees. A full suit of knight's armor stood in the foyer with an enormous, two-handed sword for killing something larger than I knew to fear. Hunting rifles and more swords from his family decorated the mantel of the fireplace in his library.

I went to call on him, thinking that if it was not my Euphrosyne it had to be him. Another copy of the novel, for him, wrapped, sat under my arm.

He would be returning shortly, his butler said, as he answered the door. Would I care to wait?

I said I would. I was shown into his library, where I seated myself on his couch.

The butler offered to take the package, but I said I had to hand it to him myself.

Of the men who had come to me at Odile's, he was the only one who had ever wanted to know me. His loneliness was different. The distinct proportions of it in his mind were like those of a theatrical that needed casting more than anything else.

He sought a playmate, almost a rival.

Almost.

There was a coda to my evening with him at Cora Pearl's those many years ago, and I remembered it as I waited. We had sat down eventually to her catered supper served on gold-rimmed china. She had caught my expression of pleasure at the gold rim, as the plate for my soup went down in front of me, and raised an eyebrow.

You should take your little doll of me out more, she said to the tenor. Get her used to fine china.

Here at dinner, as everyone ate, this wounded me, but I had been trained not to react or, at least, not to cry out. As the tenor turned toward me, I put a practiced smile on my face and said, Yes. Yes, you should. Teasing him.

The guests at table, quietly waiting for my reaction, erupted in laughter. I hadn't meant to be funny, and I knew it was dangerous to humiliate him too much, so I pulled his head in close to mine for a kiss on his cheek, at which the laughter increased. As we each sat back, I found Cora Pearl smiling at me.

We would not be friends, as she had said, but I had earned her respect.

When the dinner ended, she ordered the waiters to fill her tub with champagne and asked anyone who wished to join her to come with her into her *salle de bain*. The tenor looked on as she stood, her bare shoulders gleaming in the candlelight, before leaving silently with me after she had made her exit.

Perhaps a few weeks later, friends of the tenor's entered his box at the intermission to greet him and recount how the men who'd stayed after our departure had sat round Cora's champagne bath, filling their glasses from it as they spoke to her until her figure appeared, and the tenor made a face, as if at something disgusting. At this cue, they all began to speak of how badly she'd sung in *Orphée aux Enfers*.

He smiled a little and interrupted these complaints to present these friends to me.

She is a soprano, he said. My protégée. There were some grins, but all took my hand and kissed it in greeting. I am preparing her for her debut, he added, and they all smiled at this as if they could already hear me sing.

As I answered his friends' questions on my student repertoire, I noticed how he seemed proud of me, and I knew I was mistaken as to Cora's and my fortunes.

Cora had been discarded, for she had disappointed. He was not trying to make me over into her — he had failed to make her into what I was to become. If I failed, perhaps there would be another.

My old fear from that time, that he would give up on me, seemed quaint at best as I waited for him. From our first meeting, I had never been able to rid myself of him, and over time, that came to seem like something like or, at least, more reliable than marriage. But then I had never been married and knew as little of it still as I did at this time of what it would mean to be bought.

The tenor returned as the butler had said he would. I heard the entrance door open and the butler's voice, no doubt telling him he had a visitor and who it was.

I then heard laughter.

The door to the library opened. All this time I have had to chase you, and now you come right to my door? *Chérie*, it's too much. He came to where I sat.

I would have thought I would not see you again, unless you have finally come to kill me, he said.

I said nothing to this.

You must want something, he said. It can't be money. What is it? Is it your curse? He laughed as he said that.

I hear a rumor we are to be married. It wasn't me, he said. But I like the rumor. Perhaps . . . perhaps it is our time.

I wanted to be sure, I said, with a smile. And then laughed with him about the rumor even as I saw, at once, he wasn't probably the source.

Consider this your present in our imaginary engagement, I said, and offered the novel to him.

He unwrapped it and turned it over with real fascination.

You've never given me a novel, he said.

He was likewise not my secret tormentor. He'd never been able to rid himself of a certain wounded air since I'd won my eventual freedom from him. If it was him, this air would be gone. Instead, I saw his hopes rise to see me, to page through the novel—I had misled him even by coming—and so I consoled myself with this as I made an excuse and left, saying I hoped we'd sing together soon.

It was a game, to hurt him again even like that, but it was only a part of the game by which I had escaped him. And while it was not the satisfaction I sought, it would do for now.

You will notice I do not use his name. For this story, I never will. He was named by the rules of the Majeurs-Plaisirs—it seemed safer this way. He is always the tenor. If there had been another tenor, that tenor would have been "tenor 2," or "second tenor." Something that would have amused me.

If these men met you on the street with their friends, they were as likely to ignore you as recognize you; to introduce you might offend whomever they were with. That was their prudence. This was mine.

If there was some way they could not allow me into their circles, well, it would be the same for them somehow.

In these ways, it seems to me, you kept yourself.

Eight

WHEN I SAY he owned me all those years ago, I mean he owned me like he owned his shoes.

After that night with Cora Pearl, he bought me from Odile, bought my contract. He freed me from my unconquerable bill of fare with her but delivered me into his own.

I still remember how I stood by my wardrobe with him, packing as he sat with Odile, who tallied my bill. If he did not pay for something, she would make me leave it behind, so, as I brought each item out, he said either yes or no, and a maid he'd brought to help either set the item into a case or put it on the bed I'd shared with Euphrosyne.

I was the envy of the house. Each girl here wanted to have her contract bought and her client to arrive with cases and a maid to pack them, but the scrutiny of each object humiliated me, especially as the other girls lined the doorway, excited for me, but also arguing already in whispers over who would get what of the things I would leave behind.

Odile turned and hushed them before continuing.

We had come to the cancan shoes, which I was intent on keeping no matter what he said. I took the pair Euphrosyne had bought me and pointed to the case as I handed them to the maid.

These are mine, I said, as Odile raised an eyebrow. I wore them into prison and on my way here. I will wear them out of here as well.

In the doorway, the girls laughed.

My six other pairs, one for each day of the week if I wanted, amused the tenor. I like them, he said, as they were set in one by one. And then it was done; he paid the bill outright. He left to wait downstairs and let me dress and say good-byes. The maid stayed at first to help me, but I shooed her away. As I closed the door, Euphrosyne came and sat down on the bed.

I told them I pick first, she said, and then plucked at the few things the tenor had rejected—mostly lingerie. We will buy all new ones for you, he'd said.

When she saw there was nothing she wanted, she turned her attention to me.

It's nothing to me, Jou-jou, she said. It's a favor you do for me, though, really, she said. You'll tire of him. You'll see. Give me a kiss and let it be done. We must stay friends, for we love each other.

She had slept beside me coldly since that night I first sang for him. This had angered me, as the fantasy act that introduced me to him had been her idea, and so I had been cold in return. But she was right.

I bent down and gave her a kiss.

Just be sure to be careful. It will be harder to refuse him now. And if he beats you, promise me you'll show him that knife.

I nodded.

I have a confession, she said. Please forgive me. She withdrew something from her blouse and set it on the bed.

It was silly of me, she said. And terrible. I was . . . I loved the story, she said. I would take it out and pretend the Emperor had given it to me.

The rose pin sat there, strangely dark in the light, almost black. She'd had it this whole time.

I made myself go to the bed and pick it up.

She kept talking, not quite meeting my eyes. Her voice seemed focused past me, as if on someone listening in.

I meant to give it back sooner, for it was really childish of me, but then when our tenor friend chose you over me, it was as if you'd stolen from me, and I felt we were even. But we aren't, are we? Nothing like that will ever happen to me, you see, she said. I don't have any other talents except this, and she gestured to her figure. And when this is gone, nothing. So forgive me, please. And you! You will finally be the singer you were fated to be. He will help you, I think, yes? And you must come back often and tell me everything.

With that, she came close and embraced me.

You must kiss me; we must stay friends, she said.

I did.

The tenor's driver came for my new cases then, and as I followed him downstairs, I passed by the open door to the room where it had begun, the faux opera boxes and the illusion stage. The maid was mopping the floors clean of the previous night's exertions. I looked back up the stairs, but there was no sign of her. There was only Odile at the foot of the stairs calling for me to come.

◦

That first time I entered my apartment on the brand-new avenue de l'Opéra, I felt as if I were an interloper visiting someone else's home.

The walls were painted carefully, a beautiful dove gray, and furnished in what struck me as the most elegant furnishings I'd ever seen, though I might be less impressed to see them now. Enormous crystal chandeliers hung in nearly every room, even the boudoir. There was even a music room with a piano.

As I left the maid to set my things out in the new apartment, I knew what I'd been too proud to say in front of Euphrosyne, what she had even tried to tell me.

There was always at least one client who was reluctant to leave. This is paradise, they'd usually exclaim first. They'd joke with Odile, ask her what she would charge to stay the night; and she forbade it each time. The Plaisirs closes at dawn, she would say to them. It is the only rule. That, and that you must pay.

This was what they wanted. A house of tolerance with just one girl. The apartment like his own music box, and when he opened it, I was what moved and sang.

This apartment was not my freedom, and it would not have been hers, either. Instead, it was as if I were shut inside one of the theaters and told I was to live in there with him, or for him, or both.

As I examined the sconces on the wall of my new music room, I half expected to see Odile's eye peering at me through some hollow bottom in one of them, making sure all was as he wanted it.

As the maid unpacked me, she found my little ruby rose and held it out to me, praising it before putting it in a little jewelry box on my dressing table.

The sight of it mocked me—my charm, back with its strange luck. It was a kind of mercy Euphrosyne returned it to me only after the bill of fare had been settled. I did not have to see it discussed, or worse, valued.

I could guess what it was worth now. And while I hated Euphrosyne for stealing it and still felt she had trapped me by doing so, I could never have paid Odile back with what I would have gotten for selling it. Just as I could never have made my way to Lucerne with whatever I might have sold it for.

I was finally worth more than any of my things, in any case. This tenor, I had seen what he had paid Odile for his fantasy of making me a singer.

Let it remind you of that, I told my reflection the next time I pinned the brooch to my lapel.

And, for a while, it did.

Nine

ON A WINTER AFTERNOON in Paris, in a cold wooden room at the Conservatoire National Supérieur de Musique, I auditioned for a jury of voice professors and was told afterward, with extreme wariness, that I was a Falcon soprano.

I asked what this was.

The head music professor looked first to his companions. The voice jury, three men and a woman, shrugged as one. He turned back to face me.

At first it seemed you were a mezzo, he said, and then that was not the case. You are studying and have been helped with your audition piece, yes?

I nodded. Our eyes fell together on my own music case, gleaming in the soft light.

And this person did not tell you this?

No, I said.

Well, it would be difficult to know. In a category of fragile singers, you are among the *most fragile*. An untrained listener would assume the voice was quite strong, for your *tone* is strong. But the voice is not and could be destroyed quite easily. Especially if trained by someone who cannot tell you you are a Falcon. He frowned, shrugged, and continued. The voice itself is a dark thing, but hooded. But from this comes impossible lights. There is an upper register where the mezzo voice might thin or pause. As you sang up, the surprises became evident.

He looked away for a moment. His colleagues watched him, not me.

It was like a night and then shooting stars, he said, and smiled.

I stared. I was afraid of missing something I needed to know that I might never be told again.

With this sort of voice, he continued, it may be you have a long career. But it may be you have a very short one. It is a very odd, very beautiful, very rare sort of voice. You could sing all the dramatic soprano roles I can think of, but . . . perhaps you should not.

Should not? I asked.

For then you may have a very short career, he said. And this is what I mean. The tone is powerful, but the voice itself, delicate. You might ruin your voice in just the training we could provide. It is even possible you destroyed it here today, singing your Abigaille aria from *Nabucco*.

I touched the hot skin of my throat, my hands cold, and left them there to warm.

Do not do that, he said. Do not chill your throat like that after singing.

I put my hands down.

This voice has another name, he said.

Tragic soprano is how it is more traditionally known, said the woman at his elbow. None of the four council members spoke as the head professor paused and paged through their notes.

Accept our congratulations on a distinguished audition, he said finally. I can't think of when I knew Abigaille's first aria to be sung with appropriate force and it is an extraordinarily difficult aria, not at all what we are used to hearing in auditions. It was very dangerous but very beautiful, he said. Whoever you are studying with should likely be reprimanded. He cleared his throat and continued. You are too young, however, he said, and paused. And here the woman at his elbow looked sternly to him. And while you appear very in-telligent, you lack a proper French education, and this is another obstacle, and not a small one, he said. But we have been assured that you will work hard should you be allowed. If you are accepted, you must commit to a very disciplined training to make up for this. Do you understand me? he asked.

I do, I said.

Are you performing now? he asked.

Under my wool skirt I could feel the leather garters I still wore against my thighs. No, I said.

You must not, he said. It is very likely someone would try to exploit your voice and get you to sing too soon, in the dance halls or the cabarets. Everything you learn here, should we admit you, could come to nothing if your voice fails, he said. He paused and a silent council moved between them all, and then he said, We will confer. Please await our letter. And until then, sing nothing.

He was a tender old man, someone who had grown old here, clearly. In my fear and nervousness I stood staring around the room. Then I picked up my music case.

The woman professor, whom I would later know very well, came and took my arm, walking me to the door. She had a matronly air but a maiden's figure. My dear, she said, it is not a bird, this Falcon. The first Falcon gave it her name: Marie-Cornélie Falcon. She was my teacher. She was an elegant gentlewoman and an inspired singer, but her career lasted just eight years. I wish you many more. She clasped her hands over mine and, with a pat, released them.

She was too late. As I walked the rue du Faubourg Poissonnière afterward, I could feel the wings trailing off my back, the wind in the street beating against them.

∼

I left the area quickly and returned home. I did not want to risk arrest for conspiring against the honor of the lady professor.

All over Paris, I saw them, young men and women carrying these handsome leather music cases like the one under my arm, students at the Paris Conservatoire, formerly l'Hôtel des Menus-Plaisirs, the place Odile had studied, the state-run school that trained and educated the musicians, singers, and dancers who sang for the pleasure of the Emperor Napoléon III and his Empress Eugénie on the stage of the Paris Opera. I hoped to truly be one of them—and that my past would not prevent this.

There was much Euphrosyne had neglected to tell me of her situation, and so I alternately regretted and rebelled against my entry into the register. In this life, I was forbidden to be on certain streets altogether, forbidden to be on any street during daylight, and my head was always to be covered if I was outside. I could never be in the company of unregistered women, and every two weeks I was to renew the registration in person. The door to my apartment, if I was to live away from the brothel, was to have oversized numerals on it, announcing to all who passed the nature of the woman who lived there, and I was never to be seen at my open window. To disobey any of these rules meant I could be arrested.

While at first I obeyed these laws, I soon went about by day with a bare head, couldn't remember the forbidden streets until I was on them, and had not renewed my registration in more than a month. To go now, though, was to be jailed for lateness as well. I'd allowed my life with the tenor to take me over. I was sure, without any reason to think so, that our time together would end in my freedom. I could see it in the change in expressions from the professors—at the beginning they had looked on, almost embarrassed to see me. By the end, there was real respect.

I was a Falcon.

A Falcon, my dangerous teacher said questioningly, when he arrived a little later at the apartment he had bought for me. I walked to him as he threw himself across my bed.

He wore evening dress at all hours of the day. I am either going out or returning from going out, he would say of it to anyone who asked. His blond hair glowed blue in the winter sun coming through the window. I put my hand against the black velvet along his collar and then ran it against his beard. His eyes were likewise a pale blue. The French spoke of a color that calmed the horses and a color that frightened them. I was not sure which these were.

And likewise, sometimes it reassured me to be with him, and sometimes it terrified me.

In singing, nothing hides, especially not from your teacher. I learned quickly my dangerous teacher could tell if I had been singing too much or too little, if I was having my menses or was hungry. It frightened me at first. It was as if I could never be hidden again.

During the months prior to my audition I had been rehearsing and taking lessons inside the unfinished Opéra Garnier with him, who was better known to the jury at the Conservatoire and to the city of Paris as the Prussian heldentenor at Salle Le Peletier, the current home of the Paris Opera. Charles Garnier, the architect of the new home for the Paris Opera, had enlisted the tenor to come and sing at various stages in the construction in order to hear how the sound changed inside the theater. The tenor had suggested the place for our rehearsals and Garnier was delighted.

He is tuning it, the tenor said to me one day. Really, it can only help him.

I met Garnier only once and then never saw him, and I soon forgot he listened, if he ever did—the tenor was the sort to obtain a great deal through charm, and much of what he said was never true —we had never prodded each other on this, either, for his lies, so far, had not affected me. Not in any way I knew. In the meantime, the unfinished Garnier had come to feel like my own home, in part because the tenor had said to me, It will be your new home, and he encouraged me to treat it familiarly. To rehearse there, he felt, would give me a certain advantage over the other sopranos. This is the only place any of us will want to sing, he said, when it is done. Your first time here you will know your voice in it perfectly.

Yes, *comprimario*, I said. I am a Falcon.

Since beginning the rehearsals at the Garnier, we called each other *comprimario* and *comprimaria*, the opera terms for the supporting cast.

The Garnier was more beautiful with each arrival and even with each departure. A new corner was always being painted or shaped or plastered, or a statue had arrived, or a frieze had been finished. There was very little natural light, and as the stage lights were not yet installed, we sang by candlelight into the dark theater over the stepped slope where the velvet chairs would be someday while work-men pressed gilding across the walls and ceilings. A sketch would be a god or goddess the next time I passed, a marble statue turned to gold.

It was, on reflection, the perfect place to turn a *fille en carte* into a Falcon soprano.

We shall have to hood you at night to make sure you do not get lost, he said. Very dangerous and very beautiful, the professor said of your voice?

Yes. It is exactly what he said.

It is clear he's already in love with you. I can't allow you to go to this school, the tenor said, and drew me into his arms as he laughed at his own joke and I pretended to laugh as well.

~

He introduced me to his friends. I soon discovered it was my duty to entertain them as well, as he pleased.

They were mostly good men: a Japanese painter, an English dra-matist, the tenor's former lieutenant, in Paris on diplomatic mis-sions. An Italian baritone from Trieste who liked to stay the night. This preference enraged the tenor, though he allowed it, and so I had to allow it, though the baritone snored like a dragon.

The painter painted me as a prelude to his affections; the drama-tist gave me poems or spoke forever of his desire to introduce me to London, creating eventually a long story of turning me into a star of the Royal Opera; the former commander aspired to be a composer and rarely asked for a single erotic favor, instead asking me to sing his relatively simple compositions.

Euphrosyne's warning returned to me. *You will tire of him.* I had. What had first seemed to be a long play was, in fact, more like a repertory in which much of my role was silent and I had to manage the cues as they arrived. It was tiring to always have to please him, to always have to pretend he made me happy, to pleasure him, to pleasure his friends. At the Majeurs-Plaisirs at least there were hours when you could be left alone.

I also missed the company of the girls late at night. The dorm now seemed like a paradise by comparison to the apartment, where I had only the maids he'd provided for company, Doro and Lucy. Doro was a slight Italian woman with a fierce, hard face softened, usually, by an expression of perpetual amusement in her eyes. She seemed of an indeterminate age, her thick dark hair graying slightly. Lucy was young, a plump French girl, pink and blond, who said so little I almost thought her slow, but she was not, or her wit was not, at least. She liked to wink before she burst into the bawdy laughter I soon knew to expect from her.

I was unused to maids and didn't know how to let them do for me, and so I tried to befriend them instead, and at first they resisted. I sometimes heard them in the kitchen, or the rooms they shared off the kitchen, and tried to catch them, but if they heard me, I was met with silent, blank, expectant faces—faces waiting for requests or commands. Finally, I crept into the kitchen late one night to find them drinking gin and playing bezique. They stared at me as if at a mouse, and then as if at their lady, silent.

Please, I said finally.

They looked at me for another long moment, and then Doro, who it seemed was in charge, relented and gestured with her chin at the chair between them. I sat down as she dealt me in.

～

In the month of waiting for the letter from the Conservatoire, cards and gin were not enough, and so any night I found myself free, I went to the Mabille instead, even taking the risk of going alone when the tenor or his friends wouldn't take me. I danced until morning, relishing the walk home, my hair wet, steam rising off me in the cold like smoke.

There I was a champion. The clap of my back on the hard wooden tables, my legs in the air, my skirt a wheel, and the cold air on my thighs while I was drunk from the screams in the room and the misery of my dance-floor rivals, whether those of an hour or a week or a year. All of us were trying to kick higher or fall faster, but I had learned to win with a one-legged kick I could hold, one hand in the air, one on my hip, my skirt around my waist as I swiveled my hips. If you did it wrong or hadn't practiced, you'd fall over backward, very painful, so challengers had to know in order to get it right. A first challenge could undo you, but I could stand there and do at least four in a row.

I missed Euphrosyne even though I was too hurt still to write to her or otherwise invite her. She seemed to feel the same of me. But on the nights her gentlemen brought her, we were tentatively reunited, and soon we were joining our arms again as before, kicking and whirling as groups of men gathered to cheer us on.

Her efforts at forgiving me were aided by the tenor's never being there. Mine were aided by our both knowing she was right; I had a future unlike hers. I could be more than this, and she could not.

I soon wore my cancan shoes as often as I could, for they were very sturdy, and if I wore them always, I could dance on any evening. I liked the clip-clop they made as I walked across a street, as if I were a mythological creature with hooves instead of feet.

It was better in this life if you weren't altogether human, I would think, as I heard the sound. It was easier to bear.

～

Given the Conservatoire jury professor's warning me not to use my voice, in lieu of rehearsals, the tenor took me to the opera much more than before.

He had not relinquished his role as my teacher. It is my greatest wish, he said, that you fall in love with one of the roles you see on the stage. Your talent will lack focus until then, he said. And so I went along, waiting to be moved.

No longer did I have to entertain his friends as before. The dresses that were delivered to the apartment were finer than ever. He dismissed Doro from dressing me, enjoying the task himself. He was like a boy with the corset, which he liked to pull shut almost as much as he liked to pull it open.

In his box at the opera, he regularly introduced me to his friends now as his protégée and spoke of how we were awaiting the results of my audition at the Conservatoire.

And her voice? these new friends all asked with a thrill I did not yet understand.

A Falcon, he would say, and they would draw back, startled. As if they were in the presence of something rare.

I typically said little during these occasions, only smiled and nodded, afraid of betraying to them the quality of my French. I still could not imagine being like the women I saw on the stage or the women in the other boxes, no matter how finely he dressed me, and these introductions made me nervous. The more I waited, the more I was sure the Conservatoire had given me the audition only due to the letters of support the tenor had provided — that I was never to be taken seriously — and that his friends must know this also. And so I was nervous in the company of these celebrities and distinguished personages, and drank too much, ate too little. When I became drunk, I used the pin from my brooch on my legs so as not to fall asleep, pricking myself under my garters until he took me home.

We never spoke of what would happen if I was rejected. We acted instead as if it were impossible. Each time he left me, however, I feared it. If I failed him, it seemed to me this game would quickly reach its end.

～

We must get you to see Delsarte, he said to me one evening, as we exited the opera. That the Conservatoire jury cannot reproach me for.

I did not think to ask why, but to Delsarte I went.

Delsarte was one of the most famous voice teachers in Paris, though if you called him such, he would disavow it. He taught what he called "singing false," by which he meant accomplishing in the singer the appearance of emotions the singer did not actually feel, so as to move the audience. He taught this in his famous salon of portraits, the walls covered in paintings of the expressions of the different emotions.

Your face is a mask, he said. Do you know the masks of comedy and tragedy? I told him I did. Then think of your face as a perfect mask. A magical one. Able to assume the shapes at command, and he struck the portraits one by one with his pointer, counting them off. Anger, Terror, Laughter, Love, all of them yours to command!

Our first lesson consisted of my singing the *Nabucco* audition piece for him, and as I did so, he pointed to each of the portraits for the shape my face was to make at each part of the song. He was disappointed I could not accompany myself on the piano—a singer must be able to do so, he said, as the occasion demands—and grudgingly allowed the tenor to accompany me, who did so quite well, never once flinching as I did when Delsarte smacked each portrait.

I was anxious not to disappoint either of my teachers, but the fierce expectancy in Delsarte as I sang and he pointed to a portrait was comical to me, and I found myself moving between terror and hilarity no matter what my face did.

Stop, he said, as the tenor began at the piano once more. One moment. He came over to me and said, Close your eyes.

I did so.

He took his fingers and set them on my face. Anger, he said, and the image of his pointer at this particular portrait appeared in my mind. As my face tried to assume the expression, he pressed against it, pushing it into the shape. Grief, he said. And again pressed my face to order it. We did this for some time before he let the tenor play the piano again. The fingers of the old genius pushing my face into place.

Your face appears to be only a mask, he said to me, of his decision to teach this way. It does not appear to know the shapes. Instead, everything is in your eyes, but we cannot see your eyes from the audience. So I closed your eyes so that you would have to speak another way.

Speak with your whole face, he said. Not as a lunatic, but as an artist. I think you fear you are giving something away, yes? But not if you can master this. If you master this, you can give and never give away anything.

This I could understand, and soon he praised me as a quick student.

～

I had another concern, one I could not even mention to the tenor: My voice had disappeared before. When the Conservatoire professor had said, *You could destroy your voice just in the training*, it was like finding myself in Hades and being told I could leave, but the bargain was that there was just one candle to get me out and it might not last the way. And I wouldn't know until I'd begun.

When I returned to Delsarte next, I told him of what the jurist had said and of how my speaking voice had once disappeared, and I asked how this could be.

This problem you describe, it is very interesting, Delsarte said. Your speaking voice and singing voice are located in two different parts of the throat—this is true of everyone—but it bears examining.

He had various instruments he brought forth to observe my throat as he had me intone various syllables and then sing.

I think the disappearance, it is perhaps a part of the Falcon voice, he said, as he put the instruments away. You must be careful. Your voice, the tones it makes, it sounds so strong, as if it could never go away. But it might, all at once, without warning. Certainly it was true for Marie, he said.

He knew the woman for which the voice was named, of course,

and then he told me of how she had lost her voice midperformance as she sang Niedermeyer's *Stradella*.

The line she was to sing was *"Je suis prête."*

It might be you are the next Falcon, as the Conservatoire seems to think, he said. You could do worse. But it might also be, if you are careful, that you could do better.

~

The letter from the Conservatoire said that despite a brilliant audition there was too much to overcome, and it suggested private training. The tenor had brought it himself, still sealed.

Comprimaria, I heard him say behind me. What news? Please, he said, let me see the letter.

I tried to hold it away, and as he reached for it, I ran for the door.

No, he said. No, no, no, and he caught me and then tried to hold me. I struggled, pushing him, and then screamed.

He couldn't console me, and yet he was all I had.

No, he said, it is a mistake.

Nothing could happen with him, I understood, as he stroked my back. Whatever his intentions, for me to be a singer, to really be a singer, I needed to be rid of him.

Dark thing, night, shooting stars. How ridiculous. How beautiful and how cruel to know what I was or could be, and yet to be kept from it—and to know it could vanish as I reached for it. Still, it was enough to be everything I wanted, and this was when I knew.

I pushed away from him and ran out to the street, a street where I knew I was not to be, and having spent so much time avoiding arrest, I knew exactly what to do next. I drew my knife as I had at the Bal Mabille and walked slowly toward the police officers I saw who rushed for me.

When I looked back, I saw him at the gate to the apartment, startled. He ran to speak with the police, desperately shouting first at me and then to the police, insisting they release me. They asked if he was my husband, and when he said he owned me, they told him to come to the jail for me and bring my contract and bill of sale.

I would not look at him again after this; there was nothing more to say. I did not know what was next, only that it began here.

~

When my turn came before the magistrate, I was told I was to be taken to Saint-Lazare.

I was put in with a girl they called only La Muette, the mute. They had no way to know her name. But they were certain that, for being mute, she could not be corrupted by the likes of me.

She sniffled occasionally, weeping, leaning into the corner of the cell as if it might give way and let her go. But soon she was quiet, and the two of us were a pool of silence amid the noise as the other prisoners argued and insulted one another, alternately threatening and weeping.

All grew quieter eventually as the night began and sleep came over the jail. I unfurled my sleep roll on the floor and I lay there awake for some time before thinking to at least help my cellmate to her own sleep roll — she shouldn't, I thought, sleep there in the corner that way. I stood and went over to her to find her cool to the touch.

She was quiet because she was dead.

The magistrate had ordered her to be sent to the convent orphanage, its having been decided that she needed some sort of education in reading, writing, and a trade, as well as some protection from vice and sin. But she didn't react to most of what was said, and I was left to wonder if she even knew what her fate was.

By now it was becoming light. I could see her soft expression, so like sleep I envied her a little. Soon the tenor would come, he would pay my bail and show my papers, and I would be returned to him.

I had thought to ring for the guards. I looked down the hall to see the one set to watch over us asleep at his post. He'd be angry to be woken, I knew, and would demand to know which of us was who, and it was then I knew it was likely all the same to them which one they buried, and which they sent on to the nuns.

She had been mortally injured but unable to say so, her girl's body all bruises and infected wounds, which I saw as I undressed her, for I was now determined to take her place. I felt a terrible sadness and also fear, that to even pass myself off as her would make me share this fate or worse. *If you were damned before this,* I told myself, *you'll be twice damned now.* But I wouldn't be stealing from the dead — she couldn't use her future, and I could. The only person it would matter to was me.

I remembered the prayer I had said over my own mother's body and whispered it softly, as if she could listen, and then kissed her hand, pressing my cheek against it.

I know you can't give a blessing, I said to her quietly. But spare me a curse.

~

The guards came to take us to our breakfasts, such as they were. As I had suspected, the morning shift was new.

You there, wake her up, the first guard said, before the second yelled over him, Wake up, my dear! It is time for breakfast!

They laughed at this, but stopped laughing when she didn't wake.

They looked at her, arranged in a posture of sleep, her face turned to the wall, her feet set into my cancan shoes, visibly displayed. This had been the most difficult part, her feet having stiffened after death and me still wanting the shoes.

What's the matter with you? Are you stupid? asked the first guard to me, before the other said, She's dumb, she can't understand us. They began miming to me, for me to go over to her.

I did. I pulled at her shoulder, and she fell to the side with that unmistakable slowness of death. I stepped back, my face a perfect expression of terror, fit to make Delsarte proud.

All right then, one less mouth to feed, the second guard said, as he unlocked the door. Our little slut is dead.

~

After breakfast, I was returned to wait in the now-empty cell. I stared at the cell door for some time, waiting for them to angrily return and accuse me of what I had done. But the guards returned to escort me to the sisters, and I was handed a small satchel I understood to be the girl's effects.

I had not expected this somehow. Light as it was, it was heavy in my hands. Not quite a warning.

Her name was unknown to me, and so as I stood before the magistrate again, he asked me if I understood that he was releasing me to the care of the orphanage. I only stared as I had seen her do.

Sidonie, the magistrate then wrote for my name. He held it up and showed it to me. This is your name now, do you understand? They are giving you this name, will call you by it, he said, and then he gestured for the guards to take me off, and as I left, I felt the name close over me like a door.

~

She is most likely in the rue d'Enfer now, one of many in the hedge of skulls down in the catacombs. There's an entire city of the dead under Paris, complete with streets and corners. I sometimes wonder if it is any more merciful than this one.

As for me, I was delivered to the Convent of Saint-Denis orphanage. The sisters stripped off my uniform and burned it and shaved my head for lice, as they called me Sidonie and I struggled to remember to look at them as they did so.

I had again taken a dead girl's name to make my escape.

In the first months, I waited for the police to angrily return, to take me from the sisters and return me to jail. But they never did.

I knew my last life was truly over, my name struck from the registry, a death certificate written for me. No one owned me but me.

Alone in this new country made by my new name, as I walked the convent walls, learning my alphabet, my sewing, I felt something surely miraculous waited for me now, something only possible now that I had died and been reborn.

Act III

Un Ballo in Maschera

One

WHEN THE TIME came for me to find the Comtesse de Castiglione again, it was easier than I would have thought.

She was said to receive no one now, and yet everyone I asked knew where she lived—an apartment on the Place Vendôme, said to be painted black and empty of mirrors, the windows shrouded. The building was stately but conservative, strangely understated for her.

I could see the black curtains I had heard about from the street as I approached.

Her apartment on the rue de Passy, well known to me, was still hers, and another residence also, but it was said she treated these as museums to herself, filled with her gowns, props, and photographs, the souvenirs of her legend. She visited them occasionally but lived here. This apartment looked, from the street, as if the widow's weeds she'd put on in 1867 had bloomed over the years until they'd made a black hood over her entire life, though she no longer mourned her husband, if ever she truly had. It was said she mourned her beauty, which people still spoke of as of a vanished champion from another age. She had buried herself alive in public, on one of Paris's most fashionable streets. One final *tableau vivant* until death.

She was the beauty in mourning I'd seen on my first day in Paris. She had become for a time my teacher, protector, and, eventually, an adversary—though I had never had the power to threaten her. It was she who had crushed me, who had taken my measure and set me down according to her purposes.

This address, she had made me memorize it before I ever knew what it would become. I think, even back in the days of my service to her, she knew she meant to come to spend her last days here.

I rang her bell, waited, and presented my card to a suspicious young woman, who returned quickly, her face a shield.

I'm afraid she cannot receive you, she said, before showing me to the door.

I thanked her and left and returned the next day to try again. This time, as the door opened, there was not even surprise on the girl's face. She looked away then back to me, and said, You must know she will never receive you. Please take no offense. I always ask once, but she receives no one now. Please, do not return. It is an anguish to her.

I went across the street.

The neighborhood had many little cafés to choose from, so I found one I liked and waited, drinking a coffee and having luncheon. I wanted to see what hours she kept and if she ever left.

I had not seen or heard from her in more than ten years. I had since created a new life, one I thought of as empty of her and my service to her. But if I had an enemy who knew the whereabouts of the Settler's Daughter after she'd left the circus, with a penchant for the theatrical and the patience to plan, it could only be her. If the book I had brought with me, if it meant the old war between us had been renewed, I needed to know why and what it would take to end it.

She never appeared. Sometime in the late afternoon I saw her maid leave by the service entrance and go off to do some errand from which she returned.

The next day I went over again to the café and spent the day in much the same manner. On the third day of my vigil, a gentleman came and sat down in the café at the table next to mine.

Mademoiselle, he said. Please excuse me. Good morning. I'm an officer of the secret police, he said, very quietly, so only I would hear. The Comtesse de Castiglione is under our protection. We have been made aware that she refused you three days ago and that you are apparently conducting a surveillance of her apartment. So I must now give you a warning. If you are found here again after this, you will be arrested and taken in for questioning.

I stood and looked at her windows to see if there was any movement there.

There was not.

Ah, he said. I'm so sorry I did not recognize you. You are Lilliet Berne, La Générale, yes? I nodded. Forgive me. I saw you sing this season in *Faust;* you were extraordinary. Please forgive me. It is an honor to meet you, he said. And then his smile dimmed, and he said, Do not force me to take you to the station; it would be a terrific scandal in the press. He paused, and a terrible silence stood between us. For me to be the one who questioned La Générale.

Yes, I thought, as I took in his expression, *the papers would enjoy that very much.*

We both looked at the wrapped package in front of me.

I smiled and nodded to him, picked it up, and left.

I had managed this all badly, I saw as I made my way down the street away from the Place Vendôme. I had come here as if all were the same between the Comtesse and me, sure she was my antagonist, even that she knew my name — my professional name — and had not thought that perhaps she would refuse me or simply take my card to be that of a stranger's. I was stung, too, as I had briefly expected something more like the request for an autograph from my young policeman friend as he turned to me, and so I chided myself for my vanity.

But there was fear as well. I had not expected the Comtesse to still be protected by secret police, especially not in Paris. I believed the fall of the Second Empire had sundered all the agreements I knew of this kind for everyone, but for her especially. Instead, she and her agreements had outlasted it.

Whether or not our old war had begun again, she, at least, was armed.

How is it I am here? I wondered, as I walked away. But I knew.

I was looking for someone who'd been thrown away, she had said to me, of how she found me.

Once she was done with me, I was to disappear.

Of those I suspected had betrayed me, she was the one I was sure never thought of me. The most dangerous one of all.

Two

It is said there were four hundred Italian assassins hidden in Paris, each sworn to take the Emperor's life if he wavered in his support for the cause of Italian unification.

Four hundred Italian assassins, and then there was me.

As the Empress Eugénie didn't fit in the dark basement passageways of the Tuileries Palace once she was dressed, her many gowns were delivered there instead, where they were stored and then sent up on dressmaker's forms in a dumbwaiter to an antechamber where she would dress quickly, like an actress, and make her grand imperial entrances.

I arrived at the Tuileries in the early fall of 1868, a girl of seventeen, there from the Saint-Denis convent to work as one of the maids in the palace basement wardrobe, a *grisette*. The name means little gray one, or gray girl. I liked the word because it made me feel as if I'd become a shadow, working as I did in the basement of the Tuileries and sleeping in a small room in its eaves.

L'Impératrice, that was the word for empress, and there was just the one.

That word stayed in the air a little after it was said, a kind of glittering dark omen. The guards said it as she made her way through the crowd, or we said it in a fierce whisper, a signal to stop what you were doing and throw yourself to the ground in her general direction. Once I heard it, every moment I was not on the ground was one in which I felt my life might be forfeit. This dismayed her, I believe, though, of course, it was done to please her. She never said it—even the Empress, I think, feared this word.

The ladies of her court wore her badge on their left shoulder, tied there with a ribbon. Three wore her portrait, painted in miniature, circled in diamonds—these were her most powerful, the most senior: the Duchesse de Bassano, Princesse d'Essling, and Madame Murat, widow of Admiral Murat and Gouvernante des Enfants de France—her title made me think of her as the ruler of a small kingdom of French orphaned children, bordered in sorrow. The other nine wore her monogram, diamond letters on a black enamel background: *I* for *Impératrice, E* for *Eugénie,* and an *I* stepping through an *E,* as if someone had plunged daggers into the *E* from above and below.

She could not choose her ladies-in-waiting. Some were her friends, but many were not. Two were with her at all times for a week at a time in Paris, a month if she went to the country. Pepa, though, she could choose. Pepa belonged to her.

Pepa was the mistress of Her Majesty's wardrobe. A fellow Spaniard, she was squat, ugly, fierce, and strong, brought by Eugénie to Paris from Málaga. She might have been pitiable but for the rages she used to enforce her ways. If beauty didn't make you good, Pepa was proof ugliness didn't, either. She was assisted by two sisters, the daughters of the governor of the Château de Saint-Cloud. The governor had once been the Emperor's jailer, and his appointment, and that of his daughters, was meant to repay the man for the trouble the Emperor had made for him by escaping from his jail. But obeying Pepa offended the sisters, and as there was something each of them would not do, a girl was needed who could not refuse.

So it was I came to the Tuileries.

I was known to them as Sidonie, from the orphanage of the Legion of Honor of Saint-Denis Convent, chosen for this work as I was small, young, quick, and believed to be mute; the chamberlain felt it best to find someone incapable of speaking back to either Pepa or the sisters. I undertook my responsibilities gladly, eager to confirm for them that they had chosen well.

I quickly proved handy at climbing inside the dumbwaiter and wrangling the dress forms into place without either tearing the silk swaths of the enormous skirts or dirtying them on the walls of the chute. The skirts or the bodices or both were often jeweled, sometimes took a month to make, and were never washed—you couldn't clean something studded with diamonds in water and soap.

The Empress wore during the fall and winter, the high season of the balls, as many as four dresses in a day, and the single, finest, most expensive one was always for the New Year's ball. The seconds, as they were known to us, once they'd been worn, were often stripped of their gems and given out to the poorer relations of ladies-in-waiting or sometimes, if it was not too expensive, one would be given as a present to a favorite servant.

Someone unlikely to wear it in her presence.

And so we took great care with each dress before she wore it, as it was hers, and then great care afterward, in case it was to be one of ours.

The dressmaker's forms were made just to the size of her and she was measured every season for them. One was sent up dressed, the other empty for the dress she'd take off. When the door to the lift opened, there were always the two dummies side by side, the one bare, the other in the recently quitted dress or gown. They looked to me like two headless women, and it always gave me pause. Given how much the Empress worshipped her forerunner, Marie Antoinette, I can't imagine she didn't think of it. But Eugénie was Spanish, and Louis-Napoléon not quite French, either. There was not much French in him or any other Napoléon, for that matter. That would mean many things in the course of their lives, but I think, most of all, it meant they didn't entirely understand how it was with France and her rulers and how it had always been, how it might always be.

~

From my arrival, I was concerned almost entirely with Her Majesty's furs. They were heavy, and even if well cured, the animal musk of them made the air of their room thick and close. This was where Pepa and the sisters refused to go most often. These were not given away like the gowns, and as if they resented this fact, Pepa and the sisters ignored them all the more.

My French was of a very odd kind at this time—I knew curses and sexual positions, and how to ask for a drink, and then a few more words from lyrics learned for the tenor. At the convent I had added prayers and psalms, but in written form only. Of what I learned here, I often knew neither how things were said nor what they sounded like, and I learned as I could by listening.

When I was presented to Pepa and the sisters on that first day, for example, I understood very little of what they said to me. Pepa's French was thickly accented by her Spanish in a way I found charming; it would be the only thing I ever found charming about her. The very stout Spaniard and the two slender, quiet French women seemed at something of a loss when I only nodded to everything they said but, of course, this was the loss the chamberlain had in mind, had even hoped for; when the chamberlain indicated that I was mute, they stared, as if it were something they could see. They then walked me through the basement kingdom, showed me the dress dummies, the boxes of pins, the dumbwaiter, the bell that would ring for me, enunciating everything carefully. And then they brought me to the room where the furs were kept. Pepa gestured with a sideways grin to me. I couldn't tell the source of her pleasure, exactly. I could only think it was because her time in this room was done as mine began.

A list of the furs the Empress abandoned when she fled the Tuileries was published in the British newspapers shortly after the end of the Empire.

One Swansdown cloak, lined with Silver Fox.
One black velvet mantle, trimmed with Marten Sable.
One black velvet circular cloak, lined and trimmed with
    Chinchilla

One black velvet pelisse, lined with Weasel, with Sable collar.
One otter skin cloak.
One blue Cashmere opera cloak, lined with Swansdown.
One black Cashmere opera cloak, lined with Swansdown.
One hunting waistcoat, lined with Chinchilla.
One black silk boddice, lined with Chinchilla.
One grey silk boddice, lined with Chinchilla.
One Marabout muff.
One Sable muff.
One Silver Fox muff.
One Ermine muff.
One Otter muff.
One Otter's Head muff.
One Marten Sable boa.
One collar of Sable tails.
One collar of Marten Sable heads.
One pair of Chinchilla cuffs.
One pair of Silver Fox cuffs.
One green velvet wrap, lined with Canadian fur.
One carpet of Thibet Goat skin.
One white Sheepskin carpet.
One set of Otter trimming.
Two caracos of Spanish Lamb skin
8 ¾ yards of Chinchilla trimming.
27 yards of Sable tail trimming.
One front and a piece of Black Fox.
Four strips, a wrist band, two pockets, two sleeves and one
    trimming of Black Fox.
Two Swansdown skins, in pieces.
Fourteen Silver Fox skins.
Six half skins of Silver Fox.
Twenty Silver Fox tails.
One Otter collar.
Three tails of Canadian fur.
Two Marabout collars.
Some odd pieces of Chinchilla.

Four large carpets of black Bear skin.

Two small carpets of black Bear skin.

One brown Bear, with head.

One stuffed Bear.

One white Fox rug.

One caraco, one petticoat, and one waistcoat of chestnut
    coloured plush, trimmed with Otter.

19 ¾ yards of Otter trimming.

Two Pheasants' skins

Three white Sheepskin stools.

One Sable dress trimming.

Three Sable skins.

Two squares of Chinchilla.

One Weasel tippet and two cuffs to match

Two pieces Swansdown.

Two Pheasant wings.

One stuffed Fox.

One pair of Otter gloves.

3 ½ yards of Skunk trimming.

Two court mantles bordered with Ermine.

I knew they'd published this list to shame her; but as many furs as were found, I knew well there'd been many more.

As often as not, under one of those ermine court mantles, Eugénie wore only a flannel wrapper, brought with her from Spain. It made the Emperor quite cross when he would look over and see a bit of it showing. I sometimes wanted to explain to the Emperor that he had married a horsewoman, but if he didn't know it, it wasn't for me to tell him. He'd admired her horsewomanly ways, having fallen in love with her on a hunting party at the Château Compiègne, meant to be six days that became eleven. At the end of it, he gave her the horse she rode in the hunt and an emerald pin shaped as a cloverleaf and covered in small diamonds in memory of a moment when she'd paused to admire a clover after the rain. He had it made in Paris while the hunt went on, and it arrived in time to be his token to her.

For all any of us know, he had the hunt extended so as to give this to her before she left, all of them waiting while the jeweler did his work and the Emperor his.

She lives now outside London, having escaped the mobs that screamed for her death. A brave few of her loyal subjects had rushed her from the palace in the first moments after the Emperor's capture and the fall of the Empire. Like Louis-Philippe before her, she was rushed from the palace to London in a disguise, on the yacht of a British dentist.

I wondered how it felt to her, if she'd read the list of her furs, if she missed any of it at all, or if she was content to wear as much flannel as she liked now over there in England, the Emperor and the Prince dead.

I had a pang on reading the list, of missing my life there. I thought of the Tuileries and how the enormous buildings of the palace looked to me sometimes like the cars of enormous trains. I missed walking toward them in the night and knowing there was a small room for me within, where I could close the door and vanish, no one knowing who I was or where. In those days, the Emperor and Empress were both everything in my life and nothing to me, for I never saw them. I wasn't among the servants who were close to her physically, not at first, though through my work I had to know, constantly, the intimate details of her life — if she had gained or lost weight, if she was with menses, angry or sad or in good humor. Each day had a schedule to it, determined by her events, when she would need this or that dress or gown or fur, and when she would no longer need them. It was not constant drudgery, but instead there were short periods of intense work and then long stretches with nothing to do. Nothing of my life mattered to them except that I be present according to my schedule, which I received weekly, with some changes daily, the times I was to climb inside the dumbwaiter and get the dress on. The hours were very irregular, as the parties could go late into the night or early morning, though usually her lady's maids would leave the night's last dress in the dumbwaiter, and we were to rise and send up the new one before the Empress woke. We knew, for example, when she was wearing the flannel underneath, as there would be no requests, nothing for us to do when the schedule clearly said something like *Ambassadeur du Brésil*.

I felt she let her flannel show to punish His Majesty for how he met for hours on matters of state with his "secretaries" every night, which is to say, his whores, his wives of other politicians and royals, their daughters, women who often imagined they could be his next Eugénie. As this was conducted below, his first Eugénie wandered the upper galleries and halls of the palace alone, with little or no hope of seeing him, visiting her courtiers in their apartments and playing with their children, always staying too late. No one could send her out; she was the Empress, and she was very lonely without her Emperor. And yet because it would be dangerous for her to have a lover, in case she was to bear a false heir, her movements were carefully guarded by secret police.

None of the young women who wanted her position knew what her position was.

~

As my role had no precedent, I was given a room of my own, a luxury, up in the eaves of the palace. I had a window that looked out onto the courtyard, a bed, a trunk with my name on it, and even a lamp for reading at night. A scarlet-eyed pigeon with bronze feathers was my single regular living visitor there. I was fed regularly and well, and passed my time mostly in the company of the other household servants. All of this suited me.

I remembered the stuffed fox on that list. Also the bear. I remembered the twenty silver fox tails. I liked to set a silver fox head, the mouth open around the head of the otter on the muff, and leave it lying out to make the other *grisettes* laugh. The stuffed otter I kept up in my room with me for company. In the dark, by lamplight, the glass beads for his eyes seemed always to be almost alive.

I'd found him in a corner of the fur closet, covered in three marabout boas. I quickly propped the boas on something else and then

pushed him back behind several cloaks so he couldn't be seen. A
few nights later, as the courtyard blazed with the lights of a ball and
the staff drank bad sour wine near the pantry stairs, I went down
quickly to the basement fur closet and brought him to my room. I
knew I could be arrested for theft, but there was none who missed
him. He was tribute and sent, I imagined, from Quebec.

He had been made so he stood upright, as if he'd seen something.
There were faint black silk stitches on his wrist, repairing the tear in
the fur from the trap. In the dark, he looked whole and alive.

If he could have spoken, I would have known then, without any
doubt, that I was lost in a fairy tale, but he never spoke. The single
speaking animal in the palace was a parrot, a present to the Empress
who'd sent it home with a maid, where it learned to swear and curse
like the maid's lovers. Sometimes I could hear it shouting, *Tais-toi!*
Tais-toi! The creature had become much beloved by the Empress
after that but was thought to be too obscene to be allowed anywhere
near the apartments, and instead the bird was kept in the basement
with us.

In days as carefully measured as Her Majesty's gowns, I grew
to be at peace with my lot in life somehow. I didn't imagine that I
would stay there forever, nor did I see any opportunity to leave. I
was hidden deep inside the enormous machinery of the institution
that was dressing the Empress for her public and private appearances, and what I thought, what I looked like, and who I was were
of no importance to anyone as long as I accomplished my singular
tasks. I had found a very strange and beautiful kind of shelter, and
there was work I could accomplish easily. Here, no one knew me as
anything other than *une muette* of indistinct origin. I was sure I was
content to spend my life inside the warm circle of light my lamp
made, whether it lit my room or my passage to the vast cloakroom
of the Empress.

I was very grateful, then, to the Comtesse, for introducing me to
the chamberlain, and did exactly as she asked.

～

Once a week I left the Tuileries Palace for an afternoon, something allowed all of us. It was under the pretense of visiting an invented aunt and uncle, and so for this visit I had a dress, a careful blue one, dark and plain. The other *grisettes* liked to mock it a little when I came down in it.

It had never belonged to the Empress.

There were not so many uncles and aunts for us all, and like many of the *grisettes* who pretended to visit a relation on their one day of freedom, I went to the Bois de Boulogne, where I would present myself as if I were like any other girl who went there looking to make an extra coin on her day's leave on a ride through the park with a gentleman in his carriage. The procession of vehicles and horses was full of people either occupied at this pastime or busy looking at those occupied, a strangely public thing, like a theater's boxes spilled out into the light of the afternoon.

There was not one of our number who did not need some other way to make money. At times, stepping into or out of the carriage that picked me up, I had the sense of stepping over the death that waited if I was any poorer than I was. For me, it was always the same carriage and the same gentleman who left with me and brought me to this aunt I was to be visiting.

My "aunt," such as she was, was the Comtesse, the one woman in Europe who knew herself to be Eugénie's true rival and perhaps the only other woman who could have been empress. She felt her mother had bungled her chance at marrying her off to the Emperor, and so when she was sent by Cavour to Paris as part of Italy's diplomatic mission to France to seduce Louis-Napoléon to the Italian cause, married as she was to a man she did not love, she preferred this duty to all others and went willingly. She was so beautiful that when she entered late to her very first official ball in Paris the musicians stopped playing, causing the Emperor and Empress to look to see what had happened.

This was a story she loved to tell.

Like the Empress, the Comtesse had red-gold hair that was sometimes light, sometimes dark, but unlike Eugénie's, her eyes were a brilliant green and set off by her pale skin. Her breasts and her feet were as celebrated as she was, and she often wore no corset and no shoes, letting her breasts loose in her bodice and slipping off her slippers when receiving male guests at home.

When I met her, she was still an extraordinary beauty, but not as she remembered; she considered herself in decline. Even in the time I knew her best, she stayed inside more and more. Her eventual seclusion was still distant for now, the darkness only approaching.

Our ritual, like my appointment to the Tuilieries, had been arranged by the Comtesse, and to repay her kindness, she asked me for this simple task. There was a written schedule of the Empress's appearances prepared by Pepa and the noble sisters, and it included a catalogue of what she was to wear each time — this was done so we would know what to prepare each day. When the week was concluded, the list was taken down and discarded. I was the one who took this list down. Per her request, I instead kept this and set it in my greeting card wallet, where it stayed until I entered the Comtesse's home. I placed it in a bowl near the entrance, as one might leave a visitor's card, and withdrew from near the bowl a small envelope containing my five francs' pay. I passed on, following her footman into the parlor, where I would sit and wait.

Our ritual was unchanging.

Her entrances were always grand, even when she made no apparent effort, even for such as me; she had no need to seduce me, though she did, as she did everyone. She came down the stairs always with a great refinement of movement, usually in an exotic costume of some kind, such as a silk kimono if she had been alone for the day, but it could as easily be a gown or a toga. Her passion for *tableaux vivants* and theater meant that, even when she was alone, she would amuse herself with her clothes for much of the day, dressing and undressing until it was time for her to go to her next appointment. And what she would wear to that appointment was somehow drafted over the course of the day's changes.

The Comtesse greeted me warmly always, her hand covering my own as she entered. She never mentioned the list, and neither did

I, though I never failed to bring it. She instead showed me to her table, set out with crystal and silver; and over a bit of rabbit or duck, I ate and listened to her.

If the chamberlain had need of a mute girl to work for the basement wardrobe because she couldn't talk back, so too had the Comtesse; my second duty, though it was not one she'd instructed me to perform, was to listen to her stories, and her stories were almost entirely of the Emperor and the Empress. She sometimes teased of giving me an education in being an independent Parisienne, but this inevitably involved more stories of the imperial court, which led always to the story of her exile from the court and the injustice of it, how she was blamed for the assassination attempt on the Emperor's life but not given credit for her role in the unification of Italy. She had neither been brought to trial in Paris—and allowed the vindication of proving her innocence—nor had she been honored at home in Italy for fulfilling her mission.

I did not understand much of this, or did not initially; but with repetition, I came to know it as if I were her, as if these were my own memories. When I returned to the dark of the palace basement, rushing to prepare the Empress's gown, bent around the dummy in the dumbwaiter, pins in my mouth, careful not to stick them in wrong and thus accidentally ruin the gown, at those times I felt I belonged entirely to the dark basement and might never go above and outside again. It was only when I retrieved the day's record and brought it to my room did this strange part of my life come back into view, hidden again when I slid the list into my things.

The mother superior herself had been the one who sent me to the Comtesse personally. I have undertaken a mission near us here, the saving of a soul, she'd said. A woman of wicked sins, a courtesan, who has made her fortune as a professional beauty, regularly disrespecting the vows of her marriage and of others, and who has become very serious about repenting and joining us here. She feels herself near her end and has asked for a habit of our order to be prepared for her so that she might at least go to her last rest as one of us in this way.

It amused me to think of this courtesan springing up the stairs of her last rest dressed in a habit of the Sisters of the Order of Saint-Denis Convent. She held out a slip of paper. Rue de Passy, near the Bois de Boulogne. The note at the bottom, signed by her, gave me the privilege of leaving the convent to visit her. She will need to be fitted, she said. A soul like hers, that is a great victory to win it. A great victory . . . and she sighed. Go tomorrow.

The doors on that first visit, as I waited for the courage to announce myself, seemed to me like the doors to Hell itself. The ornate stonework on the building's façade, carved to look like a giant's roses and thorns, the wooden double doors that were more than twice my height, the knocker, a bronze Medusa as big as my face, all looked as if, were the doors to open, I would be drawn inside and never allowed to leave.

I was dressed that day in a simple dress and bonnet, and carried with me my sewing tools. Over my mouth I wore a scarf I'd made for myself that read *muette,* the word stitched there to explain to any stranger why I would not respond — and to hide me, I hoped, from any chance encounter with someone who might recognize me.

I could not have guessed how much I looked, in short, like my own *tableau vivant* or how this would charm the Comtesse.

I pulled on the Medusa's chin and let it drop, and a loud knock echoed inside. The eyes to the Medusa head slid to the side, and her large green eyes appeared, shadowed by the lamp behind her. *Oho,* she said.

The bronze eyes slid back into place, the door opened, and inside stood a beautiful woman in something like a toga but which was a black satin dressing gown, her red-gold hair loose and carefully wild. A crystal goblet in her hand glowed with champagne. She waved me in with her free arm, but I was so stunned, I only stood there. Her smile stayed on her face but dimmed slightly, and she spoke through it.

Well, she said. *Muette*. Is that your name?

I held out the letter of introduction from the convent.

She looked familiar to me, and then I knew—she was the very Parisienne I'd seen my first day in Paris. I was sure of it. The woman in mourning who had parted the crowd in her enormous dress and jewels. She was still in mourning, but she did not seem near death, as I'd been told.

As she pulled the letter open, she asked, Are you perhaps the ghost of the Chateau de la Muette, my neighbor? She gestured at the distance. Or some long lost heir to the château? I had always wondered when La Muette would come for her house. She flicked the letter with her finger and held it out to read it.

I shook my head again, unsure at what she meant. I knew nothing of this château.

You are my convent-bred seamstress, yes?

I nodded. And then smiled from under my scarf.

Come, my girl. You've come just in time.

She would always be like this. Familiar, full of vaguely oracular pronouncements, a Pythian oracle fed on champagne and pearls instead of myrrh.

La Muette, she said, as we walked up her stairs. Only in French, she said, would we have a word that can mean mute, hunting dog, or young falcon. Are you any of those?

I felt Fate reach down and trace the word on my scarf.

Slowly, I held up two fingers.

Two? You are two of those. How mysterious. I suppose we shall see which ones you mean. And with that, she threw open the doors to her dressing room.

The Comtesse had need of alterations to a nun's habit she'd once worn for a *tableau vivant*, in which she appeared as the sole resident of l'Ermitage de Passy, a comment on her social status as an exile from Parisian society in the aftermath of an affair with the Emperor. The resultant scandal of her in a habit was almost as enormous as her affair had been. She now sought to commemorate the event in a photograph. Her Paris dressmaker had claimed he did not know the details of a nun's habit, and so she had engaged in this pretense in order to engage me.

She told this all to me as I worked, and more. She was busy commemorating all of her most significant dresses and appearances in a series of photographic portraits. She praised me when I was done that first day and said she had more for me to do if I wanted the work. While the sisters were predictably disappointed, they allowed me to return again and again, imagining, perhaps, that I had bent her toward some last, virtuous response. Instead, I was repairing a red velvet toga dress for her as the Queen of Etruria. Or a fascinating Queen of Hearts costume, cut low and revealing. Or an enormous white gown with a cape trimmed with ermine, which she wore with a black mask.

After another month, she told me she had recommended me and my work to the Tuileries. This seemed extraordinary to me. She then added I was to expect a letter of employment soon from the Empress's chamberlain.

Are you pleased?

I nodded and wept, overwhelmed.

My dear *muette!* This is what she called me—she could not remember my name. How good you are and how sweet. Are you prepared to serve them well?

I nodded again.

Good, she said, and glowed with pleasure. When you are in your new position, you must come to see me every week. But our new arrangement must be a secret between us.

The attention and favor of this great woman made me fiercely proud, and I nodded again, agreeing to this condition instantly. But, of course, this was her intention. The result of those visits was not, as the good sister had thought, the capture of a great soul or, at least, the soul that was captured was not the one inside the Comtesse's famous breast. The soul that was captured was mine.

When the letter arrived, the sisters were greatly honored I was to

work at the Tuileries. They did not ask as to how my reputation had
traveled to court. I did not tell them.

~

Each of us in the Tuileries lived inside very clear territories, whether
it was the Empress or I. I could only be in the kitchens, for example,
to leave my dish and spoon or to pick them up. I ran a narrow series
of stairs from the eaves to the lower levels, and this path never took
me through the royal apartments. Though I lived in the Tuileries
Palace, I felt that I lived in a small room with a narrow stairs that
led to a larger room full of gowns and furs. Not the palace at all, but
something like a rabbit warren, dark and too warm.

In November the Emperor and Empress went for a month to
Compiègne, in Pierrefonds. The royals invited the best of European
society to join them there for a week of hunting, a hundred guests
per week. A few, such as the Princess Metternich, stayed the month.
Some of the imperial household staff went with them, but many did
not. It was usual to have the month off for most of us. So it was with
some surprise that I found myself being spoken to as I was pushing
an enormous sapphire silk gown down into a trunk to send to a girl
in Rouen who was the next in line for the Empress's castoffs.

I looked up.

The speaker was the Empress's own chamberlain, and I came to
understand that he was asking me, or telling me, that I was needed
to go to Compiègne. The girl who normally would have gone had
taken ill, which in the palace usually meant she was with child. I'd
been chosen to replace her there.

He paused here, and then, indicating the scarf over my mouth,
said, Take that off at once. It will frighten her. And you can't wear it
in the palace; it isn't the uniform.

I quickly untied it, put it in my pocket, and pressed my hand
against it for luck.

The chamberlain indicated I was to follow him. We went out of
the cedar rooms of the palace basement, and as we approached the

door to the royal apartments, I felt a faint terror, as if I might be burned. The chamberlain's movements were clockwork mechanical, a sort of stiff, persistent staccato energy drove him, and yet, as he reached out for the door's handle, he lunged a little, as if he'd held his breath while below.

An incredible light spread up from the bottom of the door as it swung open, and he dissolved in it briefly. He held the door for me, waiting as I also went through.

I walked out into the apartments of the palace and then stopped short as the impossible brightness of the mirrors flashing from the Paris morning sunlight replaced the cellar dark. The door closed behind me and my heart began to pound in my chest.

The chamberlain, already off in the distance, turned back to see me still by the door and gave me a severe glance, his left eyebrow raised, waving rigorously for me to hurry. The brightness here was like a tunnel also, and finding my senses, I moved toward his dark figure at the center of it, following him to where I would serve next.

Until then, for having so much of what I wanted, I had not considered just how I was not free.

As we walked, it seemed to me the light came from the Empress, as if around the turns of the halls in the rooms ahead she sat glowing, an unearthly radiance emerging from her like the figures in the paintings I passed. I remember the first room I entered was barnacled in green and gold, with an enormous mirror that ran the length of the wall on my right and reflected the gardens visible outside through the long, thin windows along the left. It looked as if I could walk through to another garden there, and as I ran by, I caught sight of myself and slowed, looking and then looking away. It was as if I'd never known myself, who or what I was, and I stared not so much at myself as I did at the series of strange details there that resembled what I knew of me. My face seemed to have changed shape; my eyes seemed some new color. And I was thin, very thin, too like the shadow I had fancied myself to be. The chamberlain glanced back, and I smiled at him anxiously, pulling my dress into place as if it could be made more presentable. The mirror image of me marched beside me and I found I listened for its footsteps.

The second room was red, and there were mirrors to the ceiling and paintings of men and women in mythic *tableaux,* all unfamiliar to me. The chamberlain stopped there and gave me whispered instructions on the presentation, how it was to be quick, that I would remain in the basement wardrobe service when I returned, but that after the presentation I was to be measured for the uniform I would wear in Compiègne. I wasn't to address her or ask questions but only respond to any question she might direct at me.

And then he pulled a long ribbon outside the door, a bell rang, and I heard what I instantly knew was the Empress, a tired *oui.* He pushed the doors open to the Salon Bleu.

I sank to the floor as I entered, pushing my face down into the skirt of my dress. My first curtsy to her was clumsy, and I felt her stare. The two of them had a short conversation over my head, and I slowly turned to try to peek up at her despite the terrible danger of doing so. I was presented as you might a new hairbrush or hand mirror, a tool to be put out of sight as soon as it was used.

She was not the legendary beauty I now recognized from a few of the pictures I'd passed by in the imperial apartments, but she was still a very beautiful woman. She was the Andalusian, with her red hair that was sometimes light, sometimes dark. Her pale complexion was still smooth and unlined despite her love of sport. I tried not to stare at this woman I had dressed so often but had never seen. I looked down from her face to her fan, open and paused in its movement on her lap. She held a posy of Parma violets that shocked me for being fresh. On her fan were the painted figures of a man in dark armor kneeling at the feet of a beautiful woman. When it later became my job to care for it, I would know it was her favorite fan and that the picture was of Henry IV at the feet of Gabrielle d'Estrées, the woman whose love gave him the courage to be the great king of France he became. She was never, however, his queen.

It was an odd thing for an Empress to favor. But, as I would also learn, Eugénie loved dark omens and collected them scrupulously.

I was dismissed and left, returning to the dark, airless comfort of my basement palace. The seamstress measured me for my new uniform, and as she pulled the tape around my waist and batted my hands away, clucking her tongue at my size, a strange shame ran through me as I couldn't remember the last time I'd been touched.

That night the eaves of the Tuileries constrained me in a way they never had before. Unable to sleep, I finally stood and went and looked out the tiny window. The lights made the palace seem made of a gold that glowed in the dark. I tried to imagine what Compiègne would be like. All that I could imagine, though, was the image from her fan. The man in armor bowing before the beautiful woman and the expressions of each.

Sorrow in the man, pleasure in the woman.

My role in the Empress's destruction begins here.

Three

DURING THE HEIGHT of her affair with the Emperor, the Comtesse had a special illusion door built inside her own so that the door could be open and appear closed, so that someone watching would be persuaded no one had come and gone when, in fact, someone had. I could never find it, but I thought of this each time I passed through.

I had never once seen the Emperor in the time I'd worked in the Tuileries, and as I waited in that doorway on this occasion, I understood I now likely would. As the door opened, as I entered with her butler, as I waited in her sitting room, I could feel, crossing in the air, the many paths of the man; could imagine his cloak, his clothes, his possession of her, still somehow complete after all this time. The door was still there for him to use if he should ever return. She'd had from him the passion that the Empress could feel missing in each part of the Tuileries she paced at night; it had come here and spent itself, and the air was still rich with it.

I left a note alongside the list as I passed the bowl this time, telling the Comtesse about the change in my position, and when she sat down at table at last, she held it up and then smoothed it against the wood by her place setting before looking up at me.

My dear, it's excellent news, though we'll need to be more careful. I will reflect on how this then changes your duties to me.

I only raised my eyebrows, waiting, and she laughed.

You are my "spy" in the basement. She laughed again. I'm sure he knows of our little meetings. I chose you because you are a *grisette*, because you are beneath notice. Because you are La Muette.

She paused as she said this, as if uncertain as to whether she had offended me, and then she pressed on.

When you are nearer the Empress, though, they will begin to observe you. And soon, if he does not already know, he will know. He may even have sent someone to follow you here today.

Terror at the idea of being discovered froze me in place. She smiled when she saw the change in my face.

It is important for him to know I'm spying on what she wears. I'm sure it will amuse him to think I am plotting something involving how many crinolines she wears, something like this. She gestured at her dress.

Looking up at me again, she said, It's important because then he'll allow it, and in doing so, he'll believe he controls the result.

She was lit by the single candle near her at that end of her table, her beautiful red hair rising loose in curls.

He won't, she said.

I returned to cutting the duck leg in front of me.

If anything, it's quite the opposite, she said to me. She is so odd, she said. It is, in fact, she who is always copying the fashions of his mistresses, copying the women she has lost to, as if she can win by imitating them. She is the spy of the crinolines. She is always befriending them.

And then she paused and raised her glass. All of them except me, she said. Her eyes glittered, as if she had won a prize of great worth.

During the time of the liaison between the Emperor and the Comtesse, the Empress had been recovering from the birth of the Prince; she sickened and took to bed for much of the year. If the Emperor understood this as a comment on his affair, he had responded by continuing it.

You're in no danger, she said. In fact, if you are already known to him, I would say you are meant to be a taunt to me, full of tales of what I can never have that you, my *muette*, cannot ever tell me. It is their revenge on me to bring you, I'm sure. For I am not allowed at Compiègne.

As I listened, she began to tell me of who would be at Compiègne, as well as the story of her banishment, but I could not quite hear it. I raised the fork to my mouth and paused to look at the delicate meat, pink at the center, before setting it in my mouth. I was careful not to betray any change in my expression as the thought came to me.

She was indifferent as to whether my errand for her resulted in my arrest or death.

The dinner finished soon after that. She called for paper, a pen, and ink.

I want you to copy out an address several times until you can do it from memory, she said. It is not this address, as it would immediately place you under suspicion.

I sat and did as she asked, writing it out, writing it out, writing it out with a terrible effort to keep my hand steady. *7 Place Vendôme, 7 Place Vendôme,* again and again.

Very good, she said. Now then, I would like you to record what she wears during the series, a much greater task, as she will be changing approximately four to five times a day. You will post the list to this address from town. During this period, I will pay you a raise, to be collectively paid on your return. Are we agreed?

Oui, I wrote in script under the repeated addresses.

~

When the door to the carriage opened and I was again back at the Bois de Boulogne, I forced myself to walk back slowly to the Tuileries and calmly greet the guards as I did so. They waved me in, smiling; I nodded, opening my packages for them to check, and they passed me through as usual. No one feared me. I walked up my familiar passageways, and as I did, I felt it, like a faint movement of air, even a wind, at my neck.

I waited until I could wait no longer, and then I ran the last part, and once in my room again, I bolted the door, fell on my bed, and pulled out my purse.

Away from her, the fullness of what seemed to be her madness came into view. She was bound up in an obsession with the Empress, who, it seemed, was perhaps likewise obsessed with her. To be caught between them was to be ruined, and that was where I was.

I set the coin the Comtesse always gave me next to the others. At the bottom of the purse, the napoléon I had first received from her glowed. I took it out and rubbed it for luck.

I knelt then and prayed for guidance, the coin still in my hand, and when I was done, I knew my purpose.

This coin, it had been joined by another, and another, and with this next task, perhaps a flood. This had been the first in a trail of coin I hoped I might someday lay down, leading to a world without the Tuileries, without the Empress. Without the Comtesse.

This work was not my ruin, then, but providence, a test that, if I passed, would provide a way for me to finally go to my mother's family in Lucerne. Seeing her that first day in Paris now seemed like a sign from God that she would put me back on my path. And so I blessed the day I'd been brought to her and counted the coins until I was calm.

Four

THE DAYS OF preparations leading up to Compiègne passed very slowly. For weeks, in addition to keeping up with the Empress's daily schedule, we also set ourselves to the business of packing the Empress for the retreat: a month of furs, shoes, hats, crinolines, costumes, robes de chambre, tea gowns, evening gowns.

In the dark of the morning on the day of our departure, we found a special breakfast of café au lait and a piece of toasted bread with butter and cinnamon on it floating in the coffee. This was a rich surprise and lent the work of overseeing the final details of the packing of the trunks the feeling of both a holiday and a conspiracy; I and the other *grisettes* conducted it in an unusual, even solemn, silence.

I'd never thought for a moment of what the Empress looked like in the dresses before this, but now that I had seen her, little scenes of her cast themselves in my head. As I laid the dresses in tissue in their trunks, I thought, *Oh, this will look quite fine on her* or *She will want to wear this with these*, and so on. I had never felt this way before.

To feel a small pleasure in it.

Previously, I had been like the abbess of her furs. A solitary mission. Now, dressed in the green and gold uniform dress of the autumn palace, I kissed my friends in the basement good-bye and left, as if off for war.

Her luggage was by comparison to the Emperor's the greater. The trunks were made by Louis Vuitton in a pale gray known as Trianon gray, her favorite gray. It was as if the Empress were secretly something enormous, disassembled in the morning dark, her various parts in the neat rows of boxes and trunks we'd prepared and brought up to the surface.

She was to be there for a month. Her lady guests each week were required to bring twenty-four distinct toilettes, changing three or four times a day, and could not repeat a dress or gown or piece of jewelry in the Empress's presence during their stay. And as Her Majesty could not repeat, either, and required choices, that morning we departed for Compiègne with two hundred toilettes, each of them new.

I stood near the trunks while the imperial train cars were loaded, testing the feeling of my new uniform with my hands along my hips. The crowd around us seemed to communicate an automatic respect for me, as if I were a Cent-Garde of the Emperor's, not the Empress's *grisette*.

The train gave its signal.

Eugénie appeared then. A veil covered her face, falling down from the brim of a tweed cap, but she wore the diamond known as the Regent, a diamond the size of a sparrow, and in the sunlight coming through the station, it flashed so brightly I almost expected there to be a sound. I wondered why she wore it, as it seemed dangerous to me—watching her cross the station I imagined a thief snatching it from her neck in a dash or the clasp coming loose and the diamond rolling along the floor. But I saw the people around her looking on with pride at the flash of the Regent in the morning sun of the station; at the trunks; at her careful procession, all heavily guarded; at me, waiting by the train, and I knew it was very much what they wanted of her. I'd thought of it as her own greed for these things, but that morning I understood it was also theirs.

Her guards in a phalanx around her repeated, *L'Impératrice, l'Impératrice, l'Impératrice,* and the men in the station doffed their hats and bowed, the women made half curtsies. As she approached the car, I threw myself to the ground in my now-customary way. *Vive l'Empereur, vive l'Impératrice, vive la France!* shouted the men and women in the station, and then I felt her steps on the stairs, and with her safely inside, I stood and made my way to my own car with the other servants, brushing the dirt from my skirt as the people cheered and the doors closed behind us.

We were met at the station at Compiègne by imperial carriages that took us to the palace quickly, cutting past the town's enormous cathedral and humble rain-stained square.

The palace was nearly plain by comparison with the Tuileries, cut of a stone of the color of bone, though not of ivory but a bone found in the woods. From the coach, it resembled a library or a tax office, not quite the rich retreat I'd imagined from my glimpse of the imperial retreat at Biarritz. The single greatest feature was the long park that extended into the imperial forests, where the hunts were to take place.

Orderly rows of chestnut trees, their leaves turned to gold by the new cold and beginning to fall gently in the hard autumn sunlight, bordered the palace, a bank of color high above the black iron fences with their gilt dragon's teeth, which seemed to surround any place the Emperor and Empress were to stay the night. More than the Tuileries, this place seemed prepared for some attack—black cruel spikes feathered the walls and entrances.

This palace's chamberlain stood in wait, with pages in court dress in lines to either side of the entrance. The colors were the same as my own. They took no observable notice of me, though, which was its own kind of notice—if I'd looked wrong, only then would they have glanced at me directly—and then quickly unloaded the carriages and brought us in. I followed the luggage and the other lady's maids, and left the chamberlain to his observances with the Empress.

The imperial apartments here were more familiar, hung in the same red and gold as the Tuileries, as if we'd taken the trains and cars all this way just to find ourselves back home.

In her dressing room, we waited for her, preparing for her first change from her traveling costume to her riding one; she wanted to go for a ride before the Emperor arrived. A bell rang and we stood quickly while she walked in. The dressing room was circular; an enormous pendant chandelier hung above us radiating an unearthly sparkling light. White silk hangings draped the walls and ceiling so that it was like standing in a tent, if a very well-appointed one. She looked at us expectantly but I hesitated, as no one had briefed me on my duties, mistaking me, perhaps, for the girl who always came. I waited for a moment as she stood there, her arms aloft. The first girl glared at me, an eyebrow raised with contempt, and then made a yanking gesture with her arms.

You are the new girl, said the Empress, quite suddenly. She said it in the same Spanish-accented French that was familiar to me from Pepa.

I nodded, instantly blushing.

This duty, it was once the duty of my ladies-in-waiting. But no longer. Not since Marie Antoinette.

The other girl was blinking quickly, as if whatever the Empress had said had stung her eyes.

You used to dress my dummies at the Tuileries, yes?

I nodded again.

Treat me a little gentler than that. And then she smiled softly.

I hadn't thought she would speak to us. I imagined us beneath her, not worthy of her conversation. The earlier, nascent affection I'd felt for her budded, and while I let the other girl lead in taking her jewels, which I didn't know very well, much less how to handle them, I helped her with her riding costume and found her green velvet tricornered riding hat and her coat with the Emperor's badge for his hunt. I set the hat on her head gently and pinned it into place, careful not to look at her eyes directly all the while.

She left with a quick thank-you, spoken to the walls, and only when she was gone did we relax our postures, at which point the anger in the other girl returned.

How stupid you are, she said. You should have asked someone to tell you your duties. I nodded, as if this were true.

We were walking swiftly now along the back passage. I was passing by dark mirrors, walking over ancient creaking wooden floors.

Here, as at the Tuileries, no one was going to tell me what they expected from me, and they would be sure to punish me for what I didn't know. What's more, my identity as a mute was not commonly known here. As the chamberlain had forbidden me my little scarf —it was not part of the uniform—I lacked its protections, and one had been that it kept me from speaking as well.

The first result of this, then, was that the impulse to speak rose up, to explain myself, to protest, and I suppressed it with a panicked start, catching my opening mouth with my hand.

～

While the Empress was away on her ride, we were given a tour of the palace by the Compiègne chamberlain and shown our quarters.

I was to share a room at the back of the palace with my unhappy partner from earlier and another girl. The window had a view of a ditch and the wall and the kitchen entrance at the back.

I hadn't understood the excitement in the other staff at leaving for the country. But as I unpacked in my small room, listening to the conversations taking place around me, I understood that as our wealthy charges exercised themselves, as they planned their musicales, *tableaux vivants,* operettas, hunts, and masked balls, we also plotted our own entertainments. Each week, to make sure the one hundred guests had their fill, there would number nearly nine hundred of us between the attendant valets, lady's maids, footmen, cooks, *grisettes,* and guards. Some of our company came and left with the guests, some were of the Tuileries, and some were of Compiègne. Subsequently, much the same as on the other side of the palace among the official guests, there would be affairs, singing and dancing, feasts, terrible fights and feuds. And the separation was not by any means complete; there were guests whose tastes ran toward the servants, just as there were servants whose tastes ran toward the guests. The term for the gratuity usually exacted from guests just prior to their leaving, and which the chamberlains kept in large part for themselves but were meant to distribute among the rest of us, was also what you might say if you'd stumbled into and out of an apartment with a guest. *Pour boire.*

If the guests were satisfied, they were absorbed entirely in their satisfaction, and they were not concerned with our whereabouts. And so we worked to their satisfaction in order to remain invisible and unheard and at play where possible. And in the shadow of their satisfaction, we set about our own.

The bell for dinner rang and we ran quickly from the room for our first meal.

~

The Cent-Gardes at the Tuileries had told us of how the women the Emperor had brought to him were asked to come to him naked; they left their elegant toilettes behind and were told that they could do anything with the Emperor except kiss his mouth.

I thought of this often, I found, now that I was around the Empress so frequently. I wasn't allowed to meet her eyes unless she specifically asked me a question, and even then it made me nervous, and so I looked at her mouth.

And as I did, I wondered who it was who kissed her. Or if the Emperor saved this part of him for her alone.

I had very little patience for this new job. I was extremely uncomfortable to be so very much in the imperial presence in the day and in the company of my fellow *grisettes* at night. A bench in the hall was for me or whomever was on duty to rest on as we waited for the inevitable bell—this was my only solitude.

I found outside the Empress's apartments a secret passageway that led to the Emperor's library, the door hidden by a design to give the appearance of a shelf of books. While at first thrilling, it was hard to believe it would fool either the serious invader or the unserious one. And as the Emperor would never use this to call on the Empress, I did not know why it was there, so I explored it.

There was a daybed there, in the secret passage, and doors to the back stairs and passageways that led to the kitchen, the stables, and our quarters. A servants' passage, then, for the footmen. I could doze lightly here, springing forward at the bell in any direction needed.

I was bored that first week, cross in a way that seemed new. I wanted some kind of adventure, something forbidden but harmless. The guests had yet to arrive that morning and so, after the Empress left for a morning ride, I stood up from the daybed and pushed open the Emperor's library door.

The ceiling was painted with friezes of women gods I didn't know. I had a view out to the pale gravel yard, the garden, and the forest beyond it. The chestnut trees' golden leaves took the light of the morning, glowing in their rows. The room's handsome wooden quiet spooked me. but I was relieved to feel so alone. The walls were so thick, nothing of the activity of the servants could be heard.

The velvet-backed chairs gleamed in the pale autumn sunlight, and it was easy to imagine the young Comtesse there, just nineteen or twenty, a little older than I was now, her beauty like a furnace the room warmed itself on.

The Empress had been a famous beauty herself, but hers was a queenly *froideur,* as if she could cover the windows and mirrors in frost as she passed. The Comtesse, ten years her junior, newly arrived from Italy, with her wild red hair, must have seemed more than a rival—more like a demon of pure desire.

I walked to the far window. The chestnut allées crisscrossing the property framed the horses returning from the hunt. I could imagine the imperial displeasure if I was late, so I turned to go back through my passageway to where I knew I was to be expected, but when I heard the noise of someone moving, someone who had been at rest in the next room, I stood still.

For a moment, the silence in response seemed to suggest I'd been successful in avoiding notice. Then a high, soft piano note sounded, followed by others, chords. A slowly meandering, carefully beautiful piece of piano music.

In the musical education waiting for me, I would learn that this was a nocturne, a piece of music said to have the qualities of night, usually written for piano and performed solo. Nocturnes often don't sound right by day; listening to them then is sometimes confusing. This, though, my first one, was Chopin's op. 55, no. 1, which still sounds to me as it did that day, like someone walking through the dark quietly searching for something loved and lost, and the morning light didn't undo this. Instead, it was haunting, instantly so. I could not bear to go until it was finished. And as I was convinced somehow of being hidden for being still, I stayed and listened, deciding it would be safer to move once it was over.

The playing became louder briefly, as he moved to the music's conclusion. I was sure that this music had to require all of the attention of the person playing, certainly enough to keep him from noticing me. I thought I was safe enough then to peer around the corner into the room beyond the library, and so I crept to the far entrance and peeked around the corner.

A young man sat at a pianoforte, dressed in a beautiful dark green frock coat, a pale green tie knotted at his neck, and the strange short white pants the imperial court found fashionable then gleaming along his muscular legs. He was dark, as if he spent considerable time in the sun, and had the sharp, handsome features of a Gypsy, all set off by the strict white and green of his clothes. The effect was nearly narcotic.

He turned as if he knew he was being observed and looked at me, his eyebrow crooked, over the top of the piano. He smiled as he continued the piece's conclusion, which he let fade away gently. But he looked directly at me, and our eyes met.

I stood still, unable to look away. When the music was gone, I remained a moment longer, and then it was I felt the entirety of my trespass. I quickly turned and left, curtsying as I went before anything could be said.

Unknown to me then, he was both a pianist and composer. He was young, handsome, reckless, enormously talented. He could stand while playing mazurkas on the piano and turn to face the crowd and continue playing backward while he smiled into the audience. It was ridiculous and thrilling to watch, and he didn't make mistakes. He had a young wolf's face, and his eyes looked hungry, his dark hair rising in curls. When he smiled, his huge teeth flashed. Shortly after arriving in Paris from Argentina, he was invited everywhere, including, now, Compiègne. But it was unusual for him to be early and alone with a piano, left to himself in the music room off the Emperor's library; there was to be a week for distinguished artist visitors, but it had not yet come.

Later, when we knew each other, he would tell me he had been waiting for me to leave before playing. That he had sat down and, hearing the door open, realized he was not quite alone.

He was, at this time, accustomed to using the piano to get his way with women.

~

Here then was the last one, the one who knew all, but could not betray me as he was dead. I had watched him die. He was the one I had promised to marry, the only man I would ever consider. The *hôtel* in the Marais had been his, the room there his, that ruby rose left for him.

On the evening at the Luxembourg Palace when a man approached me and told me he'd found that rose, it was as if he'd told me he'd found his grave.

Five

OUR ROOMS HERE were cold stone, cold enough to make me miss the warm stink of the Tuileries. I was sure the bed was smaller, but it didn't matter, full as it was with three girls desperate to stay warm.

Out the window, I could see bright moonlight coloring everything a silvery blue and black.

I reached out to touch the stone wall next to me, and my eyes followed my hand, and I briefly rested it as long as I dared on the cold stone, staring as if I could push out the mortared stones with my gaze like a sorceress, to walk free out to the fields and whatever lay beyond the edge of the forest. I shivered finally and drew my hand back, warming it on my leg. The single advantage to dressing the Empress over my previous position, was the time spent in the warm rooms of her apartment.

The day's events passed through me as I lay still, unable to sleep. I could still hear the piano notes in the air as if the young man were playing somewhere nearby, and the memory of his eyes, the glance, looked back at me from the darkness above my head.

The mystery of him had puzzled me, and then the puzzle had resolved itself that afternoon.

The ladies of the court still retained the privilege to enter the Empress's chambers at any time, even though their duties as her dressers had concluded; I found this unnerving. The Princess d'Essling was the least intrusive, perhaps, and the Duchesse de Bassano was the most. The widow Murat entered like a warm, matronly shadow, the ghost of a mother returned to give some comfort or advice. But Eugénie did not take advice from these women; instead, they gossiped. And with some shock, I learned they gossiped in English.

From them I heard how Louis-Napoléon had never been a very learned or intelligent man, but this was not to be required of him, either. He was descended from the first Emperor Napoléon indirectly, the son of that emperor's brother. Whatever you could say of Louis-Napoléon, he didn't love a good song nor did he love a bad one. He had very little taste for music and mostly only tolerated it. He went to the opera because he was the emperor and it was an imperial entertainment, and so his opera had to be grand beyond all others, and it was very grand. But not for his great love of opera but for his great love of himself.

There was no reason, this is to say, for there to be a consummate pianist and composer in the palace before the beginning of the series. Not, at least, there in the Emperor's library, alone.

I found I thought of the pianist each time I sat idle, wondering when I could steal out into the passageways to see if I might see him again, though I told myself, of course, that I only desired the freedom.

Why was he here? I wondered. But there was no one to ask. It was no business of mine.

Days passed like this. The first week of the series was nearly concluded when I chanced to let my eyes rise up and see the Empress as she examined herself in the mirror. She was sadly beautiful; in every portrait of her, her eyes have a kind of immortal melancholy, as if they contain in them a picture of some larger, divine sadness. But this day there was also a fierce edge of pride, which made it impossible to feel entirely sad for her. This day there was also something romantic to the way she prepared herself, something of the coquette. There was someone she anticipated, someone she wanted to have see her and, in doing so, to be ruled by her. Not for her being empress, but for something else.

The thought waited in my mind, and finally I allowed it. I looked down, afraid of her seeing it in my eyes.

He was here for her.

~

I stood by and watched her as she posed in the mirrors of her bedroom's antechamber, dressed in her first gown of the day, a chiffon of the palest lilac, before picking up the day's bouquet of violets waiting on the table. She posed with that as well, and when she was done, she went out to attend to the last-minute arrangements for her guests before returning to wait for the ministrations of her hairdresser, Leroy.

Ça y est, she said, waving me and the other girl off.

As I watched her fretting, that curious servant fondness, almost maternal, returned, and as I felt it, I was grateful, for it obliterated the fear. At this distance, seeing myself as I once was, I understand it for what it was.

It made it possible to stand there.

She adjusted her expressions in the mirror until they suited her, but the expression she put back on immediately when she looked away from the mirror was the one she had discarded: the melancholy of the neglected beauty.

When she was gone, I sat in the empty antechamber, grateful to be alone and warm. Her mirror beckoned me, but the risk of her returning quickly and finding me in front of it was too great, and so I went over to examine the day's clothes instead: a tea gown, a gown for dinner and dancing. Another in case she changed her mind or there was a tear or stain, and as an excuse to touch them, I primped them lightly on the dummies around the edges of the room.

I waited while another girl went and ate her midday meal in the kitchen; when she returned, I would go. Someone had to be here at all times in case the Empress should suddenly return and need to change for whatever reason.

I had mostly let go of the idea my appearance should matter, at least as it once did. But alone with her dresses and her mirror, this returned. I began to imagine myself in the gowns in front of me and longed to hold one up or just touch the soft silk and imagine it was mine. I contemplated approaching her mirror, empty and reflecting just her pots and brushes, when I heard, from the entrance: Sidonie, what a surprise. I had forgotten you were coming.

Pepa entered. She was very proud of her dress, a castoff of Eugénie's, which, between the corset and some magician of a seamstress, she'd managed to fit herself into. It was white and blue satins, and looked something like a First Communion gown or the dress of a matron at her daughter's wedding. She made a show of turning in it in the mirror, the exact gesture I had feared making.

I made a show of smiling.

It's good, yes?

I nodded my head vigorously and smiled. She had put on airs, as if she were also a guest, but I knew she was not allowed out to see the guests and never in that dress. She wore it only to lord it over the rest of us.

Finally, the other girl returned, and I ran to the kitchen to eat before the Empress arrived. On my return I found the Empress sitting and laughing with Pepa, talking in brisk, softly accented Spanish, waiting, I feared, for me. She stayed seated as I entered, though, and Pepa continued telling her whatever story she was relating. I heard the words *Saint-Denis* and thought to smile, but they were not speaking to me, only of me.

The Empress stood then and we prepared her first for tea, then soon after for dinner, and then after that, for the first ball that evening. While at first it fascinated — *So it was like this*, I kept thinking, after my long time in the cellar with the furs — soon it bewildered. By the time she left for the ball that evening, in my mixed hunger and exhaustion, I nearly went to my room until I understood I was to undress her at the night's end. She would also require one of us to be near her at the ball in case she needed some-thing.

The Empress chose me.

~

There was a painting that kept me company outside the Com-piègne ballroom, a night scene, figures moving through what I first thought was a night sky, flying across the clouds like angels, a dark and angry-looking earth below. I stood there night after night, and as I did, it became like a story I told myself again and again, for it was most of what I could see. Soon I thought it was horses riding across a night beach, the moon high in the sky casting a beautiful light on the riders and mounts. Then I came to think of it as swans swimming at night. Later, I was told it was a mythic scene of the first Napoléon's wars, a night battle.

This was not my post; that was nearby. A bell would ring if I was needed. Standing here, I was in the foyer to the ballroom. I could glimpse the ballroom and still be in shadow. Another tiny rebellion, though this time it was done so I could listen.

The dance master had been winding a mechanical piano for the dances before this, but it seemed the effort eventually winded him, and the guests had begun to despair, if quietly. Still, word of their discontent had reached the Empress, and she had mentioned she intended to correct it at once. I had guessed she meant the pianist.

A quadrille began, accompanied by just a piano, and vigorously so; my pianist was playing, I was sure. His nocturne had left me with a portrait of his movements, his intelligence, his emotions; all playing does. I knew this was him. He was a guest, then, but no common performer.

I stepped closer.

The blur of sparkling gems, the candy colors of the ladies' gowns alternating with the black-and-white flash of the gentlemen — each

couple as they turned went from dark to light, a chiaroscuro following the beats of the dance, and I longed to enter.

The quadrille ended, and a mazurka began. I heard something
more tender than what had come before, more lovely. They are not
as quick as some dances, but the movement of them, the triple time,
one-two-three, one-two-three, has the feeling of something that
moves again just when you think it has reached its end. They can
be quick and fast; they can be as slow and sad as a funeral march. It
seems to me you have to be a little in love to write a mazurka or to
play one, and if you dance to one with someone you don't love, well,
for me it's unendurable.

I believed two things at once in that instance. I was both entirely
sure I belonged to this pianist, and he to me, and I was sure that at
night the Empress would bring him to her room and that he was
hers. I wondered if she likewise commanded her lovers to undress,
to come to her naked as the Emperor demanded. I imagined him
under the flower of light, her antechamber's chandelier, the little
rainbows on his skin. She would still be painted, the sadness still
there on her face as she looked at him. As she perhaps traced her fan
over his heart.

Was her mouth as forbidden as the Emperor's?

This mazurka was Chopin again, the no. 2 in F minor, op. 63,
though, again, I didn't know this then, but instead I felt only the
way that this mazurka, in my pianist's hands, sounded like something undeclared and hidden, impossible — like love or, at least, the
love I felt then.

The musical education that awaited me included the knowledge
that a Chopin mazurka was unlike any other mazurka; fans of mazurkas were not always pleased to hear them. They were impossible to dance to, being very slow, proceeding in a threefold series of
movements, timid, bold, timid, or minor chord, major, minor, just
as I'd heard that night. A "proper" mazurka was to be like a jeweled waltz, ornamented, decorated with flourishes so, of course, it
was popular with the Empress Eugénie and her friends, but Chopin

liked to conceal the rhythm with syncopation, and on the whole, his resembled a lover's feint in the dark.

It was, in other words, a bit of a disaster for this dance. The frustrated dancers ambled through ably, but another piece was soon called for by the dance master, and it began promptly. A proper mazurka.

The Empress pretended not to notice and kept up her dance with the Duc de Tascher even as she surely understood the gesture. Her asking him to play as a mere entertainment, an honor in some other circumstance, must have humiliated him. The Chopin mazurka as lover's complaint was noted, perhaps, by the one who knew to find it, and for the rest of the room, only artistic caprice—the musician-composer's inappropriate tribute to a newly dead musical hero.

At this point he was simply an infatuation of hers for a handsome young artist. For him, he felt sympathy for the woman who could transform his career overnight, and had. He loved that she loved him, and while this was not quite love for her, this feeling inspired its own loyalty from him, and jealousy, too.

The bell rang, the signal she was to change, and so I left for my post in her antechamber.

~

The dressing room was dark and so I lit the lamps to be ready for the Empress's return.

After I lit the last one, I caught sight of myself in the mirror.

I was still the stranger I'd glimpsed at the Tuileries. My beauty had turned strange. My eyes looked dark and enormous against my face, my figure too small and too thin—like a boy in a dress. I looked younger than I was, my hair drawn back into a simple chignon only to be neat, not attractive. I was plain, undecorated, even rough, and the poverty of what I had compared to my desires made me turn away in shame.

After so much time spent wishing myself away, I now longed for my own return.

I contended for the affections of the pianist with no less than the famous beauty I assisted in being a famous beauty. I could not compete for him, not like this.

That moment in the music room, it was pure chance; it was not to be repeated. Most likely, I would never see him again, but what's more, I was too ashamed to let him see me one more time.

And so when Eugénie returned finally, it was very easy to keep my eyes from her, very easy to be just what she thought I was. Easy to put her gown away quickly before going to bed myself.

Timid, bold, timid. The timidity in me, so like that in the Chopin, seemed permanent, the mazurka a false mirror for my feelings, leaving me unaware of the movement rising in me next.

∼

I stood in the spare palace apartment where the Empress's dresses were now kept before and after she wore them. It had been commandeered after a guest had complained of the drafts and was moved to other quarters; the chamberlain had said he was sure it was to prevent the man's wife from being seduced by the writer Théophile Gautier, who was said to be writing her a poem every day.

The draft is from him opening the door to deliver his poems, no doubt, he said.

I batted my hand and, sure enough, felt no draft. The pink brocade walls, if anything, helped keep these rooms warmer, though all of Compiègne, I had learned, was famously drafty.

The apartment being unoccupied, if also in use, was something most of the staff had taken advantage of thus far; one girl had brought a lover in here and dressed herself in the gown in which Eugénie had received the week's guests. It was thought to be the Prince Napoléon himself who'd had her there, though she refused to say. When she told us this, another girl said, Well, you're the picture of Her Majesty from behind, and then laughed shrilly until she was slapped by the offended *grisette*.

The lovers aside, the part of the story that stayed with me most was the idea of her wearing the Empress's dress.

The Empress had just left for the hunt in her emerald-green riding costume, the green tricornered hat pinned to her head, which I knew she meant to look rakish. The palace was emptied of guests and we had a few hours of peace without them. I took off the palace uniform, folded it carefully in a place where only I would find it, and drew out the gown she had worn to the first ball, the gown she had worn to dance to his music. Rose-petal pink and white, the skirt and cuffs were covered in black lace that rose to a strange, witchy black lace collar, unearthly in its beauty.

I stood quietly, mesmerized by it, holding it up in front of me. I then reached behind myself and began to unbutton my dress, working quickly until I was naked. I put my feet into the shoes she'd worn, of the same pink, with black trim and black heels, and then threw the dress aloft as I went underneath it, pulling it over my head. It was like crawling into a tent. Her scent was still in the bodice. I found I could button and lace most of it myself, and while the dress bagged a bit on me, in the mirror I looked a little like what I remembered myself looking like at the Majeurs-Plaisirs. I had thrown myself to the floor in front of the mirror in a mock grand curtsy, pressing my head into the skirt, when I heard the door to the apartment open.

I stayed on the floor, unmoving.

A voice called out the name of the girl who'd been had here. It came closer and closer. Soon the caller was standing over me, and he laughed.

I looked up at my discoverer. I already knew him.

The tenor was a handsome man of fair complexion, but this day he was painted purple, as if to resemble a Negro; the effect was to make him look like neither race, but like something else, a demon. I did not recognize him in the first instant, then, but in the second. He wore his typical evening dress coat and the tight white pants the Empress favored. Though the style favored only a few, it favored him.

We stared at each other openly.

He likewise did not recognize me in the first instant, but on the second one; and when he did, he swore viciously in German before striding quickly to my side and gripping both my arms tightly, pulling me to my feet as he stared into my eyes.

Dead, they said to me. Dead! I begged them to release your body to me and they said it had already been taken to the rue d'Enfer. I came with money for your bond and they told me you were dead and I went and threw it at *any beggar* I found along the Seine! I then went to a church and prayed for your coward's soul. I! I prayed for you. I wept for you as I did so. Do you know whom I have prayed for in this life? You don't even deserve to know this.

His speech was the more terrifying for his monstrous appearance, and yet I could not run.

All the while, I knew it couldn't have been you who died, he said. They told me you'd been beaten to death and received no treatment for having not described your injuries. I had seen the police take you away; I knew you did not resist them.

He threw me to the floor. I did not cry out—I could not even breathe to see him.

I should beat you to death now. He raised a hand, and then it stayed up, like a lost thought.

I was the one who had faked my death, and yet here I was surprised to see him alive. That the tenor, currently at the Paris Opera, would be invited to Compiègne, this had never occurred to me but, of course, it was him; there could be no one else.

I could pull you from here now by your hair and insist the sheriff of Compiègne help me. You still belong to me.

I had moved not at all but seemed to watch from inside my eyes, though I did not look at him.

He stepped closer and stood over me as he opened his coat, and then I saw my ruby rose, worn there on the inside of his jacket, facing in over his heart.

I kept it, he said. I kept it to remember you. Along with all your shabby little things.

I saw his eyes then, the raw, angry wound of them. He held out his hand, and I flinched until I saw he waited to help me up.

And just like that, his eyes had closed up again, the terrible fire in them gone.

I stood and he circled me, taking me in. He pulled at his cuffs. I am here to perform Othello, he said. Thus my appearance. Why are you here, dressed this way? Is the Empress lending you one of her gowns? Are you . . . is it possible you're a guest?

I nodded. It seemed to me it might protect me if he believed it. To think somewhere in the palace another, more powerful man waited for me. But I did not want to speak to him if I could avoid it; to do so seemed like breaking another promise—to the girl whose place I'd taken, or to God, my mother—I did not know. An affront somehow to my renewed mission.

Well, the pleasure at our reunion is entirely mine then, he said.

I smiled, turning my chin in toward my shoulder, still afraid.

Perhaps it would amuse you, he said, if you came to see our dress rehearsal.

He went behind me and pulled the dress taut, his hands on my waist and back. He settled my hair, his fingers brushing the skin of my shoulders. I felt a shock at the familiar touch.

Like this, he said. You are a maiden; she is a matron. It should fit like this.

I nodded.

He reached out expertly to a hat pin near us on the vanity. He took it and slid it through the thick fold of silk at my back, and I nearly fainted as it passed through.

Well, he said. You've still barely a figure. I'm sure Her Majesty keeps slim, but you are a knife.

I stood still, held in place as much by all of this as by his hands, and allowed him to continue to pin the gown in place.

You're no guest here, he then said. I know this, for I am one. I've not seen you once at dinner. How is it you are here? Or does someone keep you in their chambers for their own pleasure? Is it the Duke? The Prince Napoléon? Who is it?

I made to run and he grabbed at my wrists. This time the pain brought tears to my eyes. Ah, he said. You will not cry out. You are afraid of being caught. With that he let go.

I must leave for now. But I will find out your secret, he said. We will see what happens then.

~

I undressed quickly, put the gown back into the trunk, and was fitting myself back into my *grisette*'s uniform when the girl the tenor had been looking for appeared in the doorway.

She didn't ask me the question I could see in her eyes, as to whether her tenor had been here and if I was to blame for her not finding him. I took a breath and set the lid of the trunk down.

She's back, she said to me, instead; and I followed her out.

The hunt had left the Empress in a thoughtful mood. She seemed distracted as her hunting costume was removed and we settled her tea gown into place. I imagined she was thinking of the composer, perhaps plotting an assignation or worrying that he was in love with someone else, or both.

The tea gown was pure rose pink crepe and tulle, almost too girlish. She asked for white and pink diamonds for her rings and necklace, and the Regent again. She seemed to wear it a great deal, perhaps for the way it insisted on her position. Her color was good from being outdoors, and when she was dressed, she was transformed and was lighthearted and then made to leave.

She paused in the door and turned.

Do you like it, she asked me. Does it suit? I was taken aback and blinked rapidly before nodding.

Oh, you're the mute, she said. You poor thing.

She came close to me, walking slowly, as if I might startle. I made myself still, though inside my heart beat at a run. She reached out and ran the back of her fingers against my cheek. It was strangely humiliating and affectionate at the same time. Only as she paused and held the fabric of the sleeve against my cheek did I understand what the gesture intended.

Yes, it suits you. This will be yours, she said. It should be yours. She glowed deeply, full of pleasure at the thought of giving it to me. I cannot remember your name right now, but to be sure, it is to be held for you. She turned to the other girl. You are the witness if any should challenge this, she said to her, at which the other girl gave a brief curtsy, and murmured, It is done, Your Highness.

And with that, she left us, smiling.

The other girl folded the hunting costume over her arm and left me alone in the antechamber as she returned to the apartment.

Alone, I approached the mirror, full of shame at having thought to steal something she would give so easily. But I could never wear the dress; there was no place to wear it, no one to invite me. If I was very smart, I could sell it. I'd never had any of this sort of attention before from her, and it both pleased me as a novelty— imagining myself as being so favored by the Empress—and it also frightened me.

For I longed to vanish again, even as I became, with each day, more visible, and the chance to belong to oblivion again became more remote—the chance I could belong to it and the chance I would even want it, both. In its place was something new. I became briefly unsure of what had happened to me earlier that day, as if I had fallen asleep there in the chair in the antechamber while the hunt emptied the woods of game, dreaming this all the while the tenor was still making love to his *grisette*, the one I knew he meant to find.

But then I remembered what he'd said to me—*I will find out your secret*. And with that, my partner in dressing the Empress appeared in the door, fierce, and walked calmly over to me, her eyes darkening.

I watched her as she approached, understood what she would do, and still I didn't move, but instead waited. I even met her eyes as she struck me.

Salope, she said, very quietly, as her blow, quick and stinging, rang across my right cheek.

I remained silent and didn't break her gaze. After she pulled back her hand, she left quickly and with purpose, shaking the feeling back into her hand.

I sat for some time afterward, savoring the blow as if it were a badge. Then I withdrew the silver and black silk-satin-and-tulle gown for that evening from the trunk and held it aloft. The gown unspooled to the floor, as if it were alive.

~

I had been so proud previously, had disdained Pepa so thoroughly, and yet with the gift of one gown my covetous heart awoke.

Six

THE NEXT MORNING, when I took my dress to the empty apartment, my new pride held me erect the entire way. I opened the trunk to find the dress from the day before. Clearly visible were the little black crescents across its back, invisible to me in my haste, partly because of the black lace. This from the tenor, as he pinned the dress—the evidence that brought on the attack from my fellow *grisette*, I was sure. I scraped at the marks with a fingernail and found they flaked off, so I sat there and cleaned the dress with my fingers this way, and then put it away again.

This time, I chose an empty trunk and set it off to the side and placed my new dress on top to cover it.

I'd noticed the dresses were being sent less often to favorites. Perhaps there were fewer favorites or perhaps the favorites had tired of the seconds. What good is a dress to a court favorite if it cannot be worn in front of the Empress? Still, most of these were too grand to give to servants, though, of course, there was Pepa, and the apartment's bounty seemed almost in danger when I thought of her.

Pepa was the greediest of those who received Eugénie's castoffs. For her to wear them took so much corseting and tailoring that she appeared like a caricature of the Empress, a clown empress. The more she tried to be like her beloved Eugénie, the more she showed how unlike she was, and the more I'd resolved to never be like her —yet here I was.

I chose a trunk for my own to fill with the dresses I was now sure would be given to me; I would include a few others. I lacked for an address to send them to, as I had seen them sent to others, but once I had one, I could do it then in secret and collect them. And then they would be entirely mine. I was sure no one would know. I smiled as I imagined printing *Tante Castiglione* on the side and sending it to her.

I remembered then that I was to have sent a card to her by now. A card I had not yet prepared. I had entirely forgotten. I had two missions, the one I had sworn to myself and the one I had promised to her, but my mysterious pianist and the tenor's reappearance had destroyed my sense of them both. Yes, it was silly, this thing the Comtesse wanted—this mission was the exercise of her vanity, no matter what she said. But she would be impatient, even angry, if I delayed further, and I needed the money she'd promised—it didn't matter if she was mad if she paid.

I shut the trunk, off to discover just how a *grisette* might post a letter to her aunt.

Seven

THE HUNT WAS out once more the next day. There were two hunts in the week, I knew: *chasse à tir* and *chasse à courre*—in the first the animals were beaten from the woods into a cordon and shot while helpless to escape, and in the second the animals were beaten from the woods and then shot as they ran, no matter the kind, in every direction. I couldn't remember which one this was. It didn't matter. I went alone to the apartment, sure of being undisturbed, and worked at making a fair list of the week's events, laying out the Empress's gowns in order.

I had made some good progress when cannon fire and gunshots began to fill the air until it seemed like a war had begun here, an attack on the palace while the Emperor and Empress were at play. When I heard the first cannon, I thought it a salute of some kind, but then the next and the next came, and then I heard gunshots and the shouts of men.

I imagined the Empress dead in the forest beside her horse, the entire party slain, the woods burning, filled with enemy soldiers. They would advance on the palace, setting fire to it next, I was sure.

The single way out I knew of was the road out of the palace into the town, but this would be full if there was an invasion or so it seemed to me. Or was it better to hide in the palace and wait? It seemed strange to me that there was no one to tell me what was happening or what to do if this was an attack until I remembered no one knew where I was.

I decided on changing into the dress the Empress gave me. I

could leave disguised as a guest. I took off the palace uniform, and as I did, the door opened.

I leapt behind the dressing screen, afraid to think of who had entered.

Through a crack in the screen, I saw the tenor. He searched the room with his eyes before entering quietly, and I next saw a woman following behind, fair-haired, carefully dressed, a rich man's wife, with a florid complexion on an intelligent face. Or she was blushing from what she was up to, I couldn't say. She wore her tea gown already, clearly having abandoned the hunt, but there was no urgency, or not the urgency I would have expected, in either of them.

She looked askance at the room, as if reconsidering their joint aim.

I wondered for a moment if they could not hear the noise of the battle until the battle noise was rejoined.

How much longer? he asked.

I mean, who can say how long the ambush of a cottage can take? she said, indifferently, and crossed to the window before turning back to him with a smile.

The tenor chuckled at this, but he could see her hesitation. An expression crossed his face I did not recognize. He was softening, I saw, to her. Was it pity? Here was how he was with a woman he had not paid for. He reached for her.

With the French, he said, such an attack could last a week.

They laughed, rueful.

She said something I could not hear.

Well, you could say you have not recovered, he said. There's no reason anyone should protest.

The tension of the battle seemed to thicken the air around them, slowing whatever passion there was, and then there was only quiet.

It's over, and now they'll be back, she said. Richard will be at my room in half an hour. I . . . we will try again, she said. Tomorrow the Empress seems likely to be at her councils again through tea. Perhaps then. I'm sure whatever indisposed me this afternoon will not leave me so quickly, she added, and leaned in to kiss him before slipping through the door expertly.

It was some game then, the cannons. A game of war. My own mistress would be back, then, as well. I waited for the tenor to leave, but he did not, sitting down instead and then reaching to where I had stowed my uniform. He pulled it out slowly and held it to his face.

I had never seen this before. The hunger he had for me.

You're here, he said flatly. Show yourself.

He would try to force himself on me, it seemed to me then. Was it better to go to him or to be pulled from here?

I went to stand in front of the vanity. My body was pale in the late afternoon light, the gold of the sun covering my skin. I still had something of a girl's body except across my hips, but a faint fullness to my breasts had appeared, which was new. A sense of what remained of my own beauty returned to me then. A sense of it and the powers it perhaps endowed. He had loved me best naked, I recalled. I could use this to my advantage.

You saw nothing, he said. He said this without having turned to see who it was, he was so sure of me. He held out my uniform and mastered his face back into the angry confidence of a moment earlier as I stopped before him.

You see? I told you I would have your secret.

He walked closer and circled me, examining me.

This is lucky, he said. Very lucky. So you are *hers,* then, yes?

He meant the Empress, of course. I still had not spoken and did not want to speak. My eyes averted themselves as he put his hand under my chin and lifted my face so that I was looking at him.

Understand me. You still belong to me. And when I leave, you leave with me. I may sell you; I may have you imprisoned; I will decide. Part of how I will decide will depend on if I am well pleased.

He took his finger from my chin and ran it down my front before handing me my uniform.

Dress then and return to your lady. But meet me here tomorrow, for I have something for you to do. Much depends on if you please me then.

He said this with such confidence, as if it were on the week's schedule like the dinner that evening, the ball after; it chilled me as I made my way through the back passages, which comforted me now. I walked back to the Empress's chambers and sat shivering on the bench.

How had he found me? I asked myself. *How?* But, of course, a single answer floated before me in the dark.

The tenor was sent here to remind me of what waited if I failed in my tasks. If the Comtesse was Providence, the tenor was a warning from God.

~

The following afternoon, when the Empress left again for her afternoon council, I returned to the apartment, seating myself on a sofa there.

The door opened and the tenor walked in.

He took in the scene I made as I waited, the picture of a palace *grisette.*

Where does your mistress think you are? he asked.

I shrugged.

Speak to me, he said. I asked a question. Or has the sight of me struck you dumb?

I closed my eyes, hoped for divine forgiveness, and cleared my throat.

She's at council, I said. She thinks of me not at all. She thinks I am looking after her gowns.

This thundered inside of me and around me as I said it, speaking to him in French in our old way.

Are you? he asked.

I am, I said, and held my arms out to indicate the trunks around us.

Take off your uniform, he said. And put that on.

He made me dress in the gown I'd just brought up and then took me in it, brutally. And then continued, for he was not satisfied.

He took real pleasure in it and knew me enough to try to reach me in my pleasure also, and so these discomforts mixed to create a new one. This was no blunt cruelty, but something intimate. Here then came over me the old trick of the body, the way I could pull back from the surface of my skin as someone might leave a room.

The instrument took over and saved me.

Afterward, I ached and was wet, as if from a fever, and full of shame. As if we had fought on the floor. I felt the need to clean myself and stood. He, by contrast, seemed asleep, at rest. Child-like.

A long golden beam of light traced the skin across his stomach up to his left eye, and as if it pressed there, he blinked and opened his eyes.

Leaving, he said. Does your mistress need you so very much?

She does, I said.

He laughed. Who are you really? he said. Are you the ghost of the one I loved, here to torment me? Will you vanish now like mist?

I sat down on the chaise and tried not to let him see my own anguish.

No, he said. You're not. You're like a girl from the fairy tales of the Comtesse d'Aulnoy. And you're back from the dead to kill me. You'll be the death of me, I think.

I let myself smile a very little bit as I looked down at his naked body and the unexpected, even extraordinary beauty of it.

Why was I not used to it? But, of course, each time I saw it, I sought to forget it, and so each time it was new.

He noticed my examination and laughed again slowly and slapped his naked belly. He sat up. And then I will come back from the dead for you, he said. Perhaps it will never end.

He leaned in to kiss me, and his mouth against mine, unexpectedly soft, made me feel suddenly grave. The kiss was long and quiet, and had an insistent tenderness, unlike what had gone before.

I pulled back my head and nodded my assent. If anything was

going to prevent him from exposing me, it was this, his tenderness for me.

This, which I abhorred most of all, this could save me.

What is this council you speak of that your lady is attending? he asked.

A war council, I said. Her ladies-in-waiting are up in arms over it, for it means no one has tea with her. I must go, I said. I paused a moment, aware that he was in no particular costume. Is there no performance tonight? I asked.

A recital, he said. In the music room. This young new composer. I like him. He'll accompany me.

I must go, I said again.

He shrugged. As you said. Off with you then, he said. Return to your lady. But be sure to come here again tomorrow when next she meets in council.

He laughed again, and it followed me as I ran the passageways back to the Empress's quarters.

~

Speaking had confused me; my silence had been a mask, and so it were as if a mask had slipped. I no longer felt like myself—I could feel how I even walked differently. I summoned a vision of myself as I had been even a few days ago. *Like this*, I told myself, *and like this*, slowing, as if finding the pace at which I'd once walked would return me to my disguise, remembering to be someone who could not speak and answer.

When I entered the antechamber where the Empress sat, her hair waiting for the imperial hairdresser, I hoped I again resembled her mute *grisette*.

I was late, but as I had never been late before, the Empress was generous if stern, merely raising an eyebrow as I had arrived just in time to help with the removal of the afternoon's tea gown. Service had not been disturbed. From the face of my former rival, I could see a story of me had been told, but it couldn't have been too incriminating or it would likewise ruin her fun, and it would have to avoid describing her as the loser—the mute girl was an unconvincing victor, and this would humiliate her.

The Duchesse de Bassano came to complain of the councils again—even to scold. The Empress was neglecting her guests with these long meetings, and guests were offended. All through the palace, these women sat dressed, waiting to be invited, and were not invited, and came to dinner as a group, feeling snubbed. To have tea with the Empress in the afternoon was a great honor, and she was not extending it.

White tulle again for the bodice, I thought, as I set the tea gown gently over my arm. The wrapper came off, and a skirt like sea foam spread out down her crinolines, and I clasped a long white velvet train over the skirt behind her. She added a diamond brooch to her waist, a bracelet of pearls over her sea-foam gloves, and then the Regent again at her neck.

She did not reply to the Duchesse, and instead pulled at her jewel box. She set her fingers on the emerald brooch from the Emperor and turned it where it sat. She held it up, as if to put it on, then set it down again, repeating this quietly as she waited for the hairdresser, her eyes watching the door through her mirror's reflection.

For the recital, I found a hiding place better than the one previous, able to view the piano in part, though not the tenor.

The Princess Metternich welcomed the assembled gathering. This was my first glimpse of her. She looked to me at first like a youth in a gown, her face more the face of a charming boy. The Princess's eyes were deep set and large so she always appeared intent and serious, but also always a little amused. Her nickname was Cocoa Monkey, I knew from the ladies-in-waiting, and the rumor among the servants was that she was half-caste. To me, she exuded a different kind of chic from the other women of the court for the way her features were already original. She wore a particularly sleek gown of a pale green silk, which made her look even more exotic, her thin shoulders bare and a collar of pearls at her throat. Her hair was worn slicked close to her head and parted severely like a man's. She appeared distinctly beautiful, while the others appeared only to decorate the room around her. The Princess had none of the seriousness of the Empress and wore her rank the more lightly, as I think she believed in it in a way the Empress did not believe in her own. The Empress seemed as if she could not believe she was Empress until you did. The Empress looked like an actress beside her.

This evening the Princess was full of a barely contained excitement. I arrived as she declared to the gathered crowd that the composer she was introducing was her discovery, found on a night she and the Prince attended the Bal Mabille in secret. They were so taken by the pianist, they sat at a table near the musicians and left more impressed by him than by the dancers. They at once had become his patrons and introduced him to the Empress's Monday salons.

I was so stunned to think I had danced to his music and never knew that I barely heard her as she gestured to him and then welcomed the tenor to the stage as well, praising him as the greatest living Prussian heldentenor.

She went and stood by the Empress, and they spoke to each other.

I never surrender, the Empress said.

They were rivals for him, or so it seemed—this was all I heard of what she said. I was so full of my new confidence, so certain I belonged right where I was, that I was shocked to see the Princess had noticed me.

Her expression was a steady one; she was not going to interrupt the performance to reprimand me. Instead, she looked at me as if a horse had wandered into the hall, and in commanding it with her eyes, she could get it to return to its stable.

I stepped back three quick steps without turning around; and, content, she returned her attention forward. I quickly made my

way into the service hall, walking until I was back in the Empress's
rooms.

~

There I sat and looked at the Empress's gowns, waiting for her to
wear them. In the darkened room, each of them looked as if it were
the ghost of the Emperor's next mistress. I listened to the music,
which I could hear faintly. I imagined myself in a gown, black and
fantastic, meters of silk and glittering jewels, and the composer leading me across the floor to dance. We were at a ball at least as grand
as any the Empress might have here, glowing in the candlelight.

Then the tenor began to sing, to great applause.

And then I began to see myself putting the dresses away, and
then the tenor putting them on me for his strange game.

In my bed later, as I tried to sleep, I heard it again, in memory,
the slow, meandering footsteps of the piano, of the mazurka that
was not quite a mazurka—to me more like a lover's search of the
rooms of a party after it has ended. He wanders, watching for the
object of his pursuit. The wildness has spent itself, and now there's
just caution in the step and the insistence of what is felt, almost the
sound of footsteps, something in search of what it loves. I wished it
were the composer and that he would find me as well, and I heard it
until I slept.

Eight

THE WOMAN THE tenor had brought to the spare apartment was an American soprano singer married to a French nobleman and an intimate of the Emperor and Empress.

He had gone from trying to turn his lovers into singers to turning singers into his lovers, I noted.

He told me this as he described the mission that he insisted was the price of his goodwill.

The soprano was to appear in a *tableau vivant* that evening, to sing onstage in a little salon play written that week by the Prince Metternich. In that *tableau*, I would take her place as the American Doll, shipped from America. The theme of the play was "exposition," in honor of the Paris Exposition; it was a charade. The audience of guests and the Emperor and Empress were to try to guess the theme.

I was her height; I was her size. I lacked her fair hair, but mine would be under a wig, my face under a doll-face mask and powdered. She would be with the tenor, enjoying at last the consummation of their affair.

I have not sung all these months, I said to him.

It's fine, he said. You're to sing badly. You're the American Doll, but you've been broken in transit.

Now I stood backstage in my wig, mask, and powder, dressed in a traditional Tyrolean peasant costume with a black bodice and a red skirt, both beautifully embroidered, and a Tyrolean hat, a long pheasant feather jauntily rising above me. A large turnkey sat on my back like a metallic single wing. The Princess Metternich was dressed in a coachman's costume, with a cape, pants, and riding boots, a pipe resting in her mouth. She was busy winding a very wide silk ribbon around me, as if I were a package, tying it finally in a bow. The ribbon parted at my mouth and eyes to allow me to see and breathe.

The Prince and Princess Metternich knew the tenor and the singer well, and were in on the conspiracy.

The first part of the word, *Ex*, had been performed as a skit between invalids at Aix-les-Bains competing with descriptions of their elaborate diseases and miseries. Then the Princess had performed a song the Prince had written for her, "That Was Paris, and Now It Is Gone." She had cracked a riding whip over her head with great authority, causing the audience to shriek, and smoked the pipe through the song. The audience laughed at it all, though I did not understand why. Following her had been a young man insistent on learning to fence in order to defend himself against the hordes of foreigners who had invaded Paris for the exposition. When he finished, the curtain came down to much applause, and then I was set on the stage to await my decoration.

I should have liked for the Princess and I to be friends, I had decided, watching her song. I tried to think of how to speak to her as she decorated me, but she treated me as if I were only another piece of her costume. That afternoon we had rehearsed my song and the various trills and pieces of songs I was to sing in the skit.

Your voice is very like hers was all the Princess had said at the rehearsal. You should do quite well. If she recognized me as the girl she had caught outside the ballroom, she did not let on.

The Empress had been at the councils all afternoon, something that the Princess found puzzling, and she said as much on my delivery to her by the tenor. So they are having her sit in, she said to the Prince and the tenor, as if I would not understand. She shook her head. She cannot even organize the paintings at the Tuileries, and yet here she is sitting in on the imperial council. It's too much to believe! She will easily make a mess of things.

She cannot even keep her maids in line, she added.

I flinched under my mask.

~

The curtain opened again to tremendous applause. The Prince
Metternich and the Comte de Vogüé played the showmen in this
final act. The curtain went up on a stage with clockwork pairs. Ant-
ony and Cleopatra, with an enormous pearl; a Chinese couple, who,
when wound up, clicked their chopsticks wildly, flinging the food in
front of them across the stage; a Bavarian shepherd and shepherdess
who wandered lost among their sheep.

I was last, unwrapped by the Prince, who had dressed himself as
a caricature of a butler, with thick black brows, a wild beard, and a
false hooked nose. The audience laughed wildly at his every expression. He introduced me as a Tyrolean doll singer sent from America
for the Exposition, the latest in mechanics. He was to wind me up,
and the idea was that the clockwork mechanism had gone wrong
and I would sing brokenly from a series of pieces of songs inter-
spersed with trills and shouts.

He turned the false key at my back. I looked at the candles lighting the theater, seemingly thousands of them. The audience, the
candles, the theater, it was all so beautiful, the crowd so elegant, I
nearly forgot myself until the Prince arched his eyebrow and I began.

It was a pleasure to see them laugh at me.

Eh, it's quite terrible, the Comte said. Can we stop her? He then
made a pun in French about screws and vice. *Est-ce qu'il n'y a pas de
vis?*

To which the Prince said, *Il n'y a pas le moindre vice.*

We must send her back, the Prince said. It would seem the doll
was deranged by the voyage. *La poupée a été probablement dérangée
pendant le voyage.*

There was vigorous laughter at this all. They wound my key
again.

I think she needs oil! the Prince said to the Comte, in a mock
whisper to the side. She won't sing! Perhaps we are missing a nail
somewhere?

But this is terrible! She's the main attraction! There must be a button we've missed. Look well!

And with that, they began searching around my figure, looking for the "button." More laughter.

Not one sign of a button, the Prince said sadly. Perhaps the button should be gold! he then said with a shout, and there was more laughter at this.

Ah, I think we must give her a shake, said the Comte, and then they stood on either side of me and shook me. There were still silk ribbons around my neck from the wrapping, and the Prince made as if he had accidentally caught one end in his arm as he announced, And now, she will sing "Beware!"

I did this jokingly, halted in places by his playful yanks on the ribbon at my neck, which belied a viciousness. Soon I was choking, and the line I was to sing was a refrain I had sung a few times already, "Trust her not, she's fooling you," and instead, for I had become frightened, I sang, "Trust him not, he's choking me," and the audience laughed, howling as the Prince reddened and relaxed his grip on the ribbon.

The curtain came down again to much applause. The Prince and Princess, in their costumes, went out to take bows as I rubbed my throat.

I was sure the Prince had been cruel with his ribbons to show me the value of my silence in this matter.

All at once, the Empress was before me, thinking I was her friend in my disguise. Thank heavens, I thought the Prince was really to strangle you! I was so frightened, the Empress said. And then I think she sensed the disguise, but before she could say more, I gestured at my throat and ran to the back, where the American I had replaced waited. I washed my face of the powder, and when I ascended the back stairs to return to the Empress's chambers, she walked out dressed in the costume I had removed, as if she had just cleaned herself to receive her fans.

~

The bench in the darkness was again welcome. I had not expected to be overcome, but I was, and I wept there, miserable, as I waited for the ring of the bell that would not come for hours.

As I had looked out on the audience, I'd remembered the last time I'd sung for the Emperor's pleasure, over a year previous. His gift to me pinned now to the tenor's coat.

I saw myself sneaking the rose back from the tenor, walking out into the crowd here in the Emperor's little theater to where he sat, to see if the Emperor remembered me.

It's me, I would say. Or sing—perhaps I would sing the round again, return the token to him. And thus revealed, beg for his protection.

But I would never sing for him again.

Pepa appeared, surprising me, asking me to admire one of her newest dresses.

This time I clapped, and when I was done, she gave me a calculating look and offered to buy the tea-gown gift from the Empress right there. She flashed the coins at me. Did she know a maid's weakness for the sight of gold? I think she did.

She was surprised when I nodded yes and laughed after she paid me. She even thanked me, perhaps the one time she ever had, and I knew I had struck a poor bargain—I'd not even haggled. But no matter; her first offer was more than enough for Lucerne. I brought her the dress, and as I handed it to her, I smiled at her, my first smile of real affection for her. She eyed me suspiciously, as if it made the dress suspect, and I left her to her imaginations.

❧

When the Empress had gone once again into another council, I made my way to the apartment where the tenor, sure enough, waited.

He hadn't even needed to tell me.

Afterward, as I lay on the floor of the apartment, dressed in another of the Empress's gowns, the tenor stroked my hair in the aftermath of his passion and described his plan to steal me away.

Tonight there is to be a costume ball, he said. The company of the Comédie-Française is here, and they will present a salon play, Madame Girardin's *La Joie Fait Peur*, then they will leave before dinner. You will be mixed in among them in costume, as will I. I will beg off, saying I must return to Paris on urgent business. You will follow the actors, and then we will depart.

He reached up and traced my cheek with his left thumb, and he closed his eyes, his head turning slightly.

You will come as my guest to the ball, so I can look after you, he said, and there you will join the actors. You must come to the ball prepared to leave.

What of my things? I asked.

What things? What things do you speak of?

He saw me look across to the trunk. Ah! Your gift! Perhaps we will put you in one of those, he said. When her empire is scattered to the winds, I will enjoy it as a souvenir. Or perhaps you meant this one?

He opened his coat. The rubies on the little rose glittered. He let the coat fall shut again.

Come back to Paris — and to me — and it is yours again, he said, and smiled at me. But only then.

The Empress would be hurt, I knew, even alarmed, afraid something terrible had come to pass. But the Comtesse also seemed dangerous to disappoint, as dangerous as the tenor. Then I remembered that I would be disappearing again once I was in Lucerne, and this world and its problems would be gone.

I had not told any of them I meant to go there. Once I was there, I would be free. I meant to escape him as we escaped and, in doing so, escape them all.

But whatever escape I could make began by pretending to agree to his plan.

I nodded to the tenor in assent.

Say you will, he said.

I will, I said.

My single regret was the one too dangerous to admit. I had hoped to at least hear the composer, as I now called him, once more.

For more than that, but at least for that.

~

We went to the theater for costumes, down past the stage to the costume closet. I needed a mask of some kind that would cover my face, not just my eyes.

Here, he said, and chose a bear's-head mask for me. He stood behind me and pressed his hands over my breasts, pressing them against my chest. Perfect, he said, and bound my breasts flat until, when he was done, I was the picture of a young soldier in a French general's coat. Thick gloves hid my hands and riding boots gave me the height of a soldier. A cutlass swung off my waist, though it was a stage cutlass and could cut nothing.

And then he came from behind me and settled the bear's head over mine.

Nine

AT THE ENTRANCE to the ballroom one of the guards smiled at us and asked respectfully to check my weapon.

He drew it, pushed the dull point into his palm, and then passed it back to me. He saluted as I sheathed it.

I could only see out of the bear's mouth, everything framed by the bear's teeth. Even so, it was the most beautiful, glittering moment I'd ever seen. The ball was a gathering of gods and goddesses, figures from myth, monsters. I wasn't the only member of the palace to have raided the theater wardrobe for a costume, and the sight before me suggested it was perhaps what the costumes were used for most.

As it was a costume ball, I was not asked to remove my mask, though I still had the sense to be anxious in case I was engaged in conversation and the guests tried to guess my identity, but I felt safe. My costume, to my mind, encouraged silence. Bears were not known for their conversation, even in formal dress.

The dance master appeared in front of me, in the guise of a sultan, and raised his hand with a tremendous slowness. The musicians gathered their attention, and the room waited in silence. The hand descended, and they began a waltz.

The tenor, beside me, had dressed as a shepherdess—the most powerful shepherdess I've ever seen, the Emperor declared, as he appeared at our side. He said it with a slightly odd, flirtatious tone, as if perhaps the tenor had attracted his attention in some new way. The Emperor cocked his eyebrow, examining him boldly. The tenor endured it with a coquette's stoicism. I wanted to laugh.

Finished with that, the Emperor turned to me.

I watched his mouth, oddly magical to me, as he peered into the glass eyes of the bear. I wanted to kiss it.

The Emperor wore just a domino cape and hood, and a plain mask over a plain if elegant dark suit. He was dressed exactly as he had been the day I first saw him. The day he gave me the ruby flower still hidden in the tenor's coat.

Who have we here? he asked. Are you the Prussian Bear himself? And he tapped the snout.

This bear is French, the tenor said, a protesting tone in his voice, and clapped my epaulets. He's even a general in His Majesty's army, though I suspect his only allegiance is to the woods.

With that, the tenor made a surprisingly graceful curtsy.

May they be French woods then, the Emperor said. And remain that way. Be welcome in my court, general of my woods.

I bowed stiffly, careful not to tip the mask off onto the floor.

The theatrical troupe had mixed in with the crowd too well; one of them came over and told the tenor they'd been invited to stay the night and that they'd agreed.

I experienced this at first with some relief, but then I knew this would not stop him.

I tried to think of what to do as I struggled through the ball's formalities. All of the watching of balls that I had done before this had not prepared me to be inside one. It wasn't just that I didn't know the dances; the entire costume ball was a ritual, from when we entered until we left, and I had the sense of moving constantly outside its rhythm. I was so concerned with this that I forgot my real purpose until I found we stood in front of the Empress.

She was in the company of a man in a plain suit and domino cape, but the hood had been pulled back and he wore a red-painted wooden devil mask over his face. The Empress had also dressed as a shepherdess, but by this, I knew from having dressed her in it, she meant to appear as Marie Antoinette.

The devil I knew; he was my composer. I could tell from his hair and his eyes as they studied me, trying to figure out who was beneath the mask.

Does the bear army need a shepherdess? the Empress asked, with a laugh.

Devils appear to, the tenor said, and she blushed or flushed slightly. I couldn't tell if it was embarrassment or anger. And then the devil laughed, and she appeared pleased, at least, that he was pleased.

We do, the devil said. We need a shepherdess who knows the valleys of Hell.

That is *precisely* what I am, the Empress said, and as she said it, she fingered the soft cloth of the devil's cloak and looked out across the floor to the crowd dancing there. The strange truth of it grew as we waited for her to return her attention to us.

Away with us, she said to the devil, turning to him, and they went on their way.

I was grateful I was allowed one last meeting.

A mazurka began, of a more ordinary kind, and the devil led the Empress into it. She tilted her head back, a careful mask of appreciative pleasure, looking, for a moment, just like Marie Antoinette in Hell, at home enough to dance. The other figures moved closer, a siren dancing with what appeared to be Neptune, a courtesan with massive shoulders in the arms of a slight, stern gentleman, a Spanish Gypsy woman with a huge Viking warrior.

I noticed the tenor busy speaking to one of the Comédie actors, perhaps about me. He looked away from me. I made my way along the wall to the doors, and without looking back, I let myself out onto the balcony, shutting the door with the quiet you can only learn when you are in service.

This was my chance.

A group of the goddesses from inside had hiked up their skirts to cool their legs from dancing and were lighting cigars. The Princess Metternich was visible at their center, lit by a huge flame from her match.

Salut, ma générale, she said, waving at me. She let out a curl of white smoke into the air and beat the skirt of her dress like a cancan dancer, which made the other women laugh.

How strange to me still that she should have been the first to call me that.

I bowed to her and they laughed again. And then, with a small shock, I understood that she had seen that I was a woman. The strange confidence I'd had of feeling hidden left me, and I nearly ran for the allée.

~

I followed the path as it wound into the garden and headed for the woods behind the palace. It was very cold now, almost too cold to be out of doors. The rich smell of the grapes left on the vine to rot or freeze greeted me under the canopy of vines.

The tenor had not come outside for me, or if he had, he had not found me yet. He would console himself, I told myself, with his American singer; the Empress with her composer; the Emperor with any of them or all of them.

I turned to look back to the palace and saw it light the dark, as if something bright and immense paced through the rooms, unable to be still. It was a vast *théâtre du désir,* on a scale to make Odile weep. All for the pleasures of the Emperor. All of France was, at that time, not an empire but a salon play of an empire, with a Napoléon who was not, in fact, a great general but had only a great general's name, at the head of an army that could barely take an undefended cottage in the woods, and with an empress who could not control her maids. Here I was, rebellious maid that I was, in her garden.

I remembered the tenor's taunt to me, holding his jacket open, the ruby flower there— *Come back to Paris, and to me, and it will be yours*—and it stung.

He could keep it, I decided then. He could make his American soprano wear it as he thought of me.

I was glad to leave with only the money from my bargain with

Pepa. That seemed honest. My plan, such as it was, was to make the walk to town and wait for the train dressed in my costume and mask. Some might laugh, some would have questions, but it would be a fine disguise, that of a dissipated guest of the palace. They would laugh at me, but no one would stop me or talk to me.

It was time.

I took the mask off to see better in the dark garden, held it at my side like a helmet, and walked down the allée away from the palace. At the bottom, as the garden opened out into a long slope, there was an enormous mound of dirt by the edge of the woods, where some sort of construction was being done. Behind it, from in the woods, I heard footsteps, hard and quick, and singing, and saw flashes of fire. I heard three young male voices singing at the top of their sound, singing a drinking song of some kind in heavily accented English, but trying to sound British.

Ye sons of Anacreon, then join hand in hand! Preserve unanimity, friendship, and love!

Two appeared in the air, passing to either side of me like spirits of the forest, burning pitch torches in their hands. They landed partway down the hill, still running, and headed up to the palace at a sprint, laughing. A third, singing in a rich alto, appeared also in the air above me. The light on his torch lit the small horns on his mask, tipped back to reveal his face.

My devil.

'Tis yours to support what's so happily planned! You've the sanction of the gods and the fiat of Jove!

He landed in front of me, and as our eyes met, he stopped. Behind me, his fellow singers ran to the palace, picking up the song again, and I saw him look at them and then look back at me.

If I had made my way down even a moment later, I would have only heard them run by, never knowing. The full force of what I felt for him, for this chance, filled me. I had thought I would not see him again, had thought the world perhaps organized to keep us apart. But perhaps, this seemed to say, perhaps not.

Perhaps not.

He took in the mask at my side, then my face, and I saw him recognize me with surprise. He smiled, bowed deeply, and stood again, looking at where his friends had gone. He turned back to me and said, Stay here, and then he sprinted after his friends.

He belonged to her, without question. But it seemed as if he also belonged a little bit to me.

His request was impossible, however. To linger meant I might be caught. Yet to leave meant to lose the one chance I'd hoped for in my time here, other than to leave.

I pulled my mask back on in case I was discovered by anyone else and continued up the rise of the hill. I turned back, and in the distance, by a statue of a lion on the terrace, I saw the composer with his friends, the three of them singing their song at the tops of their voices to the assembled group of women I'd passed, who now let their skirts rest near their ankles, but who continued smoking their cigars, the tiny red lights of the embers there sparking in the distance.

Voice, fiddle, and flute! No longer be mute! I'll lend you my name and inspire you to boot!

Raucous applause for this funny little song, and then the gentlemen bowed, and all at once the composer vanished from sight.

I waited to see if he would return, and at once, there he was, emerging from under the vines, intent, head down, headed back to me, an arrow in the dark, some last gift of the palace.

As he caught up to me, he took my arm in his hand and walked me farther into the garden. He led me down the stairs into what seemed like a path the gardeners used, hidden unless you knew it was there. At the bottom of the stairs, he stopped and pulled me to him.

His face silver in the moonlight. The wind at mine.

The mask fell on the ground beside me. He kissed me as his hands unstrung the tie in my hair that held it up so that it fell around my shoulders. The hands next slid down to grip the sides of my hips as he pressed me against the wall and crushed my mouth with his. He opened my coat and pulled down the bandage holding down my breasts so that they were in the open, and then pressed his face down into them. When he opened the front of my pants and pushed against and then inside me, I made a low moan against his neck that he then stifled by pressing the bottom of his forearm against my mouth. He continued to lean his hips into me. The newness of him, the urgency of him, made it sharp, and I tilted my head back, almost fainting. Our eyes met while he moved deeper into me, and in response I punched him furiously on his chest and shouted against his arm. He pushed his mouth into my hair as he thrust into me again and I heard the low sound come out of my mouth again. His face on my neck, he pulled me up until my legs crossed on his back and I rocked against the wall. It went like that, sometimes violent and sharp, urgent against the cold air and stone, smoke drifting down from the fires and the distant cigars, distant voices.

When it was done, he stood panting, still holding me up, our faces wet. He closed his mouth over mine. He pulled back, as if hearing something, looked to both sides and then back at me. He held up a finger and pressed it against my mouth before fastening himself up and slipping down the gardener's path.

And then he was back again. I paused, afraid—it was time for me to continue on, past time. I was expecting the tenor at any moment.

He gently touched my chin with a finger and drew me to him to kiss me once more. I allowed it.

This kiss, it was not like the others with him, or with anyone before him. It had the feeling of a secret between us. It was like the discovery of a new world, or an agreement that was also a new world, that began and, I would discover, was returned to and built upon each time we kissed again though, for now, there was just this one, a hope in the dark.

How the world seemed to shake with what had happened. But it was just my heart.

He drew back, the hint of a smile on his face, and then let go, and he put one finger on my lips as he put another on his own to warn me to be silent again. And with that, he was gone again, sprinting up the hill.

For the briefest moment it seemed as if I could follow him, go back inside, stay, sleep, wake, and serve the Empress and wait to find him again.

But I could not. With all I had in me, I ran the other way.

When love comes this way, the first dream of it feels like a prophecy that has come true. I had never known this feeling until now— he was my first. And so I let myself dream of him again and believe it could be the future.

The chords of the nocturne I'd heard him play that first day I saw him found me again as I made my way into the woods, and I went as if I could follow it to him, to where he would be next.

∿

Mon général, I heard someone say, and a hand shook me awake. *Pardon.*

I opened my eyes to the darkness of the mask. I remembered I'd arrived to find the station closed and hid here behind the railing when I heard a rider on a horse. I'd only meant to rest for a moment, but instead I had slept.

For how long? I wondered, as the station clerk tugged at me.

Wake up and buy a ticket, and I will not call for the police, he said, and laughed.

I stood shakily and tried to move the mask's mouth to at least see him, but then I heard his keys in the lock. I muttered a thank–you and steadied myself as he went in and closed the door.

I took off the mask. My hair was stuck to my throat and ears, waxy and damp. I pulled it out to my shoulders to dry and, anxious to find another spot to hide in until the train came, I walked down the platform. Vapor rose off me like smoke in the new cold.

A young family arrived, a husband and wife, with two daughters and a son. Their youngest, the son, noticed me and waved as their carriage was unpacked. His mother pulled him away, cutting her eyes from me in disgust. She was, perhaps, a few years older than I was, dressed in a new traveling dress and coat, a fine hat and gloves, new leather shoes. She was my dream of me as I was to have been on the day I headed to Lucerne, but made real, and I watched her as the door closed behind her.

And, as if mocking me, another like her, and another, and another all arrived to take the next train wherever it was going.

In the dawn light of the Compiègne station, my dreams of arriving in Lucerne played before me. In them, it was always morning. I drank a rich coffee in the dining car, and the sun beat brightly through the window like a whip. I wore a beautiful dress, my hair braided carefully, and smiled as the train passed over the canals filled with swans, the one thing I knew of Lucerne. The rooftops glowed dark red in the early morning sunlight, and the streets to my aunt's house were clean and quiet. I would knock on the door to her large respectable town house, a house that looked as if nothing could ever bring it low, and be recognized, embraced, welcomed inside. I would finally meet my mother's sister and discover if she is like her in any way—in the face, her smile, a gesture, her scent. I would be fed, given a beautiful room, beautiful clothes, a beautiful life with everything I wanted to eat, and I would rest at last in the love of my family. I would find it all had just been waiting for me here to come and pick it up.

I reached into my pockets to be sure the napoleons Pepa paid me hadn't been taken from me as I slept. As I did, I took in my boots. My pants, my coat.

My costume saber.

In the window by the door, I saw my reflection. The young woman in a general's coat, as if I were a favorite *cantinière* he'd left his coat with to keep her warm. The coat suited me, but to go like this meant I would not arrive in a beautiful dress. It would not be morning. There would be no coffee for me in the dining car, not dressed like this. I would arrive like a refugee from some mysterious war—one concluded by a masked ball from which I'd escaped.

I tried to judge what I thought a toilette like the young mother's would cost. The clothes I was accustomed to up until now either cost much less—a *grisette*'s dress—or so much more. If I needed more than I had, I could go to a junk peddler in town to sell the costume and the mask to him. But it seemed to me he might know these things had come from the palace theater. He might even have sold them to the costumer. And then I might not be able to afford the ticket as well.

I stepped down to the street as if to go to do this and then did not, waiting instead.

I needed one last disguise. One last disguise when I did not want even one more.

I imagined myself then, sitting before this aunt I had never met, dressed in the dress I would have to buy to make my way to her, and giving the news of my mother's death—and that of my family. And the very next question she would ask me.

However did you get here?

And I would look at her and see my mother's coffin, the dirt shining by her grave. The farmhouse burning in the night, the blood on my skirts, the horses as I sold them. The face of the widower farmer and the graveyard on the hill. The tents of the Cajun Maidens, the cheering crowds, the lights in Flambeau's hair, Ernesto as he picked me up off the horse and set me down. The Emperor and his ruby gift to me, his hand opening like a magician. The Cirque Napoléon, Euphrosyne, Odile, the Bal Mabille. The nights at the Majeurs-Plaisirs, the tenor, the Garnier, the Conservatoire. La Muette. The Comtesse and the Empress. My composer . . .

The palace garden at night.

La poupée a été probablement dérangée pendant le voyage.

Indeed she was.

To leave for Lucerne that day was to leave it all, and all of this would have to hide inside me as I told my aunt a story that I'd sold the farm and that a young, unmarried, unaccompanied girl had traveled to her, virtue intact, through the terrors between the farm and Lucerne. She would nod and smile, most likely not believing me, but accepting the story and me. And so I would be able to remain with her until she found me a man willing to marry her foreign-born orphan niece, sitting before her in the dress she likely would have stolen to get there.

The strange one, who sometimes smelled of a cigar. Hidden in her last disguise forever.

To do this felt like death. All the rest I could do except this.

I laughed and then stopped.

As I stood there, I burned like something thrown off a falling star, as if I'd crashed to earth still surrounded by the fire of the passage. The memory of the bright palace in the night behind me haunted me, as did the memory of the composer leaping down from the air above my head. I could still feel his hand at my face. I was at the edge of the victory I'd long sought over my circumstances and fate, the correction I was so certain I needed. And yet I was also at the edge of something else, something I could only see now. Where once I'd hoped to be made pure again, to be forgiven, returned to the state I existed in before the death of my family, I now longed to be loved in a way that would be a triumph over death and misfortune, over all that had been forbidden to me and all that had been taken from me.

I *had* escaped from a masked ball, one the size of the world strung between the farm and here, and I was proud to have come this far, proud enough to want a hero's welcome, and in my costume uniform, no less. I saw myself tumbling and falling through the air, in and out of disguises, on and off horses, leaping, singing, changing as I became whomever I had to be next to be here. And the hesitation I felt now was nothing like that morning in Paris when I'd only wanted to keep the one most beautiful thing I'd ever earned. I hesitated now because what I could see, here by the station, was that this trip was a mistake. There was a question I wanted answered more than I wanted anything else, and it could take my life to answer it. This question was *What could I be?* This was what I wanted to know.

On the day I had myself arrested to escape the tenor, the day

I hid myself in the clothes and future of La Muette, it was not to protect this dream of going to Lucerne so I could live on as some imitation of someone I'd never been. I'd wanted the dignity of a fate unencumbered by the tenor's obsession, and whatever this could bring me—to learn to sing again, somewhere else, under some other, better teacher. And I still wanted this, but I was remembering this only now, for I had confused myself with my disguise.

I wanted to return to Paris. I wanted to study voice. I wanted a life, a destiny free of the tenor. I wanted my beautiful composer, who I was sure I could find again at the Bal Mabille.

I would begin at once. And thus resolved, I went inside.

Ah, you are awake, the clerk said. What is the meaning of this costume? he asked.

I was separated from my troupe, I said, and set the mask on the counter. A *cirque*. And then I made a practiced pose, arms up, as if an announcer had called my name.

A woman in pants outside of a theater is a public lewdness, he said. Here, at least. We are not Paris.

Yes, I said. Sell me a ticket for Paris, please, then. And he laughed as I pushed a napoleon onto the counter.

Ma générale, he said. As you wish.

Ten

THE COMTESSE WAS not the kind to receive visitors uninvited
to her front door, so I observed our old protocol instead. I posted a
note to the address she'd made me memorize, saying I was in Paris
again and would wait to be picked up in our old location.

I did not include the list I'd made, as it was the only way I could
be sure I was paid for it. And I did not include my address, as I did
not yet have it.

I sent the note from the Gare du Nord, just off the train from
Compiègne.

I sold the mask, saber, boots, and pants to a junk peddler near
the room I took by the Palais-Royal and got more money than I
expected. I then bought from him his least ugly dress—gray wool,
with decent buttons—a plain black hat with a blue ribbon, and
what seemed to be new kid-leather boots. I added a hairbrush and
stockings and a slip. The general's coat I kept, as nothing else the
peddler had was as warm, and I still liked the look of it. With what
I had left over, I could afford the room and meals for at least a week.

The room in the Palais-Royal was barely big enough for me to
swing my arms in, and the curtains were of an ugly brocade that
may have been red once, but the curtains were mine to close, and I
wouldn't have to share the bed with anyone.

I'd arrived in Paris once more with almost nothing, but my life
was my own in some way it had never been before, and I felt some
new contentment despite my prospects. This was my newest trea-
sure, and I wasn't sure where I could hide it and have it be safe. I

wasn't sure I could live this life anywhere in Paris, but I was determined to try.

The Comtesse's promise of paying me on my return was my single guarantee of any kind, hardly secure, but better than the last time I'd landed in Paris. I'd made a plan on the train to contact the Comtesse, apologize, give her what details I had of what the Empress had worn, tell her a few stories I was sure were of interest, and then once she'd paid me, I would ask if she might help me find work again. I would go to see the lady professor at the Conservatoire afterward and ask if she might teach me privately. And discreetly, of course. The tenor could never know.

I thought to offer to do some kind of work for the professor in return, perhaps mending, but that seemed unlikely to pay for singing lessons. I would need better work than that.

Ever since my audition, my singing voice felt like something in a box I shouldn't open until I was in the presence of someone who could teach me how to keep it. If I did not use it, I would need some other way to make my living until I could.

In the spring my new composer friend would be at the piano in the Bal Mabille. I hoped by then to be able to surprise him with a song.

This was my slender bridge to the future, and I stepped onto it as carefully as I could.

On the first day, as I waited at the Bois, I sat and ate a package of hot chestnuts, purchased in confidence, until I grew cold, and then I went to a café to warm up before returning for one more hour. I ignored the many carriages that slowed or paused for me that were not hers.

It is too soon, I told myself. *The post may take longer to reach her.*

On the second day I did the same again. *Too soon again*, I said to myself, though I was less sure.

The third day was colder, and there was rain. As the rain began, I accepted first one carriage and then, as it continued, another.

The first was a beery gentleman, visiting from London, excited at all the women about and easy to please. The second, a terrified young Frenchman, perhaps even a boy, if a very rich one. Easy again, and he paid too much. After him, the rain stopped.

I used an old trick Euphrosyne had taught me, to rub them off using your thighs in such a way they thought they were inside you, to make sure the dress from the junk peddler wouldn't be ruined by their spunk. But then I had to spend money at the baths after, and then it was time to go back to a café. There I found a man who wanted to pay for the meal and gave him the slip while he was in the pissoir. I went home alone to prepare for another day at the Bois.

Not quite too soon, I told myself, and hoped I had not missed the carriage.

I came out even in the end, but it was more trouble than it was worth, it seemed to me. I hoped it wouldn't be too much longer. I made myself promise no more carriage rides until after the one that mattered.

∼

At the end of the third day, I closed the door to this paradise and sat down on the bed; I didn't feel quite as bold or brave, and doing tricks Euphrosyne had taught me made me think of her again. I knew I'd see her if I was to go back to the Mabille, but I thought I might wait and surprise her then, whenever that was. Despite how she'd betrayed me, I still loved her, and I knew she loved me. I feared she would be angry at the deception and, of course, consorting with her in public also risked my being taken in by the police and registered again—as I well knew—but I had already taken that risk twice today for men I didn't know.

Without friends, my new life was only an empty room, if a little larger than the one I'd just rented. I missed her too much to wait until spring.

And so I stood and went out again.

∼

I found my way back to the Majeurs-Plaisirs easily enough. The downstairs salon windows were lit, and I heard the chatter and laughter that I knew marked the evening's beginning. I waited in the alley, watching as the door occasionally opened and closed and guests came and went.

I was near giving up when the doors opened and out stepped a woman as richly dressed as any I'd ever seen, even at the balls at Compiègne.

Euphrosyne was a vision. In the light from the door, she glowed as she shrugged a new white fur opera cloak closer to her. An ostrich plume fluttered atop her white velvet hat and nicked the top of the doorway. She laughed and petted it down, and then came down the stairs with the flutter of at least a hundred tiny black ribbon bows on her black silk toile gown's skirt. Diamonds flashed in her ears and at her throat. A gentleman beside her, with her on his arm, was busy speaking with another coming along behind them. She let go his arm and waited for help from the driver to enter the carriage, and as she did, I stepped forward.

The driver looked at me as he might at a beggar or an assassin and glared, waving me back. She had ignored me, and I was so embarrassed to be snubbed by her, I stayed quiet, but as I stepped back, the general's coat caught her eye, and then my face came into view.

You little bitch, she whispered, a smile growing on her face as her gentlemen paused at the carriage door and the driver stared. I *knew* they couldn't kill you. And then she leapt at me with a cry and pulled me to her.

I prayed to God to bring you back to me, she said, and then looked up at the sky and said, Thank you! And then she kissed me again and again, saying it was the only way to know I wasn't a ghost. She pulled my arm to her in our old way and began to walk me down the street. When her companions in the carriage protested at her abrupt departure, offering at least a ride, she turned and waved them on before continuing with me.

My dears, she shouted. She is just back from the dead. Please forgive me and return for me at intermission.

I came back to tell you everything, I said, as she waved to hire us another driver.

Of course, she said. Tell me everything.

                             ~

She took me to a little bistro, where we smoked and had little glasses of wine. We made a strange pair, I knew, talking closely, she in her opera finery, I in my junk-peddler toilette, and soon many of the other tables were watching us. She turned at one point and said to the too-curious audience around us, This is not a show, unless it is a show, in which case give us a coin and she will sing.

Ashamed, they turned back to their conversations.

You can't return to the Majeurs, she said. If Odile knows you are alive, she'll be furious. At the least she'll have you arrested, for it shames her, too. He is still a regular client.

Yes, of course, I said, though this surprised me. Of course, during my absence, the tenor had again become a good customer.

You must go back to this comtesse, she said. Beg for her forgiveness, tell her what you know, and, most important, ask for her advice and protection. You're in terrible danger. And then she paused, and a little glint came into her eye. This woman, she is one of the great courtesans, after all.

I nodded, uncertain. This I did not know.

Perhaps she will teach you something. She and Giulia Barucci even share a lover, a rich banker. I heard he settled a half-million francs on her.

I let out a startled laugh.

Where did you get these clothes? she asked. Is this what they buried you in?

I shook my head, still laughing. No, no. A junk peddler.

Ah, she said, fingering the dress. This is what they buried someone else in. They're all grave robbers. Be careful wearing a dead woman's clothes. Don't wear them too long. I will see if I can find something I don't wear anymore until we can get you set up.

She turned to check a beautiful watch made to look like a gold brooch. I must go, she said. But when you want to see me next, leave a message with this barman here; I come in every time I can.

The man behind the bar nodded to me.

This man, I think he wants to marry me, she said. Can you imagine?

Yes, I said, and smiled at the barman. I could. For she had become more beautiful than ever, not just because of her finery.

No, not the barman, she said. The other one, with the carriage. Maybe this one will marry you. She winked and then kissed me twice. Don't you dare die again, she said into my ear before she let go. And with that, she returned to wait for the carriage he'd send for her at intermission, and I stayed for another drink with the barman before returning to my room.

⁓

On the fourth day in the Bois, in the late morning, the grand black carriage I knew so well pulled to a stop, and when I saw the Comtesse's familiar crest on the side, I leapt up and ran to it.

Little girl, came the voice of her driver. Is it you, La Muette? Where have you been?

I kept running to him and smiled as he jumped down and opened the door.

This time I was shown in through the service entrance. Her maid greeted me, a new one I'd not met before, and brought me into the parlor, where the Comtesse sat waiting.

I saw her an instant before she noticed I'd entered. She was seated, her hair bound up and then falling down her back in curls. She wore a simple black muslin tea gown, almost demure except for the way it accentuated her coiffure and bust. Her portraits were now hung all around her on the walls, turning the room into a theater of her expressions, with her at the center. The one I noticed most was a painted photograph I had never seen of her dressed in the nun's habit I'd first repaired: the Comtesse transformed into a nun, but her face a mask of implacable enmity. Her eyes were hooded and yet also flaring, the whites visible beneath her pupils as she looked up in a mockery of a prayer. This was a face that promised not so much murder as an eternal war waged for a revenge that would have no end.

In the soft light of the room, her face was a pale reflection of this as she gazed into the distance as I entered. I froze in place, not daring to move forward. I had made a terrible mistake in coming here.

She then saw me, and her eyes lit with affection, and she was all concern.

Sit down, sit down. Where have you been? I was stunned to get your note. I thought you were dead. I could not believe it was from you.

A little speech in my head, a lie about how my voice had returned, vanished as I tried to begin it.

You should have come straight to me at once, she said. I was told you had either escaped or were kidnapped or were perhaps murdered. She held a letter out from beside her and shook it once. The paper made a crisp snap.

A search party even went through the woods looking for signs of you, she said, and set the letter down. The Empress was quite fond of her mute *grisette* and was distraught to lose her. The palace chamberlain had the good grace to write to apologize to me. And yet you are not lost. Instead, you managed something few have managed, to escape from Compiègne.

Here we were both silent.

What a little mystery you are. Perhaps I am wasting your talents, and she laughed as she said this, as if she'd surprised herself. Perhaps you should do more for me. And yet you have disappointed me.

At this, a terrible coldness swept over me down into my bones.

But why the escape? I hope you are here to explain. She called for paper and pen, and asked me to write for her all that had occurred.

There's no need for that, I said, as the maid entered the room. I didn't know how to explain my voice, and any further pretense was unbearable. I wanted to be done with La Muette.

She stared, and now she was the one who momentarily seemed frightened.

I took a little pride in that, but only a little.

When I looked up again and met the Comtesse's eyes, it was as if we were meeting for the first time.

Now we moved into opposite roles. I spoke and she listened.

I passed to her the list of the Empress's gowns, such as I had been able to keep, and as she read it, I tried to think of what I would tell her.

When she finished, she set it down and said, Explain yourself. Tell me everything.

I did. I told her the story of being given one of the gowns and described it. I told her of how the seconds were not being given out as often and of the complaint of her ladies-in-waiting provoked by the Empress's attending councils and the lack of invitations to tea. Then the recital, and the interest both the Princess Metternich and the Empress had in a talented young composer, and how I had found him alone in the imperial apartments before the series began. And then last was the tenor and his seduction of me, his game of the dresses, described as if we had no history at all.

I know my escape disappointed you, I said. And I am very sorry for the trouble it caused. But he meant to kidnap me that night. I escaped as he was taking me from the palace.

My dear, how incredible. She rested her chin on her hand. It is astonishing to even hear you speak, but it is all quite puzzling and intriguing. I have a question, given this tenor character who you say was intent on kidnapping you. Why did you not simply alert the guards?

I had no answer ready and fought to think of something.

And why, after eluding him in the dark, did you go to the station and not back to the palace?

I could not return, I managed to say.

Yes, why? What had you taken? Had you stolen something from her?

She pushed at the note as I stayed silent.

What did you steal? she asked. I'm guessing this coat. Or is it in the coat? Sewn into the linings? Somewhere else? What did you take? An earring, a brooch, a pearl?

I took nothing, I said softly, but I could not look at her, and at that, she leaned closer.

A girl like you, there are two reasons you leave your mistress. You either have stolen or you are in love. If you stole nothing, then it could only be love. Who is he, then, who are you in love with?

I finally met the terrible eyes full of anticipation, but still I could not speak. It had been a mistake to speak. I had been safer silent.

Tell me or be destroyed, she said. I will have you returned to the palace as a thief. Can you imagine yourself then? When they are done beating the truth from you, no man will ever look on you again except in horror. Who? Not the tenor, it would seem. What other he?

To say it seemed to be to destroy it, but to say nothing was to be destroyed.

This composer?

At this, she stood, walked over to me, and grabbed for my chin to make me face her. She held it fiercely, waiting for my hands to come down, waiting for my answer. The rings on her fingers against my chin made me wince, and I relented, nodded finally, and the tears I'd kept back until now began.

And now you have become so precious, she said, and let go.

She waved to her maid to bring me a handkerchief.

My girl, please. Now that we have the truth, no more crying. She waited as I calmed and dried my face.

It is time to speak of our little bargain. I'm sure you are anxious to be paid. You were much more attentive than I'd thought possible, but the result of leaving as you did is that you have brought me both more and less than I'd hoped for. Still, now that we have the truth from you, I feel the balance is in your favor, and I'm in your debt. So do not fear; I will not turn you in. But we must plan.

Thank you, I said, and then went to my knees before her. Please forgive me.

Come, this is ridiculous. Get up.

I stood carefully.

What is your name, then? What am I to call you? How long did you deceive the sisters about your voice? Are you even called Sidonie?

No, I said. Call me — call me . . .

Oh, it doesn't matter, it will only confuse me. We will call you Sidonie a while longer. My driver here has a wife who lets rooms. He will take you where you are staying now, and you will remove anything you have in his presence. He will then take you to his wife's, and we will install you there until we decide what the terms will be. Do not deceive him; do not try to elude him. Do not disappoint me again. He will return you here tomorrow and report to me on the contents of your room, and then we will have our parley.

I thanked her quietly, ashamed.

Do not be afraid of him. You understand, do you not? I think you do not know what you have done. He is protecting you. You are not safe here in Paris. Perhaps not anywhere in France.

With that, the driver appeared, and they exchanged some words in Italian. He then led me back down to the service entrance to the carriage.

I returned to my room with him. The landlady protested until he explained he was removing me. I pulled out my junk-peddler things, emptied out my coat, and at his bidding, undressed so he could search even the dress. He even checked my shoes for hollow heels. The gold coins left from what Pepa had paid me mocked me, lined up on the bed.

The trail of gold I once hoped to set down had led here.

I bade good-bye to my landlady and went to meet the driver's wife, who showed me my new room. I listened as I was locked in-

side, and when she left, I brushed out my hair and I calmed as I reviewed my prospects.

As the Comtesse said, I did not know what I had done. I knew
I was still in danger, but it now mattered if I lived or died to the
Comtesse. This was new. We were now to discuss terms. My situation had somehow improved. Or so I hoped as sleep took me at last
in my strange new bed.

~

In the morning I dressed with dread, after what Euphrosyne had
said of dead women's dresses, and hoped for someone to unlock the
door, and for breakfast. Both came. Afterward, we drove off, and I
noticed we went away from the Comtesse's address into a part of the
city I didn't know.

I became anxious, even afraid I was to be killed, when we arrived
at a restaurant. The Comtesse came out and joined me in the carriage, having had, it appeared, some previous appointment.

Did you sleep well? she asked me, as the door closed.

Well enough, thank you.

Did you feel safe? she asked, with a smile.

I did, I said.

The driver reports you were honest, and while you had an unusual number of gold coins for a *grisette*, there was no property
of the French empress in your belongings other than that coat. I
trusted your tears, she said. But it's best to check. And now I know
you are a little miserly, always a good trait.

I made my face as blank as possible and waited for whatever was
next.

Now we may begin our parley, she said. You are an orphan, I recall. Is this true? Do you even have papers?

No, I said. For I did not understand what she meant. What papers?

She laughed. And have you any accounts?

No, I said.

Very well, then. Much as I thought.

This seemed some clear reference as to a method of payment and the possibility of employment. Sensing my chance, I took it.

Yesterday you wondered if you were wasting my talents, I said. You wondered if there was more for me to do for you despite disappointing you.

Yes, she said. She seemed amused.

If I might offer, I said. I would like that very much. Whatever you might require, that you might find for me to do. Given the trouble I've caused, I know I couldn't hope even for something modest, but I hope to repay you if I can.

She nodded. Very well, then, she said.

I allowed myself my first smile in her presence since the day previous.

She rapped on the door to the carriage and shouted an address to her driver.

Here is what I propose, she said. I must think on the rest some more. I cannot allow you to move freely for now. This is for your own protection. But for now, I will continue to play the part of an aunt, an elaboration of our previous little *tableau vivant*. I will set you up with a dress—we must get rid of this awful frock you are wearing, perhaps immediately—and perhaps teach you some style. The rest will wait for now, and in the meantime, you will continue to be a guest at the room we have let for you with the driver's wife. Is this agreeable?

It is, I said. Yes.

If anyone asks, you are the driver's niece from near the Alps. In public, if people address you, say nothing, and I will explain you speak no French. Do you understand? This is what I need you to do for me right now.

I do, I said.

Very good, she said. I was sure you were quick. This protects you also.

As we pulled to a stop in front of an elegant atelier, she turned to me and said, Perhaps someday, when you have the chance, you will tell me who you really are. Though it may never matter.

~

The address she'd shouted to her driver was for the dressmaker Félix.

On this first day I stood in his workshop, the Comtesse promptly introduced me as her driver's niece, as we'd agreed, and he said, Oh, but I know you, this is certainly Jou-jou of the Bal Mabille. Sister to La Frénésie.

There was an awkward silence as the Comtesse looked to me. I tilted my head as if confused. As if I'd never heard the name. He laughed loudly.

You are the picture of her, he said, if you are not her. I had heard she died at Saint-Lazare, so perhaps you are her ghost? Or her doppelganger? If so, now that she is dead, that is good luck for you; you won't ever see her. I will check later if you can cancan, though. He winked. His assistants tittered behind him as I shook my head again and the Comtesse told him I knew no French.

I was relieved to be taken behind the screen and undressed. *I had heard she died at Saint-Lazare.* As I was helped out of my peddler dress, I thought of the apartment on the avenue de l'Opéra, the tenor with my little ruby rose pinned over his heart—would he have kept it and all it contained, then, or would he have sold it all to a peddler? All of my things on a cart in the street.

I was given a muslin shift to wear and brought into a smaller room with an alcove that had mirrors on three sides, and I stood there as he measured me.

You must be the most important driver's niece in Italian history, Félix said. I have never provided this sort of service to even an intimate of the Comtesse's.

I shrugged, he laughed, and he continued to measure me.

This joke of his alarmed me—it was, of course, his way of telling me he did not believe her or me. But it also told me he did not fear her, which I allowed myself to admire. Like many who served Paris society, Félix was in the business of keeping his clients' secrets; for him to be indiscreet would mean he was dying or retiring. But he would, until then, still have his fun.

They held bolts of cloth to my face and discussed the cuts as the assistants tied a corset to me and attached a cage crinoline to my waist before having me stand on a stool. Slowly, a muslin dress shape was pinned to me with several necklines. After a conference between Félix and the Comtesse, an order was placed for a bright blue poplin dress with three bodices I could remove and replace without removing the skirt—a new modern convenience made mostly with sewing machines so it could be prepared more quickly. The one for day was plain, with sleeves to my wrist and a high neck; the one for dinner, with silver silk ribbon piping and a white machine-lace trim, was cut lower but still demurely, and the sleeves just covered the shoulders. The last, for the opera, was square cut, more daring, a black-velvet-ribbon trim at the neckline, the arms nearly bare.

Crinolines and a skirt cage were chosen, as well as shoes, gloves, and a hat.

The three bodices at least suggested a better life than the one I had known before—I had never owned a day dress. I felt like one of the most elegant prisoners in Paris and counted myself lucky again.

The Comtesse then returned to the rue de Passy, and I went back to my room and the driver's wife, where I was to wait until the toilette was ready. In my memory it was three days or five, perhaps it was a week. The days were the same—spent at a simple window, looking into a courtyard where I could watch a mother cat and her kittens at play or playing bezique and drinking peppered gin with the driver's wife, a favorite drink of hers that I grew to like. She continued to lock me in all the while, but I wouldn't have left. I had decided to see the Comtesse's offer through. And this room, it cost me nothing.

～

There was a question that I could not bring myself to ask, for it seemed sure to insult her. This question was *How does one become a woman who inspires a man to settle on her the sum of a half-million francs?* It seemed indelicate to even suggest she could teach me anything of this kind. But there was no need to ask her; her whole life was the answer.

This way, I heard her say, from inside her parlor; and then she appeared at the door, her champagne already in hand. I went in and sat down. This was the morning my toilette would be ready. She had wanted to see me first.

I was only looking for someone who had been thrown away when I found you, she said, once the door had closed. And yet you are so much more, she said. I have been thinking of your situation and how to help you best.

A review of your talents and history suggests the following. You are good at sewing, observant, and discreet. You are a natural actress. You have some beauty, but not so much that you cannot, if you choose, blend into the background. Your teeth and hands are good, though you are small and too thin for most men. Your face and head are large, and as such, suited to the stage. But perhaps you will fill in after a few meals. You should learn to eat more heartily when in private. Most men do not like to see a woman eat.

What else? She tilted her head as she asked this, as if the answers came from someone offstage.

If not for your lack of papers, you would be suited to be a diplomat's wife. You could be a courtesan, though much would depend on your enthusiasm for men. And your ability to sense how to get them to act on your behalf. Without an instinct for this, most women with these ambitions are doomed to a certain level. Consider, for example, La Païva. She is no great beauty. But she has more than beauty. She keeps no list of *prix d'amours*; there is only a sum for which, if it is not met, she is not aroused. The man does not exist. But when the sum is there or surpassed, what comes to life in her makes that man feel, during the moments he is with her, as if he were the most fascinating, most interesting, most delightful man in the world. He is not paying her for favors. Favors are nothing compared to this. He is her protector because in the moments he is with her he feels as he never does away from her. This feeling, this is everything. So he pays for her food, her horses, her dresses, her home, all so as to be able to be this man he is when he is with her. And if he must extend the realm she occupies so he can also be that man elsewhere, this is what he will do. But she never even meets his glance without the sum. And this is why she has the finest home in Paris and the attentions of her German industrialist.

With your lack of family connections, you will most likely never marry. Any man of quality would eventually marry someone else —you would be his distraction. You can offer no guarantees, you see, for your offspring. You would do best to become a celebrity of some kind. And then, once you are sought after, you might find a husband.

But who knows? Who knows what you will be. And you may never want a husband once you see what a husband is.

~

When we returned to Félix's atelier to retrieve my dresses, a gentleman in a perfectly tailored dark suit appeared at her elbow and whispered in her ear.

She thanked him dismissively, but lightly so; her scorn was not for him. This way, my dear, she said to me. As we left, she told me Eugénie herself was inside on a rare visit and that we were not to go in.

I held my breath.

I could have gone in, she said, as we neared her carriage again. But she's afraid of me, and there would be no good to it.

Afraid of you, I repeated, not quite a question, as she airily directed her driver to stay put.

She has what belongs to me, she said, turning back. And she knows it. But I have something else she wants, she said, with a grin.

And so we cannot let her see you, I think. More important, we cannot let her see you with me.

The gentleman who had spoken to her was one of the Emperor's secret police, and their duty was to walk the streets protecting the Emperor, Empress, and her court as they went about their errands. They gave the appearance of being elegant gentlemen, well-bred and well tailored, and I knew from my time at the Tuileries that they knew Parisian society's secrets better than Parisian society did. They were secrets themselves, hidden until needed and then gone. I'd only seen them in the palace, where they were typically acknowledged openly; I'd never had the occasion to see them in public.

As we walked away, I knew they likely knew exactly who I was, and if they did not, they soon would.

The Empress has a few more of these agents than I do, the Comtesse said, and gestured grandly at the atelier, distracting me from the encroaching misery at the thought of being found out. But then, she is a small woman; she has always been. This role . . . it was never right for her.

We drank a glass of champagne nearby, and when we returned, the Empress had left and I went in for the last fitting to be sure the fit was correct. I dressed in my new day dress, and when the vendeuse politely asked if I wanted the old one in a box, I waved it away. We returned to the carriage and rode through the Bois.

That day the barren chestnut trees looked to me like the black iron feathers lining the gates of the palace at Compiègne, as if those feathers had spread across the country to become a forest of iron. The parade of horse-drawn phaetons, coupes, buggies, and carriages were filled by some of the wealthiest and most beautiful people in Paris.

You're attracting some notice, the Comtesse said to me, as we made the first turn. You shouldn't accept the first admirer, however, unless he does something truly extraordinary to get your attention. And even then, consider resisting, she said. Unless, of course, she said, by accepting him you attract the competition of another admirer. Ideally there will be several. A single man's support is unreliable, she said. With three you can be secure.

What is the best number? I asked.

That would depend, she said. Three can keep you very busy. But some of us, and she gestured at the crowd circling the lake, have as many as there are on this road right now.

Our carriage rattled a bit on the gravel underneath. We sat in silence. The men driving by seemed identical to me.

The men were approximately the same men. Russian and Italian princes, German barons and French dukes, the famous Turk, Halil Bey. Prince Napoléon.

The Prince Napoléon, she told me, had been married off to a magnificently ugly and devout Christian noblewoman from Italy named Princess Maria Clotilde. He was famous for leaving the doors to his apartment open while he satisfied himself on this or that mistress or whore.

It seemed being the Prince Napoléon has left him in a permanent bad temper, she said. Or that in the arrangement of his marriage, Louis-Napoléon had played a joke on him.

She directed my attention to the beautiful if unadorned phaeton of Louis-Napoléon driving around the Bois in disguise. The Comtesse pointed him out casually. They did not acknowledge each other.

He's married to his country, the Comtesse observed. Almost every woman in it.

I turned to take in the Comtesse, who did not look away from the Emperor. Her disgrace had not seemed real to me before then. She had seemed only beautiful, powerful, shrewd. The light off the park highlighted her face starkly in that moment and revealed in her expression some unknowable grief, unseen before; and this startled me. I had meant to make some sort of joke, but stopped myself; it was as if I were not there at all.

It was then I understood that she was not disgraced, not exactly. She had been sacrificed.

And then we were back at the rue de Passy, and the Comtesse wished me a good night as she departed.

∾

The sight of the Empress at the atelier, the Emperor at his ease in disguise in the Bois, this meant Compiègne had ended. And somewhere in Paris that evening, my new love was also here.

Back at my room, the driver's wife first made a fuss over my new toilette—how beautiful I look, I am too fine for her house—and then showed me a trunk that had come for me and helped me examine its contents: a tea gown of simple black muslin, much like the Comtesse's own; a boar's bristle hairbrush, lotions, maquillage, a nightdress, slippers, hair ribbons. And room exactly for the toilette I wore and the other two bodices in their boxes.

It was if I were to be on a voyage soon, this much I could see, and yet while the driver's wife cooed over each item, my dread returned and increased until she locked us in once more, put her key in her bodice, and set out her gin and cards. I dressed in the nightdress and slippers, and we played into the night.

I was certain all of this meant I was to leave Paris, and I expected to be taken away the next morning but, instead, a note came from the Comtesse through the driver, inviting me to attend the opera with her that night. I was to wear the opera bodice but to be ready in the afternoon. And so I was.

∾

The Comtesse's son and his nurse greeted me as I arrived. He was a boy with beautiful long chestnut hair, the longest hair I'd ever seen on a boy. He looked like a faerie, neither girl nor boy, at the edge of youth, the sort of creature who could cast you out of paradise if you answered a question wrongly.

You are my mother's friend, he told me, more than asking me.

Yes, I replied carefully.

You're very pretty, he told me. It's how I knew. All of Mother's friends are pretty.

Not as pretty as you, I said, and he smiled, vanishing quickly up the stairs.

I was shown up to her boudoir where the Comtesse sat waiting for her hairdresser. She told me she had called me early to have my own hair done as well. As her maid settled a kimono around my neck and over my gown, and I joined her in waiting, she withdrew a small velvet bag and shook its contents into her hand.

Here, she said. For you to wear this evening.

Emerald earrings in the shape of leaves, three stones in each, and the stones the size of small tears.

I give this to you now because, when you have your hair done for an evening, you should always show the hairdresser your jewelry so that he may make any necessary adjustments or suggestions. Tonight I am introducing you to a potential admirer. We will go to the opera and then dine afterward at the Grand Seize, where he will meet us. This completes my part of our bargain. At dinner I will speak of yours.

Thank you, I said.

It's really nothing, she said. I ask that you wear them this evening. And that you continue your habit of refraining from speaking in public so as to keep up the alias I have created. It will only be necessary a little longer.

I turned them over in my hand, and as I did, she said, A lesson on jewelry. You only rid yourself of a gift if you are at the end of an affair—if you are sure there is no hope. If you are in need of funds, sell your jewelry last; first suggest to an admirer the nature and scope of the debt, and then if that fails, sell the separate stones first rather than the entire piece. Always avoid selling the entire piece as it would likely be recognized by the giver on someone else and this would, even if you have ended the affair, embarrass or offend him. Especially if he could have covered the debt happily. Sell the original piece whole only if it is a historically important piece of jewelry.

She sat back. Do not keep the setting and have the original

stones replaced with paste, as no one is fooled by this. Either restore the setting as you are able or reset the stones remaining. Take these with my blessing. Let them remind you of all I have told you.

The hairdresser and his assistant arrived then and began to heat their tongs, playful, speaking of new styles, admiring our clothes and hair and the earrings as I placed them in my ears. As I examined them, I could tell they were not new; they had been hers.

There was an affair she was ending or had ended. There was no hope. *But who?* I wondered. But as I admired the earrings in the mirror, I knew them.

The Empress, that day at Compiègne, waiting for her hairdresser and fiddling with the emerald leaf she had from the Emperor. These were a match, I was sure of it. They were a set, and he had split it between them.

~

In Italy, when we go to the opera, we watch the opera, she said to me, as we exited the victoria and the coachmen helped us down. In Paris we watch one another, and she gestured a little at the crowd outside the theater.

We entered and ascended the stairs of the Théâtre-Italien. A hush descended over the crowd along the stairs and ahead of us; people turned to stare and whisper. It was a strange, quiet procession she and I made. I remembered when I'd first seen her move through the crowd at the Exposition, thinking it was her beauty that made people stare, but it was also envy, fury, spite.

In her private box she cast an eye over the people entering the other boxes, who were themselves looking up to see her. Then she sat back, drew her wrap closer, and smiled at me.

Have you ever been to the opera? she asked me. You may speak freely until we are joined.

Yes, I said.

You were perfect as we entered, she said. Perfect, perfect.

Thank you, I said. This word, her highest praise.

Tonight is Verdi, she said. *Il Trovatore*. It is about a wandering troubadour. Do you know what a troubadour is?

A little, I said.

He is a traveling singer, she noted. And he also travels as an agent for his king. They are excellent spies, singers, she said. No one thinks to stop them.

There was a commotion in the hall and then the door to the box opened. Shadowed at first was the figure of a woman, her hair piled high on her head and an enormous choker of pearls covering her throat and chest. When the door closed, we could see her more clearly.

Jou-jou, my dear, the Comtesse said. I present to you Giulia Barucci. The greatest whore in Paris. Giulia, this is Jou-jou of the Bal Mabille.

The new arrival smiled at this, as if it were a royal title, and made something of a curtsy before laughing as she stood upright. *Enchanté*, she said to me, and then she threw herself into a chair.

They then dropped into conversation in rapid Italian. Giulia made occasional nodding glances at me as her eyes swept repeatedly up and down the box and my own figure. She then reached out and touched the emeralds on my ears.

Que bellissima, she said, with a sigh.

I was careful not to reply or even look at my patroness. I was nervous, though, to be introduced that way—was it a joke?

She stood. See you in Baden-Baden, then, she said in clear English to me, and left, her glass nearly untouched.

When the door was shut, the Comtesse asked the waiter to stand outside the box, and then when he was gone, she said, She meant you. I won't be going.

The opera began.

May I use your opera glasses? I asked.

Of course, she said.

I was curious and excited, but I had also become afraid and, with the glasses, searched the boxes near us as surreptitiously as I could.

This was the opera the tenor loved above all others, and as such, it contained the soprano role he most wanted me to learn, that of Leonora, the doomed lover to the *trovatore*. We'd never seen it performed during my time with him, and if I were still with him, we would have been seated in another of these boxes that night. For this reason, I was sure he was near; he would have to be ill or away from Paris to miss this. But I could not see him and decided to be content: If I could not see him, he likely could not see me, and in the meantime, I was grateful for the chance to decide on the role without him.

I passed her opera glasses back to her.

The curtain rose. Guards sat outside a palace at night, anxious to help their Count di Luna catch the *trovatore* who had been coming regularly to serenade the Duchess Leonora at night. The Count loved her jealously and, having failed to court her successfully, was anxious to end this interference. The guard captain sang to the guards of the Count's tragic history to keep them awake—how as a child, the Count's younger brother fell ill, and the Count's father blamed a Gypsy and burned her at the stake. After the fire, a child's bones were found among the Gypsy's ashes and the brother was missing. It was said the Gypsy's daughter had kidnapped the sick boy and left him to burn with her mother in revenge. Only the Count's father was sure his youngest boy was still alive somewhere and charged the Count with finding his younger brother.

But for now, the Count was in love, and his guards were ready to help him.

The curtain closed and reopened to applause. A beautiful young woman in a veil stood in a garden at night, another woman approaching her through the dark, calling for her. When the woman in the veil turned to face us, the applause deepened. Adelina Patti was tonight's Leonora, the best possible surprise. I had not seen her since she had changed my life with her Lucia. My fears left me; surely this would be the best night of my life.

She began Leonora's first aria, of a mysterious knight in black armor she'd crowned the victor at a tournament, and described how she fell in love with him then. War had begun shortly thereafter, separating them, and she'd sustained herself on her memories of that day until one night here in the garden she was surprised to hear the song of a troubadour, her name on his lips. When she came to the garden, she saw it was him, the love she'd feared lost.

The night I'd heard her sing as Lucia was nothing compared to this—on that night I had only remembered the music, which moved me. This, however, was my first experience of the ridiculous and beloved thief that is opera—the singer who sneaks into the palace of your heart and somehow enters the stage singing aloud the secret hope or love or grief you hoped would always stay secret, disguised as melodrama; and you are so happy you have lived to see it done. The singer singing to you with the full force of what you feel is transfigured and this transfigures you; you feel as if it were *you* there in the opera, the opera your story, the story of your life. And so I stared in amazement from the box as Patti sang what was in my heart, what I hoped was my secret future; and in her slow, soaring, searching aria full of surpassing sweetness I found my first real consolation since leaving Compiègne. By the time she began her defiant cabaletta—*My fate will not be complete if he is not by my side! If I do not live for him, for him I will die*—her final note sustained like a sword held to the sky, the crowd rose to its feet cheering, the flowers raining down on the stage, and I, I caught myself. I had already stood, clutching the edge of the box.

The Count appeared alone then, singing stolidly of his hopes for his love for Leonora. Also of his jealousy. And so I sat.

I knew then I would sing Leonora if I could. I wanted nothing more. I was her, and she was me.

This was, of course, what the tenor had hoped for, what he'd never been able to arrange for me or describe. The roles he had tried to tempt me with were like little crumbs he had laid out for me compared to this. He knew *this* was the quickening; he knew what I would know after this night: that it is impossible to sing opera if the singer has never felt this.

The song for the entrance of the *trovatore*, Manrico, began next. It is one of the most beautiful, I think, of the songs there are for men. He is announced first by a harp, which is his lute, heard in the distance as he approaches through the forest at night, intent on Leonora, who listens for him from her window as Count di Luna, on hearing him, hides in the dark garden.

> Alone on this earth,
> at war with his fate,
> one hope in his heart,
> of a heart for the troubadour!
>
> If he possesses that heart,
> beautiful in its pure faith.
> He is greater than any king . . .
> The troubadour king!

Leonora rushes to the garden and embraces the Count, not the *trovatore*, mistaking the one voice for the other, the one man for the other, upsetting both. I knew the story well enough from the tenor; this is a clue that the *trovatore* is the Count's long-lost brother, his hated rival for Leonora's affections, unknown to him. But I knew, even if the tenor had a brother who sang, his voice would not sound like the tenor's; there could be no mistake.

The tenor was not in the audience because he was on the stage.

You imagine it, I told myself then, for the *trovatore* was still singing in the distance, unseen. And so I even believed this little lie for an instant more until the moment he stepped into the clearing and removed his mask.

I wondered if he could see me through the dark, sense me here in the box. I glanced at the Comtesse, who held her opera glasses close to her face, intent on the stage. Was this a trap? She betrayed no sign of what I suspected.

If this was a trap, it was a beautiful one.

Never, I silently swore there in the dark. *Never will I be on that stage with you, singing this. Never.*

The scene ended as Count di Luna and Manrico fought a fierce duel and Leonora threw herself to the ground in despair.

Manrico wins the duel but spares the Count's life and returns to his Gypsy camp, where his Gypsy mother reveals she is the daughter of the Gypsy the Count's father murdered. Manrico is really the Count's brother—the bones found when her mother burned were her own son's. This is why Leonora mistook them for each other. Manrico is told Leonora believes he is dead and is entering a convent out of grief, and so he runs to stop her but finds the Count there to do much the same. He and Leonora escape to the woods where they can live together as lovers, but a trick of the Count separates them, and the Count kidnaps her and imprisons Manrico. Leonora agrees to marry the Count if he would free Manrico, but she swallows poison instead and goes to the prison so she can die in Manrico's arms.

After her death, Manrico loses his will to live without her, stays a prisoner, and goes to his execution willingly. The Count discovers the truth of his brother's identity only when it is too late for the Count to save him. He has killed the brother his father had asked him to save.

Victory, defeat, victory, defeat, victory, defeat. Such is tragedy.

The Gypsy's daughter cried out in victorious revenge: the audience again came to its feet cheering. The Comtesse rose to leave the box early. As I still expected the tenor as the Comtesse's next guest, I was relieved to make an exit. We entered the lobby just as the rest of the audience flooded out, the Comtesse and I their first sight as their eyes adjusted to the light of the candelabras.

She studiously paused, and the crowd likewise paused to see her turning slowly to display herself in the black velvet gown she wore that evening, her hair piled high on her head and spilling down the back, the hair at her brow powdered à la Madame Pompadour, the enormous rows of pearls at her neck, a necklace of hers for which she was famous. I know there would be stories of her told describing all of this and ending with the slow turn she made, the lobby briefly her theater before she tossed her hair and departed with me.

As I turned to leave, I saw myself as I must have looked beside her to the crowd: the blue silk of my own dress a contrast to her black velvet, my dark hair swept back and curled to display the Emperor's love gift to her. Our little *tableau vivant*.

She had been like an actress running for her cue. All was as she'd wanted it.

To the Café Anglais, she told the driver as we were seated, and we left, off to meet my prospective admirer.

~

When we were seated finally at our table, the Comtesse ordered for us, and after the champagne was served, she spoke.

You asked what you might do for me, she said. I have certainly found a position for you as well as an admirer. But first I must speak of a somewhat uncomfortable matter, which is that the Emperor has requested you.

I did not immediately understand her meaning, and so she waited until I did.

As I smiled and lifted a glass of champagne to my lips, she said, He does like a horsewoman. Eugénie, of course, and then also Marguerite Bellanger. You wouldn't be one of the ones he has there at night, though, she said. You're young but you're not trivial, not at all. Even when you don't speak, I think that voice is there. It comes with its own atmosphere.

All of my thoughts stilled as I understood she meant my singing voice. I had never discussed it with her.

I won't let him have you, though, she said. But he did ask and then insist. I can still refuse him, and he's not as well as he once was —I think such an audience would disappoint you. Still, the idea of being able to take the young woman who stole Eugénie's lover from her is, well, it has an undeniable appeal for him. It makes you an extraordinary prize.

There was a beat of silence amid the din of the room around us, the wing of some terrible angel overhead.

You're under the protection of the Italian embassy here in Paris, such as I can offer. You have, however, humiliated me to the Emperor. So I must set some conditions.

She said this quietly, pausing to sip from her glass.

You seduced a favorite of the Empress's and escaped from her service, leaving her short a dresser during the series at Compiègne. I admire this as a feat, certainly—I have also taken a man she loves. You are, perhaps, nearly like my own daughter to have done so. And it is very useful to me to know the Empress has a closely guarded lover, but I've had to deny I know where you are. For even though she may not have lovers, when her lovers take lovers, her guards are certain to punish the girls involved.

She let out an exasperated, dismissive chuckle and surveyed the room.

And so to prevent your being hunted as a fugitive, tortured, or even executed as a spy, I have introduced you to Paris this way. Hidden you in plain sight, in gowns, your hair freshly curled.

She finally looked at me. I hope we understand each other.

I said nothing and then remembered to nod. She continued once I did, returning to looking around the room.

All of this is better than you deserve, I think. For there's the matter of one Jou-jou Courrèges. A former star of the Cirque Napoléon and a favorite of the Bal Mabille, declared dead at Saint-Lazare and stricken from the registry. Mysteriously beaten to death despite arriving at the jail in good health. This after a bitter argument in the street with a famous tenor who was one of her amours. And who, it would seem, owned her contract, having bought her from a popular house in the Marais.

Here I was, thinking you were a poor mute orphan girl, and it would seem you have been crisscrossing Paris in disguise for years.

You are, I should say, an incorrigible criminal. And yet he is so happy at the thought of your reunion, our mutual tenor friend. And he is so dear to one of my own dearest friends. You are, he says, a rare talent.

As she said this, she sat back in her chair and smiled, her gaze again on me directly. He is our mutual friend, yes? He will be here shortly to confirm you are who we believe you are.

Your education at my hands ends here. You will now renew your relationship with your tenor friend. He is going to train that voice of yours properly this time, in Baden-Baden, at the hand of Pauline Viardot-García. There he will tell everyone you are his protégée.

She returned her attention to me. You will, to show your thanks to me for this, stay with him. She raised her glass. The single condition of this is that you can never leave him and you may never speak to him of this bargain. Not without my permission. Your stay with him repays me for my assistance to you. Leave or betray him, and without question, the dossier I have on you will be sent to the authorities. And the Emperor will then have you to do with as he pleases.

She waited, her good humor unwavering throughout. I am returning you to your owner, she said. But I won't, she said, likely make you stay with him forever.

You owe me another debt, however, for the humiliation of leaving your position, the Comtesse said. And here is the way you will repay me: The day may come when I will send someone to take you to the Emperor. You will go to him and do whatever he wishes. And whatever else you wear that day, you must wear those earrings.

Slowly, I reached for my glass and raised it. She thought it was to toast her, and she raised her own.

Congratulations, my dear, she said. Your first admirer is one of Europe's most famous singers. You have done well.

Our glasses touched. At that moment the tenor entered, and the gathered crowd stood and applauded him as he walked over and stood by our table. He bowed deeply to the corners of the room and then begged them to sit. They kept applauding. The maître d' came and pulled the chair back himself, at which the others took their seats.

He took first the Comtesse's hand and kissed it, and then mine.

So good to see you again, he said to me. Our little runaway, he said then to the Comtesse.

Yes, my girl. What *is* your name? the Comtesse asked.

The tenor reached for my hand across the table, the gesture of a lover. I looked at it briefly, cautiously.

I set my hand on the table also and slid it toward his. He then opened his palm, the ruby flower there.

His hand glowed white in the candlelight, the rubies dark in his palm, like blood.

How we hold on to what we believe is ours. How we mourn when it is lost. And how unprepared we are when it then returns to claim us.

Lilliet, I said. Lilliet Berne.

My future lifted up on the light emanating from that ruby rose in his hand, out past the tables of elegant diners and the gleaming walls of the restaurant into the rest of my life. I knew what I was to do. I saw myself take it back from his hand, pin it to my dress, look up at him, smile, thank him, smile at the Comtesse, thank her for being our intermediary, curtsy to her, and leave with him. His carriage taking me on to this education and whatever it would bring me. All of this would begin once I picked it up.

I picked it up.

The tenor was speaking of how glad he was that I'd finally seen him sing in his favorite opera and of how much he hoped one day I would join him onstage as his Leonora. He said this as I moved the flower along my dress, searching for a place to pin it. I wanted just a breath before the rest that was to happen; I could survive it if I could have just another breath.

Without stopping his conversation, he reached over and took my hand, taking the rose back before carefully pinning it over my heart.

When at last I looked up, his face was unexpectedly tender, even kind. His expression told me how strongly he believed he was in a story in which I was the contrite penitent he'd already forgiven for running away.

Thank you for returning to me, he said. He reached up and touched my chin, searching my eyes with his eyes.

The Comtesse smiled approvingly and touched the enormous coil of pearls at her neck.

The tenor's eyes changed suddenly, concerned, as he looked past me and reached to my ears. He traced one of the emerald earrings. These are an emperor's ransom, he said, turning to my teacher.

Yes, the Comtesse said. Yes, they are.

After all my time among the Empress's secrets that no one but the Comtesse would think to keep, I had become one.

Act IV

First Love

One

MY THEME HERE is love. Love and the gifts of love, love kept secret, love lost, love become hatred, war, a curse. Love become music.
Love and those who died for love.

Love — and, especially, first love. My first love, the one I could
not keep and could never, will never, lose.

If you were to have visited me in my apartment on the avenue de
l'Opéra, you would have been greeted in the foyer by an onyx falcon on a wrought-iron pedestal beneath an enormous chandelier,
displayed as if it were the most valuable thing I owned. And it was
very fine — the claws were gold; the eyes, carved rubies; the feathers
outlined carefully, so that they glittered even in the dark. A small
gold dish for visiting cards sat by its feet, and beneath that, hidden
in the pedestal, was a jewel safe.

This was a trap of a kind, bait for thieves.

Inside were some jewels I did not value, my real treasures in another safe hidden elsewhere.

I kept the emerald earrings from the Comtesse there. My hope
was that if a thief found them they would convince him he had discovered my trove and he would leave immediately and take nothing
else.

So far no thief had been thus blessed.

Jewels told you a story each time you put them on, as Faust's
Jewel Song made plain. Sometimes the story was of your future,
sometimes of your past. You sold them when you never wanted to
hear the story again. I had never found cause to sell even one emer-

ald, but neither did I wear them more than a few times in the years that followed the night she gave them to me. I was sometimes asked as to their provenance, and each time I could only shrug.

A gift, I would say.

With time, they had proven to be a spur to the richest of my admirers who sought to do them one better, jealously imagining my spending other evenings with the one who could afford such gifts, and I could never say otherwise. They'd had their uses, I suppose. But that night with the Emperor had never come to pass, and now that he is dead, it never will.

I never doubted my sense of their provenance. I'd had an education in jewels since, and the handiwork, even the color of the stones, told me the story the Comtesse would never tell. I am sure that the Emperor had them made at the same time, perhaps even from the same stone, as the color and style were a perfect match. Had the Comtesse ever worn them in front of the Empress? Or had the Comtesse, in turn, ever seen the Empress's brooch? Each would have known at once, as I had.

Divided stone, divided heart.

The Comtesse had come to Paris well after the marriage to the Empress had been made, which meant the Emperor had kept these, perhaps meaning to give them to the Empress later on the occasion of an anniversary of some kind or the birth of a son, but he instead gave them to the woman who would go to her death believing she should have been empress.

That the Comtesse had kept these earrings all this time told me she had been nursing some secret hope for herself and the Emperor. On the night she gave them to me, these were that hope's grave. And by instructing me to wear them if I went to him, she sought to create a certain moment. When I would undress for the Emperor and he pulled back my hair, these were what he would see.

I had imagined the scene in my head many times as I waited, trying to prepare if I was called, and I am certain this was her plan. Some days I imagined him enraged, some, come over with passion. Or both.

She meant even then, even as the Emperor would have me as revenge for the Empress's affair, to take some revenge of her own. Known only to her.

But I would never know the earrings' last secrets, the ones they cannot tell; I can only guess. What I know for certain is that *Il Trovatore* was a favorite opera of the Empress's, and she and the Emperor would have attended together. Certainly, I was there to be seen, on display to the Emperor, or one of his intimates, or one of his agents, perhaps even the Empress. I went with her that night as the proof she had me in her custody. And for her to place these earrings in my ears, this was her declaration of war.

In those years when I believed the ruby rose lost to me forever, I would sometimes take the earrings out and reflect on what I thought was the irony of my situation: that after the loss of one tiny jeweled gift from the Emperor, I was now the custodian of this other, far greater gift he had given to the Comtesse.

Now it seemed I was fated to have both.

These were my thoughts on that evening, many years later, when I again went to the statue, opened the lock, and took these earrings out to wear them one more time.

I was dressed in a gown of black chiffon and taffeta; sheer sleeves and a black lace ruff at the neck were the gown's only whimsy, and so the emeralds went well with this. They suited me finally. Back when I first wore them in the Café Anglais, I most likely looked like an overdressed girl who'd taken them from her mother, out trying to pass herself off as an elegant woman. I remember I sat there that night, too aware of the fortune in my ears, trying to look as if I deserved them, all the while I felt myself to be vanishing, falling further inside a story I couldn't see, in which I occupied a role that was both central and yet also minor, and that required this of me to operate—and would not give me my freedom. This story seemed, perhaps, to have begun when I put on the earrings, or further back, when the earrings were given to the Comtesse, or even further back, when they were made. Or even further back still, when the idea of them was born in the mind of the giver. I couldn't know. I only knew that something was in motion to which my actions had proven vital and that I was not to be allowed to see any further than this. Questions had repeated through me in a chorus that night. Why could the tenor not know of her arrangement with me? Who had set those terms, in turn, with her—who had the power to do so? Had he been in the lobby of the opera? Had we succeeded then? Whose story was I in?

Whose story was I in?

This was the question I had asked myself that night so long ago as the tenor led me to his carriage. This was also the question I asked myself now in my apartment each time I held Simonet's novel in my hand. Once again, I had the distinct feeling of being inside of a story that had begun somewhere out of my sight. A story around me that would also not let me inside it. A story begun with someone imagining my holding the book as I did just then. There was something this person wanted me to believe as I did so—what was it? And why?

The return of this feeling, more than anything else, was what had made me suspicious.

Whose story was I in?

I had woken that morning from a long dream that had turned and tumbled until I could no longer remember any of it except a name that stayed with me as I was delivered up from the ocean of sleep.

Simmonet? Simonet.

And with that, a memory came of the writer George Sand. Sand had a nephew by that name or something like it.

Was my Simonet, the author of this novel, her nephew? Or even secretly George Sand?

I stepped from my bed, took the novel from my nightstand, and turned it over in my hands as if some previously hidden secret to its authorship would fall out, but there was, as ever, nothing except the words I'd refused thus far to read.

Sand was dead now these last six years—if she was the author, this was the work of her ghost. After being presented to her, I'd admired her so much that I hoped to inspire a character in one of her novels some day, much as Pauline Viardot-García, my voice teacher, had—Pauline had introduced me to Sand; she was her oldest friend. I tried to remember if, on that fortnight's visit, I was ever presented to Sand's nephew or if he'd any literary aspirations. But my Simonet had been so free in speaking of other French writers, it seemed to me that if he was Sand's nephew, I would already have been told by him directly.

I set the novel down, full of the same dread I'd felt since being told of its existence and rang for my breakfast tray.

Not quite a week had passed since the *bal* and the mysterious novel's arrival, and in attempting to certify whether its existence constituted a betrayal of some kind, I had gone through my short list of suspects—Euphrosyne, the tenor, the Comtesse—without luck. Euphrosyne seemed entirely innocent to me, even of carelessness, and seeing her glittering in her elegant home reminded me that my past was not a subject she spoke of to others, just as she did not speak of hers; she would protect me much as she protected herself. She had forgiven me instantly for my abrupt departure from her salon, and now each day's mail brought me more letters from her of the *bal* she was planning for me.

My visit to the tenor had likewise reassured me that all between us was as it had been for some time. His long obsession with me seemed unchanged. I did not suspect him of being the source of the marriage rumor, either. He had once proposed marriage to me, and I had rejected him as, just as the Comtesse had said so plainly all those years ago, I was as unfit to marry him or any other men of his class as I ever had been; and this, like his social class, would never change. What he wanted from me did not require marriage nor did it derive from it. We both knew that when he saw me sing on that little stage at the Majeurs-Plaisirs he hadn't imagined our sitting with a batch of baby tenors and sopranos, and my pulling at a spindle somewhere in Prussia. He imagined us together in Paris, on the stage, at last singing *Il Trovatore* at Les Italiens.

I had rejected him by reminding him of all of this in no uncertain terms. And by denying him, I had ensured he would be a servant to this dream forever and, in a way, to me — in a way that protected me. My visit had assured me all of this was as it had been since that rejection so long ago. It would thus be too painful for him to joke in public of something he still desired.

And there was every chance he had since married some Prussian princess picked out by his family at birth and left behind to be the mistress of that distinguished, ancient, if also somewhat reduced, domain — him all the while in Paris. In the times I had seen him since the end of our liaison, he had seemed richer than before, and I knew well that for men of his class a wife was what secured you your inheritance and her dowry, and a lover was where you spent both. But I did not know, and had never asked, if there was a wife. Either way, I no longer suspected him.

The Comtesse alone remained, albeit out of reach. I had never told her of the end to my liaison with the tenor. I was sure my value to her — and our bargain — had ended once Eugénie had been driven from the palace. The discovery that she was still surrounded by agents, and French agents at that, not Italian ones, a decade after the passing of the Empire, this had only made me fear she did not agree that our agreement had ended; this left me the more sure she was my mysterious antagonist. And while the police officer I'd spoken to that day seemed content to think he knew me for knowing my reputation as a singer, if he were to check into my background, he might find that series of mysteries that could lead him even a little of the way back to the Comtesse, who knew the answers to most every question he might ask — and I was certain she could still provide my old dossier on request. For all I knew, she had my old *carte* from the registry and the record of my examinations and arrests — and death.

This novel and the opera, though if a plot of hers, had not yet revealed her style. If she sought some final revenge on me, she was unlikely to come for me this way. She had a great love of theater, yes, but her theatrics were meant to draw your attention directly to her. If she was behind this, it would mean she had changed in some way I had not foreseen and couldn't imagine. And certainly, hidden as she was now inside of her blackened apartment, this was possible.

My single consolation was that if the Comtesse read the paper as the officer had, then she likely knew the rumor of my forthcoming marriage to the tenor and might be reassured to think the arrangement she'd set was still in place. That might stay her hand if that hand was raised to strike.

This was the very slightest of consolations to me, however. And for now, the only person from my past I could find who seemed clearly intent on my destruction was me. That one seemingly harmless lie I had told to Verdi continued to hurtle through Paris, leaving a trail of rumor and chaos in its wake.

I was determined to at least stop the damage to my reputation and to repair what I could of this life. Afraid of what I had done and what I might still do, I thought to cancel all of my social engagements and take to bed, where I could at least, perhaps, finally read the novel and not lie to anyone any further. But before I did so, I still wanted some further assurance that this composer Simonet had mentioned existed—if he was real, and the opera real, that alone could assure me this was not the trap I feared it was.

This all seemed quite impossible, though, without contacting Simonet. And as that lie had been inspired by Simonet's own seemingly ridiculous confession to me—well, I mistrusted him and his novel even more.

Even worse, I had begun to believe he—and Madame Verdi— were right, and my little lie was the truth and, perhaps, always had been.

Doro opened the door then and brought in my tray. As she set it down, she asked if, as it was Thursday, I was to go to Madame Viardot's as usual, for madame had written, her note was there on

the tray, and if I was to go, what would I wear, would I dine in or
out. . .

I cried out and hugged her, at which she protested and laughed,
and left me to my breakfast and my note.

If Mondays were for Euphrosyne when I was in Paris, I usually saved
a Thursday or a Sunday for my teacher, Pauline Viardot-García —
the teacher the tenor brought me to study with in Baden-Baden.
Pauline's salon on Thursdays at her home on the rue de Douai in
the ninth arrondissement was the most exciting of its kind in Paris
and the most important. She lived with her husband, Louis Viardot,
a former director of the Théâtre-Italien and now an art historian,
as well as her friend and intimate of many years, the writer Ivan
Turgenev, the three of them living amicably together under one roof
much as they had when I first met them. Together they attracted
an audience of actors, singers, painters, composers, musicians, and
writers. It was not uncommon to attend and find Delibes, Fauré,
Brahms, Clara Schumann, and the newest genius or the oldest living one, not just in attendance, but singing, presenting, playing.
Something about her put these talented and distinguished men and
women at their ease and brought out their best performances. There
was a very good chance that the Verdis or Simonet or even the protégé himself would be there. Whoever this man was, someone there
would know, Pauline, I was sure, most of all.

Pauline's note apologized for not being able to attend *Faust*, and
she insisted I return to the salon the moment I could to perform for
her.

I heard a story about you, several, actually. One is that you are
leaving the stage and finally marrying our mutual tenor friend,
which seems impossible, for you would not dare become engaged
without both of you coming here with this news first, yes? Another is that you were a sensation at the Sénat Bal last week, with
an impromptu Jewel Song in the garden. A sensation! This I believe. Perhaps you will repeat the sensation tonight? Come, and

if you do intend to sing, wear some conspicuous jewels so that I will know at once.

> I remain your teacher,
> Pauline

She meant only one thing by her request. And so, dressed in my conspicuous jewels, I went.

~

On entering Pauline's salon one passed through a gallery of painting masterpieces separated by red-velvet drapes that led to her astonishing Cavaillé-Coll pipe organ, installed along the far wall of the downstairs gallery like a throne for a queen—a queen who could also play music. The organ had been made for her so she could face her audience seated on a beautifully carved wooden pedestal and accompany herself on the organ as she sang. At the foot of this pedestal was a piano, and chairs were set out near this for any fellow musicians who were also to play. Rows of chairs in circles ringed this for the rest of us in attendance.

The scene was somber at the start due to the news that both M. Viardot and Turgenev were in poor health. I'd heard Louis was not well, but the truth described in the conversations around me was worse than imagined—he'd had a stroke. In the meantime, Turgenev, often afflicted with painful gout in recent years, was now said to be suffering from an angina as well. Pauline took a moment to address us all and assured us we were very welcome and that our merriment would not disturb her patients—some had expressed concern. She said Turgenev, who occupied the fourth floor by himself, had even had a long listening tube installed so he could hear us. To cancel would sadden them, she said. They had asked us to carry on, and she extended it to us as a duty to be happy for their sake and improve their spirits also.

I had not seen Pauline since my return. She seemed vital still, if also weary from nursing what were effectively her two husbands.

Leonine in appearance, she wore her hair in something of a silver crown; her skin was still smooth, her large dark eyes still shining, her cheeks full. She was the youngest of the trio, but there was something else to her, some vitality that had brought her all this way and remained, undimmed by her trials.

She then went around the room to greet us, and if we at first were somber, given the news, we soon saw she was happy to see us and tried to match her. When it was my turn, she kissed me on each cheek and, touching the earrings, said, Ah! You are prepared. How I love you, thank you. Now tell me, I must know at once—are you truly marrying? And what is this nonsense about curses and retirements?

Lies, every one, I said, and she laughed.

You were away too long, she said, and set her face in a moue. You must return Sunday when you can see the men at dinner. They won't forgive me if I don't get you up the stairs. Come early, though. And wear something especially beautiful. And forgive me for not seeing you in *Faust*. I don't dare leave them alone.

With that, she swept on, greeting the next of the room's guests.

Paris had been cruel to Pauline as a young woman. She came of age as a singer amid a field of established singers who'd felt they'd only just emerged from the shadow of her older sister, the legendary Maria Malibran, who had died some years earlier, far too young. If Pauline had been only half the singer Maria was, she would have been a threat to them, but she was much more than that from the beginning—a mezzo-soprano with a three-octave range, she could sing freely in many roles.

After her debut, the Paris opera houses turned their backs on her on the orders of these older, more experienced, vengeful sopranos. She'd needed to go abroad just to sing. Once there, she made herself into someone who could not be ignored by any opera house anywhere in Europe. She eventually returned to Paris with much acclaim, basking a little in the fury of her enemies.

Now that she had retired, this salon in Paris was her revenge on those earlier enemies, whatever else it was—a stage in her own house that she commanded, where no one could dismiss or surpass her. Those other singers might have paused at her age as their voices faded; her technique and her command of her repertoire was such that she made more of her ailing voice than most younger singers did with theirs.

Here was Pauline, then, still accompanying herself on her organ, beginning the evening with a song from *Sapho,* which thrilled us all. She went on to perform songs from *Alceste, La Sonnambula,* and *Orphée et Eurydice,* and then, after applause, she gamely gave curtsies to us and then moved down to her piano, where she announced she was to play Chopin's Nocturne in C Minor, op. 48, no. 1 and began.

If Chopin's Nocturne in F Minor, op. 55, no. 1 is like looking for a love lost in the darkness, this is the descent into love, in all its richness, mortifications, and subsequent glories. It begins mournfully and then becomes tender, then passionate, then seems to rage in a movement from despair into redemption, then passion again, and at last, a plaintive, even affectionate acceptance that this will die and leave us. In Pauline's hands that night, it was a storm of arpeggios, a passion made more beautiful by the way it aspires to immortality despite the knowledge of its own death approaching—a love that knows it can be lost and still loves hopelessly as long as it can. Pauline played it as only she could—which is to say, as someone who was a dear friend to Chopin, who had studied with him, collaborated with him, played four-handed beside him, and then sang Mozart's requiem over his grave. A tenderness mixed with grandeur illuminated it all. Her performance was extraordinary, and the last bars sounded as if they were thrown over that final wall that is death, a last farewell to a lost beloved passing on into whatever lay beyond.

When she was done, the room was silent, humbled. We had been startled by the force of it, I think, or, at least, I had been—and the force of what I felt. I had wept. As I reached for my handkerchief, a movement near the door to the stairs caught my eye: a silver-haired shadow that could only be Turgenev, still in his dressing gown, his eyes bright with tears.

His listening tube abandoned, it had taken him all this time to descend the stairs.

At that moment, Pauline waved for me to come forward, thundering into the introit to the Jewel Song—she intended to accompany me, of course, a great honor. I hesitated—I wanted to ask someone to help Turgenev back to bed, remembering how painful his gout was, or to tell her to sing or play something else for him —but as I looked to the door once more, he put a finger over his mouth, a gleam in his eyes as if he were a naughty child, and then withdrew farther into the shadow.

I went to Pauline's side instead and obeyed them both as I always had since meeting them.

I was finally able to speak to Pauline alone near the evening's end when she approached me and thanked me for singing for her—as if I could have refused her.

You have truly grown into your artistry. You sing to give pleasure, she continued, but it is not with that craven approach that goes out begging for applause; instead, it is a gift given from your own store of pleasure, a pleasure taken from the music. This is the only honest way to give this, I think. The result is that your Jewel Song was exquisitely handled. But what's more, I can tell you finally understand what is in that beautiful throat.

Thank you, I said, made shy by this, but not too shy to ask the questions I had come with, all of which amused her. But Pauline had none of the answers I needed. She apologized for not remembering the name of the Prix de Rome winner from several winters before and said she had heard nothing of Verdi protégés, nor did she know of a writer named Simonet, much less his novel. She, like me, doubted he was Sand's nephew. I am an old woman at last and have no gossip to share, she said, even as I protested it couldn't be true.

Only the gossip that comes in with the doctors, she said.

And then she leaned back her head with the faintest smile and, tapping her chin, asked, Are you in love with him, this mystery composer?

How can I be? I asked in return. I don't even know him.

Almost every opera is about this, she said, her smile growing. Love *before* first sight.

I laughed.

You laugh, she said, but it is so. How I wish we were still in Baden-Baden, she said. Walking across the lawn back to supper as we used to. Do not forget Sunday, she said, with a wag of her finger.

I promised I would not and kissed her good night. I returned home to contemplate my little mystery some more.

Was this love before first sight?

Perhaps, I told myself, as I entered the foyer to my apartment and Doro greeted me there, lifting off the coat and the fur collar I'd worn out, and tutting at me for wearing the emeralds to Pauline's —they were too ostentatious for a salon! I assured her my hostess had invited this.

Whoever this composer Simonet had mentioned was, yes, perhaps I did already love him, or would. Perhaps it was time to love again. I had loved exactly once. After the circumstances under which my first and only love had died, I decided to set this heart of mine someplace safe forever. If I could not save him or be with him, I at least wanted never to betray him.

But even as I reminded myself of this, I knew my heart had at last begun to disagree with me. It had grown hungry and, at the scent of love in the air, suffered the temptations of any hermit who has stumbled onto what seems to be the preparations for a feast.

I went to stand alone in front of the falcon. I took the earrings from my ears and returned them to their trap.

The answers I sought now, they could very well set me free from at least my suspicions and fears. They could also matter not at all.

On that long-ago evening, as the tenor's carriage passed through the streets of Paris taking me to my next life, I had vowed to learn the nature of what was hidden to me in this transaction, for I was sure the answer was the answer to everything—sure the answer would free me and return my life to me somehow.

But if the earrings were a reminder of that evening's singular defeat, the falcon that hid them reminded me that when I'd at last fought my way through to my long-sought answers I discovered these answers would not have released me from this strange bondage. And, say that they had—I would never have become a singer. This was the real irony to my situation: Everything I had as a singer I owed to this bargain.

The falcon statue was a gift from the mysterious man who had set the terms of my return to the tenor with the Comtesse. He had given it to me along with my freedom.

That last artificer, hidden up above them all.

~

As a story of discovering you are in another story, *Il Trovatore* is a tragedian's sleight of hand. It is a love story until Manrico dies, and the Gypsy's daughter stands and shouts her victory, and the Count understands he has ordered the murder of his lost brother and driven Leonora to her death. In a single instant, we find we are in another story altogether, the opera only the last chapter in the Gypsy's daughter's long plan for revenge begun so long ago.

Victory, defeat, victory, defeat, victory, defeat.

And so my tenor and I had found ourselves to be in quite another story from the one we believed we were in. A story begun when the Comtesse arrived at her first ball in Paris, and the music stopped, and the Emperor and Empress stopped their conversations to see what had happened.

Only I knew this to be true, however. He never knew. Just as I never knew what, if anything, Pauline had been told of my situation when we first met. Her mock hurt at the thought the tenor and I might marry and not announce the news to her in person told me she still believed the tenor and I might still be the happy lovers she met when we went to her in those last days of autumn in 1868. Yes, if we were to marry after all this time, she would have to be included in some important way. And certainly, the tenor believed in our love then, and so why wouldn't she?

I never once suspected her as having a role in the events surrounding me now because she was too good to me, too purely my teacher—my only good teacher—to concoct schemes of that kind. And she would never endanger even one of us for fear of losing even the smallest piece of what remained of our time there.

But, certainly, I suspected her then.

It amuses me to remember how suspicious I was of her, just as I was suspicious of all I saw, convinced I moved through a country populated entirely by the Comtesse's plan for me. From the train to Baden-Baden, as I watched through the window, this country seemed made of an unbroken forest braced for the coming winter, bordered by meadows with the grass gone brown and wet from the rain. Baden-Baden, the tenor assured me, sat at the edge of the Black Forest, just over the border from France, in Germany, in a valley of extraordinary beauty and mild climate.

He had been speaking of Baden-Baden until then and describing its various virtues and history, but these had slid across me like the rain on the window at my side.

We were at luncheon, nearly at our destination, seated in a luxury dining car at the table assigned to us for the trip. I was afraid and also afraid I could not hide this fear; I had the feeling of riding an angry horse indifferent to its rider. Behind the tenor was a mirror set into the wall, and so when I did not look out the window to the landscape during our meals, I used the mirror to help me modulate my expressions so as to better perform the part of his interested fellow traveler—our meals on the train like rehearsals for the days ahead.

I was almost accustomed to him again. He had changed during our time apart. His beard had darkened and grown longer, though his hair was still golden, still worn past his ears and swept back with pomade. He still wore evening dress often, though not for this trip — he had dressed the part of a proper Prussian gentleman in a beautiful traveling suit of a dark blue wool and a waistcoat embroidered with flowers. This drew attention to how he had thickened as well, but it suited him. He seemed less a former soldier and more of a tenor.

All of this activity with the mirror, to which he seemed oblivious, sometimes distracted me from his actual conversation, and so I found I had not been listening carefully to the description of Germany, and this was in part because I was indifferent to its details for not having chosen to come — it was the same as any other confinement to me. With some surprise, then, I understood he had finished speaking to me of Germany and Baden-Baden, and turned to the subject of me.

When you died, or when I believed you'd died, he said, I couldn't tell anyone. So I invented a story that you'd gone to Baden-Baden, to study with Pauline Viardot-García. I'm so happy I can make this true.

He said this ruefully, quietly — we were surrounded by fellow travelers — and pushed at his wine glass.

Neither of us said anything more for a moment. I sat back again. There was only the unearthly sound of the crystal and silver set on all the tables ringing as we went, as if the train were a mystical bell of many parts. This strange concert was oddly comforting.

The instinct I'd had to simply act with him as I once had, to resume our easy banter and nicknames, was more difficult as time went on. Sustaining it meant some part of me had already papered over the rupture, but at moments like this, scenes from that other time intruded, alien and alarming, which chilled me, though I knew he meant his remarks to please me.

Grateful but contrite happiness, I told my face in the mirror, as if I were again in Delsarte's classroom and he was pointing to my next expression. Though I was well past his room of portraits, deep inside my own. I reached for the tenor's hand. Please forgive me, I said.

I have, he said. And I hope you also will forgive me. Madame Viardot-García is the greatest voice teacher in all of Europe, you see, he said. I have sung with her informally and learned something even just in singing across from her. I hope, in introducing you to her, she will make up for the mistakes I made earlier with your training. Also, she is not so concerned as to whether you have a proper French education; and she has room for you and was moved to hear of your situation.

What is my situation? I asked, and smiled as our soups were set down in front of us.

Wurstsuppe, the waiter said, and then left.

That you were rejected from the Conservatoire, the tenor said. And could lose your voice. She can teach you to be a Falcon properly.

I nodded.

I do this for love of you, he said.

At this, I smiled with the appropriate expression of gratitude but looked down to the creamy surface of my soup. I did not want to speak of or lie about loving him yet. But I could see he also wanted to be complimented so very much for having chosen this voice teacher, and I did not want to do it, not yet. I was still afraid of her precisely because he had chosen her.

Another maxim of Odile's came to me then: *If you cannot compliment a man but you must, ask him to speak of himself instead, this has the same effect.* I remembered I had meant to ask him of his *Fach*, and so I did.

Please, tell me what is a heldentenor?

He smiled the more, nearly preening.

I am the tenor version of you, he said. A tenor who is almost a baritone, deeper, richer in the lower range, but with a seemingly hidden high range that surprises and can sustain high notes with force.

What does this mean, *helden*? I asked.

Helden means hero, he said, making a fist and shaking it playfully, as if to smite an enemy. It is the voice you hope to have if you are a German tenor. This voice is for singing Mozart, he said. And for singing Wagner, too. I think in Germany men who can give voice to tragedy, those are our heroes or, at the least, that is how we want our heroes to sound when they sing.

He grinned at this, and his eyebrows rippled as if he had surprised himself.

I was always hoping to find someone like you, he said.

So we could give voice to a tragedy together, I said, trying my hand at banter.

Yes, he said. That is exactly right.

Before this luncheon, I had wondered who I was now. The question was not a simple one. Now I knew.

The tenor had not installed a new woman in my place during the time he believed me dead. Whatever it was he felt for me, it had not dimmed, not once, not even in death. I found the apartment kept like a mausoleum to me when he brought me there proudly that first night after we left the Café Anglais. The furniture shrouded, the clothes still there, some of them packed into three trunks, waiting by the door for the footman, who loaded it into the carriage. As I peered into the apartment from the foyer, he assured me all would be kept as it was until my return. Only as he locked the door and we descended the stairs did I understand I was the woman he was installing in my place; Jou-jou's life, for I did not think of myself as her anymore, was truly over, and whoever I was to be next had been given her things.

We then set off for the tenor's own apartment, where he showed his trophies to me: his antique swords and pistols, the stuffed kills from his hunts, the relics of his family. We drank a liqueur made from mirabelle plums from tiny glasses, and he told me the story of the boar he'd killed as a boy, which stood by the entranceway, a sentinel shaggy with age, along with his more recent prize, an elk head mounted on the wall. The taxidermist had given the elk some serene gaze as it no doubt looked somewhere into an eternal Germany, which I now entered for the first time at his side.

I had given no further thought as to who I was—it was easy to forget that it even mattered. But the question had returned just before this luncheon, in the form of the conductor, who appeared at the door to our compartment asking for our papers. The tenor had supplied them immediately and did not look at me once, and neither did the conductor, who examined them and then bid us a good day.

This had been the most telling detail to me. The woman who had left him, that woman was still legally dead and could not be resurrected without questions neither he nor I wanted answered. And she had no papers, could cross no borders on a train. I had papers, however. Or rather, the tenor had them, and he returned them to his coat. I thought to concoct ruses in order to read them. What did they say? What name was there? When he would introduce me to Pauline, what name would he use?—but I would know then, it seemed to me. And perhaps it was better, quieter, to wait. The thought of asking what my name was now seemed likely to pull this little world asunder.

After the conductor left, I understood I was still waiting for the tenor to show some sign that it was all just a game, that he would return to our old ways, but the longer he did not, and the more he continued to be tender to me, and kind, the more curious I became.

This would be easier if I could love him, I thought, as we finished our luncheon, stood, and returned to our cabin to prepare to disembark. And could I love him or grow to love him? He was handsome, devoted to me, willing to spend a considerable sum of money on me and even to forgive that I had run from him as I had twice now. He had made a case for me with this foreign voice teacher and was now accompanying me to her side.

But I did not love him as I did not love him.

This was the gift I had asked the Comtesse for, the last test of my apprenticeship to her. But how to have it?

As I contemplated his back as he spoke to the porters, and thought of the packet of papers I now knew to be hidden in his breast pocket, the Comtesse's description of the secret to La Païva's success seemed instructive in that moment.

Favors? Favors are nothing to this.

The details of who I was now mattered less than who he believed he was now with me, someone he'd longed to be all this time. A world he'd waited for to be born came into being with my return to him, and I was now the source of it. I mattered more than I ever had, lost to him twice, now his again by choice, the tragic soprano perfectly matched to his tragic tenor. As long as I was this woman, all would be well. And as to who this woman was, I had but one clear answer.

I was his partner in tragedy.

～

How I congratulate you on your triumph in *Il Trovatore* and devoutly wish I could have seen it. I have heard nothing but elated reports of your performances, and so we will greet you and your Leonora with all due glory and celebrations here in our Gypsy camp in the mountains when you arrive. And you must, you must come at once.

We were in a carriage hired at the station, riding up a hill just outside of Baden-Baden toward Pauline's villa. The tenor read to me from a letter from her and occasionally interjected, a startling affection in his face as he did so. He was merry, like someone on holiday. I'd never seen him so gay.

You may have heard that I am a Gypsy; my father did not know his father, this is true; and he is from that part of Seville where the Gypsy blood is strong, though it distressed my dear mother to no end whenever we made light of this.

He stopped reading and laughed, and then held out the letter to me, smiling. She's really quite clever at these, he said.

I assumed he was showing me proof of her compliment to him, but I stared in amazement instead to see a caricature she'd drawn of herself as Azucena the Gypsy in *Il Trovatore*. She stood next to a cauldron, a shawl over her head, and had written *Azucena implores the spirits to reveal her new student's fate!*

She plays a game you will like, where you must draw a face, and then all present invent ideas for the character's name, identity, and destiny, the tenor said.

I laughed. *Of course*, I thought, chilled even as I laughed. *If I was to be his Leonora, we would need an Azucena.* Pauline's joke but Fate's as well.

If before this I felt abandoned by Fate, now I feared that I had Fate's full attention.

Pauline was a true Gypsy's daughter, though she did not, I think, plot revenge there in Baden-Baden, only operas — operas and her students' careers. Her father, as she explained beneath her carica-ture, was Manuel García, a Spanish Gypsy tenor and one of the world's most famous singers, as the tenor noted. With her mother, the soprano Joaquina Sitchez, he raised the García children in what resembled a traveling circus family, but devoted to opera. The Gar-cía family had toured America and Mexico throughout Pauline's early childhood, performing a repertoire of Italian operas and Gar-cía's own original compositions. García, his wife, his oldest daugh-ter, Maria, and his son, also named Manuel, performed the major roles while Pauline, the youngest, looked on from the wings.

Pauline's letter explained she had nearly put me off until the following spring as she would spend much of the winter between Karlsruhe and Weimar, at work on the production of an opera she'd written as well as planning a command performance of this opera the following April in honor of the birthday of the Grand Duchess Sophie of Saxe-Weimar-Eisenach. She had changed her mind, however, as she feared treating me too daintily. As this opera of hers was something she'd written to give her students to practice with, much as her father had done with his own students, and as they had performed it originally in her *Haustheater* in Baden-Baden to audiences in her salon, and as this, in turn, led to its current successes, she had decided she would bring her students in Baden-Baden with her to Karlsruhe and Weimar, and one of them might even perform in the formal production. And as she had been educated amid tours and productions, so then would I begin my education in the wings.

Think of it as a García tradition, then, if you will, to bring her into this circus now. I can understand that you might fear she would be overlooked in the tumult, but please accept my reassurances. My own education began as we toured and continued no matter if we had been feted with all due glory the night previous or robbed by Mexican brigands—the next day my father sat me at the piano again wherever we were. He wrote airs for me to practice that I still know and occasionally sing, written just for my voice. In this way, he has remained with me despite his death when I was still quite young, and so I have lived most of my life feeling both as if I never knew him and that he is always with me. You know how strong is the force of my will; you know I will keep after her. She will have the chance to witness the various demands, successes, and failures of this life firsthand, as all my students will, all at once. They are my good luck charms, even this young woman I have not met. I feel certain this will toughen her in the best way—you see my own upbringing has not failed me. After all, once her career begins, it will be one of constant travel, so her education may as well include accommodating herself to it. So, please, come at once, without delay, with your Falcon. Join us in Baden-Baden and follow us on to wherever we go next.

The tenor smiled at the last page and then looked up. You meet Madame Viardot-García at an extraordinary time, he said, folding the letter and shaking it at me. But she promises to make the most of it and you. In fact, it seems she is set on making a García of you.

I smiled and turned my attention back to the window.

On the train I'd made a little picture of the misery I was sure awaited me here, imagining days spent in a small room like the one in Paris, with lessons of some kind, unimaginable to me. I'd hoped at least for something like the pleasures of gin and cards, which I already missed dearly. I had added to this imaginary scene with each detail the tenor offered previously, but the letter extinguished all of this and even strangely reassured me.

I knew a little of the ways of a traveling show.

Despite this elegant explanation, there did not seem to be a single pause or uncertainty in the pace at which I had been brought to her. Her change of mind sounded sincere, but was some other pressure applied? Had she been threatened or paid? And how was my education paid for, and what had Pauline been told of me, other than my needing an education as a Falcon?

I smiled, looking away, and turned my attention to the window.

Baden-Baden itself would not let me stay anxious, however, and had begun to work its magic on me through the air alone, clean and sweet as I breathed it in, a relief after Paris. Against my will, I relaxed. The mountains were the dark green of winter approaching, when the pines are the only trees still dressed. The town itself, visible from the road that led to Pauline's house, gave the appearance of a village growing a city in its midst. The elegant pale stone buildings of the casinos and baths, covered in grand statues and columns, stood beside the staid older German houses of brick or plaster and made a mix of the grand and the quaint together, their green and red rooftops shining in the afternoon sun. The summer season was more for the gamblers, the tenor had said. By winter Baden-Baden would belong mostly to the patients who came to be cured by the waters. Those who came for music, though, came all year, and the more so now that Pauline lived here—a colony had grown around her, and this was what we entered now.

Beneath my various fears and imaginings, I was aware of a growing anticipation for the teacher herself. While I was still suspicious of her, this news that Pauline had written an opera that was being produced and honored with a command performance was the most interesting detail anyone had ever told me about her, or any woman, for that matter. I had never once heard of a woman composer before this. In every respect she took on the aspect of a creature of myth. And part of the myth, I recalled, was that she was ugly.

The Comtesse had said of her, as we parted ways, She is very quixotic, very whimsical. She may even meet you at the station! You will see her right away, she is famously ugly, but she really is very well dressed.

I'd forgotten this detail until I saw the caricature, and so I asked the tenor, Is she really as ugly as they say?

You will have to decide for yourself, the tenor said. This was debated in the papers at the time of her debut, I understand — was she beautiful or not, and did this affect her art? He laughed. Once you know her, she's lovely, however. And you will know her instantly when you meet her. You will see. She is very correct in her appearance, very elegant, he noted. I think she is a beauty — a beauty like a queen out of legend is a beauty, he said. And as she is the ruler of this world of music, that, at least, is true.

We rode on in silence a little more and he said, As a girl, she was cursed to be the younger sister of a great singer who was also a great beauty. Maria Malibran. Those who've seen both will say Pauline is the greater singer, but not in front of her. Maria died very young, and Pauline, she worshipped her. He paused and then said, When people say she is ugly, they mean she is not her sister — a debased cruelty, I think. And Pauline knows she is not her only too well.

At this, the carriage made its way onto Fremersbergstrasse, her street.

Pauline came down to greet us at her gate as we arrived, waving cheerfully, and I understood what the tenor meant at once. In her presence I was embarrassed to have asked my question. She was handsome and queenly indeed — she radiated a magnetic authority. Her thick dark hair was worn close to her head that day and pulled back at her neck in the plain style of a busy woman, but it flattered her beautiful brow. Her eyes were large and dark, lit with a mischievous intelligence, and they seemed to comprise nearly half of her face, though I think it was mostly because they were entrancing. The mouth was generous and expressive, her chin soft, her nose oddly smaller when you faced her than in profile, but this can be one of the physiognomic signs, I know now from her, of a powerful singing instrument.

And with that instrument, she could speak and sing in French, Russian, Italian, German, Spanish, and English, what she jokingly called her salad of tongues. She could accompany herself as she sang with the impeccable force of a virtuoso and had been, as her father and sister before her, a legend in all the capitals of Europe. She had retired at the height of her fame after a successful run seven years earlier in Paris, singing in Gluck's *Orphée et Eurydice,* and now she was one of the most distinguished music teachers alive, as well as a woman composer. Over time, it seems to me, people called her ugly because they felt they needed one thing to be counted against her brilliance.

The question of beauty in a woman, as a result, amused her greatly, as I saw when she greeted me.

Ah, they've sent me the *cocotte* I ordered at last, she said, after the curtsy I made for her. She held my hands and took me in. You're so beautiful they'll come just to see you walk on the stage. But we will make sure they hear you also.

I stood before her in the general's coat, worn over my poplin, the ruby flower pinned to my chest like a medal. She tugged at my coat's cuffs and then looked to my four trunks—the one from the Comtesse, the three from the tenor. I'd not seen them lined up this way until now as the driver and footman set them down.

And you've brought costumes for us all, she teased.

I blushed, embarrassed—I'd imagined my luggage modest—but then I saw the humor of it and saw her wait for me to find it. This endeared her to me, and any apprehensions I had about her vanished in front of her immediately. Whether or not I knew her, as the tenor had put it, I knew I belonged to her and would do anything she asked.

She winked. Come, my dear. Let's get you inside.

And you, she said to the tenor. You rogue. When did I last see you? Was it in Leipzig with Liszt? And what will you do with yourself while she studies? Where are we to put you?

He gestured to the air. I'm sure there's something here that requires my attention, he said.

My *Haustheater*, I'm sure, she said, with a proud lift of her head. We sometimes need a tenor to sing across from the girls. Perhaps you'll do.

~

Her *Haustheater* was really two houses side by side—her villa, where she lived with her husband, Louis, and Villa Turgenev next door, built for Turgenev. The two sat close to each other away from their neighbors at the end of the road. They made for a strange pair: the Viardot villa looked to be of a piece with its neighbors down the road, but Turgenev's villa was newer, built soon after Pauline and her husband had moved to Baden-Baden, and had the appearance of a strangely new French château but in the old French style. Her traditional German villa seemed to be keeping time with a French stranger who'd snuck out of the forest, acting as if he'd always been there.

Turgenev himself was entirely at home, however, as I discovered when, on entering Pauline's villa, we found him taking a late cup of tea in her parlor. He stood, surprised to see us, and greeted us in impeccable French as Pauline tutted at him for being at his leisure with guests arriving. Mistaking him for Pauline's husband, I greeted him as Monsieur Viardot, and he laughed, if a little ruefully, and corrected me.

Mademoiselle, he said, I am Ivan Turgenev, at your disposal.

Turgenev had already become the beautiful giant I would know him as for the rest of his life, his long white hair and beard giving him a mystical appearance, as if he were the last of a great race, and this mystique was added to by his strangely high voice, startling in a man of his size. He was dressed simply and elegantly in a dark suit and white shirt, as he would be, I would soon see, every day. The white beard, in particular, glowed, lighting his face; but much like Pauline's, his eyes took you in, though his projected a calm, conquering kindness—of course you will love me, they seemed to say, and I will love you.

He saw my embarrassment at my mistake, and as Pauline introduced me—*Lilliet Berne, may I present the great Russian writer Ivan Turgenev*—he deftly turned the conversation to my toilette, complimenting me on making such an elegant first appearance in their home, and then admired my general's coat, even inquiring after the fur in my collar. But the sound of my old name had surprised me —now at least I knew whose name was on that paper—and with that, I understood why Pauline had not asked my name at her gate —she had simply greeted me as if we already knew each other, as had I. Nervous, tired, unsure of my French suddenly, with not one wit about me, I touched the collar—I had never once thought of the animal who'd given its life for the coat's trim—and said, *Lapinard?* And he laughed, and as soon as he laughed, I knew I had mixed rabbit, *lapin,* and fox, *renard,* inventing a word and an animal by my mistake.

Ah, he said. *La peinard?* Or, better, you should be La Peinard. We should all be *les peinards.* I apparently already am, he said, gesturing to his teacup as Pauline continued mock-scowling at him and I smiled through my embarrassment. Please, he said, forgive my casual manners and be welcome here.

This pun, *la peinard,* if it meant anything, meant "the relaxed one," and this did have the effect of putting me at ease—and Lapinard would become what he called me for as long as I knew him.

I then noticed a giant black pointer dog lying curled on the rug by the sofa. He raised himself up mistrustfully as we talked and fixed me with a glittering eye.

This is Pegasus, and he only loves women, Turgenev warned the tenor, as the dog rose and came over to us and the tenor reached out to pet him. All women except for Pauline, strangely, he added.

Pauline only laughed at this as Pegasus came to me and pushed his nose into my hand.

He has kissed your hand, see? Pauline said. Now you are made welcome as I never will be. Come with me, I'll show you to your rooms.

And with that, she left her own house through the rear. The tenor and I looked to each other with a surprised smile and then followed her into the garden.

However interesting I had found it that Pauline was a woman composer, I found the mystery of the conjoined houses and lives, the apparent *marriage à trois* at the heart of this kingdom, even more fascinating as we passed through Pauline's garden to the gate in her wall and then walked through to Turgenev's villa from the back.

We climbed a set of stone stairs to a placid terrace lawn, where we found a fountain with a stone Nereid at her ease in the center, water playfully pouring down her face from the tiny dolphin perched on her head. Yellow and red leaves skated on the water's surface, blown by the wind. We entered through the back door, as if we had been here all along and had only stepped out for the air.

Pauline moved here with much the same authority and ease Turgenev had shown in her parlor. We passed through the main salon, where three men cheerfully greeted us as they struggled to hang a long green velvet curtain across the middle of the room. There will be a performance here in your honor before dinner, Pauline said, as she led us by quickly, a playful smile on her face as we took the stairs.

We came to a stop in the upstairs hall, where our hostess directed each of us to rooms opposite each other with the faintest smile. Dinner will be served after the performance, across the way, she said. We will gather in the salon in approximately two hours. Please refresh yourself, and I will have tea sent up for you both if you'd like to take it here.

We thanked her; she smiled as she took her leave. The tenor stepped into his rooms and winked at me as he closed his door, as if we were fiancés to be kept separate before marriage. With that, to my surprise, I was left alone in the hall.

I went into my rooms and closed the door as well.

~

I'd not been alone once since being presented to the tenor at the end of his *Il Trovatore,* and the placid cheer I'd worn until now fell off me like a cape. No one to insist I speak to them, no need to remember who I was as I spoke, no need to feign pleasure or interest or knowledge of a language. The advantages to my new circumstances were still making their case to me, but the shock of losing the hopes I'd had from before my capture — my desire to set myself up with a little room, to find a teacher at the Conservatoire, and to wait and find my composer again in the spring — this had stayed trapped within me and still flew along my nerves, electric and unanswered, even as his example of my naïveté mocked me. Worse in some way than the future I'd never have was to contemplate the past I might have prevented.

I was going to bring you here to her before you left, the tenor had said so lightly. I could no longer ignore that little sentence. My escape, my time spent with the Comtesse, the Empress, the escape from Compiègne, all of it for nothing, then, if he told the truth — all of it for nothing, or for one thing. One man.

These rooms, like the rest of what I had seen, were nothing like I'd imagined. At first, I was puzzled to see there was no bed and then understood I was in the sitting room to a small suite. A fireplace glowed with a fire, newly set, blazing crisply. I went to warm myself at it and took in the rest of my surroundings — a dark wood writing desk and chair by one of the two windows and a bedroom with a dressing room, visible through a far doorway. Two green velvet chairs and a small couch kept watch over the fire, with small tables for I did not know what—all of it anticipated a kind of leisurely attitude I could not remember ever having taken toward my life.

The bedroom, set back from the sitting room, was very grand, the bed hidden under a canopy hung with thick velvet brocade drapes of a deeper green than the chairs. Across from the bed was a washstand and vanity with a petite chair and a tassel discretely dangling by the vanity mirror to ring for assistance. At this, I briefly felt the duty to watch out for the lady who would dress herself here until I reminded myself she would be me.

The trunks had already been delivered, set like little coffins in their place beside the dressing room's armoire.

I found I waited to see if the door would open, the tenor bursting in with plans or demands, or if he would lock me in with a key Pauline had somehow provided him secretly. But the lock stayed silent.

I opened the door and looked out again into the hallway and the stairs, and then to the tenor's door. The keyhole glowed with the late afternoon light—he was not even so much as watching me through it. I put my ear to the keyhole carefully—an eye might reflect light whereas an ear would not—and the faint murmur of his distant snore told me he was already asleep, taking a nap.

This was how much he believed he did not have to lock my door. And that I would stay as he rested.

I slipped carefully to the top of the stairs.

I was truly a guest, then. A guest of honor, no less, the welcome protégée of the celebrated tenor. Of course. Of course they would make a fuss over him, and of course they would make a fuss over me as well. The performance in our honor! Pauline was greeting me, greeting us both, with even more attention than the tenor had predicted, the tenor who seemed delighted at the prospect of joining her *Haustheater* and the newest endeavors of her famous family troupe. And this confused me—was he really here only to look after me? And yet, if so, why was his door still closed and he asleep?

I could walk out, go downstairs, at will. Ask to take my tea in the parlor.

Leave for the station.

I had already plotted one escape, done as Pauline led us through the garden to our rooms. I could claim exhaustion, stay in my room, and, as the performance began, leave for town with the emerald earrings and the rose pin and find a jeweler there I was sure would give me an excellent price, perhaps even better than in Paris, given the casinos. Between out-of-luck courtesans and suitors eager to impress, I was sure the jewelers here did a brisk trade. I could hire a carriage that might take me directly back to Paris that night, I was sure of it. With the tenor asleep, the temptation, tired as I was, was to leave for the jeweler's now.

I could make an excuse, a need to shop for the evening's event, or affect some eccentric desire to be fulfilled in the town beforehand. By the time the tenor woke, I could be on a train headed anywhere. Though for now there was only one place that mattered.

Still, even as it amused me to think of the Comtesse at the Café Anglais watching as some other woman, fresh from Baden-Baden and dressed in her earrings, walked across the room, I wondered how far I could go before I was stopped. Before the Comtesse discovered my betrayal, before the mechanism she had set in place caught me. To go now, provided I could stay hidden, would turn Paris into a lonely vigil, and me in it with a single task: hoping to see my composer sometime before the spring, otherwise waiting until then for the Bal Mabille to reopen. If I left now, all I would leave with would be my freedom, and only for as long as I remained far from Paris, far from all of France, Germany, Italy—and I was not sure this was enough.

The only real escape, it seemed, was to go through with this to the end.

The house began to fill with the sounds of scales being played on a piano and a woman singer's voice warming up. I guessed she could only be Pauline.

I returned to my room and closed the door, locking it myself.

～

I opened one of the trunks, curious to see what had been brought from the avenue de l'Opéra and if any of it would be suitable for the evening's performance. A fragrance of lavender and bay escaped, and I felt a pang of loneliness—this fragrance would always make me lonely. All had been carefully folded in papers and laid with sachets. A deck of cards sat on top, strange to me until I recognized it as the deck Doro and Lucy had used in our games.

I picked the deck up.

Had those two packed this, then? Where were they now?

The hardest part of service is that when you serve you are a custodian of something the master or mistress you serve cannot bear or they would do it and you would not be there. The cooking, the cleaning, the lighting of a fire. The taking off and putting on of clothes. Sometimes you served their loneliness or an exotic appetite, impossible or forbidden until your arrival. Whatever it is, ordinary or obscure, it becomes the center of your life, requiring all of you.

And you must bear it, this thing they cannot bear—and, in turn, bear what you become as you do so.

That first night on the avenue de l'Opéra so long ago, when I crept into the kitchen, lonely, hoping to surprise my maids at cards, I wanted to explain I was no lady to be waited on, even if the three of us were made to pretend it was so—that I was a servant, too. Yet when they let me sit and play, I knew they only humored me, and we played a lonely game. To receive the cards now told me they understood my meaning at last.

I gave the deck a little kiss and set it down on the writing desk.

This would make this easier to bear, but what exactly did I now bear? I was now both the secret and the keeper of it, but the idea that I could not know what it was I served, nor why, nor who, became nearly unendurable all at once. And why *was* he here, my tenor friend, and not in Paris? Why had he been trained around me this way and I around him? What did he serve that he also could not see?

I went to the window and opened the shutters to see the view. The sun had begun to set, the sky darkening. A stream gleamed silver in the distance, visible at the edge of the meadow that began past Turgenev's garden wall, but his gardens were blue with shadow.

From here I could see how fine the garden was and the true size of it. The grounds extended well past the corner through which we'd passed—for watching the Nereid fountain as I'd approached, I'd missed the pond below it farther down the hill, lined with stone walls and speckled with golden drifts of new-fallen leaves and, here and there, water lilies. A few leaves still clung to the branches of the trees like tongues of flame to a fire that was almost out.

I no longer felt as if I were onstage in a play unknown to me —I knew this play—this opera—*Il Trovatore*. From the moment I had left on this journey with the tenor, I knew what Pauline's letter to him had joked of as we arrived—I was his Leonora-to-be. He wanted me to sing her part opposite him; it was clearly the reason he'd had me brought to see him at the Théâtre-Italien. He had wanted this of me perhaps since he first met me. And I did want to sing it at last, just not to him as my *trovatore*. I would never sing it to him; I meant to keep the vow I made that night I first knew I would ever want to sing it. And yet this was precisely what he hoped for most. I was not his Leonora, I could never be, but for my own sake I would now need to be. And in the meantime, around us, the world seemed to take on the shape of the opera. Pauline for our Gypsy, and here a garden in which I could hope someday to see my lost love emerge from the trees and serenade me.

All was almost ready. All this lacked for was the composer, in a mask and cape, singing below my window, the tenor hidden and waiting to challenge him to a duel.

Our little tragedy.

If this were an opera, I knew, it would end with my being forced to play the role I had vowed not to play as the audience reflected on the hubris of my vow.

Victory, defeat, victory, defeat, victory, defeat.

Before I could ever hope to fear that an opera role would control my life if I took it up, I feared this role already controlled me, choosing me before I chose it, as if the opera hid some god of the ancients inside it, determined to make me his plaything. This was no punishment, no price to be paid, this hand was not my mother's God, nor her ghost, nor did it seem providential—the spiritual mechanisms I knew or feared previously were not engaged here. This was something else altogether, determined and intent on its own satisfactions.

Whatever the tenor wanted from me by way of making me his Leonora, on stage with him or in life, it seemed all of this was a mask for some other force now grinning out from behind him.

I had gotten more than Fate's attention, then—I was its plaything.

It is a peculiar thing to reach this conclusion, that a god has taken your life in hand. The sensation is not what people might imagine; it is not magic, nor is it a haunting, nor is it a miracle—there's no storm of roses, no whistle that can put a raging ocean to sleep, no figure in the mirror besides your own. Instead, the terms are stark. You may or may not leave with your life. You sense your world changed into a stage set for something done to teach only you. You do not feel mad, only very alone, for the scale of the event is so ridiculous no one else will believe you and so no one else will help you—and to say aloud what you are going through will sound like madness, and your god wants this. Your god wants you to be abandoned by all others, for your god has done this so he can be alone with you, and he is waiting.

But even then I knew, as puny as you are, your one consolation, should you be chosen by Fate, is that the god who chose you will feel the need to speak with you at the end.

No god teaches a lesson without this.

All of this, of course, is a prelude to some final transformation, one that begins in earnest once you push away thoughts of lessons and gods and their desires, and tell yourself you are mad to believe it and thus place yourself the more firmly in its grasp. But this last I did not yet know, and so I told myself I was mad to believe any of it, to even think of it, and I opened the window as if, in doing so, I could let all of these thoughts out.

The wind came in instead, so fiercely that the fire guttered behind me and the wind and sudden smoke together conspired and
brought more tears to my eyes, but this time I let them stay — the
wind slammed the shutters against the walls and threatened to
shatter the glass if I let go for even a moment. The noise was such
that I feared someone would come to see what the matter was, and
yet I hoped they would not, for now I gave in and fully wept. There
was a pleasure to it, even to the wind blowing through my suite, the
smoke, and the banging shutters — all of me, for a moment, aligned,
was honest, an emotion and my reaction matched. This consoled
me, and as I sank into it, I found the grief beneath it, submerged
until now, some deeper colder current underneath.

The woods below beckoned. They looked as if they led all the
way to those other woods — as if, were I to enter, I could follow
them and emerge on the other side of that mountain in that other
garden, that last night in Compiègne — where I could slip down the
days between now and then as if they were the backstairs to the
world and to time itself, where I might find my composer coming on
his way here to my window. Drawn in by the same power that had
put me here, until he stood, below my window, in a salute.

How we all want to be Leonora. To go to the garden and find the
love we thought lost to us singing his way out of the dark, having
survived the war.

How had Leonora done this, living on just a single memory of
one love over the years while another suitor made his case to her
daily there in her own castle? I had been braver in Paris, with my
fantasies of returning to him at the Bal Mabille, but now, by the
edge of the Black Forest, I foundered. I wanted to see him that very
night. While I did not know how to leave this room, I did not know
how to stay, either. I knew it would destroy me to go to him that
night as I wanted to, uncertain even of finding him; but the thought
of staying here and thus somehow fating him to be the one to come
here and die at the tenor's hands, sealing him into this strange game
of destiny, wasn't this sending him to his death? And my own?

The only way to save him from that fate was to leave here before it came true. If this was what I feared it was, he should never come, never walk out of that forest; it was too dangerous. If there was a way to warn him that he should not come for me should his circumstances ever conspire . . . But this was the madness I spoke of before —I knew it even as I thought of it—even if I knew how to reach him, it would be a madwoman's letter. He would not believe it. He might even try to come here to convince me it was not true and thus bring it all to fruition.

Where, to that end, would a letter find him? Where did he reside, and was he safe or in danger, a captive like me? If our little moment in the night had made me so valuable, he, under the direct caresses of the Empress, would have become much more so. Did she keep him in an apartment the way the tenor kept me or was there a golden cage, brought from palace to palace, in secret? Or a cave beneath Compiègne guarded by assassins? He was almost certainly a kept man or a prisoner, or both, and whichever was true, he would not be at the Bal Mabille come spring no matter what I hoped—his days of playing for whatever they paid were behind him. I knew from the Majeurs-Plaisirs of a house much like ours nearby, full entirely of men, and their clientele also almost entirely men, though it was said a few wealthy women availed themselves of them as well. I had never once tried to imagine this, but now I did, the composer at a piano in a salon, playing and waiting, amid laughter and champagne . . .

But the Empress would never risk such a thing, she in a domino on some velvet chaise looking on as others drank merrily around them both. She would never do this. His quarters were likely even more mysterious than any of this, and the more hidden.

There was only the very slightest chance he was still free. And if he would be there in Paris, at the Mabille come spring, the dream of our reunion would likely conclude with my being caught by the Comtesse's agents, or the Emperor's, or the Empress's; and if any of them had not found him before this, I would lead them to him just by going to him.

How stupid I'd been to dream of it.

This world is not made for us to be together came the thought.

More ordinary ways of losing him intruded. I could lose him to another woman, or I had already lost him, or I was only a bit of fun in the garden to him; and all of this was only some ridiculous fever dream—the dream of a prisoner. All of the scenarios I imagined, extraordinary and ordinary both, ended with us apart.

The wind blew even harder as these scenes proceeded in front of my mind's eye. *I have gone mad*, I told myself, this final self-betrayal, unforeseen and bitter—more bitter than the others. But as the wind surged, that sense of madness ebbed, and what returned was the very real feeling of the outline of that god's hand, as if the wind were the very heel of that hand pressed to my face.

I was not mad.

If I can be with him, let me be with him, I said, into the fingers of the wind. *Make me your plaything; do as you will. But do not give me all of this and not him as well. Do not make him the price I must pay; I will not pay it.*

I waited, fearful for a moment, as if I might hear a response. *And how would I refuse?* I wondered to myself. I knew only that I would. And I knew only one way that I could. This little game would end if this Leonora died before her lover's capture.

I will not pay it, I said again. *I will pay some other price.*

As if in answer, one last monstrous gust of wind blew so that the fire behind me was snuffed and I nearly let the windows go, but then it left as suddenly, leaving the air strangely still. Frightened, I shut the windows and fastened them. I made to close the shutters as the sun went behind the mountains, the sky darkening all at once like a lamp blown out, and as I did, the fire in the grate returned to light the room so that the view outside was obscured by my reflection, looking much as I had that day at the train station in Compiègne.

I have told you that I kept the general's coat from that fateful journey because it suited me, and it did; and I have said I kept it because it was warm, and it was. But there was another reason, of course, one I was only faintly aware of myself until I saw myself reflected here—I'd kept it because it reminded me of him. This

was the coat I'd worn that evening when my escape brought me to
him, the night I'd decided the only path back to him led away from
him first. It seemed lucky to keep it, as if wearing it had a magic
that could help me find my way to him again—as if it could keep
us both safe until he could take it from my shoulders again. That
night, when he'd leapt out of the woods and landed in front of me,
he could have landed anywhere, anywhere at all, but instead, he was
there, as was I, and I could not have made my way there dressed any
other way. When I wore this coat, I felt confident the spell survived,
confident of moving to his side like some slow arrow shot through
the dark by Cupid himself, that tiny marksman. I would find him, I
would; I just needed to be patient and wait.

I touched the window's glass with my hand.

I could still feel those threads I was sure connected us, heavy in
the growing night, hidden there. I could still feel their pull.

The nocturne I thought of as his began then, the music thread-
ing its way up from below in the salon. I recognized this with a
shock and went out into the hall and halfway down the stairs before
I saw, through the curving archway, Pauline, still at the piano, her
slender neck pale in the dark.

Pauline who, as I could see, loved this nocturne, too—she played
it with an absorption that my own listening sought to match even as
I stood by the door full of fear.

What sign was this, amid my other signs and portents—was this
a cruelty, as it seemed to me at first—mocking me and my fears
—or a doom, my strange god's way of saying there could be no bargain, or the opposite—a parley, even a mercy? A promise? I stayed
in the doorway and listened, for there was nowhere to be until she
was finished; and slowly, note by note, the tumult ended, the spell
broke, and all thoughts of meanings, signs, and omens left until
there remained only her and the goodness of her, a charm against
these fears, and the nocturne.

And him. He was there, just for a moment, an apparition in
the air before me as surely as if he'd stepped from a carriage in the

drive. The sound of the remaining grape leaves rattling above us in the wind. His face silver in the moonlight, his finger as he touched my lips. And then gone.

How will I survive this? I asked myself. To come all this way had taken so much from me.

The pleasure of eavesdropping on a musician, Pauline said then, is in how there's a performance possible sometimes when you believe no one is listening, one that should be offered to the world and yet may never be because it vanishes once the musician is aware of a listener.

She said this without raising her head. She had known I was there.

The sense of bravery and purpose I felt that night returned to me, and I met her gaze confidently as she closed the piano and stood to face me, smiling.

And yet this is what we must summon to ourselves as we play or sing. We must bring that out. Hello, my new friend, she said. Is everything well?

I nodded. Never better, I said. What is that you were playing just now? I asked.

A lovely form of music called a nocturne, she said. Named for the night. It seemed appropriate to play it just now as the night begins to fall. What did you think of it?

I thought so. It's . . . I think it's one of the finest pieces of music I've ever heard, I said.

You know it! I think so, too. It was written by a very good friend of mine, a composer by the name of Chopin. He was not at his best in concerts; it drove his fans to despair. You had to catch him unawares, she said, and waved her hand at me. A surprise audience but hidden, and so I have many fond memories of sitting outside a music room as he played alone. I think this is the best way one can listen to Chopin, as you did just now. We have guests arriving in an hour, will you be ready?

Yes, I said.

I noticed he brought you here without a maid but with all those trunks! My own is quite busy, I'm afraid, but I will find someone to assist you.

Thank you, I said, and returned to my room to wait, where I stood by the window, looking out into the dark garden again.

What luck, what luck it was that had put me here, a welcome guest in their celebrated company. And yet the one feeling stranger to me than being unable to rescue myself from an unlocked room was my growing sense, as I listened to her, that I did not want to be rescued—not from this. The menace I'd previously ascribed to her and whatever this school of hers would be was gone, and in its place was the feeling that I did not want to leave, perhaps ever. As Pauline returned to her careful vocalizes, and I heard the sure-footed power in her voice as it ran its paces, I recognized that her voice had some of the timbre and qualities of my own—a sense of recognition I'd not had previously. Before I'd had even a single lesson with her, I knew, now that I was here, I would do well not to leave her side, not until I was finished learning everything she could teach me. I'd never met a woman like Pauline and had met her at a time when I feared not one woman like her existed in all the world. In some way I had never known how to express, I'd feared I would have to become the first of my kind, whatever my kind was, should I be allowed to survive—that which history has never seen before. Instead, here Pauline lived; she had done what I feared I would have to do and now lived as the most liberated woman I'd ever met in a world she'd sung into existence with a voice much like my own. And whether or not she could teach me to sing with this strange voice of mine, I wanted to learn how to *be* like her as much as possible, and so I did not feel like a captive now. I felt saved. To leave would mean leaving this education undone.

Yes, I could stay until after tonight, or I could stay until the spring. Or I could stay until she was done with me. I knew already what I would choose.

For now, the price was the performance I was to take up again, waiting for me in the trunks by the dressing room; I had a few more moments before the tenor roused himself and it would begin again. I poured water into the washbasin at the table and began to gently wash my face with a cloth. The strange pity I'd felt earlier for the tenor returned — and while it was strange to think of him as the innocent in this, he was; and the more I did think of him this way, the more that pity began to change, though I was not yet aware of it or what it meant.

Pity, which, it should be said, is the ambassador of love. And it grows only from a position of power. And I did feel powerful, at last, as I sat, shook out my hair, and, with a fine new hairbrush found waiting among my parcels in that first trunk, began to brush my hair flat. I felt as powerful as if I'd already escaped into my heart's desire.

One day I would leave him, and I would not explain. Whether I left with a summons to go at once to the Emperor's side or because I'd earned my eventual freedom, either way I knew I would leave and he would never know, and he could never know, this was among the conditions. And if I did my best, he, in turn, would protect me and more. He would need to believe on waking what he believed as he slept there across the hall, and he would need to believe it constantly, so that he would never see the moment when it came. *There should be no falseness to it*, I told myself, as I prepared to put my hair back up.

What I did next, I would do every night after. *Whenever you think of the one, think of the other*, I told myself. *This is how you will survive.* And so I built a secret second heart inside my heart, a little theater full with my memories of my real love, such as they were — a gilded cage for him made of this music, the torch in the night, the music room in a palace. All of it would be hidden at the center of the other heart, the one I'd always had, now an alias as surely as the name I had given the world. There was a secret door, of course, hidden by a view of chestnut trees gold with autumn in the afternoon sun.

I recalled the two of them as they were that night at the ball when they performed together, when I watched, hidden, until the Princess Metternich scared me away. My true love and my false one. If I could see that memory each time I saw the tenor, I could smile as I ought to, touch his neck as I ought to; I would behave entirely like the lover he believed was here, and I would travel safely to my true love on the other side of these days before me.

Wherever the Empress still kept him, this was his home with me.

~

The garden was dark now, the night too dark to see anything more from the window. A knock came at the door, and so I set down my brush and opened it.

I was not the first *cocotte* to arrive. There were at least three others, my classmates, and all beautiful, if differently, and more beautiful than I, or so it seemed to me that first day. They appeared in my doorway, haughty like cats and arranged by color, from dark to light, brunette, lighter brunette, and blond, and introduced themselves. They were Natalya, Firéne, and Maxine, Russian, Hungarian, and French, respectively. They resembled one another, dressed alike in simple dark jackets, skirts of wool tweed, and plain white blouses. No visible crinolines. Sensible dark leather shoes peeped from under their hems.

I was a flare of color in front of them while they were like a tidy squadron.

We openly stared at one another at first. I had supposed there would be other students, but I didn't yet expect them.

Mademoiselle, Natalya, the brunette, said, Madame Viardot sent us to introduce ourselves and to see if you needed any assistance. She saw you came without a maid, and her own is quite busy with preparations for tonight. At this, they half curtsied together, and I half curtsied back. Natalya, I noticed, held a tray with the tea.

Thank you, I said. Please, call me Lilliet. Come in.

Natalya and Firéne entered but Maxine lingered in the door. You look as if you came for the casinos, Maxine said. What an exquisite toilette. May I ask where it is from?

Félix, I said.

Your father sends you to Félix? He must be very rich. Are you from Paris, then?

I suppose I am, I said, cautious. For I could tell I was entirely unprepared for this interview. The tenor was so incurious, he had never asked me questions of this kind, had never sought to know me because he felt he knew me at once — I was for him that love with the power of a prophecy. And he was so sure, he'd never bothered to see who he had captured under the cloak of his fantasy.

But then, I could be said to be incurious, too, as to my captor. Perhaps they would be incurious also, I hoped. They then proved they were not.

I am from Paris, Maxine said. And I've never been to Félix; my family refused me when I asked. Are these all Félix? She gestured to the trunks as we made our way back to the dressing room. Your father sent you from Paris and to Félix for clothes first? What family are you from?

I am an orphan, I said, attempting to begin here by telling at least one truth.

Ah. An heiress, then. What is your *Fach*? Natalya is a mezzo, Firéne, a spinto. I am a coloratura. What of you?

A Falcon.

Falcon?

Tragic, I said. But with more strength in the top notes, I'm told.

Of course, Maxine said. Our orphan. You were born to it. Tragedy belongs to you.

She said this watching my eyes as if she were testing the edge of a blade on me. And so I made sure not to flinch.

We were conducting our conversation in French — the Viardots were quite German in many ways after their time here, I would soon see, but this colony of theirs was a French colony, if a tiny one — and so I had used the word *orpheline* just now. I'd never described myself this way to anyone and found I liked the word — *orpheline* sounded to me like something mystical and small, like an enchanted cat.

In the years that would follow this day, when asked questions of this kind about my family, I would tell the story I began to tell that day of a family in Lucerne struck down by misfortune. My being sent to Paris to be raised there by an aunt. I tried to make it sound as terrible and vague as possible, as I did that day, and to use this word I liked, *orpheline*, almost a new name.

Behind me, Natalya and Firéne had already begun examining the contents of my trunks so I went and joined them to see if I could prevent them from discovering something unwelcome. Natalya was holding a pair of my cancan shoes up with a smile.

Have you made your debut? Natalya asked. And in what role?

Not yet, I said, though I have been in Paris, training privately. Perhaps to debut as Lucia.

I glimpsed what could only be my perfume bottle's case and brought it up, setting it on my dressing table.

Eau du Lubin? Maxine said, and came closer.

I opened the leather enclosure and took out the bottle, quickly brushing my neck and ears with it and then my throat before I replaced it as if I hadn't noticed her interest.

This? I then said to her. Yes.

I'd not mixed much with her kind previously. She was the first I was to meet of a kind of Frenchwoman of the haute bourgeoisie, constantly aware of her social class and yours. She was quite the opposite of incurious, and her interest was not the beginning of a friendship but more of a measuring. She was the sort of woman whose husband would go to the Majeurs-Plaisirs to be away from her before and after marriage. She and I would not usually meet, and so we did not know how to speak to each other when we did.

Who performs tonight? I asked.

We do, they said, in unison.

They began to speak to me of who would be there, and why, who knew whom, who could provide what for you vis-à-vis an entrée into this or that salon and so on; the salon gossip of Baden-Baden, but also of Berlin, and of Paris, and even of Saint Petersburg. Giulia Grisi was coming, I was told, a famous soprano in retirement on her way to Berlin from her home in Florence. Brahms was to be there, he was working on a song Pauline was to debut. Royal titles were mentioned, meaningless to me. Through the talk, I noticed that they were not so very alike in appearance, not at all, but rather the similarity came from an attitude inside, the faintest sense of some indomitable will; each was animated by the belief that they mattered and that their futures would matter as well.

They were all like little Paulines in this way, as I hoped to be soon.

We must choose your dress tonight, Natalya said, eyeing the trunks.

As various toilettes were held up and considered and taken from their papers, Maxine continued her patter of observant and condescending resentments, somewhat confusing, for she was still quite actively helping me all the same, a task I knew she saw as beneath her. She seemed both scornful and jealous, handing items to Firéne and Natalya as if they worked for her, and I didn't know why she was leading the unpacking until I understood she did it for what she hoped to find. I was most likely about to be exposed. All that would be required was for her to find something I'd forgotten about, some incontrovertible proof—much as I knew her kind, I was sure she knew mine.

The door across the hall opened then, and the tenor emerged to see who had come to visit, knocking on my door and calling my name. My trio abandoned me to go meet the famous tenor, and I finished dressing alone. I chose the opera dress I'd once scorned, one of my first, the dark blue with the machine-embroidered bodice, fine but not too fine for a night in a private home. I called for Natalya—I'd liked her right away—and she helped me fasten the back. She returned, and as I entered, I saw how they tried to test themselves on him. His celebrity, his previous relationship to Pauline, his good looks, any of these would have made him desirable, and I could see they envied and even resented me a little for whatever fortune it was that had brought him to me.

Please, I nearly said to them. Do your best.

I wondered, if I were to meet him now, if I would flirt with him and then remembered the night I'd first met him when I nearly had. That was the smile I used as I walked to his side, and he took my hand, smiling back, and kissed it, his eyes only for me. Which I did all while not looking once at Maxine, so she would know; I had my edges, too.

~

The Théâtre du Thiergarten, as it was called in the handwritten program we were given later as we entered the salon that evening, announced it was proud to present *Le Dernier Sorcier*, an operetta by Ivan Turgenev and Pauline Viardot-García, as if it could do anything else. The room had been transformed since my earlier visit. The enormous green curtain confidently divided the salon, behind which oleander branches painted white peeped at the top. A fire was set in the fireplace, and the elegant chandelier lit, both somehow aloof to the curtain's provocation. A beautiful piano sat directly under the chandelier at the room's center and was lit by a lamp as well. The effect was a kind of suspenseful charm. If the forest beside Turgenev's villa that led up into the mountains was magical, the entrance to that magic forest seemed to be here, behind the curtain.

The salon was the heart of the house, much greater in height than the other rooms, almost like a chapel, and faintly visible from here were the library and dining room. The audience was a small one, intimate—perhaps twenty or thirty people—and distinguished. The tenor was quickly busy in an animated conversation with the Prussian ambassador to the Baden-Baden court, and no sooner had I said hello, in a halting German, but I was introduced to Giulia Grisi, the famous retired soprano my fellow students had spoken of, who asked for us to be excused, drew me away, and sat me down beside her with a proprietary air. She told me she was visiting with Pauline, who'd told her all about me, and how excited she was to hear me after I'd finished my training. I love a Falcon voice, she said. Her interest in me bewildered me, and I tried to understand it as she went on about how she lived mostly in Florence but loved Germany and Pauline's Baden-Baden set, and came often. She was a formidable woman, if not a tall one, with the appraising air of an assassin that vanished only when she smiled. Her dark hair sat in a severe crown of braids coiled on her head. Her black velvet gown, trimmed in black lace, nearly made her seem to be in mourning except I could not imagine her wearing anything else. She looked as if she might be an aunt to the Comtesse, and I was sure they knew each other—now she was admiring the tenor's figure, telling me how handsome he must have been onstage at the Théâtre-Italien, and wasn't I proud? I nodded and said I was.

Christmas is very charming in the Black Forest, she said, and patted my hand with hers. You must be sure to be here if you do not have plans. The way they celebrate it, one can imagine Christ being born again just to see for himself.

I said I would.

I'd not thought of a Christmas in some time. The idea was strange to me, as strange as choosing where to spend the holiday, all of it entirely alien. I'd spent exactly one Christmas in the Cajun Maidens—I recalled mulled wine that night in the food tent, and goose, as I recalled, and a tree lit with candles at the center of the wagons—and then it seemed as if I had not celebrated it since, except I must have. But the record of my time since then seemed not to reach all the way here, as if it had been cut somehow. My dress felt correct, though, and this reassured me: it was fancy enough to make me presentable without making me too much of an outsider, not so much with the other guests as with the other students, who had vanished, no doubt to prepare. I was anxious to adapt as quickly as I could to the prevailing culture of the household, though as I sat there, I was very aware I still wore my crinolines—a dress made for them would look woefully deflated without them, it seemed to me.

I would need new clothes, and I made the note to myself even as Giulia, who'd been examining the tableau in front of us, returned her attention to me.

How fortunate you are to be about to begin your training with Pauline, she said.

I nodded.

How fortunate indeed. I think I might have sung longer if I'd had her as my teacher, she said. But who can say. What a life it is, she said. You will never know each day if the voice is any good until you begin your practice. Each morning could announce the end. But I shouldn't frighten you, forgive me, she said.

What do you do when it leaves? I asked.

She held her hands up, palms facing up, and gestured to the scene around us with a smile. You see friends, she said. Be sure to have friends. And if you are lucky, you can give a farewell concert. But sometimes there is no chance, not if the voice goes quickly— for you want to be remembered at your best, always. Nothing less can do.

A wand tapped against the piano's music stand, and then there were three knocks on the floor behind the curtain. The crowd went silent, and the curtain parted for Pauline, who smiled as we applauded. She then announced that the evening's performance was to be dedicated to her guests of honor, and would we please stand and be welcomed. I waited for the tenor to stand first, and he was greeted with much affection and a few shouts, and then he gestured to me, and I stood also as my name was said, and Pauline announced I was her newest student. I waved as I had seen my hero, Adelina Patti, do, and then curtsied; and as I did so, I noted Giulia's approval.

Pauline then sat down at the piano, and as she began to play, the curtain drew back, revealing the oleander trees to be in pots, enormous flowers made of paper, and the outlines of what looked like a little house, inside of which sat Krakamiche, the last of the sorcerers, who was received with much applause, for he was Turgenev, smiling to the audience before resuming the aggrieved face of a sorcerer on the wane. He opened his mouth to sing, and I heard a delicate soprano voice appear, to the laughter of the crowd, for it could not be his, high as his voice was—another was singing for him somewhere in the wings.

The tenor who sings for him could not be here, Giulia whispered to me.

Stella, the sorcerer's beautiful daughter, was played by Maxine, who clearly relished the major role and was beautiful in her modest costume as the unmarried noble daughter supporting her father during the decline of his powers.

An *opéra-bouffe-féerie*, *Le Dernier Sorcier* told the story of an aging sorcerer living in a small hut in the woods with his daughter, Stella, who has enchanted a young Prince, Lelio. The Prince, having seen her while hunting in the woods and fallen in love with her, cannot find her to woo her and despairs, but luckily for him, he is overheard by the Queen of the Fairies, the ruler of the woods. She is plotting to make some mischief at the old wizard's expense, seeing him as an interloper she has longed to be rid of. She knows of the beautiful Stella and offers the Prince a magical rose, which allows the bearer to be unseen, though only at night.

Giulia continued her asides to me, explaining who it was I saw as they appeared, the delicate girl in the costume of the Queen of the Fairies—a rose wreath in her hair, a diamond star flashing at its center—was Pauline's daughter Claudie, and the girl acting as the head fairy, Verveine, was her other daughter Marianne. Krakamiche's no-good, troublesome servant was played by Paul, Pauline's son—he would sing an aria, to my delight. Prince Lelio was Natalya, who made a surprisingly handsome young prince. This left Firéne absent, but only she could be singing as the voice for Turgenev's Krakamiche, it seemed to me.

The diminutive Queen, having helped the handsome young Prince in his pursuit of his love, plans some mischief. She sends a delegation of her most loyal fairies, disguised as Cochinese, claiming to bear a gift for the wizard—a magical grass that will restore the sorcerer's youth and powers. When it instead causes him to dance a waltz that leaves him weak and humiliated, he vows revenge. The second act opens with him hunting through a book of Merlin's spells for a spell that is a protection from all other magic, the most powerful spell of all. The beautiful Stella tries to get the sorcerer to be content with his decline, saying he has all he needs there in their modest house; but as he won't hear it and instead keeps searching feverishly, she begins to sing to herself. After two verses, Prince Lelio, made invisible by the rose's magic and hidden near her, sings the third verse in response, causing her to startle and then, when he drops the rose and is revealed to her, to smile. But this only convinces the sorcerer that his spell has succeeded and his powers are restored. He tries another, summoning a monster to rid his hut of this intruding prince, but instead a goat comes up from the earth and runs from the hut.

This, of course, was Pegasus the pointer, horns hanging from his neck as he struggled to rid himself of them.

In despair, the sorcerer collapses: his daughter and the Prince comfort him. In the final scenes, Stella and Prince Lelio marry and bring the sorcerer out of the woods to live in the Prince's castle. As they depart, the Queen and her fairies celebrate having the woods entirely under their control again.

The green curtain rang down to much applause and then was parted by the sweetly shy face of Claudie smiling as she led the faeries out to calls for encores. The grateful room shouted bravos and bravas as she curtsied and her diamond star flashed. Cheers changed to laughter when, as the rest of the cast emerged, Turgenev appeared at last in his wizard's robes, and the laughter increased as Firéne came out behind him, smiling gamely as he touched his throat and pointed to her. Pauline gestured to the tenor and me both, thanking us for making the occasion of the performance possible, and he blew her a kiss while I could only stand still in amazement.

That poor man, Giulia said softly, under her breath.

Thank you for these calls for an encore, but I think we must go, Pauline said. To dinner! Pauline called this from the stage as if summoning us to a charge, and the crowd, already standing at attention, made its way out through the back into the cold garden, the women accepting shawls offered by Pauline's maid and all of us following the lanterns hung to guide us along the way.

Giulia had relinquished me, off speaking now to someone else, and the tenor appeared at my side, smiling as he gave me his arm. Do you feel honored yet? he asked, and I said I did. This might be all I ever thought to dream of, he said, and as I took his arm, he planted a single kiss on my cheek. The warmth from it stayed there at least half the way to the other house.

The entire performance had moved me deeply, from the well-mannered, beautiful voices of Pauline's children to Pauline's continued command of the entire night and, it seemed, the world around her. The story struck me as quite clever, the music also. One thing troubled me: I knew from the expressions of dismay visible on some of the royals around me during the performance that as Turgenev played the sorcerer in his decline on the stage they felt it beneath him. Another decline happening in front of them. This saddened me. I already felt protective of him and thought of him as my friend.

Pauline and he and the rest of the troupe were still in costume, walking just ahead of us, and in the dark garden, they looked as if the opera would now continue to a new chapter, as if we were on our way to the castle to see the wedding of the prince and Stella.

This was the first opera with a happy ending I'd ever seen, and despite the contrivances of Fate at work in it, this one I could see staying inside of, as they did now. We entered the Viardot villa to find Pauline's real husband, Louis, at the table, smiling genially. He was introduced and apologized for being late. He had been feeling poorly but was now a little better. He was quite small in stature by comparison to Turgenev, who kissed him on both cheeks — Louis looked a bit like an old fox in evening dress, his whiskers and sharp eyes quizzical as he took me in — all of his weight was in his eyes, his gaze — all of his body raised up so he might see. I had no sooner finished our pleasantries than Turgenev appeared at my side, picking at the sleeves of his sorcerer robes, rolling them back so he might eat.

La Lapinard, he said, smiling. How did you enjoy your show?

An enormous pleasure, I said, thrilled to be reminded of my new title. Your soprano voice was a miracle of tone.

Indeed, I thought much the same, he said, and laughed. She is wonderful. I look forward to when you join us there. Which can only be soon, I'm sure.

We looked to Louis then, who was smiling at Turgenev with real affection. He drew back a chair and sat down and urged us to the buffet. The true *dernier sorcier,* then, I understood, here, setting his napkin into his lap, at home in the castle with the two lovers.

Dinner was cold hams and a salad of potatoes the tenor told me was traditional to Germany served with a cool red wine. Seating was informal, in Pauline's salon, with small tables set throughout with candles and crystal. Giulia reappeared to sit with me at one of them, gossiping about how the imposing woman speaking to Pauline, strangely anxious to be at her ease, was Queen Augusta of Prussia, there unofficially, now a patroness of Pauline's. She has just commissioned an opera from her, Giulia said.

I tried to be interested, but instead I could only watch as Maxine sat beside the tenor at the table and did the same with the tenor as she had with me, going through her questions as if she were at a briefing. She was interested in him differently, more intensely than the other girls, who had only wanted to flirt. The effect for me was like watching a mouse dance in front of a cat, thinking it was the cat. The prospect of their pairing amused me such that I smiled, and Maxine noticed this and this confused her—her confidence dimmed. The tenor noticed and looked to see the source of her discomfort.

I nodded. He grinned back and took her hand, holding it up.

I smiled at this, and he laughed and turned back to her as she struggled to regain her previous air. Giulia smiled also and we resumed our conversation.

I understood that to Maxine I was already living the life of dramatic love and connection she and the other students hoped for after they finished their education, but it would be some time before I understood that my apparent indifference to losing the tenor passed as confidence, or sophistication, and urged Maxine to greater lengths. I had not yet learned to be possessive of a lover I did not love. Instead, whenever I thought of it or noticed her at her game, the absurdity of it would freeze me in place with the same mix of fear and hope each time.

Maxine would never quite believe I was who I said I was, and at times she treated her mission of seducing the tenor as a kind of rescue of him, as if he'd been led astray by a pretender. She would try to captivate him for a very long time after that night. And one day, many years from now, she would succeed a little because I allowed it.

Until that time, when I thought of Maxine, I mostly would hear her say that strange greeting of hers from our first meeting. It would stay with me for years.

Tragedy belongs to you.

Soon I would say it to myself.

Tragedy belongs to you.

Two

MY FIRST LESSON with Pauline that morning was a lesson in all I did not know about my voice and singing.

I went to her music room, and she invited me to sit beside her at the piano, and so I did. As I sat down, I saw we did not wear crinolines at Pauline's because we needed to sit beside her on the piano bench.

I would direct the tenor to place a dress order for me immediately afterward.

I have heard a story, she said, of your audition for the Conservatoire, but I would hear it from you directly.

I told her about singing my *Nabucco* aria and the reactions and comments of the jury. And the warning.

I wouldn't dare ask you to sing such a thing for me today, she said. What else can you sing?

I suggested the Lucia, and she shook her head.

Let us be very simple, she said. Why don't you sing your vocalizes for me?

I had none and admitted as much.

Ah, she said. He really did poorly by you. I will have to punish him! We will find something suitably humiliating, I'm sure. Perhaps I will teach him to teach. Here, and she played a simple progression for me. Now follow along, singing on each tone just the letter *A*. Do not push or strain; let the tone be natural.

She demonstrated, the sound much as I'd heard her sing privately the day before.

Your voice is quite fine, but you have not really been singing, she said to me, after a few of these exercises. Your voice has simply been misused. It is like a horse that was allowed to run wherever and whenever it liked, and then was found by someone who enjoyed it that way, and somehow it has not lamed itself, she said. Though there could, I think, be some secret wound not quite audible to us. For now we will proceed. For our purposes, I want you to begin as if you have never sung before and do all I tell you.

She handed me a book that looked like a score to an operetta in which one only sang the letter *A*. This was a lesson book, she explained, a program carefully constructed over the years to train her singers.

Each day I was to begin at the piano, and to begin with my posture at the piano—I was to sit erect, head slightly lifted. Once the posture was correct, I would begin not by singing but by playing the notes to the lesson on the piano until I knew the music well enough to begin—unfamiliar music, she explained, was a danger to the voice, like running through an unfamiliar landscape. A singer's voice could trip on too fast a change, especially if untrained.

As I played the notes without singing, I was to practice breathing through my nose only, practicing for when I began to sing. As I did this, I was also to soften my tongue so that it would not go rigid. When I was ready to sing, I was to use my practice in inhaling through my nose to take a breath this way first, and then hold the breath for a moment, before releasing the note in as natural a way as possible. I was to sing only that letter *A* and never change the vowel sound during the lesson.

When I began to sing, I was to sing slowly at first, legato and moderato, and then faster and faster. A mirror sat on the piano so I could watch my mouth's movements and modulate myself accordingly. Once I knew the lesson comfortably from memory, I would then stand and sing it unaccompanied. There were instructions for standing as well, of course—I was to stand in second position from ballet, one foot in front, the other in back, so there could be no unseemly slouching or swaying or any extra movement whatsoever. The back was arched ever so slightly backward, the head slightly raised, as if I were maintaining my stance in the face of a great wind and I would not ever lose my ground.

I was to practice fifteen minutes at a time and then rest and do this only when my concentration was greatest. I was never to force, never to slide toward a note, but instead launch it boldly, precisely, never loud when I was to be soft or soft when I was to be loud. If I sensed a mistake or a problem, I was to stop at once and begin again, but only once a natural softness had returned to the throat. The plus marks over or under the notes were warnings as to where the voice was most likely to go sharp (over) or flat (under).

I cannot play so well, I told her, anxious not to fail at even this.

She pointed at the keys. So, your playing will improve first, she said, and then your singing. Now begin, and I will return at your first break to speak to you some more. She picked up an hourglass timer, turned it over, and left.

Hesitantly, my fingers found the notes. I'd had no instruction in the piano previously. I pecked in the manner of all who cannot play, first slowly and then more quickly. I resisted the impulse to hum.

She returned. My child, you did not tell me you could not play at all.

And so she became my piano teacher also.

In several weeks' time I was ready to sing the lesson. The voice felt made new after the long rest, stronger, surer, as if it were rooted the more deeply somehow. The noise of it was thrilling. Here in the lessons were the ways to attempt the vocal flourishes, the trills and diminuendos and crescendos I had only heard and never understood. Only when I was ready to stand did I realize how I had been raised up very slowly by degrees. Until I was singing in that position in which I would not ever lose my ground.

I made my way like this through that first winter into the spring in Weimar and Karlsruhe until we returned to Baden-Baden. By the summer, Natalya had moved on, and when the opera was performed, I replaced her onstage as Prince Lelio, singing of love to Maxine, who was still in the role of Stella. This amused the tenor to no end. Especially when I decided, with a flourish, to use that ruby rose gift from the Emperor, the one he had kept for me, as the flower the Queen gives Lelio to pass invisibly through the night.

At this distance, these lessons with her are, to me, her autobiography written in musical instruction. At the least, as I sat and learned to play beside her, they were a mirror to the story of a girl who had watched her older brother and sister both break very publicly—her sister singing herself to death after a horseback-riding accident, her brother losing his voice very young—and she, all the while, their talented much younger sister, who loved the piano more than she loved singing, picking out the notes before she sang. Doing as her father and mother said.

And if it was not her autobiography, it was at the least the door by which one could enter a life like hers.

At Madame Viardot's school, her many successes were confided to us mostly by either of her two greatest admirers: Louis, who'd once managed an opera house in Paris, or Turgenev, who fell in love with her during her triumphant first season in Saint Petersburg. They spoke of her enormous capacity for memorization and her ability to keep many roles in her repertoire at the same time, even within a single opera, and in several languages. Once, in Berlin, during a performance of *Robert le Diable*, she replaced another singer as she also continued singing her own role. Later, in London, in *Les Huguenots,* she found herself tricked by a rival into performing the lead in *Norma* in Italian—but her tenor that night was going to sing his part in French. She taught herself the French as the opera began, in the wings, and her Norma was also French halfway through the performance. To the audience, Louis said, as he paused with a rare wit in his eye, it was as if the druidess had cast a spell on her own throat.

These were not lectures but they acted as such: We were to be as ruthless in the pursuit of a performance and as able. I soon inquired about learning other languages, and learning my parts, when I was

allowed to, each in several languages, all of which pleased Pauline
—and all of which she could teach. I began the practice of learning the other major roles of opera. I wanted to prepare for a life of
sudden transformations, of enemies singing at you across the stage
dressed in the costume of a lover.

I was consumed by my apprenticeship and paid little attention
to the tenor's affairs. At first, on our return to Baden-Baden, he enjoyed himself at the casinos and baths as if he were on some extended vacation, and he was a hit at Pauline's many dinners and
events, sometimes even singing at the *Haustheater*, much as she'd
suggested. Soon he was excusing himself to go on trips, at first for
a few days and nights and then increasingly for longer—a week, a
fortnight. But he would always return for the *Haustheater* events, as
if they were to him a regular engagement at any other theater. The
proximity of Baden-Baden to the major capitals and its strange role
as both a sanitarium and a casino to the rich meant a variety of no-
tables passed through, and all of them sought a place either in her
audience or on her stage.

Each time the tenor returned from his trips, he found me further
along in my education and praised me. He brought gifts, always. He
kept an apartment in the town I rarely saw; it was impractical for
me to live so far from the house. Each time he returned, some part
of me was surprised to think I had not fled, but that part became
smaller and smaller as time went on. I was content with my situation, happy to see him, happy to be with him.

This last, in some ways, was the most confusing for me, the part
that would be the hardest to forgive.

~

It's for the best they rejected you, Pauline said of the Conservatoire
after she had heard me sing a little. Pauline then launched into a
critique of their system. Too many teachers confuses, she said. The
tenor tells me you studied with Delsarte, yes?

Yes, I said.

Delsarte will tell anyone he lost his voice to the Conservatoire's methods, she said. It may even be true.

She let this stay in the air a moment before continuing.

There are two voices for an opera singer, Pauline said. Your speaking voice, which can be as ordinary as a wren's. And then the singing voice, which can sound as strange as something the wren found and holds in its beak, as if it comes from some other place entirely. For most singers, that voice is something made from the first, carefully, with both passion and patience. A patience born of that passion. For a few, their voice is a gift and can improve with training, but it has qualities that cannot be taught. And because the singer did not make this voice herself with careful training, she does not know what those qualities are except that she finds them by singing.

She paused and then said, She also does not know when the gift will break.

She smiled at me as she said that. Be careful of your roles, she said. I sang everything out of youthful pride in my three-octave voice, and I should not have. Yours is much like my own. It will not last forever, this voice. I know this seems very cruel, as you must give everything to become a singer and then it may be taken from you all at once. The voice can go quite suddenly or slowly, but even with a slow departure, once it is underway, it will sound as if the original voice has already left you.

I said nothing, alternately warm from her compliment — she believed my voice was like hers! — and chilled entirely by this warning, which was, of course, meant to chill me.

She then began to play a slow scale and then went faster, the movement between high C to high E flat and back down again.

There, she said. Did you hear it? That's one place you may fall.

She played it again, the notes sounding this time almost like a trap.

Don't be afraid, she said. It's not just the melodies we should know. We must know also where we could fail. Learn them and you will never fall, not, at least, before your time.

~

After my lesson was done, I passed by Pauline's library, where her autographed manuscript score of Mozart's *Don Giovanni* stood on a music stand. I went in, as was now my custom. The Mozart manuscript lay open, turned to a new page every day, as if each day Pauline came in and looked over the handiwork of her hero now that she was also a composer.

Le Dernier Sorcier had been a success in Weimar and Karlsruhe, and this had filled her with some new courage and happiness. She was now busy with her commission from the Queen of Prussia. Turgenev also had brightened in the reflected glory, though he sometimes seemed still pained by the regrettable controversy he made when he published praise of the production, for which he was intensely criticized — he was, after all, the author of the libretto, beyond all other personal relations to the opera, the singers, and the production. The scandal had wounded him and Pauline both; in the *Haustheater* we understood it as an excess of enthusiasm, the madness of love, and forgave it. But out in the world, it was egotism, nepotism, and, given the way they lived here, a disgrace.

This scandal would subside, but after I left there, in the years that followed, I would often have a chance to reflect on the doubled irony, the twin fictions of Pauline as "ugly" and the temptress who brutally controlled Turgenev. Whenever it came up in conversations, I would recoil and sometimes want to assure them as Natalya assured me, that Turgenev was the one who'd urged Pauline to take her composing more seriously as her voice began to fade — he did what he did out of his faith in her talents as a composer, as well as out of love. We all knew Pauline's mother had forced her to sing — Pauline had wanted to stay at her piano, out of sight. I thought of this often when we sat down to our lessons there — how, as her singing voice left her, this voice, the piano, remained — the one she'd preferred all along.

When I saw them working together, their heads bent over the score, making adjustments and speaking intensely over this or that part of the new drama, I saw a kind of love I'd not seen before, a devotion unlike any other. To the extent he'd disgraced her and himself, it was born of an excess of his fear that the world—that world that had judged her voice by her face—would not accept this from her, either. And yet I also understood that he should never have published that essay. There were too many of his readers who believed our strange little paradise, these two houses side by side, were a disgrace.

My own devotion brought me to Pauline's Mozart shrine, though I did not come for Mozart. A portrait of Pauline's sister, Maria, looked down from over the mantel in that room. I went in and stood before it.

This was my talisman. I had memorized her long white neck, her large dark eyes as familiar to me as those of anyone else's in the house. The lesson Pauline wanted us, her students, to take from her stories of her sister was that she had died too young, a victim of her own reckless ambition. But I, increasingly certain I lacked Pauline's genius, had become enchanted with the portrait and had, more and more, taken another lesson. While Pauline was not the same kind of beauty as she and had suffered for it, at least Maria would not know the ignominy of being a voiceless singer with no other talents.

I understood Maria's recklessness differently. Nothing waited for her if she could not sing, much as I suspected nothing would wait for me. But I still believed that fame could save me, somehow, even from this, and I would for some time.

This movement—between my room, her music room, this library, this is how I spent my time in Baden-Baden until the war began.

Three

IN THE SUMMER OF 1870, when French society declined their usual visits to the spas and casinos in Baden-Baden, it was clear to Europe there would finally be war between Prussia and France.

For nearly a year Pauline had hoped to at least have her good friend, George Sand, come to see *Le Dernier Sorcier* performed and then, when that failed, had begun to plan a trip to her—we would perform for her there, in Nohant in her theater instead. We were to go in July, around the time of their birthdays, and the performance would be in her honor.

It was a great compliment to be asked, and as the tenor had been gone for a month at least, with no sign of returning, I said yes, excited at the thought of a trip without him.

The news of the possibility of war cheered me at first, as the talk in Germany was of how quickly it would be over; the French, we were assured again and again, could not hope to prevail. Surely it would be the end of the regime, Pauline said one night, when this sentiment was expressed at her dinner table.

The end of the regime meant, to me at least, if not my outright freedom, the beginning of it. Inside France, the idea of a France without the Emperor and Empress had seemed impossible for me to imagine. But from inside Germany, it seemed certain. When this was done, I would be able to leave the tenor then, I was sure. This trip could be the first of many without him, I hoped.

We must go to her sooner than July, it would seem, Pauline then said to the table and us, her assembled troupe. She did not need to say Sand's name.

Several weeks later, as we packed to depart, Pauline appeared at my door, stricken, a letter from the tenor in her hand. He's gone mad, she said, holding it out to me.

Thank you for informing me of your plans, and I'm so sorry I won't be able to join you there except very briefly; for you see I must return to Paris, and Lilliet should come with me—I think she has learned all she can from you for now. I will collect her from Nohant then, as I will already be in Paris when you arrive, so be sure to tell her to pack all and make her good-byes and send what she will not need in Nohant to the avenue de l'Opéra address. I will be making arrangements for her debut there for the spring season, where I know she will be the talk of Paris.

The letter read as if it were from a stranger, almost a forgery, except I knew his hand by now. Pauline had been carefully training me for a year to debut in Weimar, in Bellini's *La Sonnambula*, performing the role of Amina. This was an effort she and the tenor had both undertaken, and so I knew she felt variously betrayed, as did I. Pauline was famous for her Amina, and as I could have no better teacher for it, wouldn't my debut and my safety be assured if we continued as we were? Why this change? He'd discussed with us how, even after the debut, I should remain a student of Pauline's for at least another year, perhaps two.

How could he do this to us? And to you most of all, Pauline asked, though I knew she knew I did not know the answers. This is just so disappointing. Well, I will send my maid to help you pack everything, then.

None of the agreements we'd made from before this letter were visible except in his insistence I return to Paris, the one only I knew of, the one that required me to be with him. Something had happened out of my sight, a cord pulled tightly where I'd expected it to go slack. I understood then that I knew nothing of what would happen next.

~

My fortnight's introduction to Madame Sand, then, was also to
be the end to my life as a member of my adopted family. We left
Baden-Baden first by train back into France in a grim procession—
Pauline, her children, Turgenev, and I—while Louis stayed behind.
All that we said to one another sounded as if we were calling to one
another from very far away, not from the next seat. It had been one
thing to mock the Second Empire around Pauline's table in Baden-
Baden, quite another to enter it on the verge of war. But whatever
we feared from the French did not appear as we crossed the border;
the conductors, the passport officers, the police, all were as cordial
and formal as ever. The peculiar spell broke only when we were met
by a carriage waiting for us in Châteauroux, sent by Sand and driven
by her servant Sylvain. Only after he had greeted us warmly and
made sure we were all packed in, only then did Pauline seem to
relax, and the desolate worry that accompanied her until then left;
her normally confident and bemused expression returned, and it was
as if we had passed through enemy territory between her house and
Sand's, and she were somehow home again.

Here was her other kingdom.

If the war should begin, oh, that I could spend it here, Pauline
said, as we exited the carriage, and laughed; and we all laughed with
her and went in, pleased our queen was happy again.

It was her held breath, you see, on the train there—all of us
holding it for her or with her, as if we could help.

~

We found Nohant empty of Sand, but her handsome son, Maurice,
received us, having arrived just the day before along with a family
friend introduced as Edmond Plauchut, a funny, sly explorer, dash-
ing in the way of a fraud, who immediately began to tease Turgenev
as if they were brothers. Sand was still in Paris, detained on business
with her publisher, and would arrive the next day. That night we sat

down to a cheerful supper, followed by backgammon and charades, at which Plauchut — who they had long ago renamed Plauchemar, a mix of his last name and *cauchemar*, or "nightmare" — proved quite adept.

The next morning, after breakfast, I explored the château and grounds with Maurice, as the others all knew this place well. We must be sure you do not get lost, he said, half joking. I made sure to be dutifully fascinated by the botanical garden, the billiards room, the park around the house with meadows and woods, the moat, and the river Indre, close enough for bathing or a boat ride, both of which Maurice assured me would happen soon. He then showed me with great pride the elaborate puppet theater he and his mother had created, how he and his mother made the marionettes together — he crafting the bodies and painting the faces, and she designing and sewing the costumes.

I was, I admit, fascinated with him.

The library, where he left me to amuse myself, still seems peerless to me, with her vast collection of books, paintings, and drawings, the Louis XIII furniture and Venetian chandeliers suggesting a life of opulent thought. Here was where I felt I could sense the spirit of our absent hostess, as if the room shook with her when she was not there.

Maurice did not mention a father and I did not ask after one. There was no question of it. Madame Sand was, I could see, Pauline's match, or more so. Each of them was a formidable artist and a woman who had made her own indelible mark on this world. I had thought to never meet another woman like Pauline, and now I knew I would.

I knew of Sand only by reputation, the writer said to wear men's pants and affect men's mannerisms. On the train, Turgenev had mentioned in passing she'd written a novel about Pauline, a little in the way she'd done with all of her lovers, though it wasn't thought that she'd bedded Pauline, he'd added warily.

This all made her fascinating to me.

In Sand's library, instead of finding the novel about Pauline, I found a copy of Turgenev's *First Love*, inscribed to her, and sat down to read it, to the exclusion of all else—I had not read him before, ever. The conceit of the book took me in from the first—a group of friends, telling stories, ask one another who their first love was. I secretly hoped to discover that it was also about Pauline. When it was soon clear that it was not, I continued reading it and had nearly finished it by the time our hostess returned.

~

Sand, when she finally appeared, was, disappointingly, not dressed as a man but as a genteel woman of her age, stylish but not too stylish. She looked me over graciously, with a smile that suggested she knew at least some of the stories about me. You are the prodigy *cocotte*, she said, and when I curtsied to her, she laughed. You are a delight, she said. You will sing for us later, yes? I looked to Pauline, and she nodded, smiling.

We had a very late dinner, and afterward, the group became maudlin with drink and talk of the possibility of war.

A drama, Sand said, finally, prepared to put an end to our sad mood. She stood up. She waved her arms up, lit by the candelabra.

Pauline raised an eyebrow. Which one?

Hamlet.

Hamlet, Pauline repeated. This is how you mean to cheer us up? But she was already smiling as she said it and stood up.

No, not that one. Not the *whole* one, Sand said. In honor of our future rulers, the Prussians, we will do the German traveling version of the play, in which we find Shakespeare's play like a captive, much abused and much shorter. And hilarious.

Will we do it in German? Turgenev asked, his voice very quiet.

Sand laughed. We should, to practice.

She waved us to the small theater within her beautiful house.

All night long, after we'd tried not to speak of the inevitable coming war, it was easier to acknowledge now with jokes. It would be *Hamlet* as farce, and we would each have to pay multiple parts.

Pauline was to be the Queen, and Sand Hamlet, of course, Turgenev the King's ghost. Maurice exclaimed with dismay at having to be the King and also Ophelia's minister father. Is there nothing more interesting for me? he asked.

The King is very interesting, said Sand, and we laughed.

I was Ophelia, but also the Queen of the Night, which thrilled me.

Why is there a Queen of the Night? Pauline asked. Was she in the original?

No, Sand said. A German affectation. Done because they love her, I suppose.

There'll be one in every opera once the Prussians are done, Turgenev said.

You'll see, she said. She's terrific. I like her very much. You will, too. You won't mind when they eventually include her in *Don Giovanni*. They also call her the Queen of Silence.

We laughed at this, Pauline most of all.

Sand chose Plauchut for the head of the troupe of actors, who were, in the play, from Germany, made to perform a play that reminds the murdering royal couple, Hamlet's mother and uncle, of their guilt.

We need Furies to accompany the Queen, Sand declared, and appointed Maurice, Pauline, and Turgenev as the Furies — Alecto, Megaera, and Tisiphone.

I stood before them, cloaked in a blue wool blanket for my starry mantle of night. I wrapped it dramatically around my head, but as soon as I did, to my surprise, I felt something sad descend — something sad but nobly sad. Outside, the lightly fervid humor of the night.

Where are we? murmured Turgenev, from just offstage. Is it her land of women from *The Magic Flute?*

Well, they are Furies, Sand said. That is all you must know. Now let's start.

This version of the play begins when the Queen of the Night calls her Furies to her. *I am dark Night that sends the world to sleep,* I recited.

I am Morpheus's wife, the time for vicious pleasure.
Protector of thieves, guardian of illicit love;
I am dark Night, and it is in my power
To give the whore her rest, and cover up her shame,
Give Evil its free rein, all mankind to betray.
Ere Phoebus arise, I shall have my prize.
Ye children of my breast, ye daughters of my lust,
Rise up, rise up, you Furies, appear before thy mother!
Regard with care all that she is about to share!

The Furies appeared and welcomed me. The comedy of it had fled at first, but it returned at the sight of Turgenev in the light from the fire, both hilarious and very convincing as a crone.

Maurice, as Alecto: What says dark Night, Queen of
   Silence?
What new game does she propose? What is her wish and
   will?
Pauline, as Megaera: From Acheron's dark pit come I,
   Megaera, hither,
To hear from thee, mother of all evil, all thou might
   desire.
Turgenev, as Tisiphone: Dark Night! Speak!
What wishes wait in that dark heart?

Pauline giggled.

Listen, ye Furies all three, listen, ye children of darkness
   and mothers
of all misfortune. Listen to your poppy-crowned Queen
   of the Night,
patroness of thieves and robbers, friend and light to all
   that burns,
lover of stolen goods, dearly loved goddess of unlawful
   love:
how often are my altars honored by it?

This night and the coming morrow, stand with me;
The King of this land burns with love for his brother's
wife,
Whom for her sake he has murdered so that he might
possess both wife
And crown. Now is the hour at hand when they lie
together.
I shall throw my mantle over them both, that neither
may see their sin.
Make ready to sow the seeds of their disunion, mingle
poison with their
Marriage, put jealousy in their hearts. Kindle a fire of
revenge and let the
Sparks fly over this whole realm, till murder burns in
Hamlet's heart, and
Gives joy to Hell, so that those who swim in this sea of
murder may soon drown.
Begone, hasten, and fulfill my command!

As this last was said, it left my mouth with the whistling of
something terrible set loose in the dark.
That those who swim in this sea of murder may drown.
The Furies gave their last speeches.

Tisiphone: I have already heard enough, and will soon
perform
More than dark Night can herself imagine.
Megaera: Pluto himself shall not prompt me to so much
As shortly I'll be performing.
Alecto: I fan the sparks and make the fire burn;
Ere it dawns the second time, the whole game I'll shiver.

Then they scattered to rip the royal family into blood and shreds,
and fill the world with justice. More giggling ensued, and all was as
it had been, a comedy again.

Sand made for an amusing Hamlet. Every line she spoke made

us shake with laughter. Pauline was regal as the Queen, whom she played as a bit thick and wintry toward her son. Maurice turned out to be an able and elegant choice for the young soldiers as needed, vanishing and reappearing in yet another costume—borrowing hats and helmets from the coatroom and, in one case, a long ostrich feather that made us all laugh as he entered.

The night was like the play, familiar and unfamiliar—and hilarious, as Sand had promised, and we got through it, murder after murder, to the end.

Ophelia, in this version, to my mind, could only be ridiculous, and so I played her that way. Befuddled as to why her world had gone mad but certain she had not changed. Her death a moment of unexpected happiness for her.

After it was done, cognac was brought, and we sat outside on the lawns. It was still very dark but it was morning. I lay back, my hair in the grass, a slight chill to it.

I watched Pauline with Turgenev—they were the opposite of the play we'd just enacted. The brother had not murdered a brother for his wife, but had instead gentled himself.

Sand came over to me. She'd lit a cigar and looked like an old elf. And how are you doing with your studies there with my old friend? she asked.

She is a demanding teacher, I said. But I love her.

That sounds exactly as it should be, I should think, she said, and tapped an ash into the lawn with a cast-down grin. I look forward to hearing you sing, she said. Somehow I am sure you are extraordinary. Pauline does not trifle.

Thank you, I said.

This was when I looked up at her and wondered if she would one day write a novel about me. This was one of the first vanities of my career, that I could somehow attract the literary attention of Sand. I hoped she would, that I would someday be famous enough, interesting enough, and find myself browsing a stall along the Seine, her newest novel there, and opening it to discover it was finally of me.

On the day I open the novel Simonet has written of me, I will remember this moment. Of staring up at her and wondering if I was to be her next subject. It was what I had always imagined it would be like to see God as He made up His mind. As He decided whether or not I was to be forgiven.

～

The novel, when I finally read it, disappointed some of my suspicions, resupplied others, and confirmed one.

I was initially amused that Simonet had transformed the Settler's Daughter into a sort of female Baron Munchausen, the Baroness Munchausen, if you will. All it lacked for was a ride on a cannonball, a fish for me to crawl out of, and a ship I could take to the moon.

After the Paris Exposition Universelle, the young circus rider who sang before the Emperor and was rewarded with a ruby rose falls under its spell. Unbeknownst to her, the Emperor had the rose enchanted with a love spell. She escapes from the circus, intent on pursuing him, but outside the Expo waits a tenor who had seen the performance and lusted for her, determined to possess her. He seduces her, promises to make her a singer, and brings her to his house in the Marais, where he keeps her prisoner, jealously guarded.

The tenor finds the spell has affected her singing, however; she lacks the passion she might have if she was free of the enchantment, which troubles him. She also keeps trying to escape and will not let go of the ruby rose. The tenor goes off in search of a remedy.

While he is out, she goes to pray in the chapel of his enormous mansion for forgiveness. As she does, a net is thrown over her and she is dragged away, kidnapped this time by faeries who live on the rue d'Enfer and are determined to cure her but also save her. Faery jewelers make the enchanted flowers the Emperor gives to women and know the rose's peculiar magic has bonded to her heart—if it should be removed by anyone but the Emperor, she will die. The faeries are now remorseful due to the Emperor's excesses, but they find they cannot undo their spell. They devise a plan—they will go to the Tuileries and sneak her in front of the Emperor in the guise of a doll. In the Emperor's presence, they can remove the rose and she will be released from the spell. As they begin the process of applying her doll costume, one of the faeries perceives the rose is killing her heart the longer she has it. There is not much time to save her.

The faeries manage to get her inside the Tuileries and deliver her to the Emperor's chambers; but the Emperor is not there so they depart, running the palace in search of him; the singer, meanwhile, still enchanted and finding herself in the Emperor's rooms, believes her wish has more than come true—not only does the Emperor love her, she is also to be the Empress. The faerie who has stayed to guard her sees her dress in one of the Empress's gowns to prepare to go to the Emperor and casts a spell on her so that she falls asleep; for if she leaves, she may die.

She wakes to find herself in a circus again. At first, she's happy to be returned, as she imagines it, but soon she discovers this is another circus altogether—she is the newest member of a circus of magical creatures hidden inside Paris within the Jardin des Plantes zoo. During the day, the regular creatures of the zoo have a secret —they are the magical ones, hidden by a spell. There she keeps company with an Italian gryphon, a Hungarian vampire, several acrobatic wood nymphs from Greece, a tiny Spanish dragon as big as a cat, and two Indian *makaras*, elephants with the tails of fishes. When the sun rises, she is transformed into a falcon and can fly. When the sun sets, she is herself again and performs.

The circus belongs to a wizard who tells her the faeries were unable to find a cure for her so they have sold her to him. He explains she is there because he knows the truth of her voice—that she had made a bargain long ago with a Navajo witch for an enchanted voice at the cost of her speaking voice. If she was ever to use the speaking voice again, her singing voice would leave her.

She is to perform with a recently captured angel as the circus's featured act, singing as he flies overhead. To keep him from escaping, they have removed his wings and return them to him for performances only, during which he flies on a leash. To her surprise, she falls in love with him—the enchanted love for the Emperor seems gone—and together they plan their escape. During their next performance, she cuts the leash and he flies away with her.

They rest on the top of the Paris Opera, where the angel has stopped, for he realizes she is dying of the enchanted rose's spell—she had thought her love for him was a sign the spell did not work, but it was only proof of the strength of her heart. She has never told him the truth of the ruby rose she wears, but as she dies, the angel thanks her for freeing him and vows to wear the rose so she will know him when she sees him next, after death. He promises her they'll be reunited in Heaven.

Instead, she wakes to find the circus was only a dream during her long enchanted sleep. The Empire has fallen, the reason the Emperor and the Empress are gone. She has been asleep for nearly a year, her stolen dress in ruins, and wakes to find herself a curiosity inside of a hospital, with young student doctors marveling over her sleeping form, for she has been singing even in her sleep. She finds the rose is gone, however, and, terrified, runs from the building despite the shocked protests of the students.

She makes her way to first the Jardin des Plantes, empty after the Siege and Commune, and eventually to the outskirts of Paris, where she is reunited with her circus, which joyfully remembers her and prepares for her to go on. As she does, she discovers that one of the men who works the ropes is the wizard who ran the magical circus in her dream. He warns her that he will have his revenge on her for stealing his star act—a test awaits her inside the tent.

You will have to choose, he tells her. Choose well.

She goes into the ring confused and believing her dream was just a dream until she sees in the audience a seemingly ordinary man.

He is wearing the rose on his lapel.

She calls out his name. He does not recognize her. He is her angel and has given up his wings forever to be with her as a mortal—but with that, he was lost among men, with no memory of his life before.

Heartbroken, she sings a final aria of her grief to have both found him and lost him. As it concludes, the voice leaves her and she runs from the stage even as the former angel in the audience finally remembers her, leaps to his feet, and chases after her.

I closed the book.

Each writer, even each form of opera, uses Fate differently. Usually an *opéra bouffe* ends with forgiveness. Offenbach's Fate was a kindly if canny grandmother with a pragmatist's eye for the main chance. Verdi's Fate was a punisher—a Fury.

I thought next of the Prince Metternich and his play at Compiègne. The sort of drama I was involved in, this was how he passed his days. *La poupée a été probablement dérangée pendant le voyage.* The story was in some ways a grand elaboration of the broken American doll at the Paris Exposition Universelle, singing to the crowned heads of Europe in a disguise within a disguise. Had the Prince Metternich written the role for me in his salon play at Compiègne or was it for the tenor's American soprano, a taunt aimed at one or both of us?

If this was his work, Simonet treated Fate as a punishment, a lover's revenge. This rose the singer cannot take off, the flower that always returns to her, I had left that rose for my beloved in a room Simonet seemed to have no knowledge of. I had left it as a taunt for my love, a last insult in a ridiculous argument, not knowing it would be my final word to him. The novel, with its foolishness about faeries and spells and love for the Emperor, read almost like the same taunt thrown back to me. Was Simonet's secret, then, my composer sitting by his side, dictating the story to him, his angel wings wrapped closely about him?

Still so angry at me, even in death. Still in that room.

I still believed a mortal to be behind the novel and the opera, but whereas before I had excluded my love's ghost, I no longer did so entirely.

It is at last time to tell you the story of the rose and the room.

Four

IN THE FIRST month of the Siege, it was said the Germans were going to empty all of our *pétrole* supplies into the river and set the Seine on fire.

In fact, it would be Parisians who set Paris on fire, almost a year later, but not one of us would have believed it then. After I heard of this plan, whenever I saw the Seine I imagined it aflame, a river of smoke in the air above it.

I saw an advertisement on the street, a poster: AMAZONES DE LA SEINE! A woman in a black hood and cap peered proudly down out of it, dressed in black-and-orange–striped pants, a rifle slung over her shoulder. A man was passing out broadsides and handed one to me. It was a call for a corps of women soldiers to defend Paris, asking for volunteers to train and serve in the National Guard. They were to carry needles filled with prussic acid and had only to reach out, if their honor was threatened, to prick the offender and watch him die.

It asked the women of Paris to donate their jewels to the effort. A hundred thousand women were to be armed this way.

I was not yet starving; it was easy to be defiant. I imagined going to my Prussian tenor armed this way, his opening the door to me, my face hooded as I reached out. I would stand over him as he fell and died, turning blue from the poison. Prussian blue. I would walk away, free at last, forever.

But, of course, this is not what I did, and he was not the man I would leave for dead.

This also I would not have believed.

~

On my last night at Nohant, Sand had urged Pauline to sing a favorite song of hers, "Que Quieres, Panchito." As I watched Pauline
sing her song, and Sand looked on, enraptured, the sense of how I
would be leaving the next day and what it might mean stole over
me.

The grand house and its inhabitants, from these great ladies before me to their lovers and children to their children's lovers and
children, all of it would be gone. I would vanish into whatever
strange future the tenor had planned for me.

As I came to the end of my time with these women and their
families, I was aware, too, that I had no family of my own; would
I ever? I somehow had been spared both marriage and children
thus far, mostly as a condition of my class, but not entirely. I had
been spared worse, as well—the clap, tuberculosis, smallpox, wasting—and till now, I had given it little thought. Your health, when
you have it, is invisible to you. I only thought of myself as lucky
and that this was my only luck. But was I lucky? Or did I have a
spiteful womb, as Euphrosyne had once said of her own? Or was
it the horseback riding, as Odile had once suggested playfully, or
something else altogether? At the Majeurs-Plaisirs, I had taken the
teas Odile supplied, cleaned myself as directed; I had gone to my
required doctor's visits, and none of the familiar misfortunes associated with my former livelihood had come to pass, as near a miracle
in my life as anything.

But I had since left the circle of Odile's protections. The tenor's
attentions to me, however, had continued, though his carnal interest
in me had been transformed by affection. He no longer sought to re-
lieve himself in me as before, but now acted as a man in love—hus-
bandly, at at times like a fiancé. But he and I could never marry, I
knew; our time in Baden-Baden had meant being surrounded by his
aristocratic peers, and while these German royals deigned to attend
Pauline's salon, I knew well the invisible line around me that would

keep me from ever being the tenor's bride, and I was grateful, in a way, for that.

I was concerned, though, with another line, visible in the light of the candles illuminating these happy families. My luck seemed to me something else: a decree from that hidden god, or my mother's God, or perhaps Fortune, whom Pauline often invoked—a sign that I was to remain in this world until my lesson, such as it was, had ended, and only then would I join my family in death, at which time we would pass from the world forever. No family and no children for me. I was to be the last of my line, I was sure of it.

The tenor appeared in a hired carriage the next morning, seeming much as he had the last time we saw him; there was no visible sign of his transformation. He was handsome, witty, charming Pauline with his jokes as he always did, and Sand as well. Pauline did not let on in the least that she was angry or disappointed or afraid, projecting only that same benign queenly power. And just as she did not complain, he did not perform an apology nor did he explain his reasons for changing our plans. Sand invited him to stay for lunch but he begged off; urgent business, he said, and this was the single moment when a faint pall appeared. What business could there be?

After the carriage had been packed and I had kissed all of them, Pegasus appeared then to push his snout into my hand one last time.

Your true love, Turgenev said. I cannot think of when this dog has ever said good-bye to anyone.

May Fortune protect us all, Pauline said, and the door to the carriage shut behind me.

As we traveled back, I believed the tenor was bringing me to Paris to die with him. Some final act of spite in the face of the war. Having failed to arrange for us to perform together in a tragedy onstage, he would make a tragedy out of our lives.

There was no other way for me to understand why a Prussian tenor would return to Paris if there was to be war between France and Prussia. Why would he not return home? Would he not be captured or expelled, kept from crossing the border? We would be going deeper into the war on the enemy side, not away from it.

The answer to my own question was visible in these questions. I simply wasn't prepared to understand it.

~

The tenor had reassured me repeatedly on the train back from Nohant that Paris would be the safer during the war — it was so widely loved, the idea it would be destroyed was madness; after all, who could shell the Louvre? And this was what people said in the streets on my return.

My calm lasted until the drive back from the station in our carriage, when we passed the Conservatoire National des Arts et Métiers, which seemed already set to the task of manufacturing cannons. From the street, the machines inside sounded like thunder.

Whether or not the Louvre was shelled, it seemed it might be transformed so as to shell the Germans itself.

All of Paris was to become a weapon; we were not so much at war as in the belly of a machine that was going to war. There were regular predictions in the newspapers of methods for the waging of war with Germany: guns mounted on balloons and fired from the sky; poisoning the Seine against invaders; setting loose the animals at the zoo if Paris was occupied. None of this was done. Instead, late into the Siege to come, when the zoo animals were finally remembered, they were not set loose but instead butchered and eaten.

Most never found money enough to try the blood pudding made from the elephant's heart, though. For them, there was the bark on the trees, which cost nothing, and would soon all be stripped bare by the hungry from the ground to just above shoulder height.

Given the transformation at work around us, it would have seemed to be a foregone conclusion that we also would be changed;

and yet, for longer than I might have believed, we carried on as if nothing about us could be changed.

I found the avenue de l'Opéra apartment mostly as it had been, as if it were aloof to my absence, though all had been prepared for my return. Fresh flowers sat in vases, the shrouds had been taken off the furniture, the rooms aired out, the floors swept and dusted. Lucy and Doro appeared from behind the kitchen door as if I had only just gone out earlier that day. Their faces were expectant, and I shouted and hugged both of them, to their embarrassment and evident pleasure. The tenor deposited me with my trunks and left to settle himself as well.

I sat down at the piano in the music room, intent on doing my exercises, to find it out of tune. Unable to practice, as was now my habit, I was reminded again of how the tenor had been unequal to the task of guiding my voice before. This had been a courtesan's piano, not that of a soprano. I was once again alone with the unsteady hands of his obsession.

Yes, at Baden-Baden, I had been inside it also—but there he had made up for abuses like this. We had returned to those old ways in some way, I feared, as well as to Paris, and I could not foresee a happy end.

I dressed to go out and take a walk. I dressed simply, still in the style of the Baden-Baden camp, as if the clothes might keep me there at least in spirit. I added a parasol, hat, and gloves, for it was now summer. As I stood there, about to exit, the doorbell rang. I was nearest to it and opened the door to find the tenor there.

The piano is out of tune, I said to him by way of greeting as he bowed deeply and I offered my hand.

Forgive me, he said, as he stood. I'll be sure it's seen to at once.

Thank you, I said.

Are you . . . headed out? He asked this in a lightly incredulous voice.

I am, I said. I am so sorry. Please excuse me. I must go. But Lucy and Doro can bring you whatever you might need for refreshment while I am out. I won't be long so you may wait or return for me, as you like. I have no dinner plans.

We stood there as he took this in, unmoving.

Shall I tell them to set one more place? I asked.

His face darkened as he looked up to answer me.

Apologies, *mademoiselle princesse*. I should have sent a card to say I was coming. It was rude of me.

I do belong to you, I said. But we both prefer it, I think, if it feels as if I belong to you of my own free will, yes?

Yes, he said. His smile returned to his face.

So then, I said. Let us have this as we would prefer it. Escort me, I said. It was a long way, and I would walk. I waited expectantly, like a lady might, and he offered his arm.

Where shall we go? he asked. He set my hand in the crook of his arm.

Let us go to the Garnier, I said. For old times' sake. I would like to see if there has been any progress.

Construction has been halted, he said. Due to the cost of the war. A lack of funds. There had been some complaints in the newspapers about the cost of the Empress's diamonds. She had promised to buy fewer of them. Soldiers are more costly than an opera house. For now. And that is as it should be.

And with that, we went out into the street.

∼

The sun was low in the sky, a gold light on the gold leaf of the Garnier. I wondered if they would peel the gold off to make coins for war.

The Garnier rose grandly, covered in the busts and names of famous men, and surrounded, of course, by those black-iron dragon's-teeth fences, the imperial *N E N E N E*, and the bronze muses with their lanterns.

I studied the nearest muse's face carefully and wondered who had posed for it.

With time, it had become less bitter, this life; the tenor had come to feel more like my companion, the man who kept me safe, fed, clothed, and even educated in exchange for what he needed from me, which was that I would not leave him. This life with him, this enclosure, the fine clothes, the fine apartment, the fine meals, all would be fine, fine, fine, and yet none of it moved me. I already knew to take my pleasure from among his pleasures, certainly, but those moments were like trying to dine from the crumbs off his meals, snatched as I could while he ate well from all of life.

I had learned to hope for a certain future during my time spent with Pauline and her circle; this was all that had made this life bearable. Here in Paris, alone with him, I could only feel the madness of his mission and that doom it seemed he sought for us both. There was some final scene he hoped to enact, and I could not apprehend it. I could only feel him arranging us on this stage to his purpose.

The tenor had said nothing since our conversation at the door. He raised an eyebrow as I looked his way and turned to face me.

How did you find Baden-Baden in my absence? he asked.

Like many, I gambled, I said.

Did you win? he asked.

Sometimes, I said. Enough to have an appetite for it now.

He nodded at this.

Careful of your appetites, he finally said. They make for poor masters.

Yes, I said. I've masters enough.

Here another expression came over him, new in this light, which turned to copper as the sun set farther. I'm too fond of you, he said.

I had never expected him to say this.

Is it a fondness? I asked.

Take care, he said. For it is.

I reached to his cheek and placed my hand there, and he ducked his head down against it.

Men often complain of the wickedness of women. Of how we

delight in what power we have over their hearts. But they reign over everything else, so of course, they grudge us this, should we ever come to rule over this thing the size of their fist. I had to restrain in myself the urge to laugh at him, at the idea that he loved me, that he truly loved me. And yet, as he had granted me my little freedom, or my illusion of it, to follow my whim to go outside, to refuse his immediate physical gratification, the idea that he perhaps did love me filled me for a moment with something like tenderness.

I harshly corrected myself.

I was only back in his little theater again. I had never left it, not really. I would need to, for it would soon fill with death.

I did not understand his apparent nonchalance at the prospect of the war, and I did not understand how to ask after the source of it, and so I could only pretend to share it and hope to learn in the process.

You are so quiet, he said. Have you tired of me, then? He said it lightly, but he did not look at me.

No, no. This place saddens me, I'm afraid, I said. Please take me home.

He offered me his arm again, and together we returned to the apartment.

～

The very next morning, having slept the night beside me, something he rarely did, he slunk from the bed, looked at my clothes, and said, I buy you all the dresses you want, but I shouldn't.

The tenor had taken to saying this often.

I shouldn't buy you any dresses at all, he continued. You are better nude. But these Baden-Baden dresses will not do.

I sat up.

You can wear them once more to be fitted for new ones, he said. Order at least a dozen. Go to see someone decent, have them present the bill to this address. He slid a card onto my vanity table. Go to your favorite.

He fitted his collar into his shirt, tied his tie, and then sat to put on his stockings and shoes. As he stood and straightened himself, he turned back to me, and said, Welcome back to Paris.

I presented myself at the dressmaker who knew me well, the only place I knew to go, the one the Comtesse had sent me to—Félix. Jou-jou! he said. Welcome back. It has been so long! How was your time in Baden-Baden?

Fantastic, I said. I did not bother to correct him as to my name.

It has agreed with you, he said. The Comtesse said you were very happy there.

I smiled as if I knew this. I look forward to calling on her shortly, I said, though I knew I could not bring myself to do so. I gave him the tenor's card. He handed it back to me. I looked at him questioningly.

He laughed. My dear, we have his card already—we expected you! He wrote just the other day that we were to see you soon. Follow me, he said. This time I will show you the new fabrics. They have just come in. And it's just as well, he said. These may be the last dresses made in Paris. He pushed back the curtain to his atelier and withdrew his tape ribbon from his watch pocket. I have not even seen the orders yet for the Empress's series at Compiègne.

~

After the constant company in Baden-Baden, Paris felt empty. I went to see Euphrosyne's barman, to leave her a message with him, but when I entered the café, another man stood behind the counter. I left at once.

I returned again another time at a different time of day, and it was still the same stranger. Again, and it was yet another stranger. There was no sign her friend worked there any longer.

I had not written to Euphrosyne during my absence, for I blamed her for what had happened—for her advice that I go to see the Comtesse. But it was the summer again, and I was sure the Bal

Mabille would be full. She would be there. As would my fantasy composer.

For I did think of him as a fantasy now. I had imagined him so often, he had become a figure of imagination, almost as remote and mythical to me as my hidden god. That old fantasy, my imagined flight from Baden-Baden, in defiance of my circumstances, had been a hopeless one. It is better, I had told myself, to wait. You would be destroyed. By waiting, I hoped we would be reunited in some future where I was finally a singer and he a composer. The Empress dead, the Emperor also.

Would we recognize each other then? I wondered.

The belief we would be reunited, that the world would organize itself to bring us together, this seemed comic at best set against the very real city around me now. All I risked, if I went to the Mabille that night, was to enter and find another woman beside him, leaning over the piano, pushing his hair back as he played — though that still had the power to keep me away.

This, at least, was what I told myself each time I took out and then put away my cancan shoes, which were too old now and, no doubt, out of style. And besides, it would be August; the city would begin to empty from the heat.

I instead took to returning to the opera house on my own, to sit outside of it, almost as if I were keeping it company; soon it became a regular pilgrimage. I stood on the sidewalk opposite the entrance and imagined my own likeness there, not among the busts of the composers, but along the roof, perhaps in the place of the golden Apollo, or joining him. I'd once thought the Empress to be ridiculous, having herself painted as a goddess, and yet there I sat at a table outside of a bistro sipping a coffee and imagining an image of myself shining down from the top of the Opéra Garnier.

After a month of these visits, I heard a voice behind me say, Can I enlist you to help me knock some of them off the roof?

I turned. My composer sat at the table behind me. He raised his glass and nodded at me.

There's no room for me up there, he said.

The sight of him, a reproach for all of my doubts. The path to him had indeed led away from him to here.

I did recognize him. His face had thinned instead of thickening, a sign of, perhaps, difficult times for a man. I wondered for just an instant if he recognized me as well, and then he said, I searched for you.

I sat still, shocked, unable even to move.

The other *grisettes* said you had run off. With that tenor singer. I wondered where you could have run off to, and it would seem you ran here. I hoped it would be.

He was here, he was talking to me, he had looked for me.

I had hoped it would be me. I never had the honor of your name, he said.

If I had to die here in the war to come, at least he was here with me. Though as I looked at him, the old fears—that we were watched or would be discovered—returned the louder. I studied the area around us for signs someone was watching us, but there were none. Perhaps our watchers had abandoned us.

I wanted to imagine my fears were senseless, but I knew better. That seemed to be the mistake I made each time.

Please excuse me, he said, and he came to my table and made a bow. I am Aristafeo, Aristafeo Cadiz. My name means "ugly knob." My mother invented it, as she felt I'd ruined her looks. But I like it, as I don't think anyone else has this name. I've been watching you come here for several weeks and wanted to be sure it was you before I spoke to you. It is you, yes?

Lilliet Berne, I said. And then I added, Falcon soprano, most recently a student of Pauline Viardot-García's in Baden-Baden and newly returned to Paris. I am here in case of war, apparently. Should Paris need to be defended by sopranos.

He smiled. I devoutly wish it will not come to that, he said. I congratulate you. You did well to run off; you must be an extraordinary singer to have been her student. I'm honored. This means you have seen her copy of *Don Giovanni* written in the master Mozart's own hand?

I said I had.

I look forward to hearing you sing. I must ask you, I thought I knew you another way, he said.

What way is this? I asked.

I used to play in the band at the Cirque d'Hiver, and there was a rider there I fell in love with. She was beautiful and so quiet. The other girls were so crass and loud, but she said nothing, not once. She was let go before I could speak to her. I would see her also at the Bal Mabille, where she seemed more lively. But I was playing in the orchestra there and could not stop playing to ask her to dance.

You should have, I said. You should have asked her to dance.

Then, I suppose, she was let go again, from whatever job she had, he said, for I saw her next as a maid at Compiègne.

I stared at him, uncertain as to whether I should laugh or run.

How many women are you? he asked.

A legion, I said. How many orchestras have you played in?

All of them, perhaps, he said, smiling.

I heard the chiming of the clock behind us and knew I had to return.

Monsieur, I said. If you'll please excuse me, I must take my leave of you.

Mademoiselle Berne, please, he said, still holding my hand. We were just getting to know each other.

I nodded and could not stop the smile on my face.

I did not dare let him into this life here, not yet. It was too soon. And yet I did not dare let him go. But surely the tenor could not begrudge me an accompanist.

I slid a card from my calling-card case, the one the tenor had given me to give to my dressmaker.

Is it beneath you, I asked, if I ask you to rehearse with me? I must prepare for my debut.

I have looked for you everywhere, he said. Everywhere but here, and he smiled, holding up the card before putting it inside his jacket's ticket pocket. Consider me your servant.

Call on me there, I said. Tomorrow. Come for tea. I will try to explain everything.

He laughed out of surprise and shock, and then said, a little louder, Until then, and then he bowed until I walked away.

~

When Aristafeo arrived the next day, Doro showed him in, her surprise at his arrival kept from her face except, as she entered, her eyes, full of fear.

The tenor was in rehearsals, I knew, and would not be free until well after dinner. We had hours alone.

Thank you for coming to rehearse with me, I said, loud enough for Doro to hear as she left. My skills with the piano are rudimentary at best, and the piano is out of tune.

Aristafeo did not flinch in the slightest. Of course, he said.

The music room is this way, I said. If you'll follow me?

He followed, and I drew the doors shut. As he passed me, I whispered, Play anything.

He smiled as he sat and began something that began in arpeggios and wild flourishes, and then settled into a melody, sweetly sad. As I walked to the piano bench, the pleasure of hearing him play again filled me. It was like it had been the first time, being admitted to a place where only the two of us existed. But on this afternoon, it was also exactly like being somewhere only the two of us could speak to each other.

For I was sure Doro would have to listen in on me as part of her duties.

Now it is harder for us to be overheard, I said.

Yes, he said. You're good.

Will you remember this? I said. This theme you are playing?

Of course, he said.

Play it for me always, then, I said. When I ask for it.

Of course, he said. He met my eyes and did not pause. What am I here to help you with? Or is this song the one you wanted?

I set out the music for Bellini's *La Sonnambula*.

You can adapt it for piano? I asked.

He raised his eyebrows in mock contempt. Of course, he said. I won't refuse you anything I can do.

Please, I said, as he studied it. Let's begin.

I sat silently, afraid even to meet his eyes, as he found his way through the music confidently. I only watched his fingers as they moved along the keys. The long hours of sitting on the Empress's bench, waiting for her to ring for me, listening to him in memory, had become the long hours of listening to Pauline play the Chopin nocturne in Baden-Baden almost every night as night fell. I knew it well enough to ask for it by name, though I didn't dare to, not yet. I still felt guilty that I had given up on him, that I had believed myself foolish to think he cared for me. This man now beside me, playing for me, hidden in my past, who had somehow kept watch over me this whole time, close but not close enough until yesterday afternoon.

And yet we were too soon. Cupid's slow arrow was still too fast. All those years ago, I had told myself I would look for him only after the Empire had fallen or the Emperor or Empress died; that seemed safe. I did not have the luxury of taking risks. I did not ask him, but I felt sure he didn't, either. I could have waited, I suppose, a little longer then, except I could not. And neither could he; he leaned in and kissed me once more, his hands still playing evenly, as if this were the most ordinary of gestures.

Five

ON SEPTEMBER 2, 1870, after an earlier false report of French victories, the Emperor surrendered to the Prussians and was taken captive along with the Prince Imperial.

There was no negotiation for the Emperor's return, but instead the Sénat noisily convened and declared the new republic without him. The Empress was chased from Paris.

There were wild celebrations in the street for the birth of the new republic. It was as if in defeat, Paris dressed in the air, briefly, of a liberated city—liberated from empire. Crowds descended on the Tuileries and it was looted before the new government's troops took control and continued, at least, the posture of a continued war with Prussia.

All over the city, old newspapers immediately covered over the imperial *N*'s and *E*'s, soon to be replaced by *immortelles*, the symbol of the new republic.

I received the news from my dressmaker, who admitted he was in mourning. His eyes were red from grief.

I am ruined without her, he said. Without Compiègne alone, it would be a disaster, but now there will be no winter balls, either. Will these senators have balls? My congratulations on taking receipt of my last dresses, he said, and bowed ostentatiously.

When I then informed him I was there to order even more clothes, the dressmaker prolonged our visit, urging me to try the newest dress forms on. When I left him, he was all smiles again. As was I.

I had kept my impatience from showing—I nearly ran all the way back to the apartment.

All over Paris, I passed workmen busy chipping off the imperial seals. The imperial seals had been taken off me as well.

This was the day of my liberation, the end of my bargain with the Comtesse. I would leave him soon, I decided—within a day or two. I would have to leave the apartment as if I were going on one of my walks and take almost nothing with me except the jewels, which I would sell as I went to pay my way. The departure should be sudden so that he would have no way to stop me, as if he turned a corner and I went another way on to another life entirely.

But where to go? I thought to go to Pauline, back to Baden-Baden; the jewels meant I could afford to pay my own way this time. Or, if it was too dangerous to be in Baden-Baden—the tenor knew her, he could be there in an instant—perhaps Leipzig, then. Pauline had spoken fondly of it and had a good friend there, a composer. I could debut there instead of Weimar. I knew I could simply go to her unannounced. She would take me in.

Back at the apartment, I planned a dinner, thinking to have a last grand meal with the tenor. I would give him one last happy memory. I gave directions to Lucy for the shopping, named some of the dishes I knew he liked from our days in Baden-Baden, asking if she thought she could make *carré d'agneau boulangère, poisson vert,* even something as festive as punch *à la russe.*

She looked at me strangely. I had never suggested or planned anything of this kind to her. Lucy and Doro had adjusted after my return to my new schedule of rehearsal, the new clothes, the new bearing, but we'd also resumed many old habits, like our game of cards with gin, and this house still ran itself without my guidance, as if it were still the petite *théâtre du désir* it began as. I had never intruded on Lucy's duties this way, never acted the part of *maîtresse.* I had never had the tenor to dinner, either, not this way. Sometimes, after a night spent here, he would make his way to the larder and return with a sausage, bread, and cheese.

No sooner had I wondered if this dinner was some unwelcome intrusion or if the menu was eccentric to her at best—the French could be quite strict about what was eaten when and how, none the more so than servants—when Lucy spoke.

Mademoiselle, I will do my best, but . . . and she gestured around us, with a laugh.

What is it? I asked.

Well, she said. *Poisson vert,* perhaps. But *carré d'agneau?* Most likely *filet de chat.*

When my expression showed I did not understand, she said, You may recall the Siege?

Of course, I said, chastened. Of course. But . . . didn't the Emperor surrender?

She gave me a cutting look that surprised me. Yes, she said. He surrendered himself. With his prince, poor child. But we have not surrendered. We've lost the man who could never lead us to victory, but we have not lost. Now, it seems to me, we very well might win.

I tried to seem cheerful at this prospect or even to believe her. She noticed, and I could tell it offended her.

There is mail, she said. And with that, she pushed a letter from Pauline my way.

The letter had taken almost two months to reach me. Pauline had stayed until the third month of the Franco-Prussian War. She'd stayed later than most, remaining even when the fighting came close enough so that the smoke could be seen and the cries and cannon fire heard in the mountains near her house. She left when the Germans she'd loved so much, and who previously had loved her, began picketing her home.

These protesters were unmoved that their side was winning the war and cared not at all that Pauline had moved to Baden-Baden along with her husband in protest of the reign of Napoleon III— they did not know nor did they care that at the war's start she'd even hoped it might result in the removal of Napoleon III, as that meant she could return home to Paris. She was almost on their side, except for their new belief she was an interloper. Eventually M. Viardot left first, for London, to secure accommodations for waiting out the war safely. Turgenev then took Pauline by train to the coast and put her on a boat with her children before following soon after; and with that, they were in exile. By the time she had returned home to Paris, Paris was her exile from Baden-Baden.

> I know that when I see you again, whenever that is, it will be as if we each carry a piece of that vanished place with us against the day it might be reassembled or returned to glory. I hope you are still well and happy and safe, and that you continue with your lessons. Keep your piece of our lost home well. Do not let the voice rest; you have gained too much to let go.
>
> I am, as ever,
> Pauline

She was in London, then. I would have to get to London.

I'm delighted to see you take an interest in these things, the tenor said to me that evening as Lucy wheeled in the first course, a potato soup with leeks. I understand you have begun rehearsing here at home.

The rehearsals had been in part a test to see what Doro or Lucy said of my doings to him, and I quietly registered the success even as it disappointed me.

I am glad to hear of your rehearsing for your debut, he said. And how are we paying for our young accompanist?

I shrugged. I am helping him, I said. He is writing something new. An opera, if I understand correctly. With a role for me.

The tenor smiled. So he loves you, he said.

It is not love he feels, I said, joking. He did not laugh.

He set down his knife. A toast, he said. To your original role. An honor rare to the greatest of singers and rare certainly for a singer who has not yet debuted.

I raised my glass and touched it to his, and it did not shake.

I would not have this *amant de coeur* staying past sunset, he said. I looked away at this to treat it as ridiculousness, but it was generous and surprised me. He raised his glass to his mouth.

Of course, I said to the tenor. And never past sunset. For my accompanist.

Good girl, he said. Thank you. I'm moved by the thoroughness of your preparations for this role. He brushed his hands on his napkin and then lifted the spoon to his soup at last. I will help.

I would never ask—

You're not asking, my love. I insist. I know the Elvino role quite well. He smiled at me, glittering through the dark. We'll begin the day after tomorrow. That way you can tell your pianist to prepare.

Amant de coeur—this lover, he pays nothing, he visits only after the others have their fill of you, he must not interfere. You never give him a ride in a carriage provided to you by another lover, you never make a gift to him of anything that was given to you. You never entertain him at any hour the others might prefer. The affair is tolerated entirely on the premise that it exists in the realm of pure love, untainted by the touch of money, and so, this *amant* is envied, of course, and so it is better if his identity is unknown, but it is good for a courtesan's reputation if she is thought to have one of these, it shows she has the normal emotions. The fantasy is then alive for her other lovers, that if circumstances were different it might be any of them who held court in her heart instead of him.

Of course, if a man has a courtesan, he does not more than tolerate the fantasy that her love could be freely given.

It was time for me to have something only for me.

You must always leave before sunset, I told Aristafeo as we sat at the piano, and he played for me again.

Is he a vampire, then?

I smiled as I considered this. I saw myself in black, the needle of prussic acid at my fingertip. No, I said. It would be easier if he were.

He kept playing.

He knows that we've been rehearsing, I said.

I thought as much.

That he knew—

It does not surprise me.

Several bars passed before we spoke again.

He will join us tomorrow, as well, I said. To sing Elvino.

He nodded without comment.

I returned my attention to the music. You are composing this now? I asked.

Yes, he said. You're too kind, however. It's terrible.

No, it's not, I said. But now you must make an opera with a role for me, for I have said you are.

Is it just music for now, or is there a libretto?

I did not answer; instead, I listened to him play for nearly an hour more like this.

Escape with me, I said. Can it be done? Could we leave now?

The light shadowed his face. He seemed to be thinking of it, but he had not answered immediately, and I instantly doubted myself. You are asking me, he said, but you, I think, are the escape artist.

What will you say to him tomorrow, I asked, when he asks you about the opera I have said you are writing for me?

But I am still planning our escape, he said, his smile like thunder.

~

I found Amina first in the wig room at Pauline's Baden-Baden *Haustheater*, one wig among many on the shelves of blank-faced wooden mannequin heads, some with their eyes scrawled in with pen to make hideous glares, jowls, sly winks. Or rather, she had found me. I had not known it was one of Pauline's most famous roles, that it nearly belonged to her. Under each wig was a card with the name. Madame Viardot walked purposely toward this one, with black curls in a ridiculous pile, almost like shearling. Small pink satin bows glowed here and there among the ringlets.

Amina, the name read. She shook the wig at me.

I took it from her and held it up, examining it from underneath. There were small loops to pull it with. It was a small cap sewn with hair.

Put it on, Madame Viardot commanded. There's not much trick to it. She walked over as if to help me.

I slid it over my head.

I pushed and pulled at it to settle it into place. When I looked into the mirror, I had the oddest experience when it was in place. I knew exactly how to smile, different from my own smile. As if the wig were a door for this other girl to walk through the moment I wore her hair.

I went home with the libretto and the music, a little afraid of it.

The opera began in a village haunted by the ghost of an angry young woman, her eyes on fire, her hair like smoke as she ran the streets at night. She is not a ghost, though, but a sleepwalker, an orphan girl engaged to be married to the town's most handsome and suitable bachelor. One night she walks all the way to the hotel room of a visiting gentleman and awakes to find herself in his bed. This sets in motion a plot that unravels her engagement—she is thought to be untrue to her fiancé, Elvino, who breaks their engagement. As he prepares to marry her rival, she tries desperately to prove herself to him, failing until, as he marches to his wedding, he sees her asleep, walking the roof of the town's mill, singing in her sleep of her love for him. He rushes to her side to rescue her from falling to her death, and she wakes to find herself in his arms.

It was ridiculous, and yet the music was extraordinary, and I loved it—and it was not *Il Trovatore*. I had found a role to focus me that was neither the role I lived for nor lived inside of.

The tenor had adjusted his disappointment and kept assuring me we would perform this together at the Paris Opera next spring as my debut, a season I doubted would come. And yet I knew there was the slightest chance that I would still be allowed to debut, and so I knew there was nothing else for me to do. Whatever was to happen to Paris, it was time to leave. He would wait for us in the music room; I would be gone. And would try to convince Aristafeo to come with me.

～

The next morning, after the tenor had left, I asked Lucy to have the phaeton rigged up, then thought better of it and asked for just my horse.

I wore the general's coat, my jewels bound in plain pouches hidden at my waist and ankle. My face hid even the slightest hint of a good-bye. Until later, I said.

Pardon me, but if I may say something, Lucy said.

By all means, I said.

Take a driver, she said. Or perhaps your horse won't be there when you return. If you take ours, he may still sell it while you're away, but if you tip him, he may fight for the horse and wait for you.

I hired a driver to take me to the Place Vendôme instead; and near there, at a chapel I didn't recognize, I asked the driver to stop.

I haven't had confession, I said, and stepped out of the carriage, though I didn't need to explain to him.

In case I was being followed, I entered the church, slipped a few sous from my purse into the slot by the door, and took a candle, following the line of women ahead of me, kneeling and lighting it, crossing myself as the sisters had taught me. I looked up. A figure I didn't recognize presided above a thick field of candles — so many had come to ask for favors, the flames had the warmth of a hearth fire, so I lingered until the women behind me glared and then I left to find Aristafeo.

There were no men in the line as I passed out of the church; the men of age to fight were at war. We were a city of women, children, and old men. The streets had filled with garbage that was no longer collected. The stench overpowered any fear I had of being caught.

At the address Aristafeo had given me in the Marais, I found an elegant town house within a courtyard, which impressed me. I rang the plain bell knocker and heard the sounds of dogs running and barking inside, vicious. I drew back from the entrance and was close to leaving when he pushed his face out, straining with the exertion of holding back two large black dogs. One moment! he said. And then his face vanished as the door closed again. I could hear the yelping and begging of the dogs and his voice, weary as he spoke to them in stern, swift Spanish until they were quiet.

He unlatched the door again, smiling. Forgive them, he said. They are loyal protectors but also quite hungry. I had not expected you, and so they were outside.

I stepped cautiously through the wooden gate, pausing at the sight of the dogs before entering completely. What are their names? I asked.

Gaston and Frédéric. Or, as I call them, the Lords of the Lower Garden.

I took in the courtyard. The dogs, both large black hounds nearly the size of ponies, sat grinning at me, anxious to approach but clearly having just been disciplined.

Come this way.

He walked so that he stood between the dogs and me. Once inside, he closed the door, and they began to whimper. He shouted to them again through the door and then turned to me, and said, I have nothing to feed them, of course. I am worried that soon they will turn on me.

I unfastened the ribbon on my hat and then undid my hair.

Take me upstairs, and then we will speak of food. And everything else.

He stepped close to me, studying my face, curious, amused again. His eyes betrayed nothing of the bitter appraisal I'd seen the day before—if he had not forgiven me for the insult of the day previous in rehearsal, he had upon my arrival. In the carriage over, I had been full of fears, each of them turning over to reveal another one underneath until, by the time I stepped through his door, I had a single mission I could be sure of: I was here to see him this one last time and to ask if he would leave with me. Here in his house I could admit what I hadn't previously, that I did not know him—I only desired him. Was it only lust, the lust I might feel for any beautiful thing, for he was beautiful, how had I not remembered? Had I somehow reduced his beauty in memory or had it grown? Why did I love him? Did he love me? And what if he would not leave with me? I might not have the strength to leave him behind and go on alone —and I would need to, to live; and yet I could not bear it if he was to die, even if it should be that he did not love me; and thus went my mind even as he reached for me and unlaced my dress at the back with a nimble, practiced hand.

How stupid you are, I told myself, *and yet how wise to finally be here.*

As he kissed me, I entered again the world that existed only with him. I fought the old habit I still had of retreating from the sensations of my own body as I delivered myself over to the pleasures of others. To be here felt like pulling myself out of my own grave. This impulse to stay hidden in this life that was death, the fear that it was the only safety, this was what I hoped to smash now in myself. To break the lock on the cage I had made of myself.

His hands pulled open my corset and his face pushed into my hair, stopping when his chin touched my neck.

He paused. What is it? I asked, as he brushed his fingers across my back, finishing the unlacing.

You don't know how long I've dreamt of this, he said, touching his brow to my own.

Dream no more, I said, to him as much as to myself, and drew back, leading him along behind me as my dress fell off me in waves.

I stepped from the traveling costume and lay across his bed on my back, making a display of myself before him as he smiled down at me, my smooth belly and breasts, my nipples pinking in the cold.

I enjoyed this no matter the man—the power it gave me over him to simply appear naked before him. But now it was my turn to be in silent wonder. Aristafeo stood over me, and as I watched, he stripped off his waistcoat, his shirt, his pants until his long slim body rose up, a dream of him in the afternoon light, as soft as smoke. He was like a faun, in that way I suppose most men are — it is right to paint them as half beast, I think, especially from the waist down; and his was a trim waist, too, and a long one. In the garden that first night he'd been only a silver violent desire, the night's hot center, but here in his bedchamber, I could see all of him. He smiled as he came near, reaching out to trace a line from my hip bone to just under my breast so that I cried out softly, surprised by pleasure. I could feel the warmth of him just before he touched me, and as he completed his descent, our skin touched in the cold air of the room and then he burned across me.

I went into my own hunger for him and stayed there under him until it was gone.

He took me three times that afternoon — the first like a race, hard and fast, as if it were just to be done with to make room for the others; the second slower, gentler, tender, if excruciatingly so, the pleasure drawn out until it was almost agony; the third a true descent into another place altogether, where I felt afterward as if we were finally revealed to each other, who we had each been all along and perhaps had never known until then. Each of the first two times, he would rise up, smiling, and I would say, Again. After the third time, I said nothing. For at least an instant, there was nothing of who I'd been before, nothing seemed to remain. I lay quiet instead, wanting to hold only this oblivion, and as it receded, there came the slow rise and fall of his chest as he slept against me in the gathering dark.

I smiled in satisfaction and then fell away until I slept as well.

∼

After some time, I opened an eye. The room was nearly the color of the inside of my eyelid. I knew the sun had set and remembered my lie to the driver, who, if he still waited at the church, was no doubt beginning to wonder how many sins I might confess to and was still likely hoping to be paid. I could see him finally going in to search before driving away, the church door opening as he looked in and closing as he left.

When I did not return, I knew the tenor would go through my rooms for signs—and there he would find my clothes still waiting, the shoes all there except the one pair. He would ask Lucy as to my whereabouts, and she would say I'd gone to confession and that she'd told me to take our driver. He would notice I had not. It was then he might go to see if I had taken any money and my jewels.

I had left the money. I wanted him to imagine I was still preparing to leave, not that I had left.

Whether he believed this or not, today was the beginning of all the tenor would never forgive, and if there was the slightest chance he learned I was still alive, it would mean our deaths unless we left now.

Wake up, I said.

He rolled to the side, his beautiful face smiling at me as his eyes blinked open and he kissed me.

Have you finished our plan of escape? I asked. For we should leave, and soon.

He laughed. Ah, he said. Yes. Where are we going?

London, I said. Or if not there, perhaps Leipzig.

I see, he said. And how will we eat?

I reached out to my dress and withdrew one of the little bags, this one with my earrings and the rose pin, which I dropped on his stomach. *Bijoux,* I said.

He pulled it open and held one of the earrings up to his eye. You have also been a baroness of some kind, it seems, he said.

Gifts from admirers, I said, and shrugged. You may know of this tradition.

I once played with the Conservatoire orchestra for a very rich baroness, he said. She had been trained to sing and wanted to have a concert with a soprano friend of hers. She hired the entire orchestra of the Conservatoire and brought them into her vast ballroom, where we played accompaniment to the two women for more than three hours.

Were they talented? I asked.

The friend had some talent, he said. We laughed.

We were rented for less than the cost of their bracelets. Our director asked the one with talent if she gave concerts, and she said her family would be scandalized if she took to the stage. She laughed at the idea.

He sat up and looked off into the garden, brushing his fingers across his moustache.

I had a fantasy of barricading the room to make them listen to us instead and to take, for our pay, everything they wore, he said. Leave them naked, tied to the chandelier. And the baroness, she liked me. He winked. Instead, we took our pay and drank. I have lived on the generosity of women with bracelets that could pay for a room full of men like me. But this is not how I wish to live with you.

He set the bag back on my thigh and sat up to push back my hair.

You may notice, we are surrounded by Communards who would shoot us as deserters, he said. And should we escape them, Germans who may shoot us as spies. And then, apart from the patriots, the siege takers, and the partisans, there are the ordinary thieves who would kill us just for one of these. He pointed at the bag.

I must leave, I said. I must leave him, and Paris, and he must not know where I go, and you must come with me.

So it's like that, he said. I had wondered. This was your first stop.

I said nothing.

I've just only found you again, he said. I am not ready to lose you or to die as quickly as that. But we should not go now. He touched the little bag with a finger. But don't go back. Does he know you're here?

No, I said. Well, he may. I left no evidence of a next address. But he is clever.

Stay here then, he said. We will be safe here until it is safe to leave.

You don't know him, I said. He'll find us if we stay in Paris. And then he'll kill us both.

You don't know me, Aristafeo said, smiling, and he kissed me again. I keep the dogs a little hungry for a good reason. He may try to kill us. But he'll die first. And if not, then at least I'll be sure we'll all die together.

This silenced me.

I won't let him have you, he said.

I only nodded.

He helped me dress again, laughing at all of the strings and undergarments, but he was very able at it all the same, and it was then I looked around at his surroundings.

A few touches seemed to be entirely his, like a walking stick by the bed, topped by a silver fox head. The rest was a bland elegance: In his study there was a golden velvet couch and a Persian rug in red, blue, and white. A dark walnut chair with legs like corkscrews and dark leather upholstery sat by an old desk painted black wood with gold leaf. A sword on the wall and a musket.

I felt myself looking for a sign that the Empress had been here, but I could not see it.

Welcome to your new home, he said.

With that, he leaned in and kissed my head once more, and whispered, as if he'd guessed at what I suspected, *She was never here.*

In those first days I was anxious; I stayed inside as much as possible, and when I went out, I wore kerchiefs to shadow my face. I did not know the tenor's regular path through the city; I did not know where to expect him. I did not even know which markets Lucy attended, which butcher and so on, but I knew enough to know they would not come to the Marais for goods. I knew to avoid my little perch at the Opera, but this no longer mattered as it once had.

And while thoughts of the market and seeing Lucy or Doro sometimes gave me pangs of missing them, the moment I understood that one of them had betrayed me to the tenor on Aristafeo's visits meant that among their tasks was spying on me, and the memory of my affections for them now humiliated me instead.

I would spare you such trips, Aristafeo said. I assured him I would do my best to help him with whatever errands could still be attended to as I didn't want to stay only in the house. This was another Paris I was meeting there in the Marais, one without the tenor, and I began to enjoy the city in my newest disguise in some way I never had before.

Soon enough, there was less and less need of going to the markets for there were only long lines in the cold for what little was there.

Is it time to leave? I would ask him every so often.

No, not yet, he would say each time.

By December, the food crisis in Paris was in extremis. The cold at least kept the smell of the garbage down, and there was less garbage also, and what there was had less and less in it that would rot.

The Third Republic had proved no more effective at ending the Siege and fighting the Prussians than the Second Empire, though, of course, I wanted to know only when we could eat again. As winter started, the hunger became unbearable, and now there was also a need for wood for fires. I sometimes longed for my dresses, but the last dresses made in Paris would bag on me where once they had fit perfectly. I could no longer wear them even if I could retrieve them, for fear of appearing a woman of means. I instead contented myself with my one dress and took hat pins and pinned it for some time so it fit until I became too thin, and then I let it hang loose so people would not stare.

To eat, I went to the Bois with Aristafeo and the Lords of the Lower Gardens, and watched them as they hunted for animals while I collected chestnuts for roasting later. Soon I also gathered the leaves, and sometimes pieces of bark, to make soup. I did this until the trees were all bare, stripped from root to just above where the tallest man could reach.

The walking stick was for disciplining Gaston and Frédéric.

Aristafeo let them range over the Bois, where as late as November they found rabbits and rats and sometimes a cat. We let them eat first, and then they would hunt for us.

To be so hungry again, hungrier than I'd ever known as winter began, I felt with certainty that my death was coming for me; soon I'd be reunited with my family, called before the Lord; for all of my sins, my lies, my selfishness, and my lust, now I would finally be caught.

And each time I arrived at this conclusion, I put it out of my head until it became a trail I walked regularly in my thoughts, from waking to the hunger, from the remembering to the forgetting.

∼

To stay sane as best we could, we adopted a schedule to which we stuck regularly. He would wake first and start a fire for tea—coffee was no longer available. When I woke, the tea kept hunger at bay for a time, and we would then rehearse. I would do my warm-ups first, my Viardot-García scales, at the piano, and then he would do his own warm-ups and play, and then in the late morning we would rehearse together. We would break to hunt for our luncheon, and then we would return, and then I might read, or he would, with more tea to keep us from hunger, and then it would be time for whatever supper we could muster. Sometimes he taught me Spanish, and more and more we drank wine in place of tea, which also kept the hunger at bay and cast a lightly drowsy light in which it was easier to bear the day. But he never took a single visitor, he seemed to have no friends to speak of, and he did not seek out friends at their homes. We had no society except each other and the dogs. We made love still, but I no longer made a display of my body; it was too cold and I was too thin. I wanted his last memory of me to be one of a plumper breast, such as it had ever been.

I no longer asked when we would leave.

Time, for that matter, seemed to have stopped altogether, each day the same until some new shortage would occur, and soon after the streets would fill with hearses and coffins as whoever could not survive this newest famine died.

One afternoon, after we returned to the Marais with a few thin rabbits the dogs caught for us and he had skinned them in the kitchen and I had stirred the fire back to life and set chestnuts to roast, he appeared in the kitchen's door. He had asked if he should save the blood for blood sausage, which I did not know how to make, and this surprised him some. That is not the woman I am, I said, and he laughed.

When the rabbits had finished stewing and the chestnuts were done, I left the kitchen to find him. He sat staring into a glass of red wine, and without looking up, he poured another for me.

These rabbits I watched stew, they were rare, I knew it. I wished I knew how to make the blood sausage.

Have you never seen him, then? Aristafeo asked me, and I knew without his saying who he meant.

No, I said.

Then the dogs' work is done, he said.

I nodded dumbly.

There aren't even rats anymore. The dogs will be taken from me soon, I think, he said. I would prefer they die at my hands.

He had never once spoken this way of them. What do you say? he asked.

I couldn't say, I replied, and shrugged. I had never loved them, but I knew he had—I knew he did not say this lightly. I knew he had become proud of the way he'd never eaten them. But we risked becoming weaker than those who had eaten their dogs already and becoming prey to them.

Game is better than carrion, he finally said. It is Christmas in a few days. I'll do it before then.

I laughed to think of dogs for Christmas.

We'll feast, he said, and pray for an end to the Siege. Though it has brought at least one gift.

I watched him, expectant.

Is it that the Siege has set you free, then? he said.

It may be.

It was good of the Germans to do this for you, then. He looked up at me and raised his glass. Cheers to them. From his pocket, he removed a gold ring with a large green stone, and then he went to his knee.

This ring belonged to my mother, he said. A gift from her for my future bride. It is Roman, very ancient, in her family for generations.

I took it from him and held it up, turning it over in my hand. The ring looked like something that had fallen out of one of the paintings in the Tuileries. It did not fit on any of my fingers, though, and it began to slide off. I held the hand up and examined the beautiful color of the stone in the light.

Will you be my wife? he asked.

If I was to be married, it would be like this. I drew my hand across his face so the ring grazed his cheek.

Yes, I said. I was always yours, but, yes, I will be yours.

～

At the end of the third week, Paris was shelled for three days straight. Aristafeo's house in the Marais was unhurt.

Parisians, starving and bored by the long siege, had taken to watching the shells land as a sport, with picnics of only wine; while lacking for food, we did not lack for drink. We were told to keep buckets of water by the door in case of fire and to leave our doors unlocked in case a passerby required shelter from a shell.

Occasionally, they exploded and there was terrible death, but then also came children anxious to collect the fragments, which they hoped to sell as souvenirs. To whom I did not know.

I remember a woman who had died in the shelling. Her body stayed for nearly a week; no one dared or cared to move her. If you did not look closely, she seemed to be a peddler's bundle. I thought to try to remove her, but I did not know where to bring her or whom to call on to remove her body.

When she was finally removed, I was almost as afraid as when she was there.

I remember a man passed me on the street, moving with an eerie quiet. Only as he passed me did I notice he was covered in blood, smeared all across him. He carried against his chest a bundle soaked in blood and filthy. He had torn his sleeve to tie it up.

I thought to ask if he needed help, but he did not ask for any. He moved quietly instead, intent. I did not exist to him. He was trying to go unnoticed, I think, or he had gone mad. I let him go by.

His package, I had noticed, was the exact size and shape of someone's head.

When news of the armistice came, we were initially relieved for there were not even chestnuts now in the Bois, much less anything that fed on the chestnuts, and Aristafeo had pledged to me again that he could eat his dogs if needed.

Many had been less scrupulous than he.

You stood before a tree and had to decide what of it could be eaten and what used to heat your house.

And yet, hungry as we were, we did not know the hunger to come.

Six

THE PRUSSIANS MARCHED into Paris in a parade after the armistice was signed — a parade that was among the conditions of the treaty, culminating with a coronation of the German Emperor at Versailles. From the papers, we knew the German Emperor had already been declared Emperor at Versailles — done to demoralize Paris — but now it seemed he wanted to sit there and have the crown dropped onto his head while surrounded by all those mirrors.

First, however, we were to endure the soldiers at their victory feast in our midst.

These well-fed German soldiers marched in orderly rows onto the Champs-Élysées, and I looked to see if the tenor was among them. There was the possibility he had been conscripted; I knew from him that all German men were forced to enlist. But while many of the soldiers looked to have been the tenor's brothers, I did not see him.

Despite the talk of ambushing them or burning them with Greek fire, in the end our conquerors went unharmed, free to enjoy the bistros, newly stocked by the "Refurbishment," as the return of food and drink was called, and to drink to their content, even singing songs.

Some were very good singers.

Some became lost in the Bois de Boulogne and had to ask for directions from passersby.

Aristafeo and I enjoyed the parade from a table at a café, seated with some bread and wine. We had been alone together so long, it had seemed as if we might be the only people left alive and, instead, here we were in a crowd. I was painfully aware on seeing the soldiers of how thin I was and noticed how they paid me no mind. *I must look like a ghost*, I thought, and was relieved there were at least no German women for Aristafeo to compare me to; the only beauties in sight were the soldiers.

I was watching the *filles en carte* entertaining the Prussians in the café where we were. When the soldiers were gone, men pulled these women into the street, shouting at them, insulting them. They tore their clothes off and shouted at them some more as they sobbed, holding the shreds of their clothes over their dirty ribs in shame.

Let's go, I said to Aristafeo, as it began.

I was shaken; it could as easily have been me. I wondered where it would end. They may as well have burned the tables where the soldiers sat, the bars where they drank, the streets where they walked, even Versailles.

When the new government of the Third Republic demanded that all back rent and taxes owed from the time of the Siege were due to be paid within two days, only the butcher who had sold the meat from the animals of the zoo had anything with which to pay—the butcher and the coquettes. Most had nothing, unable to make a living for half the year.

There was a revolt. The new government troops were evicted, their weapons confiscated, and the Commune of Paris was declared. And as costly as food was during even the Refurbishment, months later, as I waited out the Commune, I would think those prices bargains.

∽

The moment to leave, between the armistice and the Commune, came and went with such suddenness that only after the Commune began did I understand we should have left then. Instead, Arista-

feo and I continued as we had in his house in the Marais, living as
husband and wife. I wore his ring on a leather strap at my throat,
where it would not fall off. He played his piano and I sang, and we
returned to drinking wine to stave off hunger once the shortages
began again.

There had still never been even one sign of the tenor, and perhaps it was all of the wine, or the hunger, but I came to believe at
times that he'd been killed in the war and that I was, as Aristafeo
had said, free at last. My curiosity to know the truth got the better
of me, however, and one day in March I returned to the apartment
on the avenue de l'Opéra to see what was there that I might take
—and see if there was even one clue as to his existence.

From the street there was no sign of looting, just closed shutters,
and there was no sound when I slid the key in the door and turned
it. I was greeted by the sight of muslin covers again on all of the furniture. Dust and soot feathered the floors. A man's footprints made
a path.

I followed them. They led me into the music room, where, on the
shrouded piano, sat a handkerchief tied over a letter. I opened it and
read the letter.

Comprimaria,

I write knowing there is every chance you are dead and will
never see this. Or that if you are alive, you are with your accompanist, and that either way you will never return. I write on
the chance that you miss me and have come here, hoping to be
forgiven for whatever has befallen you. We have been separated
and returned to each other too many times before this for me to
believe you are truly gone.

If you do read this, and you would be reunited with me again,
you must make arrangements to leave at once. The Commune
will not last. I was, of course, called off to war and returned with
the armistice, hoping to find some sign you had survived, but
found nothing. I returned once more through enemy lines to find

you again, and as I have not found you, I will leave you with an escape plan: There are mail balloons released from the roof of the Paris Opera. You must hide in one and leave by no later than the first week in April if you can. Do not warn the accompanist or anyone else — I will be unable to protect you then.

The Versaillaise government has struck a deal with our side to retake Paris, and when this happens, all of the Communards will be killed. There can be no mercy. I had hoped to take you myself; this was my single chance to return once the Commune began.

When you decide on the date you will leave, take an advertisement in the London *Times,* addressed to one André Lavertujon, and with the date on which you will leave, the numbers only, in a row. Underneath this letter are some francs for you to pay for it. In this way I will know to expect you. Show this handkerchief with my family crest to the mail agent, who is an agent of ours and knows to watch for you — that will admit you to the balloon. Tie it then to the riggings.

I love you, my Falcon. Come to me if you are alive; I will protect you.

I remain,
Your comprimario

His footprints led throughout the rest of apartment, and I followed them — to the closets, where my clothes still hung; the empty larder; the empty servants' rooms. He had searched for me in case I hid here. As I went, I looked for any food I could find and found nothing. There was at least the gin I'd missed, and I took it, with two of the most sensible dresses.

Before this, when he said he loved me, it meant nothing to me. Now I knew love. Had he never? His belief that he loved me, this was the belief of a madman. *How could he?* I wondered. *How could he still want me?* I thought of Euphrosyne's assurance the day he bought my contract, that he would tire of me. If I ever saw her again, I told myself I would have to tell her, no, he never tired of me, not once. All those days we thought we wanted a constant lover. What I would give for him to be a lover who would tire of me.

I had been a fool to stay, and now we would die.

~

As I returned to Aristafeo's house, I passed a doorway I had only ever seen closed. Today the doors were open.

The courtyard was empty and the wings to either side seemed abandoned. A bronze plaque still sat atop the center of the door. MAISON EUGÈNE NAPOLÉON, FONDÉE EN 1856, PAR SA MAJESTÉ L'IMPÉRATRICE.

A charity, apparently, named in honor of her son, the Prince.

I walked to the door and then did not go in.

Instead, I walked back to the street, to where I'd turned the wrong way, and went to Aristafeo's house.

The back wall was shared, it was clear.

She was never here, he'd said.

All of the ways I'd imagined the Empress kept him — in that secret dungeon below Compiègne, in some gilded cage, on a leash — I had not imagined anything like this, an office that she would visit regularly so as to look like a woman of good works and then to pass through the back wall into his house. Or he, through the wall to her.

Aristafeo hidden just under the surface of her life.

This house, it was an Empress's *théâtre du désir.* As clearly as if Odile herself had set it up for Eugénie.

I found Aristafeo in a remarkably good mood, at his piano. I showed him first the letter from the tenor and then the handkerchief.

He read the letter through and grimaced at the end.

Do you think he is having you watched?

Perhaps he was always having me watched, I said, as I walked to the back wall where it adjoined the building behind. It would not be a servant's door, it seemed to me. Or would it? Perhaps it would be disguised as one. Or it would require some secret switch, some ordinary item, which, when moved, would unlatch it.

How to feel, then? I wondered. It seemed he had lied to me about her being there, this was clear; but the reason was not, not entirely, except I knew well you only lied to keep a secret if it mattered.

Was this why we could never leave? Was there some vigil she had required of him, or someone else had required for her, some invisible hand that kept him here, like my own? Or was the vigil all his own?

~

That night I woke from my sleep and left his bed. I went downstairs.

Along the back wall were his study, a butler's kitchen, and a dusty, empty butler's quarters. I traced out the butler's room then the kitchen to no avail. His study seemed likely to be also possibly protected in some way; he had by no means confided in me despite our time together.

It was a handsome study, fit for a gentleman, I thought with some pride.

After some reluctance, I lifted books from shelves, picked up lamps and candelabra. I was as quiet as I could be.

I stood at last before the musket and the sword in the middle of the wall. I had never seen him take either down or clean them, not once in the time I'd been there.

I reached out and lifted the musket up.

The mechanisms of the door opened smoothly with almost no noise at all. So quiet, in fact, the loudest noise was my gasp.

Her scent, which I remembered, was still in these rooms. The door opened into a windowless suite with a bedchamber, a *salle de bain,* and a sitting room. In the bedroom was a handsomely appointed bed done in her red and gold, gold candlesticks, an armoire, no doubt where she could hang her dress. On opening it, I saw one of her dressing gowns. I wondered how many times I had sent a dress up for her before she had come here to visit her charity for the afternoon.

I saw him undressing her, dressing her again, and remembered how well he undressed me; he had practice. As many times as I had tied her corset, his hands had often undone my work.

I sat down on the bed.

The rubies and diamonds in the two bracelets on the side table glowed softly in the light of my taper. They lay one on top of the other. Two of the stones in the one had been pried out. I remembered them from Compiègne when they were whole. They were gifts from the Princess Metternich. The Empress had often held her arm out, admiring them before setting off to dinner.

They looked to be a last gift, the Empress no doubt guessing she was unlikely to see the Princess again. And unhappy, perhaps, to have gifts from her German friends, no matter how beloved.

Did he still come here, take down her dressing gown, and press it against his face? He had not washed it. The room was unchanged since her last visit, it seemed, except for the stones he'd removed from the bracelet to sell. I had grown so accustomed to the myth that I was the one who'd stolen him away from the Empress, it had not occurred to me it might not be true.

A draft blew faintly, shaking the taper's flame and reminding me the door was still open.

I followed the breeze, found my way to the far wall, the way to open it easy to see—a simple bar and latch. I stepped into what could only have been the Empress's office, decorated much as her other rooms had been and then undone by a storm. A massive directoire desk sat near another for a secretary, but all their drawers were thrown about the room, the contents strewn, and the chairs kicked over. The place had been ransacked. Several empty bottles sat on the desk.

I went back through that secret door and dressed quickly, slid the little pouches with my jewels back into their hiding places on my body. He slept through this all, deeply; his thick snore told me he would not know I was gone for hours.

I passed through the secret door one more time. As I did, I left the ruby rose by the Empress's bracelets and then was gone.

That, then, was the room I speak of. And there that cursed flower would sit until so many years later when it would somehow leave this room and return for me.

Seven

A LONG DREAM HAD closed its doors to me.

I walked away into the dark, into the street, the buildings huddled close like kindling, rattling emptily in the winter wind.

He seemed nothing more than a story I had told myself, a way to stay alive as I passed the days in Baden-Baden.

And it had led me astray.

As I walked through the deserted Marais, his ring at my neck grew cold in the wind and reproached me.

I could not return to his bed and I could not stay.

If I could save myself, I might forgive myself, but only then.

Never love came Cora Pearl's warning, floating back to me on the air and her mocking eyes in the mirror reappearing before me, enormous in the night. Her advice that night had seemed to me that of a cruel fool; her wanting to keep a distance from any of her admirers so she could dispose of them or add them as she saw fit. But I had misunderstood her. You kept yourself from love so you could always leave, yes; you did this so you would never stay a moment too long in harm's way. They would never have your interests in mind. Most men would be more careful with a horse.

He was a prisoner to something I could not see, as I had just been, and I would die if I stayed, waiting for him to free himself. My asking him to leave for London was as impossible for him as it would have been if he had appeared in Baden-Baden the year before and begged me to return with him to Paris.

I would have told him no, just as he had told me no to London. And so I at least forgave him that.

I still wanted to live, and to stay there was to wait for death. And to wait for death this way was to die in advance of death. If I could not have the dignity of my own life, I at least wanted to have it in death. And so I would not die in a house the Empress had bought for her lover, I would not die in the night for having led the tenor to that house, I would not die obeying the tenor's ridiculous instructions. I would instead prefer to die trying to escape as I should have escaped. As the Commune was now in charge, I would go to them, and I could bribe or charm whatever guards or officials I found, I could make my way to the nearest boat.

I would try to get to London and use those francs the tenor had left me to leave an ad in the *Times* to pay my way.

I consoled myself with this new plan of mine until the sight of the ruins of the Tuileries came into view, and I understood I had walked here through the dark like an automata, a girl in a cuckoo clock, returning as if drawn along a wire beneath my feet.

The palace looked broken open, like something monstrous had hatched from inside it, scorched, pocked, and cratered, but still somehow very beautiful, graffiti scrawls coloring the walls like bruises.

An entrance had been shelled and fallen in, but the stairs beyond were still good and so I walked in, finding my way into what was once the Salon Vert. Mirrors there had been tossed to the floor and smashed, curtains burned and cut to pieces, the beautiful floors charred and the wood sticking up in places like broken black teeth. I walked through the glittering refuse and smelled smoke somewhere inside; the palace still burned.

I found the stairs to my old room remained intact. I climbed them carefully, my thoughts full of the Empress's flight. I couldn't imagine her running—had I even seen her run once?—the sisters and Pepa throwing clothes into cases, too serious to cry out until later. Pepa would have been the one to have with you when you needed to escape, perhaps that was always the secret of her, the reason the Empress kept her—she would know which guard to trust; she would have a cache of coins for bribes, horses, and supplies.

If I had stayed, I would have been expected to flee with the Empress past the crowds screaming for her death as the Tuileries became a pyre they hoped to burn her on. How surprised she would have been: no parley for the Emperor's return and no thought of keeping her without him. Instead, her people had moved to expel her viciously, as if some honor of their own could be saved by destroying her.

And I had learned from Pepa. I had my own cache of coin, I recalled, as I pushed open the door to my room. The one I had kept safe, hoping to take with me, abandoned when I ran from Compiègne but still, I hoped, hidden in my bed post in a chamber I'd hollowed out with a knife.

I lit a match as I pushed open the door. My little stuffed otter friend greeted me, still at his post. The room seemed whole, as it once had been. No one thought to defile this. But as I went to the bed, a young man moved in sleep in my bed, using his coat as a blanket, his arms tucked carefully underneath, and still wearing his boots. It was all done so carefully, I first feared he might be dead, as if he were laid out here, until he started and sat up as I blew out my match.

I lived here, I said, when I served the Empress. This was my room. Who are you?

I am Eugène, he said, part of the Commune force here to protect the palace from further attacks on the property that should rightfully belong to us all. And who are you?

This question could still confound me. I could say anything; anything could begin as a result. But I surprised myself.

Lilliet, I said.

Saying the name was like catching something that had briefly fallen from a table. I could not give her up, not yet. Not when so much had been destroyed. There was something in this little lie of a life I had found that was real; I would keep it a little longer.

I have information I need to get to a Commune commander, I said, and am uncertain to whom I should speak.

You are in luck, he said. And he gestured to his chest. I present Eugène, Communard commander.

It made me smile, that the palace had once belonged to a Eugénie and now to a Eugène.

I told him about the tenor's message to me, of the deal he said the government had struck with the Germans. And the dates and his plot to get me out of the city.

Do you trust this man? he asked.

No, I said. But I believe him . . . I believe this. I paused, for the next I'd never said aloud. He is a Prussian agent.

It is possible he has done this to save you. But not one of our balloons returns to us yet — they can only leave. And the Prussians took to shooting them down or chasing them to meet them as they land — this explains the signal you are to tie to the rope. He might also have done this knowing you would come to us and tell us something to get us to prepare for the wrong day. It could even be just to kill our spirit. And, given the record of survival for the balloons, to kill you. Or all could be as he says. We simply do not know.

As Eugène said this, he seemed placid in the face of certain death.

Did he know you came here? he asked.

No, I said. I did not go out knowing this was where I would come.

I want you to come here and speak with me again if he should communicate with you. He may leave another message. Out of all of his wrong information will be some that is right, and perhaps we can find it out.

An immense weariness took hold of me as he said this. I was again on a stage of the tenor's making, always performing as he knew I would, even out of his sight.

I would ask you a favor, I said.

Please, he said.

May I sleep here tonight and leave in the morning? I have nowhere else to go.

Of course. Share my coat, sister, he said.

I agreed and then slept as I once had, next to this stranger.

There is the great love of one's life, and then there is the first to come after. Eugène taught me to love in a very simple way, without dreams or hope, to simply set something inside my heart and let it be. From the very beginning, it was easy to be with him. In the morning, I woke before he did and slid my cache out from its hiding place. We parted happy, and he again asked me to come see him at the Tuileries if another letter came, or if I was hungry or cold. He seemed content without me, and this was one of his most charming qualities.

❦

I returned to my old apartment—there was nowhere to go. I could not return to Aristafeo, not yet.

I sold the furnishings for food until I had just the small table in the kitchen the maids had used, a chair, the piano, and my bed. I took to sleeping there again.

The food was nearly as expensive as the furniture had been.

I returned to something like the silence I'd once enjoyed, speaking to no one sometimes for entire days at a time. This silence was broken only by my regimen at the piano; mine was the only voice I heard most days. For all the training I had done before this, to sing now meant something different to me. I could no longer believe in secret gods, I could no longer believe in love, I could no longer believe even in finding my heroes again. I could no longer believe in fame—I could barely believe in life. Alone with myself and my talent, I chose it in some way I never had before. I chose myself also. The person I was and had been all along, the one who had not belonged to the place where she was born, nor to the places she found along the way, the one always under the mask, here she came out and breathed the air and felt at home. I had always believed that to be this person might destroy me or the world, and so as the world seemed to end, this made the end of the world seem nearly a paradise.

When Pauline would say to me many years later that I finally sang for pleasure, here was where I learned to do so. I took possession of my voice at last, though at the time, it only felt like simple survival. When I sang, I thought of nothing else. Only when I stopped did the world around me rush back in.

April began with a decree from the Commune closing the pawnshops, accusing them of criminal lending practices. I had also suspected this of them, but the decree put an end to what income I had, though with little furniture left to leave with them as it was, I understood it was time, yet again, to find another way to feed myself.

On my return from a final visit to the pawnshop, another letter waited in the apartment.

Dearest,

The agreement I spoke of is now in force—we are releasing French prisoners into the custody of the French government, giving them numbers sufficient for the Versaillais to defeat the Commune and reclaim Paris. The violence I spoke of is at hand —they will kill all of the Commune, taking no prisoners. You must make plans to leave by no later than the twenty-first of May. And tell no one.

Do not fail to take out the ad in the *Times,* addressed to one André Lavertujon, and with the date on which you will leave, the numbers only. Tie the signal to the ropes of the balloon you choose. To forget this will mean certain death.

I went out to find my new Communard friend.

~

I have an idea, Eugène said. He swatted the tenor's folded letter against his thigh.

Yes, I said.

We sat in chairs in front of the Hôtel de Ville in the sun. Thousands of National Guard soldiers, paid in bread, sat in rows in front, their loaves stabbed through by their bayonets, smiling grimly as they bit down. It made me hungry to look at.

I am sure he is here, in fact, he said. I do not believe he is running in and out now that the Commune is in charge; it would be too dangerous for him. I believe he is here.

As you like, I said.

No, he said, and sat forward. This is quite serious. Now, did dressing the Empress require any feats of dexterity? Are you at all nimble?

I was an equestrienne before my service, in a *cirque*, I told him. I sang from the back of a horse.

Truly? Now you will be an aerialist, he said, and sat back with evident delight. I will get you to that balloon, he said. And, in fact, I will train you in how to ride it. Because, make no mistake, we are going to die. But you must live.

We looked at the men seated with their bread.

Listen, I will put you in that balloon myself and slit the throat of the Prussian agent waiting for you. He sat back. I believe that "agent" your friend speaks of is, in fact, your friend himself.

Why would you do this? I asked.

There is a very good chance you will survive if I do, he said. That is enough.

~

Eugène took me on a tour of another Eugène's work, as he explained it, that of Eugène Godard, the pilot who had masterminded the national hot-air balloon program during the first siege.

In the empty station of the Gare du Nord we found the remaining balloons he'd manufactured sitting empty, like the gowns of giantesses laid out to dry.

They stopped the program, Eugène said, as he walked around

the enormous shellacked balloons. It became too expensive, the one-way departures. Each balloon is very costly to make and they never return. It was too much to spend for the one trip. There is no air current to bring you back, he said, and grimaced. You might end up in Bavaria, or Belgium, or anywhere other than where you are to go.

Hell, for example, he said.

Hell is here, I said.

Here is Paris, he said.

He took me next to the Gare d'Orléans, where we found the station hung with empty balloon baskets hanging from the girders, laced by riggings that allowed trainers to simulate for student pilots the conditions in the air. They were dusty and abandoned.

By order of the Commune, he said, as he tugged at one of the lines, I restore to service the balloon program of the Commune. Now then. The pay for the job of balloon pilot, he said, is three hundred francs. To be paid in full once you agree to the conditions of the contract. You are to surrender, he said. And you must go in disguise. You cannot wear the uniform of the Commune. To do so will mean certain death, or worse, rape and then death. On landing, you are to pretend to be a private citizen of Paris with no affiliation.

He handed me a vial and something that looked like a thimble with a thorn.

What is it? I asked.

Prussic acid, he said. If you are captured and it appears they will torture you, this means you will die swiftly instead. Or you dose this, and with one prick of your finger, your foe is dead.

I remembered the poster for the Amazons of the Seine, dressed in black, with their poisoned needles, and laughed, which confused and amused him both. I didn't explain. I put his gift in a pouch I kept at my waist.

I accept, I said. I am proud to reopen this important program for the security of the workers of the Commune of Paris.

He seemed to struggle for what to say. He still wanted to live.

Thank you, I said. You honor me.

It was a love gift, for all his talk, one with no strategic value. The last gesture of a doomed man toward a doomed woman. If he had been a count, it would have been a diamond bracelet, but he was Eugène.

Per my plan as the new and only member of the aerial balloon program of the Commune of Paris, I went to the newspaper's office after I left him and took out the advertisement as the tenor had asked. Addressed to *André Lavertujon, Oui, 2151871* is all it said.

In response, I received a last note.

Comprimaria,
Be sure to leave before nightfall, my Falcon. And be swift.

~

Eugène trained me at the Gare du Nord nearly every day for the next few weeks as we prepared. Afterward, he would make love to me in the training basket suspended from the girders of the abandoned station. A caution against a casual observer, he said each time. He liked to sit underneath me on the balloon basket's floor, reaching up to trace my neck in the aftermath.

I did love him, such as I could—I loved him because he loved me. I wanted to find a way to betray him in his plan, to force him to live, and for me to find some way to do more than leave. So today I asked him, This impulse to save me and not you. And not your men. Have you given up?

No.

He said this clearly, quickly. The answer ready. I was prepared to lecture him, and he continued, almost amused.

Just because I feel prepared to die here doesn't mean I've given up.

It would be a better world if you lived, I said.

Perhaps, he said. But perhaps it will be an even better world if I may die as I choose.

I had shown him the new note; he said it only confirmed what he believed, that I was observed by the tenor. He then asked why the tenor called me his Falcon. What is this? "My Falcon"? Are you his spy?

It is only a kind of voice for a singer, I told him. A *Fach*. I explained what it meant.

Falcons are what the Prussians use to kill our pigeons, he said, smiling ruefully. All our hopes of communicating with the world dead in their hungry mouths. But if you are a singer, you must sing for us before you leave.

He described the Commune's plans for a concert at the Tuileries with fifteen hundred performers. I said I would.

Why do you believe he is still here? I asked.

Eugène pointed above us to where the balloon would be. We have not flown the balloons because they are all shot down, he said. But what's more, we lack the coal gas to fill them. Not even the Versaillais could launch such a thing. Of the people to fly a balloon from the Commune now, only a Prussian spy would have the gas for this flight. And worse still? Our flag flies from the Opera. He spat after he said this.

He loves you, yes?

Yes, I said.

Is this his ring you wear at your neck?

No, I said.

Good, he said. I will see him die as you leave in his balloon.

Eugène kissed me. I am off to attend a meeting at the Hôtel de Ville. We are to discuss food shortages, he said. But do not worry. We have little food, but because there are more desertions, we will not starve. You're nearly ready, he said. Think on what you will sing for us before you leave.

I stayed in the basket for some time. I imagined it lifting from the roof, the floor littered with mail. Letters from men and women about to die, letters from the already dead. I would fly at last. Perhaps I would go to my death, my body broken and the pieces strewn across the forests around the border with Germany or tossed into the sea. Or perhaps I would land in Belgium, a place no one knew me. I would land, survive, walk free into a new city, raise a family there, teach them to sing opera. My very own García family.

I took the ring from my neck, slid it off its chain, tried it on my finger once again. The finger nearly took it. Another month of meals like the last and it might fit.

Eugène's question about the ring had directed me to my own feelings, quiet all this time—the owner of the ring had not come once, had not written. He seemed to have accepted my departure. I thought of him standing at the door to the Empress's chamber. My ruby rose glinting there by her bracelets.

The only death I feared was the one that kept me from him.

I loved him still.

~

As I undressed slowly in front of the mirror that afternoon, a terrible truth became visible.

My figure had returned but the color of my complexion had not. I was as white as the tree bark I'd eaten. Only my mouth, the aureoles of my breasts, my notch—only these had the faintest pink. I had undressed in some anticipation of preparing to undress entirely for Eugène. Aristafeo's ring was a lurid green spark at my throat.

I took a rouge pot up and then set it down and withdrew to my bedroom instead, in horror, climbing into the bed and pulling the curtains at the sides shut, as if that could help. I remembered a story Natalya had told me once, in Baden-Baden, of a story her grandmother told her. We were speaking of Amina, of her nightly walks through town, how she had terrified her neighbors in the night, and Natalya said, She was most likely a vila.

Vila? I asked.

Vilas are very pale, she said to me. One day they wake up all white like a good tooth, and she pulled her lip and pointed. My own grandmother explained it to me this way when she told me this, she said, laughing. She didn't have one good tooth. She was trying to get me to behave, to be a good girl, and told me they were women who wasted their lives in selfishness, she said, made to care for the forest.

If you hear them singing, you must run, Natalya had said. They sing so beautifully you will sit and listen forever until you die of hunger or grief, all your needs forgotten in listening to them. They can take the shapes of wolves, or swans, or . . . falcons.

She gasped then. Perhaps you know this! Perhaps you are one. This is your secret, is it not? And she laughed finally, and I relented and began to smile.

They are also equestriennes! They can ride horses without a saddle. Clearly, you are one. She told me if you charm them, you can get them to punish a man who broke his word. Will you punish a man for me? How can I charm you?

The present must be very fine, I'd said to her. We are a fickle kind. But, of course, I loved her best, and said I would do anything she asked.

How I missed her. I missed them all.

A crack of thunder came from outside, shocking me. The thunder shook the mirrors in my room, rattling them against the wall so that I swept the curtain back to see a swift blaze of lightning go by the window, like the passing of a god.

Rain fell next, hard, a torrent. I sat listening to it, my eyes closed. It had been so long since I'd heard thunder, I went to the windows and opened them then closed them, thinking to do better. I wanted to feel the rain on my skin.

The building was empty—if a neighbor or the concierge remained here, there was no sign. The tenor had taken me to the roof to show me the view early in our time here, and so I remembered the way as I climbed it.

I feared I would find him there, but there was nothing, not even the cats.

The streets below were empty, there was no one to see me naked on the roof as I let my bedclothes flutter around me in the wind. Paris seemed entirely empty but full of blooms—the flowers had returned with the spring, and someone, most likely the Commune, had lined the Place de la Concorde with bouquets at the monuments. The effect was like that of flowers for a vast funeral. Paris for a tomb. The rain now come to wash it clean, as it cleaned all graves.

The wind turned and the rain flensed me then, the cold spray shocking me. More lightning came, more thunder. I watched the bolts fly down and strike Paris and wished to be struck also. To be consumed by the storm. I wanted to run the silver rooftops of the city until I was taken up, and if I was a Vila now, watch as my arms turned to swan's wings lifting into the sky. Wreathes of lightning for my crowns, and palaces of thunder, the size of mountains, mine to command. This would be how I would leave, and I would never return.

Instead, I stood there until I was sure I, too, would die soon. And I did not wish to die just yet, not before I could sing for Aristafeo one more time.

After that, I would welcome it.

I had no intention of leaving, of surviving Eugène, you see, despite his plans. There was no life after this. Nothing I wanted would remain, certainly not me. If everything I loved was to die again, I would be sure death took me, too.

∿

The next day I wrote to Aristafeo. I told him of the concert, of the need I had of an accompanist. Would he join me? I need you, I wrote. I sent it by the only post I knew I could trust, my own hand, sliding it under the door to his empty courtyard before I ran away.

Eight

ON THE DAY of the concert more flowers lined the streets than ever before, and by the late morning, the crowd was much larger than I had expected. I think everyone remaining in Paris had come. The Tuileries garden was full of picnics, wine, children—and it seemed as if my funereal feelings could only be wrong.

Eugène had said I did not need to dress fine, and so I had not dressed fine. They will believe you are putting on airs if you do, he'd said. I sat happily in the grass, as I had as a child, listening to the performers until I was hungry.

As there were many acts still to go before mine, I left and walked to the Marais, to Aristafeo's house, to look for him. He had not written back. As the day of the concert approached, I prepared to sing a simpler song if I needed to accompany myself, but even as I made my way into his neighborhood, I still hoped he was on his way —that if I walked the route I was sure he would take I might find him. And I was intent on keeping that hope all the way to his door.

The streets grew quieter the farther I got from the Tuileries until there was too much quiet. At first, I thought it was because all had gone to the concert. I knew it before I turned the next corner, though, the silence of death, and so as I came to the corner of the street, I stopped.

I saw first the terrible color in the street, mixed blood and wine running out of doors. Broken glass glinted like smashed ice everywhere inside the one café I knew to still be open and the nearby buildings. The doors had been shot to pieces, as had the wood, not

broken as much as torn. The men in the café, the women, the children, all were dead, also torn, their expressions like masks dropped
at the moment of death.

I stood very still, afraid to move. The terrible flood of the broken
red street.

They were here in the city then, the Versaillais. The destruction
was so recent, I could smell the burning food on the stove. The time
the tenor had given me was indeed false. I could hear guns now in
the distance, but a sound like a thousand guns, an impossible sound.
A sound like the end of everything.

We could not hear them over the concert.

I pulled my skirt up and walked through the blood and wine into
the café, past the smashed people on the floor, past the smashed
mirrors and tables, the only sound the crack of the glass under my
feet. I had moved on instinct away from the noise, out of the street,
and this was the one open doorway. I stepped into the kitchen, the
stove fire still burning, to find the chef on the floor, the pans smoking; and I pushed them to the side. There was a pail of sand for the
fire and I threw it on. An unmarked wrapped ham sat where someone had taken it out. The Germans or the Versaillais, whoever had
done this, they would not steal the food, I knew. They would have
come well fed. The dead had no need for the food left behind and
I didn't know when I would be able to find such a thing again, so
I put the ham in my bag and made my way through the shelves to
leave by the kitchen entrance through the back.

I stopped again by the door, as if there were something more to
do, but I paused. If I stayed here among the dead, I would be safe.

It was all undone, emptied into the street. I would not sing tonight, I would not get into the balloon, I would not escape.

I continued, followed only by my own dark steps across the floor
when I looked back. I went into the street to continue to the next
and the next. The ham knocked against my back.

I heard now the screams from the Tuileries and again the terrible
noise of the guns. The guns they used on us that day were terrible
things, the like had never been seen, able to shoot hundreds of bul-

lets. This was the day we learned guns like this existed, shooting with this terrible speed.

There were so many of us, and they needed to murder us in crowds.

As I stared down the street at the people running from the concert, I saw a shape I knew.

Aristafeo.

I screamed his name in my voice made for crying out in terror. A harpy's bark, the full force of my voice. I'd never once made a sound like that before, and it shocked me. Him as well, for he heard it and turned and ran toward me instead, and as he did, the people behind him fell, exploding into storms of blood and bone, their terrible cries cut short as their hearts burst or their mouths were shorn away.

He was a fast runner, faster than I. He knew his streets well, and he pulled me along behind him.

~

We ran.

We ran until the streets were quiet again, away from the fighting, and soon found ourselves at the Jardin des Plantes. Aristafeo made to enter, and I questioned him, and so he explained. The zoo animals had all been eaten or died. No one would search there. The soldiers would go through the wealthy homes around the palace first, even into the palace itself, looting for valuables or food or both, killing as they went. No one would bother to search an empty zoo.

In we went. A few surviving monkeys still lived in the monkey cage. No Paris butcher had managed to defeat them. They shrieked defiance as we passed.

~

We did not speak of death. We did not speak of the secret chamber, the Empress's bracelets, or my little gift. We did not speak of the strange guns of the Versaillais.

Instead, we lay together in the back chamber of the lions' cage. It was larger and cleaner than the elephants', and fit us, lions being of an approximate size.

Tell me a story, he said finally. Anything. Tell me the story of your escapes. I want to hear everything you have escaped from.

I told him of my family's death, my time in the *cirque*, and how I had tried and failed to get to Lucerne. Of the Majeurs-Plaisirs and learning to beat men as if they were horses, as if I were racing them to their satisfactions. I told him of the secret of the scratched looking glass, of the long chamber for spying on the secrets of men, of learning to sing my first aria, *"Regnava nel silenzio"* from *Lucia*.

This is quite a beautiful aria, he said. Will you sing it for me?

Softly, I sang it as he lay against my chest, his hands tangled in my hair.

I told him still more—of my escape from prison into the convent, and my service to the Empress and the Comtesse; of my capture at Compiègne and my performance as a doll; of my being made to return to the tenor and my study at Baden-Baden.

As I came to the end of my stories, Aristafeo had fallen asleep. In the dark I saw again the tenor as he sat up in the box of the illusion theater with his look of intent surprise, ignoring the angry Euphrosyne. I wondered when he had decided it was time for me to die along with the rest. If he had decided this earlier, say, before he vanished. Or if it was later, when he knew I was with Aristafeo.

Or earlier, when he had taken me back from the Comtesse.

All his little notes, the dance of it all. And then it didn't matter; he didn't matter. He couldn't matter, not now.

∼

When we became hungry, I remembered the ham, and we cut off a piece each and ate.

Our shoes were black with blood.

Night had fallen but there was still light from the fires. We climbed to the top of the zoo to see where the fires were and if we should leave, and so from the roof, we watched as Paris burned.

⁓

In the morning we woke to find the neighborhood had been barricaded and occupied by the Commune, but still no one had searched the institutes and the zoo. Periodically, we heard the screams of fighting, and then, after two days, an enormous explosion rocked the palace.

We cannot stay, Aristafeo said to me, as the noise ended.

We stay until there's no ham, I said. And then we leave.

⁓

Our monkey neighbors awakened us. Their screams of defiance, I guessed, meant new visitors.

I shook Aristafeo awake, my hand over his mouth so he wouldn't say a word.

As the soldiers shot at the monkeys, we left, slipping into the nearest of the greenhouses. We made our way through the silent rows of plants under the vast pleated glass-and-metal roof until we were in the street. We went first to the Luxembourg Gardens, thinking to hide there next, but instead we found the fountains and gardens full of thousands of bodies, all Communards, newly dead. The grass was soaked in their blood. So many had died, the Versaillais likely needed more room for the dead, and so this was why they had turned their attention to the zoo.

We did not dare speak and fled silently until we reached the Seine, pausing only when we were down under one of the bridges.

What are we to do here? I asked him, as he waved at me to go no farther.

Aristafeo smiled at me then.

Why are you smiling? I asked.

What can you not escape? he asked.

Paris, I nearly said, and then *Fate,* and then *the tenor*—in the end I said none of these for back then I took more seriously the idea I might curse myself. Instead, I said what a lover would say.

I hope it's you.

It was then I saw it, the most beautiful horse I'd ever seen, up on the quai. It had gotten loose somehow, or the rider had died, it didn't matter—and no one had shot it yet for steaks and pies. It was most likely the mount of some dead Versaillais—the only well-fed horses in Paris were coming into the city with them.

A handsome stallion, pale gray-white and fierce, it had its bridle but not its saddle.

I snatched some grass by my feet and walked slowly toward him, holding it out. He whinnied and backed up some before coming a little closer, testing me. So I stood stock-still, hand out, waiting.

You, too, I said to Aristafeo, anxious that he help. If we were to ride the horse together, it would need calming from us both. But I could not see him, for he was behind me, slipping his elbow around my throat.

Even you, I thought, before the blackness came over me.

I woke with my own bag over my head, in darkness. The smell of the ham thick in my face. We were riding the horse; I was in his arms in front of him, my face against the horse's neck.

Paris still smelled of burning and worse. The banks of the Seine were littered with the dead, I could tell.

We rode for an uncertain distance, an instant and an eon, and then he had me off of the horse, on his shoulder, climbing stairs and more stairs, until he opened a door and I felt wind.

Are you awake or did I kill you? he asked. I could hear him making some preparations.

Still here, I said faintly.

I must confess something, he said. Of your tenor friend.

I waited.

He paid me to bring you to the roof of the opera that night, he said. I was to be his agent.

It doesn't matter, I said. Why did you agree?

How could I not want you safe? he said. Who else could it be?

But you would have stayed and died, I said.

He was silent to this.

Nothing can happen to you, I said.

You were never going to belong to me, he said. Except here.

No, I said. No. I don't want this, I don't want this.

They are killing the women, he said. I don't know why, but the Seine was full of women.

Now it was I who could say nothing.

The city has gone mad, he said. When you kill the women, you are murdering even the future.

I was quiet as he worked.

I could as easily die in the balloon, I said.

But you might live, he said, against my face, suddenly, and he kissed me through my hood.

He threw me into the basket then, reached in, and removed the hood. As I struggled to my feet, shouting, he threw the ropes in with me.

The balloon lurched into the air and then stayed a moment. He held the last rope and a knife.

I do this for love of you, he said.

The city had darkened around us, strung with lights again in places—the fabric of the night still broken by fire. Above me, the balloon, glowing in the horrible light of the flame filling it.

It was small, but I knew it would be enough for me. It glowed like something brought up from hell.

He reached in and cut the ties at my wrists quickly, and as I reached for him, he let go.

No, he said.

I fell into the basket as the balloon shot into the air. I struggled to

get to my feet again and then stood, grabbing the straps and steadying myself as I remembered.

He stood looking at me, and then I saw a dark figure moving
quickly behind him and I screamed, but I was not fast enough. He
fell to his knees, gasping, arching his back forward.

The killer's face turned quickly to the balloon, and I saw Eugène
had waited all this time.

His knife hand rose and came down again.

I screamed with all of my might this time, and the balloon shook
as if from it, already at a terrifying height, the basket tossing in the
winds as it rose, pulling me into the sky. I screamed for Eugène to
stop, though I had gone too high for him to hear.

When I woke some weeks later in a hospital in Metz, the nurse
asked me who Eugène was.

Nine

I CAN'T TELL YOU how astonished I am, the Prince said, that you're alive. Twice over now.

The Prince's family is one of the country's oldest, the tenor had told me as he brought me to this audience by train. They are nearly sacred in Germany. They are one of our sacred families.

My balloon had crashed to earth in Metz. I survived the impact but the straps around my arms broke my arms when I landed. It is traditional to punish mortals who fly with worse than this, the nurse said. You are lucky.

I had spent weeks in the field hospital until I was well enough to be moved. At some point, in and out of my morphine sleep, I knew the tenor had appeared before me. His face red, wet, his coat still on.

Ah, thank God! he shouted, and I turned my face away.

His letter and handkerchief were still in my pocket. The nurses had contacted him at once.

I had not tied his signal to the ropes. I had hoped for certain death.

In my dreams during the week after my escape, I dreamt I was in flight, dressed in the Amazon of the Seine uniform, stepping off the balloon into the cool embrace of the night wind, lifting up into the air and lighting my way by the cold radiance of my moon-white face as I fled into the farthest reaches of the sky. Below me, Paris burned. And then I woke each time to find myself in Germany. Where I truly was.

No dream, this.

The tenor had insisted he bring me to meet a man he called the Prince, who wanted to thank me. But now in his throne room, I saw he had already introduced us.

In front of me was his young officer friend, the one who wanted to be a composer. I remembered him as the one who liked to bring his compositions to the apartment and sit at the piano while I did my best to sing them through. He had told me he was a composer forced to be a soldier; from his compositions, I had never been sure if he was to be a composer, but to see him here suggested he was the better as a soldier.

If *il trovatore* is an agent of his king, this was his king. Here was my secret god, surely, the one who ruled over us all, hidden from view until now. Which meant the audience, in which he would explain all he had done, was next.

I was here finally. I had made it past the veil.

I sat before him in a wheelchair, all of me covered in a wolf cloak, my arms splinted over the dressing gown I'd worn for the trip — an invalid was allowed such things — but the cloak was meant to make me presentable for this initial greeting. The doctors who received me protested to the tenor that I needed rest, but I was brought all the same into the royal chamber to greet my host.

We were in a massive and ancient castle overlooking the Rhine from atop a sheer rock cliff — the same color as the rock it sat on, the castle looked to have grown there. Every surface inside seemed intricately wrought with carvings, and the walls encrusted by tapestries, paintings, taxidermy — snarling wolves, elegant deer, birds of kinds I'd never seen before; and along the elegantly arched walls, a forest of mounted horns and antlers rose to incredible heights.

They, too, seemed born out of the rock, all of it of a piece. I couldn't imagine moving a single item from its place.

The Prince was addressing me from a modest throne of ancient carved wood nearly black in color. He spoke in the excellent French I remembered from when I first knew him; back then, he'd intimidated me into a sort of watchful silence, not so different from the one I kept here before him. The effect was uncanny. He was fair, upright, small for a German, with a thin, delicate nose and beautiful bowed lips beneath his full moustache. His small bright eyes shone with real happiness when he saw me. And yet this seemed like a mask, as if it could fall away. He wore his dress uniform decorated with a sash of a beautiful pale blue, as if to tell me a military operation had concluded or was still under way. I remembered him in more of a Paris poet's attire, simple suits, a more bohemian, relaxed appearance; but even his beard and moustache were carefully waxed in place and his hair pomaded close. Though he had never really seemed to me to be a struggling composer, he appeared as out of place here as he had before in my Paris bedroom. Neither affect seemed like a disguise. Instead, it was as if he had a twin appearing before me now as a conqueror.

Perhaps he belonged nowhere. Perhaps he was like me.

I offered my hand, and he bowed as he took it, pressing a faint, warm kiss that surprised me.

You are surprised to see me again. Your surprise speaks well of our mutual friend's discretion. Please, have some tea.

I was unable to hold a teacup, and so I looked first to the cup and then to my shoulders. He motioned to one of my new maids, who came and held the cup up to my lips. I took a drink.

First we thought you were dead, then we were sure you could not survive. Perhaps you are not a woman at all, he said.

This was the sort of remark I knew he thought was gracious. In my wheelchair, I shivered.

He said something quickly to one of the butlers observing from the side, and a fox cape was brought out and settled around my shoulders over the wolf.

It may be you cannot die, he said, but there's no reason to let you get a chill.

He sat back.

We have always been a correction to France, he said. We routed the first Napoléon at the Battle of Leipzig. We have routed the second one now as well. I think any time a Napoléon grows to power, we will be ready to mark the place past which he cannot pass. It's a pity about Eugénie, however. Did you love her, your mistress? he asked.

I did, I said.

I did also, he said. She should never have been an empress, but she was wonderful all the same. Please be welcome here, you are an honored guest. Whatever you need, please ask, it will be made available. We will spare no expense to nurse you back to health, and I hope you'll be well enough to join us even briefly for the celebration this weekend.

The maid held my teacup back to my mouth, and I drank again. And as I did, I watched as, behind the Prince, the sight of that monstrous fountain of death in the Luxembourg Gardens returned. The bodies in their awful disarray, the pale stone stained red and black, as if the bodies had come out of some terrible well of death in the ground.

I said nothing; they could not see it. They would never see it. They would never see it, and I was sure I always would.

I focused instead on the smiling visage of the Prince, who seemed so strangely kind, though all of his proffered hospitality had a hidden distaste in it. Distaste or something worse.

He was looking at me with a studied interest, as he would at a hurting dog. He still needed me alive.

The muscles in my arms groaned as they pulled across the broken bones, anxious to clench my fists. My stupid heart, it kept beating; I could feel it against my chest as I was wheeled from the room.

~

Afterward, I was shown to my apartments, where I found trunks waiting for me. As the maids unpacked them, I shooed them away and sat in the corner under my new cape until the tenor came for me.

You haven't even dressed, he said. Come, be quick. We cannot be late to dinner.

I only looked at him, empty of anything to say.

What's wrong?

I shivered, not from the cold this time, but from fury.

My dear, I went to a great trouble for these. These are from Paris. From your dressmaker. He reached in and removed a dinner gown, unfolding it slowly. It was in the colors of the court, blue and white.

He snapped his fingers and maids appeared from outside the doorway.

Dress, and at dinner you will hear plans for the coming victory celebration. It is my hope you will be well enough to sing for our host then, for it will be partly in your honor.

My honor.

I waited for even the slightest recognition from him at what he'd done, but he avoided my eyes and was not looking at me even as he said this, looking to my side instead. As he bowed and left, walking past me to the door, I wanted to rage at him, to leap from this chair, grab the sword at his side, and stab him through.

All those nights while you slept, I should have killed you, I said to his back. I wish I had. Even if it would have meant my life, at least I would have died before losing him.

He stopped short.

I would have died before I met him, before I could have lost any of this.

I could see him in the mirror before me, his back still to me. He went to leave again and then paused.

I *saved* you, he said. You should have killed me? You owe me everything. I saved you, you belong to me, you belong here with me. Someday you'll see why, and you'll forgive me. And I, I will wait for that day. But remember: Anything you ever lost to me you had from me. Don't forget this.

And with this, he turned the corner and was gone.

The maids brought me to the mirror to prepare, the one letting my hair down and beginning to brush it. My broken arms were setting still, and I could feel them at times, the bones reaching for one another across the break.

I shouted the maids away and took to the bed, where I stayed for days. When the tenor came to my door, I refused to respond to him. I refused the food and the water as well, taking only a little water when the maids held me down and the tenor poured it into my throat.

They began to tie me to the bed, forcing me to drink cool broth as well.

Has she gone mad then? I heard the Prince ask from the hall before one such session.

She is not mad, the tenor said. She is only stubborn. He sat down on the bed once my arms and feet had been bound to the posts. He reached to stroke my forehead and then pressed my hair back tenderly.

A new life awaits you in this place. You're a guest of honor. New dresses wait in your trunks from your dressmaker in Paris, also furs, jewels. And an honor awaits you as well, he said. We could as easily bury you with it, but I would prefer to see the Prince pin it to your breast.

He took my face in his right hand. It was his sword hand, his trigger hand. He had killed with that hand, and I knew it every time he touched me. He met my eyes at last.

You don't fool me, he said. You can't make me kill you. You don't want to die, not like this.

I wondered if I did.

That black tower of the dead I always saw behind the tenor seemed to change shape then, as if it were a shadow to something much larger, and then it shifted again, rising up until it became a storm —a storm of the dead, the river of dead I had seen that day, howling and shrieking as it wheeled about the room before changing again, suddenly somehow now a black horse and rider circling the room, rearing and turning.

It was the horse I had found the day of the massacre, surely dead now; this was its ghost—and the rider? I could not see his face, but as he came for me, I knew who I wished he was, and though I could not be sure, I reached for him, screaming as I did so, an inhuman howl that terrified me even as I could not stop making it. I could hear the maids shouting for the guards and feel the pain in my arms as I struck at them with all my strength, and said, *Don't let them keep me here, don't let them!* I begged, *not here, not here,* again and again, and then I was so very light, I could hear nothing but the hooves as I sat on the horse at last. I was gone into the blackness with my rider, for how long I am still uncertain.

Ten

WHEN THE BLACKNESS released me at last, it was early summer.

I found myself seated in the music room of the castle. My arms had healed such that they were bare of their splints, but my wrists now were bound to the armrests of a sturdy wheelchair. I wore a simple dress of a light gabardine I didn't recognize and slippers on my feet. My hair, I could feel, was tied up behind my head, tucked into a cap.

I pushed at my feet to see if I could move them, but found they, too, were bound. Wrists, hair, legs, all bound. What of my mouth? I opened it, licked my lips. That, at least, was free.

Across the room, three men and a piano beneath some enormous glittering chandelier that blazed blue in the summer light. These men were the tenor and the Prince, who conferred with a young man seated there whom I didn't recognize, playing scales in preparation for some rehearsal. They were deeply engaged with one another, and did not see me.

I recalled the Prince considered himself something of a composer. It may even be the memory of his compositions, played to me so long ago, that called me back, or it could just have been as simple as the sound of a piano in the German summer air—and with that, something like the call of my lost paradise in Baden-Baden.

I watched them for some time, silent. Given my state, it seemed I had most likely tried to escape. I wasn't yet sure if I wanted them to know my senses had returned. It seemed better to play dumb a little longer. I felt relief knowing that at least, even insensible, I had still clearly tried to escape.

That I was myself even when I was not myself.

I knew this music as the rehearsal began. The song was about roses. The Prince had me sing it for him a long time ago. He likely meant for me to sing it again with the two of us as stars in his own private music box.

She is awake, the tenor said urgently. I knew music would bring her back! And with that, he ran to my side, kissing me and then sinking down to his knees to praise God for my return, kissing my knees, pressing himself into my lap like a boy all while I hated him for knowing how to bring me back.

~

The next morning I woke to singing. The tenor was making his way through something unfamiliar to me; he was accompanying himself, too, on the piano, elegantly, and I was struck to think I had never heard him play this way for pleasure.

I rose, unsteady, and slowly followed the sound down the stairs from my room, waiting outside the music room in the hall, anxious not to disturb him. I was sure if he knew I was listening, he would stop; and to listen now was like listening to a secret.

How does a monster sing? I wondered.

When he sang, all his monstrousness vanished. Yet this was sinister, too.

I looked across and started to see the Prince listening much as I was, leaning against the opposite wall.

He's incredible, isn't he?

I nodded.

Do you know this music? It's the *Winterreise*. Schubert. He set the poems of the poet Wilhelm Müller to music. It was one of the last things Schubert wrote music for before he died, and Müller died before it was done. This one is "Die Krähe." "The Crow." You don't speak any German, no? A little? The crow is following the poet, and he is wondering if it is waiting for him to die. He decides he will let the crow wait for him.

We stood together silently as the song passed around us.

He is the perfect singer for these—listen carefully and remember, you may never hear a better rendition.

We listened together, silent as the tenor finished, and then he began another song.

Our mutual friend will be very sad to lose you, he said.

I looked at him questioningly.

It is clear to me you cannot stay, he said, as much as he might like it to be different. You will die here, I think, if you stay. Yes? Or did you decide to let the crow wait for you?

We paused, listening again. I was careful to neither agree and offend him nor disagree and offend him.

Where would you be, if you could choose? he asked.

Paris, I said.

Even now, he said, and smiled. If you think you are sad here, what would you be in Paris, where they are still cleaning the streets of the dead?

I closed my eyes then willed them open again. The Prince still smiled.

Is it still your wish to be a singer? I could make arrangements at any conservatory in Germany. You could go to Leipzig. Or I could return you to Baden-Baden easily if you so liked, he said.

After another silence, he said, Ah. I understand. Of course, Pauline has left, unlikely to return. You cannot be in Germany at all? Or is it something else? He loves you, you know. Do you not harbor any feelings for him at all?

I think, perhaps, I can only love him like this, I said. Only here, listening to him sing.

I turned back to the Prince, who smiled to hear this.

I can love him even when he is not singing, the Prince said. And so I cannot wound him easily, I think. Not like you, and as he said this, he reached out and brushed the hair at my temple. And while I bear you no natural enmity, over time, despite your charms, I *would*. He paused. Your charms such as they are for me.

The gesture, so like the tenor's, said more to me of what he meant.

I do enjoy hearing you sing my compositions, he said. But even so . . .

I understand, Your Highness, I said.

Do you? I wonder, he said. I wonder if you do.

I did. All of the mysteries of my arrangement with both men were finally clear to me. I was something the Prince had bought for his favorite. I waited, saying nothing. I wanted us to arrive at the next moment, the one where he told me what I needed to do. I was sure it was next.

For love of him, I cannot destroy you. But perhaps we can cooperate. You want to leave, and I also want this. I will give you your freedom on the condition you act as if you were escaping. The reward is rich. Will you hear me out?

Very well, Your Highness, I said.

Excellent, he said. Let us plan your escape.

The reward was rich. The apartment on the avenue de l'Opéra would finally belong to me outright, papers drawn up to that effect. An account also would be created in my name, with an annual income to be drawn until my death.

He handed me a Paris banker's card with the sum of 500,000 francs, written in pen.

Was this the Comtesse's secret, then? I nearly laughed.

It would offend me greatly if a hero of this war was to live the life so many of your kind do, he said. I would not want to pass the rue des Martyrs and see you eating in that little café for impoverished singers. If you should still end up there, at least hide if you should ever see my retinue.

I promised I would.

He will speak to you the next morning of how we hope to honor you as a hero, the Prince said. When he does, you will see, right then, what you must do, what I am asking you to do. You will then depart, and a horse or a train or anything you like will be provided.

Simply tell me now. Do this one thing more for me, then, he said. And all will be as you wish.

No one who had ever had my life in their hands had tired of it yet except for me. But I'd met the author of the tenor's strategies—he as eager to keep the tenor as the tenor was to keep me—and so as I left his presence, a wild hope ran through me like a fever.

If anyone could free me from the tenor, it was the Prince.

~

The tenor came in the morning, as promised. I had not slept long, but deeply all the same. He brought a tray of coffee with cream as well as bread and butter with gooseberry jam. He set it down and went about the room opening windows. Good morning, *comprimaria*, he said.

Good morning, I said.

He cleared his throat as he sat down on the bed and began spreading jam on the bread for both of us. He set mine in front of me.

This is a breakfast my mother used to make for me, he said. He pointed to the gooseberry jam. She made this from a tree that still grows in her *Garten*. If I was very good, she brought the jam out. We used it very sparingly. It was precious.

I brought the bread to my lips. The flavor was sweet and tart. All food was still too rich for me, but I was slowly getting used to it. I didn't want to retch up my hero's breakfast, though, so I took just a nibble, and smiled.

We owe you a great debt. You were instrumental in our victory. You began as an important ally in the service of the Comtesse, bringing crucial information to us on the activities of the imperial consort. We had suspected that the affairs of state were more and more her responsibility—the Emperor was in the grip of a nervous decline, in increasingly great pain. Thanks to you, we were able to know just how often she met with visiting heads of state during an important period diplomatically.

I was still in my nightgown, still in bed. I could smell the wind coming off the river, the freshness of it commanding me like a spell. I longed to leap from edge of the castle into the river in one long dive, to feel the relief of the water taking me in, down to the bottom. A Rhinemaiden at last. I would never survive it, though it would be a beautiful death, but I no longer wanted death. I wanted to live again, stupid as that had seemed even just the day before. I wanted my freedom. And, I understood, I nearly had it. I had only to pass this last test the Prince had set.

There was always a last test and never any guarantee this would truly be the last. And yet I had to try once more.

Did you ever guess what the Comtesse did with that weekly accounting of her clothes?

He smiled, his hands behind his back, as if the answer to his question were there.

I shook my head—half a lie. I knew whatever he had in mind would go better for me if he believed I knew nothing. I also wanted to hear what he would say.

She asked me to never speak of it to you until after we had succeeded, he said. When the secret would not matter. Her plan was to make the Emperor believe your mission frivolous, a bit of theater concocted from her desire to know the Empress's styles so as to imitate her first and best. Instead, your little lists told a tale of how often Eugénie sat with the Emperor, or even in place of him, and sometimes even with whom she met and for how long.

This cheered him to think of it, and he spoke it all through a smile.

When I found you at Compiègne, hidden in that disguise, I did not suspect your mission, and I admit I was furious at your escape. But even though each of us did not guess the other's purpose that afternoon, we helped each other even then. When you told me of those angry ladies waiting for their tea invitations and how the Empress kept them waiting, I knew then the Empress sat on the council for war. Nothing less would have kept her from those teas. This confirmed that our actions in Spain would bait France into war— when we chose a new king for Spain.

He hesitated here.

Yes. We were set to do it, but when we knew Eugénie held the command, we knew she, a Spaniard, would take it as a powerful slight and would act. And so she did. This woman who could not even manage the affairs of the Tuileries Palace set France on the path to war. You gave us the ability to strike without doubt.

These Napoléons, they just play at being emperors. They think it is all clothes and jewels, parties and parades. I am sure she was the one who sent the Emperor and the Prince to the front. This put the entire imperial line of descent at risk. When we captured the Emperor and the heir, we had everything. The only person who did not or would not understand this was the Empress, who believed she still held power back in Paris—she was only ever the vessel for an heir no matter how much of the statecraft he let her play at. She believed in her power until she was chased from the palace, I think.

Her mocked her, his hands twirling by his head, as if running while wearing a very heavy wig.

When I did not laugh, he said, We should make her a present. Send her flowers. He laughed at this as if to laugh for us both.

How I longed to surprise him, to shock him—him and the Prince both. I wanted to do the one thing they did not expect or plan for, even as I knew I couldn't be certain of what that might be —it seemed they had planned for everything.

The tenor continued to speak, certain of his goal, whatever it was.

Only after you escaped and I returned to Paris, and the Comtesse contacted me to arrange for our reunion, only then did I know you'd left precisely because I'd interrupted you. She explained you had to return to her with your report despite your desire to return with me. I was amazed. I think I laughed in terror for an entire day at what could have happened if I had succeeded that day in taking you with me. I was so angry at you, but you were right. You were right to escape me. Please forgive me.

This little lie of hers was strangely poignant to hear as he took my hand in his and kissed it gently, kneeling before me. When he looked up, though I knew he meant to be impish, his face was only a mask for the hurt; I could see he still felt to think of that time when he had nearly failed his mission. And the love he had for me there, protected by that same lie.

He did not know, then. He still believed I had returned because I loved him.

Ah. You pity the Empress, he said, as he searched my eyes for a clue to my thoughts. But you should not. He shrugged and then smiled as if to console me for the foolishness of my sympathies.

I tipped my head down, and he reached to pull my chin back up, checking to see if I wept. When he saw I did not, his earlier uncertainty seemed to grow and overwhelm him.

He withdrew a package from within his coat, tied in another of those blue and white handkerchiefs. He tugged and off it fell to reveal a bronze medallion, a cross hanging from a blue and white ribbon with gold bars, one that read PARIS and the other, COMPIÈGNE. At the edges of the cross, *Gott war mit uns, Ihm sei die Ehre.*

God was with us, to Him the glory.

With our thanks, he said. For your invaluable service.

He pinned it to my chest.

He withdrew a scroll then and tied it tightly with another of these ribbons and unrolled a declaration honoring me as a citizen of Germany and a hero of the war with an income to be given in gratitude for my service.

I rubbed at the bar along the ribbon of the medal that read PARIS. Should this say TUILERIES instead? I asked.

No, he said. Paris. It is correct. He looked to the medal on my chest and smiled at it as if it were greeting him. There was some discussion as to whether you should receive the bronze or the steel, he said. The bronze is for combat duty, soldiers on the front line only. The bronze medals are made from the rifles of the defeated

French—there's more honor in them, he said, and placed the scroll down beside me. Steel for everything else. But I insisted, as you were there at the front like the rest.

A memory of the Commune soldiers' bayonets, their bread perched on each one, passed through me as I looked down.

He smiled at me, still uncertain as he knelt again. Will you forgive me? he asked.

What am I to forgive? I asked.

He blinked. Yes, he said. And here he seemed truly ashamed. I did use you, you see. I sought to punish you. I never expected you to come to me. I was sure you'd betray us to the Commune and choose to die with them, and so I conspired to use you quite foully. I gave you bad information I was sure you would pass to them. But when I heard you had made it as far as Metz, it was then I knew you had faithfully done all I'd asked, that you were mine; you truly belonged to me.

He had said this to me before, and as I heard it, I felt as if I were vanishing into all the other times he had said this to me, returning to a single place where I was always leaving him, and on my return, he was always saying something of this kind.

This occasion was different, though.

This was, to be sure, quite a spectacle, his kneeling before me, tentative, even afraid, but it was also not the moment the Prince had told me to watch for—surely I was not meant to repudiate this gift or insult it—and if this was not the moment, then why was he here and what was the moment? I knew the tenor meant for all this to enlist me, somehow. This gift was meant to deny the very real distance between us, a distance he at least knew was there even if he could not admit to it or know it for what it was, and this was what he sought to close now in order to begin whatever next life he believed waited for us. He wanted me to believe I was as he believed I was, his beloved, the recuperating invalid, nearly well, and apparently, if I understood him, a hero in the war, if unwillingly and unknowingly. But he could never close this distance between us because he still did not know why I had been returned to him. He was gathering everything in himself to keep me here forever, sure he would succeed even as another plan was already in motion to keep us apart —a plan set in place by the man who had always controlled him.

He did not know. He did not know his place here, and I did. Mine was the upper hand. And so I listened as if I believed him and waited for my moment.

We must speak of something of great importance, he said, his voice hard and confident again. I nodded for him to continue.

After your debut in Leipzig, I ask that you do the honor of becoming my wife. We can be married in the very church where Mozart was choirmaster.

This, of course, was what the Prince had meant. I knew at last what the Prince wanted from me now.

You must never escape me again, he said.

I laughed.

The tenor, descended from a noble if not too noble Prussian family, one of the younger sons with an eldest brother who'd bred heirs early and successfully, had once told me the best he could hope for was an estate of his own some day and a few dutifully produced heirs, though their fates would have circumstances even more diminished than his. The gift of being his father's third most important son was that he was free to have his musical career and live as he liked there in Germany or abroad. For him to marry an untitled woman from an uncertain background would guarantee he would lose his claim—not just to his money and lands, but to the company of his family. And as I knew well, he loved them still. He would not give them up for me no matter what he believed, and they would never accept me.

The challenges before me were precise. I had to fulfill my agreement with the Prince and yet I could not cut the tenor so deeply that I lost my value to him, and thus to the Prince. If I did that, I would be dead before I reached the border.

I also needed to protect myself. I would be a fool to rely only on the Prince's word and his little declaration, which the tenor had shown me so proudly. I needed to ensure my own safety and perhaps enact even a little revenge. And as I had spent this time among my captors observing them, I knew there was one way to do all that I wanted, and at that moment, I saw it as clearly as the tenor's eyes before me. I nearly smiled into them in anticipation as I began my surprise.

I stood and removed the medal from the nightdress, which I let fall to the ground until I was naked before him.

What is this? he asked, with a faint smile.

Do you remember? The first time you took me to a dressmaker, you told me you weren't sure you wanted to dress me at all.

He smiled.

Do you remember that day?

I do, he said. Very well.

I stand before you this way to remind you. We will never marry, I said, and put the medal and the letter together on the mantle.

What is this?

We will never marry. We cannot.

What do you mean?

What do you not understand? If you were to marry me, you could never present me at court. This letter may make me a citizen, but it does not provide me with a noble family or title to match yours.

But I will, he said. And as a hero of the war. You don't understand.

I do, I said.

I walked to where he stood. He was studying my body, which I understood would look new to him with this monstrous new pallor —it excited him. He was trying to contain this, even acting as if we were playing at an amusement of his devising.

I held out my hand, and he took it, and I drew him with me to the bed. There I sat and crossed my legs and extended my right leg before him. He took it and ran his hand back and forth, smoothing my foot.

The foot never so white as it was then.

I do not refuse you lightly, I said. I do not refuse because I do not love you. I refuse because of the Comtesse.

The Comtesse? She is our friend, he said. And a friend to you. She is even a friend to Paris. You all owe her your lives. Do you know why the shelling stopped? She made it so. She intervened with Bismarck. When she got word he was set to shell Paris to rubble, she left Florence at once and arranged to meet with him. She convinced him it was the greatest possible sin to risk the destruction of the Louvre. She and the Prince, they are very old friends, he said, and gestured at the mirror as if at the Prince. You need not worry about her.

At that, I understood the Prince watched us, hidden. Of course.

Yes, I said. For now. You say she has Bismarck's ear? What will she say there next? If this great friendship with Germany and Italy was to ever go cold, she would use me as she has used me before, without hesitation. And if I was to refuse her, to hurt you, she would need only to expose me for what I was. If I was your wife, and this came to pass, you would be disgraced before Bismarck and all of these ancient families. Can you ensure she would never do this? I think you cannot.

His face fell at last. He looked down to my foot.

You would never forgive yourself, I said. So we cannot marry. You will thank me one day.

I let myself reach out and touch his brow, and he moved against my hand until he kissed my palm. I leaned in then, as if to kiss his ear, and my hair fell around us like a hood. I pushed my finger against his lips.

I said then, in the faintest whisper against his ear, *The Prince, he is sending me away.*

He turned his head and looked at me, still pressed to my hand. There was death in his eyes, but not for me.

~

Back in my apartment, the Prince waited for me.

At his instruction, evidently, the maids had already drawn me a bath, and I stepped into it as he watched.

Did I do as you asked? Am I free? I asked.

You have won your freedom, he said. He was smiling a thin, thin smile.

He withdrew from his coat an envelope and set it on the bureau by the tub.

Thank you, I said, and stood to check through the contents — my citizenship, the record of the bank draft and the account's number, the deed to the apartment.

My Serene Highness, a word? I had used his formal address to charm him, and he nodded, smiling.

I insist, he said. Speak freely.

The day will come when my life won't be worth so much to you, I said. I know you imagine you can kill me at will. And it may be you can. But you should not.

Why not? he asked, amused. What could kill you? You are the deathless one; you have nothing to fear from a mortal like me.

I didn't answer this question. I held my arms up to be scrubbed by the maids, and as I watched, even under the hot water, I could see myself turn only a faint pink.

Deathless or all death, who could say? he asked.

I shrugged — we both knew he could say.

Do you love him?

You know I do, he said.

You imagine I am an obstacle to your love for him, I said. And I am. But I am a greater obstacle to you dead.

He laughed. Why speak like this, on this happy occasion? he asked. And risk offending me?

I mean no offense, I said. It is a happy occasion. I will leave shortly for Paris, and he will now marry a wife he can bring to court, one who will never suspect you.

Yes, he said. You will live on in his memories. He will live on here. And so why must you live?

And so I knew I was right to do as I did.

He will come to Paris again someday to sing, I said. And to see me sing.

I could see in his eyes he knew I was right.

You are very alike, I said. He kills everything that stands in the way of what he loves. You as well, I am sure. And so I know you will try to do this as I leave today, or later when you imagine he will have forgotten. But he will not forget me. He will expect reports of me, reports of the glory of my debut in Paris, my career. He will go one day to see me for himself. And if he does not hear these stories, if I am not there when he comes to Paris to see me, and tragedy befalls me instead, he will go to discover who was the author of my death. And if it was you, he will learn it was you. He will come then to kill you himself. And he will.

I paused as the maids finished and I stepped out of the water, steam rising around me in the cold air as I stepped into the towels waiting for me.

Or you will kill him as he tries.

The towels were switched for a robe, and the brushing of my hair began, which told me I was nearly ready to be dressed.

The Prince was silent.

It's so rare when the world allows you to be with the one you love, I said. Enjoy each other as you can.

He met my eyes now at last, as if after all that scrutiny he finally understood what I was.

With that, I entered the dressing room. When I emerged, there was no sign of him. I left, I did not look back, and there were no more good-byes.

～

There are times I remember my question, the one I had been so afraid to ask of the Comtesse: How does one become a woman on whom a man would settle 500,000 francs?

Now I knew. My life was now the answer to this question, too.

I would never be able to say I had avenged anyone that day I left for Paris.

I remember how I crossed the landscape, still broken from the war, and took out the scroll and the other papers from time to time, if only to believe them.

I could not make war as they had, I could not burn cities as they had, I could not kill their women and their sons. I could only rob from them a little of the sweetness and sureness they felt as I left. That I could do.

I was not followed as I made my way back to Paris; I was not stopped. My papers were accepted with a salute at the border—I wore the medal that far. I could feel in the air at the station, on the train, all the way to the border and then again once I was over it; I could feel it as I kept on right to the door of the avenue de l'Opéra apartment and stood at last, with some amazement, before the falcon statue on its pedestal just inside the door where it commanded the entrance. A note read *Please be our falcon.*

This gift from the Prince seemed at first more like a tomb marker, but soon, when I passed its smooth dark stone surfaces, I knew it marked my life, not my death; it told me of how I had made my way past all of my mysteries, had reached, past all hope, the secret architect of my life—and had won from him and his agents this freedom, such as it was.

I had set my enemies against one another and won for myself a place I could live in relative peace. Each day I lived after that was a day won from the bargains struck that morning so long ago. But I suppose I also waited to hear for news of their mutual destruction.

This was the balance I had feared disturbed, then. And the amber I spoke of at the start of my tale, the one I lived inside, the one I hoped to break free of, was the waiting I had inflicted on myself. That long act of listening for either the signs of my victories or the footsteps of my killers—a listening that would endure so long I would forget my purpose, until the day Simonet and his novel appeared, and I was sure I heard in his stories that night at the ball the sound of my killers coming at last for me.

Eleven

I DEBUTED AT LAST in the role of Amina in Bellini's *La Son-nambula* in the fall season of the Théâtre-Italien in Paris in 1872. Amina, the beautiful orphan sleepwalker who sleepwalks her way into the bed of a stranger, losing her fiancé to the ensuing misunder-standing. Her climactic aria, *"Non credea mirarti"*—"I didn't believe I'd see you"—is among the most beautiful in all of Italian opera and wins him back. This is the song she sings while walking through her town in a dream of grief, ending on the roof of that mill, where she wakes to find herself in her fiancé's arms. He had been passing by, off to marry another woman, and when he sees her, he finally believes her and rushes to rescue her from certain death.

The aria demands tremendous delicacy and range—she is griev-ing, raging at her fate, in love, ultimately despairing of all hope, unaware she is in terrible danger until she wakes to her rescue, exul-tant. I returned to scrupulously studying the role with Pauline again until then, and she cheered from the boxes. I was credited with bringing wit to a role not usually known for its humor. One reviewer even called me "tragedy's soubrette," the funny girl who knows the master's house better than the master himself.

The crowd that evening laughed, roared, wept, and then, to my pleasure, rose to thunderous applause and shouts. Flowers pelted the curtains as they opened for our bows, and as the shouts for an en-core increased, I performed one at the urging of the conductor, and then another, and another, in what felt like a fever.

After the performance, admirers surrounded my carriage, unhooked the horses, and tried to carry me through the streets, an honor reserved for only a few. My horses screamed and reared, though, as unfamiliar hands grabbed their reins; and when my driver whipped at the men to let go, they held on tighter instead, afraid of dropping me. I leapt from the carriage into the street, wheeled onto the back of one of my mounts, and rode away from the scene as the other three followed. My stunned suitors then finally dropped my carriage into the street and set after me.

The first illustration of me appeared in the newspapers the next day. I was drawn in a gown with a bustle of a size that can exist only in drawings and that general's coat, my souvenir of that costume ball at Compiègne — I wore it all winter, that night in particular — and so it was I was drawn as a general on horseback riding down a Paris street, the hem of my train and the tails of the coat billowing out behind me and breaking apart into the shapes of men chasing after me.

You could barely make out the horse — the hooves looked nearly like my own feet.

The caption read *La Générale et la légion*.

You were an ordinary woman until you earned your sobriquet. La Païva, La Malibran, La Présidente. Cora Pearl was, in fact, such a famous horsewoman she was sometimes called La Centauresse.

The coat, the drawing, and the riot would all make me more famous than any reviews of the debut. The driver was unharmed, the press and the public were electrified, and my admirers loved me more than if I had stayed in the carriage, but I was furious. The end of the night of my debut found me weeping in anger, wishing it had never happened, even that it could all be undone; but then it mattered less than it might have, and I was soon too busy to notice — La Générale it was. Off I went to make my name in the capitals of Europe.

And so it was for eight years until the time when this story begins.

The story of the undoing.

Act V

The Undoing

One

IN THE PERFORMANCES of *Faust* that followed the Sénat Bal, there were times when I was onstage and the gaslight border erased all but the most stubborn features, the flashes off the biggest jewels, the three tiers there like a portrait of the afterlife—Heaven, Limbo, Hell—the chandeliers the angels guarding each circle, the crystal points the blazing light of their fiery swords.

And then it was like looking at the rooftops, and the streets, and a vision even of the streets beneath Paris.

And then it was only crystal and flame and the rattle of the crowd.

The worst seats are the highest and are called the gods. If they were to sneak in among us, that is where they'd hide.

Those were the only gods I believe in, I would tell anyone. No more secret gods for me. Not my mother's God, not one. This was what I had sworn to myself when I left Germany. No more omens, no more prophecies.

But now I was back in Paris, waiting for an opera invented out of my life, and as I waited, as I thought I could decide whether to accept, decide whether or not the curse was true, my whole life had become the opera. The curse did not seem to care as to whether I believed in it. My secret god still waited for me to reach my lesson's end.

The house lights were going down. The stage lights would soon go up. My turn was here.

～

During the years after Aristafeo's death, I sometimes met those who said their loved ones were still with them — they came to them in dreams, appeared in mirrors, left some token on a pillow — their scent, at times, or a touch. I reflected then on how I was not one of those lucky enough to claim a connection between this world and the other.

His ghost had never found its way to me before this, if this is what this opera was.

I had seen him stabbed twice. This pallor that would never leave me was, in its strange way, a daily reminder of the distance between us.

You are alive and he is dead, this color said to me when I saw my reflection.

I believed in his death more than I believed in God. And yet I had not properly mourned him, it seemed to me, as I sat in his house in the Marais again these ten years later and waited for Simonet to return with the Settler's Daughter's things that I'd asked to see.

The house was not entirely unfamiliar now, but no trace remained of what it had been inside, having been redecorated entirely. As I waited, I wondered if it was easier or harder to be there, given how different it was from before.

I decided that it was both.

I stood and went to the wall where I knew the secret room to be and hesitantly reached out my hand to the new soft blue paper and for a moment felt fear as if, were I to touch it, I might feel his heart beating there.

I had come to see for myself, in much the same way I'd gone to see Euphrosyne, the tenor, and the Comtesse. I wanted, if not a confrontation with his ghost, then to see the house and my things at the least. More important, Aristafeo had never shown me the opera he'd been writing for me. I never knew whether it even existed. If it did exist, I now suspected Simonet of discovering it. This seemed a more likely answer than a ghost in that hidden room, still writing it, handing off pages to Simonet, a last act before oblivion called him from this plane.

The puzzle for me was how to ask after it, given I was supposed to be innocent of the house and its past. As my hand lingered on the paper, it was all I could do not to peel it back from the walls.

There was not even a sign of the mechanism, however, and then I heard Simonet's footsteps on the stairs and returned to my chair so that I was sitting as he came back into the room with my old circus trunk in his hands.

I'm so amazed to think you've finally read it, he said, smiling and nervous.

Yesterday, I said, and smoothed out my skirt. I did nothing else.

He patted at his hair, still wild. I could see that he had dressed hurriedly from his half-tucked shirt front, which he then tucked as he noted my notice.

I was not expecting company, he said. I was up until quite late last night, forgive me.

Forgive me for surprising you, I said. I was near and thought to call. This is, to be sure, a whim. But I was very moved, and after finishing the novel, I wanted to see her things.

In truth, I had hoped to surprise him. Perhaps even to catch him and the composer at work.

In his hands, the object he held looked so small I wondered that I had ever carried it.

He set the trunk down on the table between us, undid the latch, and pulled the ruby rose out first. Do you see? he asked. It's incredible.

Yes, I said. It is.

I took it from him, turning it in the light; it was as whole as it had been the day I received it.

Am I to understand you are with us, then, truly with us? Simonet sat back in his chair.

I am nearly with you, I said. I've still to see the music. But this is truly inspiring. I remain interested.

I set the rose down and then picked up the diary, as my new friend had called it. In a circus they called it a route book, and in it I'd kept the entries of my passage during my time as the Settler's

Daughter. It was one of the few things I had taken with me when I'd left, as I'd thought I might someday want to find them again. I had not.

Instead, I had turned it into something of a composition book, a practice book, where I wrote lists of the words I did not know alongside lists of the ones I'd learned. I only occasionally wrote my own entries.

There were no entries from the time I'd spent in Compiègne, to my memory, and yet . . . how had he guessed this? It was more than a guess, it had to be.

We were concerned, he said, in a tone I found strange.

We looked at each other for a moment, uncertain. There's a rumor, he said finally. That you are turning down roles . . .

It seems to me I have always turned down roles, I said. Even as I have accepted others.

And then it came to me—Where is the chapel you spoke of? I asked. Where you found these objects? May I see it?

I was sure it would be the unveiling of his deception when I asked. I was sure it didn't exist. But instead he raised his eyebrows in surprise. Of course, he said. Follow me. I will stage it for you.

The courtyard had, of course, belonged to the dogs. I'd spent almost no time there, passing through quickly into the house or to the street. Yet in this one corner a chapel hid, apparently. I felt rebuked for my suspicions as I passed through the door.

It's in terrible disrepair, he said. It was filthy with the bones of the feasts of the cats I imagine . . . as well you know. He pushed the old doors open, making a fast sign of the cross as he did.

I did the same as a precaution.

The chapel glowed blue. The light came from a stained-glass warrior angel behind the altar, sternly beautiful, his sapphire wings lit by the late morning sun.

Simonet crossed himself again.

In Italy it's said there's an angel who watches over all who love.

I think differently of this now. I no longer believe he has my best interests in mind.

I had never discussed religion with Aristafeo. This was yet another secret of his, a place he'd kept, apparently, for himself.

Simonet stood before the altar and admired the stained-glass angel with me. At first, he said, it seemed as if nothing of worth had survived except this—and as you can see, it is quite beautiful. But as we cleaned, we found these here, he said. The ruby rose atop the diary and beside it the dagger, all of them on the altar.

And with that, he pulled out my knife and set it with the other objects on the altar.

Can you imagine her here? Praying? Asking the archangel Saint Michael, perhaps, for some forgiveness?

His excited face was rapt at the scene. He waved at me. Come, he said. Kneel here to see what she saw.

As I had come on the pretense of understanding my own character, as it were, I had to follow through. I came closer, but as I did, I did not see "her" kneeling there. I saw him.

The private ceremony had been his.

What does one ask Saint Michael for? I asked Simonet, who seemed to be a Catholic, as I walked over and knelt where he'd knelt, looking up as I clasped my hands.

What I had taken for the earth under Michael's feet was the figure of a man in agony and terror, falling.

Protection from the Devil, Simonet said. He's casting Lucifer down into Hell here. If he is carrying a sword, he is at war, as you see here. His shield carries the words *Quis ut Deus. Who is like God.* It's what he said as he threw Lucifer down into Hell. If you see him carrying scales, you are near death and he's come to weigh your soul. He is the one who offers the last tally of the good and evil in a man, and then, if the balance is for evil, a chance, before death, to redeem yourself.

He is also the protection of sailors, he added, and then said, though I have never asked the sailor what he asks for.

I'd always hoped Aristafeo was spared that final humiliating gesture—that our time together, hidden inside the Jardin des Plantes, was innocent of this. But I had also noticed Simonet had not included any of the Empress's bracelets in his little tableau. It seemed Aristafeo had pocketed her bracelets, walked through the house to gather my things, and brought them here, instead.

What had he prayed for?

To my right, Simonet offered his hand. Shall we?

I struggled to my feet.

The ending, I said, seems . . . cruel. For an *opéra bouffe*. Are the lovers, in fact, reunited? Or does he just go chasing after her, and we never know? Would the composer change the ending?

Well, I suppose I've left that as a last mystery for the reader, he said. But I understand, of course, that drama operates by other rules. If you have concerns, I'll gladly entertain them. Let us go into the library; we can speak of it all there. I will get some refreshment sent in for you.

We looked at each other, and I could see the strangely cold air to him then, the one I had been looking for all this time, never visible until now. I knew at once he had not written the story. And I could see that he knew I knew, the rising panic on his face when he knew he had played his part false in the one moment he should have been true.

You'll excuse me, I managed to say, as it was all I could say, and then I ran from the chapel into the street, out of his sight, as he shouted protests at my back. I did not stop nor did I turn, but I ran as fast as I could, as if I might be pursued.

How close it had been. How very nearly I had set my neck back into whatever collar waited for it on the other side of Simonet.

I sent a letter refusing the role officially that very night. I offered no explanation.

No response came in return. Not the next day nor the next week. The strange storm out of my past, with my own life painted on its face, seemed to have gone all at once. Only the novel, which stayed on my table, ominous and still oddly mute, beside its twin, the copy I bought to give to the Comtesse, remained as proof that it had happened at all.

I had consoled myself with the thought that in refusing the part I had somehow protected my memories of Aristafeo. This gradually became the feeling of having defended him somehow, a sense of victory that lasted perhaps a day until I went to discard the novels, believing I was done with them—and yet I could not, not yet.

He had gone to the chapel to pray for me before he left to go to the performance—and take me to the balloon. When I screamed for him in the street, it was the answer to those prayers. If his final opera for me had been found and misused, I would be foolish to pretend what was in this novel could not hurt me. Whoever it was on the other side of Simonet was still there.

I had one more delivery to make if I was brave. And I was.

At a Paris dinner party I attended several years into the Third Republic, a guest told the entire party a story of the Comtesse. *She came to the Exposition on the arm of Prince George of Prussia! He drove her up the Seine in his enormous* bateau mouche, *no less, all just to view the portrait of her by Pierson on display in the Exposition Hall.*

He spoke as if this were some disloyalty of hers, the vanity of an aging professional Paris beauty once again betraying the nation like the rest by accepting the aid of any patron who would pay, even a foreign enemy. Talk at the table roundly scorned her for associating with a Prussian prince, as if she owed France any loyalty, having once seduced its Emperor.

I experienced a strange shock on hearing this—I'd nearly believed the connection between the Prince and the Comtesse was my own invention. I remembered well how the crowd that day had looked on her in awe, not hatred, as they'd parted for her. How eas-

ily that awe had turned her into the dinner party joke she was to
them that night.

Next, another guest told a story of the Prince. Some years after
the fall of the Empire, he'd found himself at the same hotel as Eugénie, and as she had entertained him at court, he sent her flowers
— *She left the hotel at once! Can you imagine? He was part of the army
that had turned her out of Paris and he sent her flowers.*

None spoke of how Parisians, not Germans, had chased Eugénie
from the Tuileries.

A line drew itself in the air that day between the end of the Emperor's affair with the Comtesse and her entrance into the Paris
World Expo on the arm of the Prince, extending all the way to Eugénie's fleeing the Prince's flowers in her hotel. But as I pondered
my possible antagonists, I saw now I had not drawn the line all the
way to me.

Much of Paris mocked the Comtesse as her beauty faded, yet she
lived in an apartment on the Place Vendôme, and Eugénie was in
exile in London. So many of those who had lost to her before had
done so because they believed her beauty was her only power, but I
knew better.

As I tried to think of why she would involve herself with me
again after all this time, I thought back to her at the time I'd met
her. She was in the first year of her mourning, the free woman any
widow was, her mission in Paris now entirely her own.

I remembered how she sat and told her stories to me, luxuriat-
ing in the victories of her past, preparing to pose for more of those
portraits, angry at the glory she believed denied her but rightfully
hers. As I remembered those stories, I understood I was mistaken
to think my value to her was based entirely on my affair with the
Empress's lover. With the Empire gone, another picture came into
view.

On the day I returned from Compiègne, when she discovered the
mute girl she'd told her stories to could speak.

A last game of hers, then. What better as a message than to write
a role for me in which I ended as a mute again.

And so, sure the Comtesse was my antagonist, I pushed my way into her rooms.

The day the policeman sent me away from my vigil outside the Comtesse's apartment on the Place Vendôme, I first left in the direction I'd seen her girl take, thinking to myself that I could wait there until she passed and try to bribe her into letting me in. I tried to guess as I walked where she might stop to do the shopping and what she would take as a price.

A girl, as I well know, is the key to a household. A maid is often her lady's only true confidante. Whatever it is you need you can often get from her, but she must be vulnerable to bribes or flattery. Or threats.

I was sure she was lonely working for the Comtesse. I knew there were likely no great pleasures and little gratitude. But then I passed the window of a new atelier and paused, examining the display.

I knew her well enough to also know she would never let her dressmaker go. No woman would.

As I also knew this meant her dressmaker was my dressmaker.

I let her girl pass on. There was no more need to follow her. I knew I could pick my moment later.

I already had an appointment with Félix, and it was time to begin the dresses owed me from what I had come to call the Dukes' Bargain. I went to him looking for the opening I was sure was there.

That first morning, as Félix moved among the dress forms, the muslin shapes were like a garden of the days ahead.

There is, he said, a new silhouette.

I'd made him promise no copies, but sly one that he was, he would have me debut a new silhouette. This he could reproduce innocently, and I could not forbid it.

There were to be crinolines that began at the thigh, not the waist. The fit was tight; the hip, more natural. There was already a new, looser sort of corset to the relief of a number of women, the dismay of others. He pulled drawings out.

Will you debut the silhouette? he asked. A formality, for he knew I would.

He did not look up as he said this. I held a cup of tea and traced its warm porcelain sides.

I only nodded, knowing he would see my answer. The shape under his pencil spread down the page.

Satin, velvet, chantilly, *point d'Angleterre,* sable, ermine, fox, red and white nutria. Gold thread and silver. Ostrich and peacock and pheasant. Jet, garnet, glass. The dresses I was ordering, some would take months to finish. The way the other women in the rest of Paris lived made its way in front of me for my regard: tea gowns, visiting dresses, afternoon gowns, riding suits, robes de chambre. I would rarely if ever use an afternoon gown, for example, preferring the quiet of my apartment in the afternoon and receiving no one then who would ask for such a formality from me. I was not a member, precisely, of polite society. I did not have the needs the rest of them did. But tea gowns were another thing; I had not thought of tea gowns in some time.

The most extravagant of these would cost what I could earn singing in a year. I loved to think of the different elements to be trained by Félix's thirty seamstresses' hands, buttons and silk made to practice until the shape was right.

I knew my dress orders would be seen as gluttony, but appetite was an excellent disguise for motive. I did not ask about her on my first few visits, only observed to see if I would see her. I did not. After two weeks without a sighting, I went to where his appointment book lay open. Félix exclaimed and ran to my side. Yes, my dear? he said, placing himself between me and it.

I think two more, I said to him. A visiting costume and another gown for evening.

I glanced down at it for the name I knew would be there.

Nicchia. I had seen this name on some of her correspondence. Only her intimates knew it.

He saw me see it. Ah, he said. Do you know? How your teacher has fallen? She comes to me in her old clothes and asks me to mend them or take them out. I do it, of course, for love of her and for who she once was, but she has asked that I don't book appointments alongside her as it shames her, though it is a great problem for me. For her as well.

He paused. She spends almost no money here now, he admitted.

I raised my eyebrows pityingly.

Have you seen her since your return? Or, rather, tried? She refuses all. He turned the book away from me. Ah, but you cannot see any more of what's here, you naughty child. Do you know the problems you all create? So many of you who cannot be seen near each other. Tell me, are you having any affairs? You must tell me right now. For I must know. I cannot book you alongside the wife of the man you are seducing.

I shook my head gently.

Very good. He looked over the book again. But you know, he said, she will be so happy to see you, of course. You were like her daughter, I think. Here, he said, doing what I had not even asked. Allow me to reacquaint you. And he wrote my name into the book beside hers.

When the day of the appointment came, I entered and heard her quietly greeting the vendeuse, and from the entrance, through a corner mirror, I could observe her. She was dressed in one of her favorite costumes, though it now fit poorly. She still had a commanding presence but seemed lost, like a sleepwalker in a dream.

As she spoke, I could hear she had lost most of her teeth.

She was asking for an alteration to one of her gowns, and the vendeuse was examining it. I could see she was impatient not to have the dressmaker pay attention to her himself. She looked around then to see him smiling as he motioned toward me.

Her eyes blazed as I came into view.

This was a fatal mistake, I understood at once. The air in the shop went thin with it, and Félix stood frozen in place, humiliated. Though not as humiliated as she.

So, she said. You. You wanted to see me this much? Call on me

tomorrow, then. Come for tea. And with that, she drew herself up
to something like the imperious height she had once commanded,
and left.

I went back to the Place Vendôme at the appointed hour. The young
woman I remembered took my card and showed me in without any
further explanation.

All was painted black, all was hung with black, and there was almost no light to speak of, only enough to see my way. The Comtesse
lived inside a permanent night of her own making.

I was shown into a salon and seated, and candles were lit. To my
shock, as the light came up off the chandelier, the Comtesse was
already seated in front of me.

I did not remember you until I saw you, she said. It was so long
ago, and so many things have happened. What is it that brought you
to my door, however? I would know.

I handed her the book. She took the candle nearest her and held
it up.

This? she asked. I know nothing of *this*. But you can be sure I
soon will.

I believed her, as when she lied, she usually suppressed emotion
instead of inventing it. All her rages were sincere.

Have you kept to our agreement? she then asked.

I stayed with him as long as he wanted me, I said. And even a
little longer than that.

I wonder if that was the agreement, she said. Perhaps it will suf-
fice. How will you repay me for this humiliation, I wonder. She
reached out then and pinched one of the candles out. I will think on
it, she said. She pinched out the next, and the darkness around her
said our interview was done. There would be no tea.

Show her out, she said to her girl, and I was shown out.

She had not been my tormentor then, but now it seemed she
would be, one last time.

Two

AFTER THE SPECTACLE of my failure with the Comtesse, I did not want to be alone in the apartment with my fears, and so I pushed myself out into the whirl of dinners and balls and midnight drinks and nights ending in breakfasts, supplied as I was with my Dukes' Bargain of gowns.

As I did, the press began its chorus—I was a favorite of theirs after the news of my curse, the scandal of the second grand entrance in the new dress, the brother dukes on each arm. The press now made reports of daily fittings with the new dressmaker, Félix, the new silhouette he introduced with me, and where I wore each new dress in its turn, from the Louvre Palace to the Café de Paris to the markets at Les Halles. No detail was too small. Doro cut out the illustrations as they appeared in the papers and pinned them to the mirror, little paper dolls of me running around the edge of my reflection. She glued them to matchsticks and made them run in puppet shows by my makeup table to make me laugh after she and Lucy had strung me in.

You're terrible, wicked women, I said to them, cursing them, for it hurt to laugh in a corset, but soon the joke we had, if the dress was awful, was *Best get the dukes*.

And just when it was said to be over, the next scandal came: the dukes had their choice of women after all of this, and by the end of that month, the dressmaker Félix was likewise overrun, but a disappointment awaited the women the brothers entertained after me as the dukes' promise to me included that none of the women to follow me were to be allowed the gift of a dress from that house for one month. The dukes' new loves could be allowed any other dress-maker except mine.

With that came a new illustration of me, running down the street again on a horse, but this time the shapes falling from my dress were the shapes of these other women springing up to chase after me in fury.

While this amused me, it was time for me to protect myself from these follies: I needed to find some way to attach myself to the tenor again—at least in appearance, publicly, and in a way that would appease the Comtesse—and then to prepare for the ball Euphrosyne was to throw for me and, lastly, to repair my relationship with Verdi. The question of who, if not the Comtesse, was behind the novel and the opera was now too much to consider—or too little. There was too much else to do, and so I set myself to the tasks I understood. The plans for the ball were the most pleasant of these and thus the most urgent. And as I'd never sung the Queen of the Night aria Euphrosyne had asked me for, as it was outside my *Fach*, I would need to prepare it very carefully.

Euphrosyne wrote to me with her plans for the ball and made an appointment with me to attend my fitting at Worth for our costumes. Worth, who, she said, was contrite at my displeasure with his last offering.

He really is so very sorry and has said he will make you a magnificent costume, she said. He has vowed it.

In the meantime, proof arrived daily that I'd been a fool to think the news of the curse meant the end of my career. Doro no longer brought my mail in on my tray as there was too much. I was besieged. Offers arrived as never before.

I should always be cursed, I joked to Doro, who did not approve.

Despite failing to find anything more to my mystery opera than what had presented itself, I now only waited. The result was that the season itself became something of a masked ball, the masks, the faces of the people I met everywhere I went. *Is it you?* I'd wonder each time a stranger pulled out a chair, or offered a light, or refilled a glass, or smiled in greeting as he was introduced. *Is it you?* It became a light refrain as I passed through crowds potentially as full and as empty of an answer.

And so I went through the days between that Sénat Bal and the one Euphrosyne threw for me, dress by dress, rehearsal by rehearsal, detail by detail, night by night, holding on at least to the hope of the ball, not quite knowing what was real, what was phantasm, each day still empty of an answer to what had filled it the weeks previous, until one week before the ball when amid the day's offers one distinguished itself. The solution I'd been waiting for arrived, the answer to all my troubles.

The offer of the role of Carmen at the Opéra-Comique, with the tenor as Don José.

This, to be sure, was an unlikely savior. If there was one opera I had never wanted to perform, it was *Carmen*.

I had known Bizet a little from my time at the Conservatoire, which had finally admitted me on my return to Paris after the war. Pauline wrote to my old address, searching for me, with the news that she had been asked to return to Paris as director of the Conservatoire. If the letter found me and I lived, she asked me to return and work with her, though an audition was required.

I did not write back but instead left at once and went to her house as my answer, where she threw her arms around me, and we hugged each other and wept, grateful to be alive and reunited.

While I had initially feared living in the avenue de l'Opéra apartment again, I knew if I had not returned to the apartment, I might never have been thus blessed. The Prince had spared no expense; beyond the falcon statue, I took note of how the walls had been repainted, the music room now red, the very finest new piano waiting to be played. The walls to the boudoir gleamed curiously to me until I understood they were covered in pressed leather embossed with falcons. As I ran my hands over their wings, I knew I would always keep it.

The concierge told me Doro and Lucy had asked her to tell them if I returned and to say they would return if I agreed, and I did.

Over cards and gin, they told me of their own escapes from the vagaries of the war—Doro had hidden with her family outside Rouen, and Lucy spoke vaguely of a hospital for the wounded—she hid something there, but I did not ask. Instead, I tried to remember how to play bezique and then finally set my cards down, and said, Promise me from this day forward you spy only for me.

At which they started, then smiled, then swore to on the cards we played with, as if they were our Bible.

I passed my second Conservatoire audition easily this time, nearly pro forma—the jury would not rule against Pauline. This education was not the same as her private instruction, however, and the work overwhelmed me initially. Music pronunciation, vocal techniques such as bel canto and coloratura, yes, these I'd expected, but not music history or theory. There had been a kindness in that earlier rejection I had not understood, and so there was a tinge of cruelty to my education now, which then proceeded with the difficulties I'm sure that earlier jury had imagined.

The other students could see I was not properly prepared, and they resented my prior relationship to Pauline, though she showed me no other favors except occasional affection, but this was more than she showed them, enough for them to hate me.

My name here was soon La Donnée, the Gifted One.

In the mornings when I was early to my classes and rehearsals, I would sit alone and listen to the violin and cello students as they warmed up. I liked to feel the notes along the bench under my fingers, in the floor beneath my feet, at my back—they bounced along the wooden walls of the Conservatoire as if we were all inside an enormous wooden instrument of many parts.

I also liked these young men with their intemperate musician's dispositions, their various pettinesses, they reminded me of unbroken colts. They did not know me by sight, and so they smiled at me as they entered and left unlike my fellow singing students.

Aristafeo had mentioned his time here to me, and it was strange to be here after him; I was helpless to think of how I might have met him earlier had I passed that previous audition, though, of course, what separated us then would likely still have kept us apart. On those mornings, though, it felt sometimes as if I'd been admitted to his past, empty of him, a little victory over his death.

Here I learned that the first classical stories of the House of Atreus and their ilk had been sung but the music was lost—opera was new clothes for old tragedies. I liked this idea, the opera stories as refugees of some ancient conflict accommodating themselves anew among us—much as I suppose I was, along with many others. I remember I wondered if there would ever be new great tragedies and then came Georges Bizet and *Carmen*.

Bizet I knew as one of these young men, one of their heroes, a recent graduate who himself was at the very edge of succeeding. He hid gentle, pale eyes behind gold spectacles, and under his suit jacket, the soft shoulders of a man who couldn't lift a crate. He had quietly married the daughter of his mentor at the Conservatoire, a composer himself.

It was said he was too proud to teach, but many times, when I arrived at rehearsals, he was at the piano working as an accompanist to earn extra money to pay for rehearsals of what he was sure was his masterpiece, *Carmen,* a commission from the prestigious Opéra-Comique.

Students often bragged to one another about the clear successes among the school's graduates. I think we imagined that before a career began there was a bargain to be struck with Fame and that the way to learn how to do this was to study those Fame had chosen. Bizet's story was told with every possible detail, for at any moment it seemed as if some deciding success or failure would descend and supply the lesson the story lacked. There were as many signs supporting a good end for him as a bad one.

Bizet had won the Prix de Rome, but the students spoke assuredly on how he'd chosen his previous librettos badly and that this had held him back as a composer. The libretto he'd chosen this time, though, came from a famous novel, and the librettists, Meilhac and Halévy, were widely considered to be the best. And Halévy was related to Bizet by marriage. This was thought to be a good omen.

Pauline told me what she had heard of his struggle from Louis, who knew the director of the Opéra-Comique well.

The story was of a young seductress, murdered when she steals a young man away from an arranged marriage and then rejects him. This troubled the theater's manager, for the Comique was a family theater and marriages were regularly arranged between performances or even during them. The bourgeois families paid for boxes in order to have a better view of one another, not the stage; and they typically talked all the way through, believing the real drama was with them. They were famous to the singers, composers, and musicians of the Conservatoire as Paris's most ungrateful and wealthiest subscription audience, and so when the management began canceling rehearsals of Bizet's opera, saying it was for lack of funds, the students scoffed. Bizet only took them at their word and earned the money required, and so the rehearsals continued.

It soon seemed there was no one who would not betray him. The most famous song, the Habanera, he rewrote thirteen times at the insistence of the soprano who was creating the role of Carmen, and she still hated it; the orchestra complained, incomprehensibly, that the music was "Indochinese." This made me laugh—there was a pidgin used inside of a *maison close*, I knew, that this referred to— but then the soprano put her disappointment in a letter to a friend, delivered by what would seem to be a very deliberate accident to the director, who, in turn, kept the dress rehearsals empty in order to protect the debut. More letters still appeared the next day, published in all of the newspapers, denouncing the opera as immoral—the complaints of ghosts.

The opera finally opened. Many of us from the Conservatoire attended, proud as the audience applauded vigorously at the end of the first act—but this was when the very proper young Micaëla brought a note to the young soldier from his mother that was the opening of a marriage negotiation. Carmen appeared, and by the time the aforementioned Habanera concluded, it was clear, as the soldier picked up the flower Carmen dropped for him, that the marriage negotiation would be for nothing. Next the cigarette girls lit real cigarettes and stabbed each other with knives; Carmen wed the soldier in a Gypsy wedding in the mountains, their hands soaked together in a chalice of red wine; and then at the end, the young soldier murdered her for rejecting him. After he stabbed her to death, the audience sat in silent fury. No applause from them — though we, his claque, did try, full of dread.

The next day the papers were filled with reviews declaring it was "a revolting display of animal passion." Bizet was heartbroken, refused our congratulations, and went away to his family's country estate and did not seem to return. On the night of the thirty-second performance, the unlucky letter-writing lead soprano fainted during the third act, and when she was revived, she refused to go back onstage, overcome with a premonition of Bizet's death.

It seems to me if she'd known what it would bring she likely would have stood and gone on.

By the thirty-fifth performance, after it was published that Bizet had been found dead of a broken heart at his country estate very close to the time of the soprano's fainting, Paris rushed to see the opera, and the remaining performances sold out. It closed after the forty-eighth performance to go to Vienna, where the director sought to shock audiences further by adding real horses and a bullfighter's parade. There, it triumphed.

For those of us students seeking a lesson in telling the story of his career, Bizet's tale had finally concluded. The lessons were that sometimes the composer died in the third act and not the soprano in the fifth. You could devote yourself relentlessly to art and there would be no great reward; you could go to your death for all of your talent thinking you had failed at your great work. There was no bargain to be made with Fame, who was, perhaps, the most fickle god of all or, perhaps, the bargain was this — Fame had taken his life as its price for conferring fame on the opera. In this way, while Bizet did not teach, he did teach.

And so there was one opera, perhaps, in the history of music that I never wanted to sing, and that was *Carmen*. And yet I saw over the years the success of the imperial productions, the theaters across Europe eager to perform it, and the sopranos lined up to sing the "Indochinese" music as if waiting in a queue for eggs and milk after the Siege. I knew one day it would be offered to me, and I would have to choose.

This was that day.

I sat in bed and read the music pages and came quickly to the Habanera. I remembered the cold-eyed girls of the chorus exhaling their smoke that first night toward the virgins in the boxes and giggled in my bed.

This chance was too delicious to refuse—it was even its own kind of revenge. The Opéra-Comique had decided to return *Carmen* to Paris for the first time since the debut and had done, as reported in the papers, a *Carmen* with no cigarettes, ballerinas made to stand still, and a young Don José who dropped his knife when he went to kill his murderer-seductress. She stood waiting for him to stab her. Amid the screams from the audience that it was a desecration, and the screams of laughter, a new production was decided on. The cigarette girls' cigarettes would be lit again, the horses brought back onstage, the bawdy jokes told.

And, as the letter indicated, if she would consent, La Générale for the title role.

The letter requested that I be borrowed from my contract at the Garnier for the performances, scheduled during my typical break in between performing Gounod's *Faust* there and my departure for Verdi's *Un Ballo in Maschera* in Milan.

The break I took between productions was a necessary one, but I'd not previously been invited to perform with this company, which was composed, perhaps more than most, of former classmates of mine from the Conservatoire. They, like the rest, no doubt all hoped the cursed soprano would increase sales, the house filled with audiences eager for a daredevil act—especially from Carmen.

I decided to let the rumor be. There was nothing I could do to disprove it to the public now, after all, except to live—and to take their dare and perform *Carmen*.

In the meantime, I hoped the news that I was performing with the tenor again would show the Comtesse I intended to continue my bargain and was preferable to some false attempt on my part to renew our affair. The illusion of a rapprochement was all that I needed here.

I signed the contracts that morning and returned them with a note indicating my great pleasure in accepting this honor and then made arrangements with Euphrosyne that after I performed her Queen of the Night aria the tenor would be Faust to my Marguerite in two of the songs from *Faust*, at the end of which we would announce our news. I reflected on how neatly it had all been resolved as I dressed the night of Euphrosyne's *bal* in an apartment she'd allowed me to use as a dressing room.

All's well that ends well, then, she even said to me over my shoulder as Lucy and Doro put me into my costume, and then she asked me to meet her by the stairs.

I was sure it wasn't him, Euphrosyne said. It's really him?

She was speaking of the tenor, whom she remembered quite differently. She had not seen him in years, and his new girth hid him well.

We stood at her stairs, each of us with a glass of champagne, as around us the guests made their way to the buffet.

I like you as a married lady, I said.

I don't, she said, petulant, and raised her jade cigarette holder. She lit it with her left eye closed, as if she were shooting a rifle, and drew on it hard. The tip burned brightly and then faded. I'm very serious!

Above, I heard the announcement of the names of the arrivals ringing out in sturdy voices. I did not ask after her husband then. She looked at me with mock evil, understanding as much, and then, briefly, an expression of hurt crossed her face as she looked away, banished as she exhaled.

I'm sure I preferred it when I was his fantasy, she said. I didn't take all this trouble just to be ignored. Now, let me return the guest of honor to her rightful place. She tried to put her arm through mine and gestured up, but our skirts were too enormous to allow us to walk arm in arm, and so we laughed as she let go.

She turned to me just at that second and said, Never marry.

I don't intend to, I said.

What, Euphrosyne said, did you not hear me? I only laughed and leaned in to kiss her twice.

Come, she said. Let us look down on what we've made.

I reached down and grabbed the flounces until I caught the loop in my hand and set it on my wrist, and Euphrosyne and I ascended the stairs.

I had never been able to correct Euphrosyne about the Queen of the Night and *Faust,* and tonight I was glad. The *bal,* for size and splendor, had surpassed my expectations, as had my costume. True to his word, Worth had driven his seamstresses hard. In his vision for the Queen of the Night, Worth had created a costume for me that made me look to be covered in a shower of stars and comets. The embroidery was hand stitched in a technique original to him that shaped the fabric as it was sewn, and the silhouette of the bodice was sculpted as a result. One comet outlined my left breast and wound down to circle my waist, meeting others, all beaded in crystal and leaving long white silk satin crystal-beaded trails that ran across an indigo velvet train. More comets created a gorgeous bustle and the edges of their trails scalloped the skirt down to the floor—the comets looked like wings. On the front panel of the gown's skirt, more comets streaked across a night sky of indigo silk satin, and clouds hid a crescent moon as rays of white and gold light spread from it, embroidered in silver thread. The moon was beaded in pearls.

At my throat I wore a diamond pendant, and in my ears, diamond pendants also. For now my head was bare, but a glorious headdress waited upstairs, to be added just before the performance. The star shower would begin in my hair and descend from my headdress, a net of beads, diamonds, and diamanté stars, my hair added to with false hair and crystal pendants, and at the center of these was a diamond tiara.

I could barely move my head when the headdress was on, but this was not a nuisance. It was steadying, somehow, because of the focus it required.

Euphrosyne had been done beautifully by Worth also. She'd had him create a version of the Marie Antoinette shepherdess costume Eugénie had been painted in, so she looked like Eugénie as Marie Antoinette as a shepherdess at Petit Trianon. She'd worn a pale powdered wig and painted a beauty mark above her mouth. She did not at all remind me of the Empress—if anything, I think she looked the way Pepa must have wished all those years ago.

Wherever you are, dear Pepa, I wished silently, *I hope you are happy now.*

We were to descend in a cortège from the second-floor terrace of the salon to the floor at the beginning of the concert. The other beauties Euphrosyne had gathered were new to society, mostly unknown to me. Another friend of hers she had assured me I knew I did not recognize in her magnificent Cleopatra costume. Still another was the Empress Josephine; another, I soon recognized, was Madame du Barry—and then I saw it was Maxine. My erstwhile nemesis from Baden-Baden.

She nodded to me. I had not known she even knew Euphrosyne. I turned to say something, but Euphrosyne gave my gloved hand a pat, as it was time for us to go wait along the balcony for the performance to begin and then make our entrance.

My *bal* came into view.

The staircase we were on was a stately one that led to a second-floor terrace library that circled and looked down onto the entire ground floor of her conservatory. To our backs were books, and below were the celebrants. Grand Persian carpets spread across the golden herringboned marble of the floors, and guests had begun to gather on the red-velvet loveseats limned in gilt. Banquettes were sheltered by the enormous tropical plants that rose above them, and above each plant, as if a mirror to them in crystal, were flaming candle chandeliers hung on chains from the ceiling, which itself had glass canopies to let in the light, though it was the night we saw just past the reflections of the party below.

This was the light of that old world, the light by which I'd first encountered Paris. Euphrosyne's *hôtel* was a grand one. No gaslights here.

We each grasped the slender brass rail as we watched the milieu below. The guest list I'd left entirely to her; I'd given her a very short list of the people she should *not* invite, however, which had made her laugh. I'd forgotten to include Maxine.

Euphrosyne tapped her cigarette holder clean into a plant by her side and withdrew her cigar case. She smiled as she cut the tip and walked to a candelabrum behind her and pulled a candle loose. Not for me, I said, not until I've sung. She lit her cigar, and she turned and put the candle back.

I heard a story about you seeing the Comtesse at Félix's atelier, she said. How? No one sees her! Tell me. I must hear about it.

She was there to have a dress taken out, I said. But she still has her face.

Not her teeth, I hear, Euphrosyne said, and let out a cackle, and I allowed myself a laugh.

The Emperor loved her once, I said. Perhaps only her, I think.

Euphrosyne pushed at my arm. So . . . you were never with him? she asked.

I raised an eyebrow.

She gestured to the room. Half the women in this room have likely had the pleasure of watching as the imperial butler folded their gowns. She turned toward me with a bit of a swagger.

I let out a mock gasp.

Of course, she said. And the Prince Napoléon, too. She squinted at the crowd. Just to be sure.

To be sure?

We didn't know how that was going to turn out, did we? I wanted to be sure both Bonapartes were fond of me. The first was duty to country; the second, insurance within that country.

I shook my head and laughed.

No butler ever folded the Comtesse's dress for her, I said. If anyone had, it was the Emperor himself.

Euphrosyne's laughter at this rang out so loudly the people below looked up.

For all I knew, she was why he never kissed any of his mistresses after her. He hadn't saved himself for Eugénie.

If you'd told me, back when we met, that someday I'd be in this room, married, and he'd be dead in the suburbs of London, I'd have slapped you for lying to me, Euphrosyne said. Are you ready for your little concert?

I am.

It's almost time. Another hour, I think, she said. And then we'll prepare your hair.

Ladies, I heard then. I turned to see my novelist friend Simonet. He had a bottle of champagne with him. He blinked slowly, his pleasure at seeing me considerable. That vaguely guilty shadow hovered still in his eyes.

What is it? Euphrosyne said. Have you met my friend here? I extended my hand to him, though he seemed almost afraid of me.

I have, I said. Thank you. I gave you his novel, if you recall.

Ah! I knew there was a reason I had invited him. Is there some story here that I should know, not in the novel? Euphrosyne teased.

Nothing she would fear you knowing, he said. *Le Cirque du Monde Déchu* is being taken to the stage as an opera, however, and despite her recent refusal, it is still my hope she will have a change of heart and originate the role.

Ah! It is that protégé of Verdi's, Euphrosyne said, and ran to the stairs, a conqueror's gleam in her eye. I will introduce you.

Simonet and I looked at each other and smiled, nervous. I'd heard nothing from him since the rejection I sent, not a single note to complain, nor was he to be seen out—not in the theater, not in the balls, not at the dinners, not in the salons, not in the restaurants. Until now.

In an opera, masked balls only ever hide lovers and assassins. I'd thought only of assassins. I saw Simonet's expression become very grave as he watched over my shoulder as Euphrosyne drew near.

Who is this? I wondered to myself. And then came that refrain, *Is it you?* And just this once, it was.

It was him.

The mystery composer I had been so sure did not exist was on her arm, neither young nor old, his hair dark but gone silver in a distinguished way at his brow. He had dressed in elegant white tie, his vest a pure white also, and he walked with a slight limp, using a cane.

On his lapel, like blood, the ruby rose pin sat glittering.

The reason his ghost had never appeared to me in dreams was that somehow he was alive.

Did I love him already, before I knew him?

Yes, yes I did. But I also knew him.

My dear, he has been talking of nothing but you, Euphrosyne said. Lilliet Berne, may I present Aristafeo Cadiz.

We had both passed through Death's land and returned, then.

Too late, you're too late came the thought as he crossed the room to me, smiling, tentative. I nearly laughed to think of it. *You've made your miraculous return to me from the dead and you're too late.*

He was the very picture of the twinned joke of it—he there with the flower, this his own sly joke, and then all around him in the air, Fate's joke on me.

I wanted to make you something worthy of your gift, he said. Once you had become my patron, too.

Three

MAY I HAVE this dance? he asked. He stood before me, impossible and mortal at the same time, and set his cane on the rail.

I said nothing—I could not speak—but I could not be in front of Euphrosyne and Simonet a moment longer, either, and so by way of consent, I instead offered my arm to him, and he took me down to the floor below.

At the least I wanted proof he was mortal, and I had it when he took the lead.

His clothes, under my hands, were new and well made, even expensive, and the wings of hair I remembered so well were combed close to his head with pomade, his whiskers evenly trimmed. He had come from nearby, it seemed, neither reborn from the bones I had sometimes imagined to be still on the roof of the Paris Opera nor having clawed his way through the earth from the underworld. He had made some other bargain, a more ordinary one, and had chosen to live in secret, apart from me, and so the shock I felt, and the happiness, transmuted from happiness to fear and then anger. The sight of him alive burned me as his death had before.

We danced silently at first, his hands on my hands, his face glancingly touching mine, and then he said, You must leave him and come with me, tonight if possible. He must not stop us.

I could see the tenor along the far wall, seated, speaking to someone I could not see.

I cannot, I said.

Hear me out, then. If you do not leave with me tonight and you marry our tenor friend, if this is true, then I will never speak to you again so we must speak now instead.

Speak, then, I said. Tell me everything.

The crowd swirled around us, their faces flashing by in the turns of the dance like a storm of masks. I watched them as he told me of his time away from me.

The knife wounds had taken away his playing somehow—the hands were mute. But my cries that day had been heard and saved his life. Eugène, hearing them, finally guessed Aristafeo's identity and stopped himself before he made the killing blow.

He was not, as he'd hoped, about to murder the Prussian spy.

It's your ring she wears, isn't it? he'd said. When Aristafeo weakly nodded, Eugène swore and said, My friend, I've cut you badly. I apologize. Let me help get you to a hospital.

Aristafeo never saw him again. His attacker brought him to the temporary hospital kept in the home of the courtesan La Païva, who took an instant liking to him and made him her new cause. When she understood he was too badly wounded to likely play again but that he was a composer, she was moved and became one of his biggest supporters and eventually brought him to the attention of Verdi.

Verdi's protégé, after all.

While he would never again play as he once had, he did thrive all the same, though his wounds and long convalescence had changed him. His hair had gone silver; he walked now with this limp and a stoop, the wolfish confidence changed into something else, something more forlorn, even a little ragged.

His time as a Prix de Rome winner afforded him travel after a long struggle. There, encouraged by Verdi, he collaborated on the libretto with this new friend, a French novelist he'd met who was in need of a story and who then bought the house Aristafeo once owned in the Marais after he'd told him the story of his affair with me. With the help of their powerful friends, the opera was under commission to the Imperial Court of Russia as an entertainment for the young Alexander, to be presented in honor of his birthday.

On the night of the Sénat Bal, he had waited upstairs for me and had meant it to be our grand reunion.

As he'd waited on the Luxembourg Palace balcony amid new friends, he'd found himself next to the tenor, who did not seem to recognize him; his habits of long nights and drink meant he lived in a steady riot of acquaintances, everyone equally familiar and unfamiliar, with friends of longstanding whom he could not call by name and strangers he was sure he loved. The tenor relied constantly on his celebrity to keep up his friendships. That evening he had been busy narrating the evening for the party of men on the balcony that night and never once recognized Aristafeo.

Aristafeo, however, knew him instantly.

As my fame had grown, the tenor's had as well, as someone who dined out on his stories of me. Earlier, over dinner at a restaurant in Les Halles with these same men, he had begun with the story of how, after attending a performance of *Lucia di Lammermoor,* I had turned to him and tried to make him laugh by, with no training whatsoever, singing in imitation of the diva in the street outside the Paris Opera and he believed I had surpassed her. To his amazement, the other theatergoers mistook me for her in the dark, thinking perhaps she'd come outside to greet her fans.

A lie told to hide my past at the Majeurs-Plaisirs.

He described the secret lessons inside the unfinished Garnier and the first audition, the discovery that I was a Falcon and the rejection by the first jury, at which they all shook their heads in amazement.

Over the second course, he told a false story of my childhood, one I had not heard: that I was the illegitimate daughter of a former nun, fathered on her by a man of the cloth, the powers of my voice the Lord's way of being merciful to a girl otherwise innocent of sin —this I attributed to some fantasy of the tenor's. Because of this unfortunate childhood, it had been his duty, he said, on discovering

my voice, to train me, and it had been his pleasure to introduce me
to the great Pauline Viardot-García, who had graciously taken me
on—and then provided the vindication of bringing me with her to
study at the Conservatoire once she had assumed the directorship
there after the war.

Alexandre Dumas, *fils,* had added, for the tenor's new friend
mostly, that he'd known me to move both assassins and those who
commanded them, and had watched surprised as his friends wept in
the dark boxes of the theater around him like children. They talk
through the other singers, but when she sings, the theater is otherwise silent, he said. I like to imagine she could stop an execution.

This was met with both general laughter and agreement.

By the time the wine was nearly gone, there came a friendly argument about recent reviews hailing me as the greatest voice of my
era, saying that I was a sign the north of Europe had been civilized
at last and that the light of that civilization was alive in my voice,
moving now through it to the rest of the continent. The world could
only be next.

On the balcony at the palace afterward, as the men smoked, the
tenor kept his new friend company with a few glasses of cognac.

You want to know more? he asked Aristafeo as I came into view.

I do, he said.

He told of the men who had seized my carriage the night of my
debut and carried it through the streets, whipped by my driver to let
go and whose hands still bore the scars.

Others were more impertinent, he added, and so she lives at a
carefully guarded secret address as a result, known only to her closest intimates.

The tenor traced for him what he knew of my days: I did not
speak between morning and my arrival at the theater, my servants
were instructed to attend to my needs by leaving me notes and returning for my written answer. The same acts were performed at the
same times of each day as if to a metronome, meals prompt and un-
varied, the foods to fit the needs of a performer who could not gain
weight or afford the slightest cough. I gave my costume mistresses

the tiny weights used in the nets of Brittany fishermen to help give my costumes their slow, wheeling movements as I walked the stage, and my preference was for only the best jewelry for presents when it was not couture.

Is it true her maids have found diamonds in her garbage? Aristafeo had asked.

A bluff. She told them to search for them there afterward, the tenor said. She is pure theater.

What gift do you suppose she'd prefer? Aristafeo asked.

I couldn't say, the tenor said. Nothing I do seems to please her.

They laughed. The other gentlemen joined them, taking in the view of the guests arriving; each outdoing the other to tell the new friend, this protégé of Verdi's, something more interesting or sad or scandalous about each person. As the breeze moved the smoke of the cigars along and the view of the crowd was commanding, the group stayed content.

From there, he saw me announced. He watched as the writer made his plea to me and became worried as I left with him for the garden. He waited for me to appear again, even saw me emerge briefly before turning back. He waited for the writer also. When he saw neither of us, he even suspected us of beginning an affair, but he had come this far, and so, having worked up his nerve, he waited.

And then I did reappear.

That is her, indicated the tenor.

His eyes searched the gardens and the crowds of celebrants wandering through. The trees were strung with paper lanterns and lamps burned brightly along the edges, candles lit throughout the garden, but he did not see me until the aisle of raised swords told him I was returning from the palace.

But she was here earlier, Aristafeo observed. Had she left?

Yes, the tenor said, and grinned, slapping his arm. Though in quite a different gown altogether. It would appear she's had some sport. He then addressed the reputation of the dukes at my side.

That dress *is* the better one, Simonet said, having rejoined them.

Aristafeo held himself in place, gripping the rail as I was announced a second time and entered to applause, the crowd shouting my name. *La Générale! La Générale!* The men and women standing on their seats to see in the uproar had the men on the balcony joined by their dinner companions, all anxious to see me as well. They screamed with laughter as the one woman's dress caught fire and she was rushed to a fountain.

When I began the Jewel Song aria, the voice in the night came with a green flash through the dark, the ring he knew well finally on my hand as I waved my hands to the song's gestures in the gaslight below.

Always, the tenor said to him, as he took out his handkerchief. Always she is giving the performance of her life.

The tenor then joked to the assembled gentlemen that I had done him the favor of agreeing to become his wife. Some of the group demanded the truth; the rest, who knew better of our history, laughed, and he refused to say more, only grinning.

Here then was the real source of the published rumor that I was to marry him, this joke.

This news from the tenor, for Aristafeo, it was as if he'd been thrown from the balcony.

When the writer reappeared and offhandedly said our meeting had gone well and that he would speak to me again after he had sent his novel, Aristafeo thanked him and then asked if he had obtained my address. When the writer apologized for not having obtained such a thing, he fumed.

The tenor, overhearing this, slid a card into Aristafeo's hand. My good friend, the tenor said. On seeing it, Aristafeo raced away before the ball was done.

He knew the address too well. He went and waited in the street for me to return, smoking himself sick.

Now he believed the worst. He wanted to be free of the errand that had brought him out that night, but instead, he stayed, helpless, determined to see it through.

How could I be there still? Why would I stay there of all places? He had put me in that balloon, and yet he found me again in my cage.

Somewhere near dawn, my carriage returned.

He had meant to cry out to me as I stepped out, to confront me, but he could not think of what to say; he then thought to go to my door or return in the morning. But in each instance he could not bring himself either to speak or leave, and so instead he stayed there through the night. He followed my progress in the distance, me moving through my rooms by the light of my taper until I blew it out and the shades were drawn.

He had asked the Verdis to say nothing of him to me, and so when I arrived at their house that night for dinner with no apparent knowledge of his return, they then affected ignorance, improvising, believing he'd had a failure of nerve and wishing to protect his wishes.

Do not blame them, he said to me.

By now we had danced together for nearly the entire hour previous to my concert. We had allowed each other no other dance companions, and so there was talk at the edges of the floor. The most recent music finished and this last dance concluded, I brought my head up to meet his face.

He led me back upstairs, back to our party.

The opera was his, then, the mystery solved, and he was here in answer to my rejection of the role—the counteroffer I could not turn down. Or so he believed.

~

Upstairs, his general aspect seemed restored—he believed himself close to success and exerted the magnetism I remembered. He bowed and kissed Euphrosyne's hand, and then mine, then embraced the novelist, smiling.

You must tell us more of this opera, Euphrosyne said to Aristafeo, before turning to me and chiding me, You never spoke of this to me. Perhaps we can convince her of the wisdom of it, she said, turning back to the men, conspiratorial. They had enlisted her, or she had volunteered, or both.

I would like her to create the role of the equestrienne dance-hall queen in our opera, Aristafeo said.

So you must, Euphrosyne said to me. It's perfect.

But she is leaving the stage, Simonet said. Or so I've heard. Is this true, the curse?

What is this talk of leaving the stage and of a curse?

A rumor, nothing more. But she is leaving the stage, I said. This one, at least, for now. If you'll excuse me, I must prepare.

With that, I turned, picked up the train of my dress, and walked away from them, making my way toward my dressing room and Lucy and Doro, as it was time for the mounting of my headdress.

Aristafeo ran after me and reached out for my arm. I paused. From behind him, over his shoulder, Euphrosyne did her best imitation of indifference, and the novelist tried as well.

I must sing, I said. This must wait.

I continued away, but Aristafeo walked behind me still. A banquette of young women in dresses the colors of *macarons*, looking for all the world like a set—as if they should be consumed together —followed us with their eyes.

We had the air of something about to happen.

I stopped again. Nothing of this is as it seems, I said. But you must wait for my story. I paused by the entrance to my dressing room.

In the dark, his face briefly silver again as it had been that night in the woods at Compiègne, my anger at him softened.

You are angry at being deceived. Forgive me. I couldn't bear to return to you and have you only pity me, he said. I wanted to return with the opera I'd promised you. I wanted to return in glory.

The rest, then, after, I said, and he nodded.

He came closer then for a kiss in the shadow of one of Euphrosyne's palms there in the hallway.

His hand felt for the ring on my hand and it was not there.

Did I imagine it? he asked.

No, I answered. I brought his hand to where it sat hidden in a pocket at my waist. It is here, hidden to be safe. After I sing, I will explain everything. Promise me you'll stay, I said. Stay and hear me out, as I have heard you.

I promise, he said.

~

The kiss had felt almost like nothing at first, but as I sat down before the enormous mirrored Louis XVI vanity in the guest apartment Euphrosyne had assigned to me for a dressing room, and watched as Lucy and Doro briskly brushed my hair and attached and styled the hairpieces that they then crowned with the diamond tiara and then draped the resulting tower of hair with that rain of crystal stars, I was like the wick that is slow to light, which, as you reach for the next match, has instead guttered into flame.

They were rapid and clever, my maids; they had prepared the hairpieces in advance with irons, knew my hair and even my hairpieces intimately. As we admired the result, the many glittering stars drew my attention to my own hand, where the little green light of the emerald from Aristafeo's ring had always been, now strangely bare.

Is it lost? Lucy asked. Do we need to look for it? She had noticed my sadness, also guttering within me.

No, I said. No, it is not lost.

But you're never without it, Doro said.

It's not in the costume tonight, I said, and they humored me, acting as if of course this was reason I did not wear it even though I wore it always.

The ring had kept me company for so long there was the faintest print of it by the knuckle from the many years of twisting it around and around, as if it could loosen the sorrow. Sometimes, as I did, I remembered the night he sank down before me and believed in his love for me enough in the face of death to ask me to be his wife. I would remember all of it: all of the nights, even when I had fled from his side into the dark, off to the Tuileries, which set me on that trail that led somehow here.

Here was the return of what I had lost, the loss of which had driven me mad, and now his return threatened to drive me just as mad as well.

I think you can never know what you can live without. I think you can never know what you will live through. Only when the disaster arrives and you are there does the depth of your real inner resources reveal itself, and not a moment before.

The disaster was here.

I had thought I could not live without him, and then I had lived on, creating the world around me now. A world that had no room for him — and this was perhaps worse than losing him the first time.

Did I still love him? Yes. Yes, I did. When he had asked me to leave with him, I had wanted to, at once. I always would love him in some way I would never be able to change and that might never die. If only he had come to me directly . . . He was so proud of what he'd done, so sure he knew my fate, he could never have known that nothing on this earth had the capacity to injure what I once felt for him quite like his returning to me this way.

As much as I had longed to be in his arms again, to see him live again, as I had danced with him and listened to him and his account of his long misunderstanding of me and my life, a sickening sort of pity had grown up in me, much like I had once felt for the tenor. I pitied him, and I also feared him now — yes, I feared him, and feared the immensity of what he'd done. This elaborate plot of his to surprise me with this opera told me he was not so different from the tenor, preparing a rival imaginary landscape for me to inhabit with him, sure all the while that I would join him once all was ready — and unprepared when I did not or could not.

I could stand before him, be in his arms as I was just then, and still be lost to him, some phantom of a desire he cherished more than he cherished me, the woman he claimed he loved.

And so I felt more alone than before his return, and I was no longer sure what I was protecting or why. My earlier piety on his behalf for nothing.

Were we at last in that garden, then, the tenor, Aristafeo, and I? The one I had fought so hard for us to avoid? But the black knight was on the balcony with his love; the duke was in the garden, raging alone. And Leonora wanted only to leave them both to their duel and be done.

If this had been funny at all, it would have been *opéra bouffe*. What was *opéra bouffe* when it turned tragic? Did such a thing exist? My Leonora was in her own duel, to be fought with Fate instead, which could choose any weapon against her. Even her own life, even the man she loved.

Cursed indeed.

It seemed to me I had one other weapon against Fate, if it could be said to be that: This role I had prepared to sing, the Queen of the Night. To sing the aria was to prepare for *The Magic Flute*. I had prepared the role of the Queen of the Night. I was never going to be asked to perform it again—I was right for neither role, not the Queen nor Pamina, her daughter. But for this reason, it had amused me to prepare it—one solution to my curse, it seemed to me, if it existed, was to sing outside my *Fach*.

I had only ever seen the opera performed once, in the company of Pauline and our *Haustheater* troupe shortly after arriving to begin the Weimar rehearsals for *Le Dernier Sorcier*. Pauline had arranged for us to see *The Magic Flute*, the opera ahead of hers in the season's schedule.

The Magic Flute begins with a handsome young man journeying at night who meets an evil serpent in the forest and, overcome with the terror, he faints. As the serpent prepares to finish him, three sorceresses arrive and defeat it, and then they debate as to which one of them he shall belong to as a lover. This bargaining is interrupted by a mystical communication from their queen, the Queen of the Night, who arrives and tells them he is to be her daughter's rescuer and, if successful, be given her hand in marriage. When he awakens, the sorceresses convince him he is the one who killed the monster and then tell him the story of the Queen's daughter, kidnapped by a demon and now a prisoner of the vile wizard Sarastro, in need of a brave hero to rescue her from his Temple of Reason. The Queen then appears to the young hero and awards him this quest. She shows him a portrait of her daughter, and he falls in love with her. She gives him a magic flute, which, when played, will quiet all hearts and keep him safe, and she then sends him on his way.

To her daughter she had given a knife for Sarastro—to kill him.

Pamina tries to escape but is captured again and returned to Sarastro's Temple of Reason. There she is made to wait until her hero arrives to rescue her. Several times she feels driven mad by waiting for him, but she is always reassured that he will come, that he loves her, and despite never having met him, she allows herself to be reassured. He, meanwhile, is captured by the wizard when he tries to sneak into the palace and is made to become an initiate in order to rescue her. Sarastro tells him he will give her to him if he passes the tests he sets for him. Tests of silence, fire, and water.

I remember I waited in vain for the hero to use his flute to defeat the wizard. He confused me—he was a handsome incompetent who could not slay monsters or defeat wizards, good only for obeying whomever seized him until his next capture, the Queen first and then Sarastro—and he betrays the Queen and his mission immediately. At the end, when the Queen is plunged into Hell for daring to try to rescue her daughter, we are told the daughter and the hero are now followers of Reason and Wisdom and that they love each other and repudiate her.

The story seemed cruel to me.

I could see *The Magic Flute* was a story of love before first sight —but at least for Pamina, it seemed the sort of story a man might tell about love—a man deluded about love, deluded as to how love comes to be. Love is never governed by Reason.

The rest of the story is mysterious. There is no reason Tamino is the hero except that he is beautiful—he looks the part. There is no reason for Pamina to wait for him to rescue her—she almost rescues herself—except that she is told that he loves her. She is a captive to that more than she is to the wizard—she had nearly been free. There is no reason for them to believe Sarastro is a figure of Reason, either, beyond what he says, unless Reason is a kidnapper who uses demons to obtain his goals. But the ending is called a victory for love.

I, however, loved the Queen. The lovers were nothing to me. I loved the power she commanded and the terror others felt at her appearance. I, too, wanted to be feared, even just once—I wanted to be feared especially that night in the Weimar theater, caught as I was in my strange cage made from my own ambitions and mistakes—what a joy it would be, it seemed to me, to summon her spectral power, to appear out of the air before my captors and have the power to force them to cower before me.

All these years later, what remained in my memory of the opera was the desire to perform a part that I would never be asked to perform because it was not in my *Fach*. This was perhaps the most dangerous form of envy for a singer on principle. The aria of the Queen of the Night is one of the most difficult in all of opera. To sing it, you must have a tremendously controlled voice capable of moving from its depths to its heights with a capacity for both softness and then enormous power. When sung correctly, it is beautiful, but as Pauline told us that night, it is almost impossible to sing without destroying your voice forever. In all of opera, it is the most like a real test of virtue and sincerity, of the kind gods, sorceresses, and magical creatures set for mortals, and unlike the hero's tests in the opera's story, it is one that can be won only by ability. No magic could help you here.

Am I complete? I asked Doro and Lucy, and they answered that I was, but I noticed my mouth was too pale, and I startled Doro by reaching out, the stars shaking as I did, to apply more rouge to my mouth as if it could remove the memory of the kiss. Yes, it needed restoring. I smiled to think of Aristafeo in the ball downstairs, his own mouth faintly made red by mine.

Had he brought her here? Whoever she was, whoever had paid
for his beautiful suit? Whoever she was, he had come prepared to
abandon her at once for me if I had left with him. Would she see the
red mark or was he even now with his handkerchief by a fountain?
The ruby rose pin on his lapel, his smile. Had she watched him demand I leave with him?

And what of the kiss?

I touched the ring where it sat at my waist, gently smoothing it
with my thumb as I thought of what to do—as if there were any
choice in it.

My reflection made a credible Queen of the Night, it seemed to
me. The column of hair, the drape of stars across my face, the comets on my bodice, the paleness of the skin that would not change
against the renewed red mouth. What I was about to do would ap-
pall Pauline, I knew—Pauline who would be in the audience if
Louis and Turgenev were well enough for her to leave.

Doro's eyes met mine, and then I saw Lucy's smiling approval
behind her. I stood gently with their help, to the faint tinkling of
the crystals, and all at once I felt that paralysis of the heart that
could only be fatal, as the sickened pity in me changed to anger and
the blackness that had once meant madness came back to me now
like my own servant. The Queen of the Night did not wear a cloak
of night, she wore the night as a cloak; she swept mightily from
within the darkness, it was hers. I heard the music change in the
house through the walls then and knew it was time for my entrance
even before the footman Euphrosyne sent for me reached my door.
Doro and Lucy helped me stand.

The evening's performance began with members of the ballet from
Faust re-creating the Cave of Queens and Courtesans within the
salle de danse, the ballerinos and ballerinas entering as the guests
danced and joined them. As dancer after dancer entered, I could
hear the gasps and cries of the guests, startled to find them in their

midst. As this went on, we, the queens and courtesans, descended from the stairs above in single file. Euphrosyne went first, as Eugénie, then came the mesdames Pompadour and du Barry, Cleopatra, Helen, and Josephine. I knew none of these new beauties Euphrosyne had chosen; I had been away from Paris for too long.

They were cheered and applauded, and they waved to their friends, ballerinos waiting for each of them to bring them into the dance. I saw mine move to their place in the crowd and stepped forward.

I was last, and the applause began for me as soon as I appeared at the top of the stairs. There were cheers at the sight of my completed costume, and at first I was pleased, but I didn't understand until I could see the many stars appearing across the dress and the stairs around me as I descended, the light coming from the chandeliers turned into tiny slivers by the headdress's many crystals. Worth had not told me of this effect, and the surprise of it brought real joy to my heart. I suppressed a smile as I passed through the crowd to the dais set up for me, the ballerinos making a path for me, applause deepening as I came to a stop.

I lifted my arms in greeting and heard my name shouted in the way that still pleased me.

The Queen of the Night aria, you cannot sing it angrily, but instead must muster the complete control that can deliver false anger. Yet I was angry; I was full of rage. It was dangerous for me to sing it this way, but still I had to begin. So I began.

> The vengeance of Hell boils in my heart,
> Death and despair flame about me!
> If Sarastro does not meet death at your hand,
> You will be my daughter nevermore.
> Disowned you will be forever,
>   Abandoned you will be forever,
> Be forever broken, all bonds of Nature,
>   If by your hand Sarastro is not made a ghost!
> Hear me! God of vengeance! Hear this mother's vow!

The sound of it coming from my own throat was surprising, terrifying, and difficult to believe; I had warmed the voice earlier in the evening in preparation; I had sung it for days; but only tonight could I hear the nearly inhuman rage the song describes and it thrilled me.

I was succeeding. Perhaps I could even change my fate.

At the conclusion, the crowd separated again and the tenor emerged at the side of the stage holding a casket I knew well—the casket of jewels for the Jewel Song. The tenor had borrowed it from the props room—the very one I had used night after night as Marguerite, seduced by the enchanted jewels Mephistopheles has charmed to turn her from a chaste young woman into a vain beauty in love with her appearance.

I looked to the walls of the room, still searching for a sign of Aristafeo; I saw him at last. He was leaning against the far wall with a row of waiters.

He tipped his head to me.

The tenor, now even with the dais, set the casket at my feet to the eventual laughter of the crowd as he saw I could not lean forward to retrieve it. He gallantly raised it up, the lid open, and a flash of green light came from a stunning emerald necklace there beside an emerald ring made to match—the laughing audience gasped, as did I.

I knew the danger represented by the ring and picked the necklace up from the casket instead, crying out the entrance words much as I had that night at the ball. *O Dieu! Que des bijoux!* I sought to begin the scene before the tenor could act, but the tenor had gestured at himself, which led to more laughter as he mugged to the audience. As I waited for the laughter to die down in order to continue, he withdrew the ring and, taking my hand, set it on my finger.

I wished for the Queen's power of flight; I wished to throw the ring from my hand, to slap his face, to do anything at all other than what I did, which was to look at the ring admiringly and then to smile at him in the manner of the role as the room cheered us on —believing us to be the lovers we were rumored to be and they the witnesses to our engagement. I looked away, to enter the song, and as I did so, I searched for a sign of Aristafeo but could not see to the wall past the blurred garden of dark faces, an occasional costumed figure stepping into the light in violent contrast suddenly and then moving on.

The tenor reached for my hand and bowed to the audience then retreated, and I continued with the Jewel Song. I remember nothing of singing it. I felt as if I had vanished, returning only when the Jewel Song concluded, and it was time for the final mad scene, the theme for the entire ball.

Here the ballerinos and ballerinas had been instructed to begin the dancing again, much as they had for my entrance. The whirl rose up once more, and I could feel Aristafeo receding, leaving, breaking his promise to stay, believing the lies, his faith in me gone. If only we could have stayed in our little paradise, if only I could have borne it, but I could not—could not bear the Empress's shadow, even as I knew that I had come to live inside it; it rose around me even now.

This dark was not my servant; I was the servant still.

When the mad scene concluded and I had finished begging the angels to take me, to rescue me from this prison, the crowd applauded again, sounding like the roar of a single beast, and as they finally quieted, the tenor raised my hand once more and announced our joint appearance in *Carmen*, at which they took up again.

The figures parted. I could see at last clear to Aristafeo's place on the wall. He was gone.

~

You were magnificent, Euphrosyne said. She sat before me on a divan she had her footmen place near the dais, and she kept eyeing the casket as if it might offer up more jewels. The emeralds had excited her. A glass of champagne glowed in her hand. She patted the seat next to her and I went over dutifully. A waiter brought me a glass of my own.

Magnificent!

I was trembling, to my surprise, and so I held the glass out so as not to spill, and a footman appeared and set the glass down on a side table placed there for this very purpose.

What's wrong? Euphrosyne asked. Are you ill?

I'm sure I'm just tired, I said. I've not had supper.

Euphrosyne had been the one to find me again, long after I had given up on finding her. Backstage at *La Sonnambula*, flowers had appeared, along with her card, inviting me to dinner after the performance. This just after my debut. The card said only *You promised you would not forget me—all my love, E.* I had rushed out of my dressing room with it in my hand to find her waiting for me outside. I wept and laughed to see her again until the backstage manager came to fine me for the noise. *Always fines with you*, I remember she said, pulling out her purse grandly.

I was still here. The angels had not rescued me. Perhaps *Faust* was not the opera to come true after all, or perhaps the curse did not work this way or were there angels still ahead of me? But I had tried my foolish bit. I had tried to sing outside my *Fach*, had tried to add to my Fates—and now they ran at each other like rearing horses. Either way, it was done, and I was right where I had begun. And I knew the worst of what Aristafeo had said to me was that, in his way, he was in the right.

I smiled somewhat weakly at Euphrosyne as she laced her hand in mine. I felt neither brave nor bold now, but I was determined to try.

I'd changed into a new dress, a black silk velvet gown. I'd not worn my new emeralds nor had I put back on Aristafeo's ring. I instead wore my diamonds, diamonds I bought myself, my hair decorated by a few of the strands from my headdress, something Doro had improvised quite beautifully.

I had decided to belong only to myself.

You *should* marry him, I think, she said.

I looked around us.

Of course. One moment. She gestured, and I saw the waiters and footmen wince and run close. This little act of yours. How hard it must be! She turned back to the waiters. The screens, please, quickly!

I know you prefer the view of the room, I said to her, once they were in place. So I won't be long. I won't marry him. Not him, not any other.

Why not? Whatever could keep you?

My work. I have agreed to *Carmen*. I will stay in Paris a few days longer after that, and then I am off to Milan for Verdi. All is well. I am not marrying, and I am not leaving the stage.

She seemed to have forgotten the evening's original purpose to celebrate my triumph and repudiate the curse; instead, she focused on the tenor's performance as a suitor. She also seemed to have forgotten the way I had met the tenor all those years ago. She was my only friend from that time with the gift of letting the past really die to her, to live like a beautiful happy animal in the present among her newest pleasures. I wished I was like her this way, but I was not. And she would never understand why.

She said, It's as if you were married before you met. So many have been separated as you have and not reunited again.

And at this, I thought of Aristafeo instead.

I will never marry him, I said. Also, you only just earlier told me never to marry. I prefer the advice of my friend from earlier. Where is she?

I had an instant conversion, she said. But I suppose it is settled.

She looked down at her hands. One question, though, she said.

I waited for it.

What if the curse is real? What then?

Then he'll kill me, I said. And I'll be spared the marriage.

We both laughed into our fans as we used to, and then I said, That's all I have to say. And with that, she waved away the screens, and we returned to watching the room.

As I searched again for Aristafeo, I saw the tenor instead.

He was dancing with one of these beauties—the Madame du Barry—Maxine.

In the years since we'd met in Baden-Baden, her slight blond beauty had become something arch and more lovely. She and the tenor were a perfect matched pair, nearly brother and sister. Her eyes found mine over his shoulder in recognition, and she smiled, nodding her head at me. I returned the nod.

I did not have the strength to look away.

The waltz ended; applause rose around the room. Maxine and the tenor made their way to our side.

She says she knows us from Baden-Baden, the tenor said, smiling, as Maxine threw her arms around me in an embrace. I don't recall her, but I'm ever so glad I sent you there. She's to be our Micaëla. Isn't that fantastic?

Congratulations, Lilliet, Maxine said. She kissed me quickly on each cheek.

I flicked open my fan, and said against it, to Euphrosyne: Maxine de Crecy and I were slaves together of Pauline Viardot-García's.

You are so . . . droll, Maxine said. I suppose you were so quiet then I never noticed.

Euphrosyne waved the screens back into place around us, and chairs appeared for Maxine and the tenor, and then she said, Lilliet, quiet?

Was I? I asked. I see you have been reacquainted with our troubadour, I said.

He's been a remarkable help this evening. I had ever so much trouble just now with a rather too-eager suitor. He dispatched him swiftly.

He is good for that, I said.

If Maxine recalled our former enmity, she was at the least not eager to renew it this evening, and so I let it go slack as well.

Maxine, how have you fared? I asked.

I did not have as fine a debut as you, but I have done well by our mistress's honor, she said.

We laughed and toasted her. To Pauline.

It was then I heard Pauline announced just outside the screen, with Turgenev. We laughed in shock as they entered. Are we so comic as that? Pauline asked, and then she noticed Maxine, and there was much kissing of us both from her.

We had just said your name and you appeared like magic, Maxine said.

Turgenev stood back, quiet, clearly still very ill, but smiling to me all the same. La Lapinard, he said, and embraced me, kissing my cheeks. I was moved. More chairs were brought for them and more glasses, champagne was poured, and we sat down again. The screens returned.

I want to say I am so proud of you, Pauline said to me. Your Queen of the Night was a revelation. But never sing it again, not ever; it terrified me.

Thank you, I said. I will never sing it again, I promise.

It was thrilling, Turgenev said. But, yes, do as she says.

I'd not expected you, I said to him, and clasped his hands with mine.

He is one surprise, Pauline said. It seems there was another.

She and the tenor looked at each other and smiled.

We dined and chatted amiably as if we had all always known each other, as if we were all on a train and headed together for some distant and placid country, someplace where we could all be together with all our conflicts the most distant of memories, behind us forever.

This, of course, was an illusion, if a beautiful one.

Some hours later, Pauline and I stood on the catwalk, watching as the guests danced below in graceful pirouettes across the parquet floor. Some of the candles had burned out and new ones been lit, but it was darker all the same.

You were angry tonight, she said.

Yes.

When our tenor friend brought you to me, I knew very well he was your patron. It was never unclear. Was he brutal to you? Did he beat you?

I thought to try to explain, but as I thought of what to say, she said only, My dear. Why are you with him? Why would you marry him?

I am . . . not. And then I paused. He is not mine, I said.

But you allow him, she said. You do not drive him away.

I'm grateful you taught me how to sing opposite enemies, I said.

As necessary, though, she said. Not by choice. The sacrifice is usually chained to the rock. She does not usually dance out to meet her monster.

This left me silent.

I wanted to see you at least once, she said. At least once before this retirement came to pass. Are you very sure? I always feared my sister's fate for you; you were the most like her of my students, God knows; and here Pauline crossed herself, though I felt a flush of pride to hear this. Has he really proposed then? she asked.

Oh . . . so much talk of marriage, I said. No, no retirement, it's a rumor. No one has proposed yet.

Yes, are you very sure? she asked, and I knew she meant the tenor's present onstage. I'd assumed this story of the curse was just that, she said. If there's a curse, it's in leaving the stage, not in staying. Or the curse is in being a little fool of a woman for the sake of a man. Her fierce expression softened only slightly. Did you never find your composer?

I embraced her then, surprising her, hoping to hide the tears that had surprised me, but she was not fooled.

It is not love that drives us mad, I think, she said. But all the rest of life around the love.

Turgenev appeared then, out of the shadows. I couldn't tell if he had been waiting there as we spoke or not. When he was silent, despite his great size, he was as a ghost. He offered his handkerchief with a flourish, and I thanked him as I dried my eyes.

Call on us anytime, she said, kissing me three times as she took his arm. Good night.

It was the end of the night at last. There was coffee on all of the buffets; carriages were being called. Men were asleep, slumped on tables or in chaises; and the air was sick with the smell of wine that had been left out. The waiters moved swiftly across the rooms inside rescuing crystal and silver from the tables, and with everyone leaving or gone, I was free to be alone, and so I lingered, neither going to my suite upstairs nor asking anyone to stay with me.

A figure entered the dark garden from the house, and I nearly took it for a ghost. I soon saw it was two figures, in fact, the tenor with Maxine on his arm.

My old prison, so close to having another prisoner.

He blinked, nearly stupid with interrupted lust, and I saw his face change to the peculiar intensity he had earlier.

There you are, *comprimaria*, he said.

Not at all, *comprimario*, I said. How easy it was, our old joke. No one is here, I said, when he did not move. Please, don't let me interrupt your game.

Don't be foolish. I was looking for you. Come with us; we're off to Les Halles. Where are your emeralds?

My maids know, I'm sure, I said.

Where are they? he asked. They're your engagement present. Go get them and come with us.

We stared at each other, silent. Be a good girl, he said to Maxine. Go get them to call our carriage.

Our carriage, I noted. He had seen her for some time.

I should choose my own present, I said. And you haven't yet proposed. Let me choose *then*, when you do.

In the cool dark, something like the heat of Hell's own door opening passed between us.

She won't likely find a footman, I said. Or if she does, she won't remember her duties.

No, the tenor said. I suspect she knows her duties well. Even in front of footmen.

She's a better match for you, I said. You should marry her instead.

A moment passed, a duel of a kind, silent.

We both know better, he said. You are my one match.

You're only proposing because of him, I said. A test. He knew instantly whom I meant.

No, he said.

Propose to me when he is nowhere around, I said. But let him live. He smiled then nodded. I'd added that perhaps only just in time.

Only then I will consider it, I said. But only then. Do I have your word?

On the asking or the living?

Both. I'll not accept you otherwise.

And why not? How could you refuse?

Think again what it is you ask of me, I said, refusing to answer him. I'll return the emeralds if you like. There's only one engagement present I want, and I've asked for it.

Maxine returned then, beckoning the tenor; she was not as drunk as she had seemed before. And he turned as if in a trance, remembering her, before he looked back to me.

Keep them also, he said softly, so only I could hear. As for the rest, I agree. I will ask you again — though I have asked you once before. For now, I will let him live against the day you say yes and become my bride. Name the hour you will say yes, and it will be done. He leaned in then, kissed my cheek, and waited to hear my response. But refuse and I keep no promises, he said.

We are at terms, then, I said.

We are, *comprimaria*. But do not take too long.

He kissed me once more before heading to the door, where he took Maxine's hand in his and led her out.

I sat back into the chair and drew my cape closer. The night air was cool, too cold for me to remain much longer, but I could not bring myself to enter yet. I looked into the candelabra, the only light in the garden. The flames took turns erupting in little gouts, like little fire-breathers at practice, and all at once, oh, how I missed Flambeau.

To my surprise, I missed the rest as well, as it paraded before me in the dark: the show, the act, my old horse, my buckskin. I missed Ernesto and Priscilla, the tiny city of tents and carts, the feeling of the world moving in the night around you rather than you moving in it, of being on a long journey without a destination, the tour your home. I wondered where the *cirque* was then and if they missed me, even as I knew there was sure to be another girl in my old costume, wheeling a horse around a ring, firing my old rifle into the air.

Another girl practicing with Flambeau, perhaps, hoping to give herself a voice made only of fire.

I took out my cigar in remembrance and lit it on the candle. As I shot smoke rings into the air and poked them with the cigar, I heard from behind me the click of the cane on the stones and knew it instantly, as if it searched across my own heart.

I did not move or even look to him.

I thought you gone, I said.

He came a few steps closer. I thought I could stay and then I could not. But I have returned for the story, he said.

There was no longer anything to tell him. The tenor would likely keep his promise to me, but he would do better if Aristafeo was far from here. If I was to tell the story I promised, Aristafeo would stay, insist I try to leave with him, be with him; and if he stayed and insisted, I might relent; and then he would most likely be killed; and I would fail us both. All I needed to do was to play the part of that pretty petty liar, the courtesan driven only by the pursuit of luxury, prestige, fame—to become the woman he feared I was. This was what would drive him from me, back to his mysterious benefactress, back into the secret hiding place he had emerged from, where he might live on in safety without me.

The one way to save this love, always, it seemed, no matter the place or time, was to refuse it.

Will you really sing *Carmen* with him? And not *Le Cirque du Monde Déchu*?

Yes, I said.

He looked down and was silent, and so I continued.

I have refused you, I said. You, you said you would leave if I did. So, please. Leave. Leave and let it be done.

The candles burning were the only sound as now we stared at each other.

I wrote the opera I said I would, he said. With the hope one day I could get it to you and it would remind you of me — me, but also of you. Of us.

Keep your word, I said.

I closed my eyes. When I opened them again, he was right in front of me.

What were you to tell me? he asked. Why did you ask me to stay?

Keep your word, I said again. Keep your word and go. Leave and do not return.

At this, he finally looked away.

I was always happy that at least one of us was saved, he said. He turned to leave and then paused and looked back.

I will still try to be happy for that.

And with that, he was gone.

Four

THE SETTING IN *Carmen* for that song known as the Habanera in the first act: Carmen has been surrounded by young men who are insisting to know when she will love them, on what day. She spins, acting as if she were ignoring them as she walks and sings:

> *Quand je vous aimerai? Ma foi, je ne sais pas,*
> *peut-être jamais, peut-être demain.*
> *Mais pas aujourd'hui, c'est certain.*
> *L'amour est un oiseau rebelle*
> *Que nul ne peut apprivoiser.*
> *Et c'est bien en vain qu'on l'appelle,*
> *S'il lui convient de refuser.*
> *Rien n'y fait, menace ou prière*

> When will I love you? My faith, I don't know,
> maybe never, maybe tomorrow.
> But not today, that is certain.
> Love is a rebel bird
> that no one can tame,
> and we call in vain
> if it is convenient for it to refuse.
> Threat or prayer, nothing will work.

Carmen is accustomed to the attention of every man everywhere she goes. It insults her to have one who will not look.

There is a rose between her breasts. Near the end of the act she throws it to the young soldier who will not look at her for shame over the feelings she arouses in him. He wants to keep himself for the young Micaëla, the girl his mother wants him to marry. His mother is dying and would like him to be settled with a good girl.

He picks up the rose and smiles at Carmen, and the string section trills with the premonition of death.

I was still singing songs with roses.

L'amour, la mort, she sings, by turns gaily and seductively. Love, death. Love. Only in French do they rhyme.

~

The weeks went by with no word from him. The autumn deepened; the trees turned black and gold again. *Faust* ended; rehearsals for *Carmen* began in earnest. The rumor of the curse, that I was leaving the stage, meant, as I'd expected, more new offers came in and the tickets for *Carmen* went at a run. Nothing had been repudiated by my accepting the role, and it did not matter except to me.

Now my plan was underway. I had only to survive it.

Aristafeo's opera would succeed without me, and he would find future patrons, lovers, and stars. And the honor of originating a role, of performing in his opera, was nothing beside the honor of protecting him as he returned.

For this was how it was possible for me. All of the love I had for him, everything I would have said, all became this performance of alienation. I needed him to believe what I did not want him to believe, that I no longer loved him. We were done, and there was nothing between us now except his ring, which I had found that night as I undressed.

I put it in my jewel safe. I knew to wait before returning it. I'd endured repeated proposals before, but always as a kind of crisis of my connection with an admirer. You needed to reject them in such a way that the liaison was protected, and yet to do so also required an affection from you or the liaison was over. A proposal repeated in the face of rejection required more of the same, though I suspected

some admirers of proposing, at the least, to receive the repeated re-
assurance that came with my rejections.

If the liaison was unwanted, then the proposal allowed you to
end it gracefully. *No, of course, my dear, we cannot see each other now.*

Rings had their own protocols. If I returned the ring too quickly,
it would be cruel; too slowly, and it would encourage him; to keep it
kept him encouraged against a day that could never come. And so
I decided to write to him as to the ring after two weeks' time, and
then *Carmen* began and all of my attention was there.

Three weeks, then, I said to myself. And then it was four.

At the first rehearsal, the director warned me to consider an approach that would not offend the conservative audiences who, when
the opera had debuted, he said, were repulsed by her.

He was a delicate man with a trim, clean beard and bifocal glasses
low on his thin nose.

He was, I decided, determined to make the same mistakes as last
time.

As we make our return to the original the audiences now say
they want, he said, there's every reason to expect the show may have
the same problems here it had before. The French do not change so
much.

I took out my notebook and wrote to him, *She has not yet seduced
them*, with a little smile for the stage manager beside him, and when
he shrugged, I added, *Don't worry. Let's begin.*

The effect of working with so many former classmates from the
Conservatoire was to feel a little as if I had returned there, to those
days spent in the dark muddle of sounds made by beginning singers
at their lessons, practicing at being surprised by love or the knife.
Again. Sing it again, your teacher would insist. And in front of you
would be some former legend looking like the ghost of the character
you were trying to master. You could not sometimes guess at the
force they'd once mustered. If you did not know what they asked
for, if after many attempts this was still a little outside your imagin-

ing, then the singing teacher would straighten—they had always
warmed up, of course—and the ghost would come to life. There,
through the unsteady air, came the notes that would remind you of
their legends.

You took custody of something when you learned a role that
could make your fortune or ruin it (or leave it untouched, which, in
some ways, was worse, to my mind—but then I was still sure glory
was the cure for me). All the while, that first real lesson of singing
—you don't choose the role, the role chooses you—it seemed I was
always learning it again. Your *Fach* was your fate as a singer, as far
as roles went, and so no wonder if we felt our fates came from our
Fächer as well.

I knew I had succeeded when it felt as if my throat were a spindle,
the voice a thread, the stage some vast loom for something drawn
from me into the air, where it caught and filled out to fit the shape
of something greater, greater than all of us onstage and that only
visited me there.

So I studied *Carmen* as if I were in school again. I started a new
notebook, like the one I kept one for each of the roles in my repertoire. I always began learning my music by copying out the lyrics
by hand, and I marked the music above them. My mornings before
rehearsal were spent with a pencil and the blank pages of a journal
that came with me to the rehearsal, where I made notes, writing
down thoughts the director and the conductor gave as well. I translated the libretto in order to understand, as much as possible, what
I sang and what, if anything, might come of it. But she would not
come to me.

I could not reach Carmen at all.

～

The night of the dress rehearsal for *Carmen*, the tenor arrived wear-
ing a new black velvet frock coat and with red silk roses for me.
He brought my maids as well, a dress rehearsal tradition for me.
My maids had become quite expert at music, and I relied on their

opinions. Mademoiselle is flat in the end of her aria near the middle of the second act, Doro might say. Mademoiselle could extend her pause in the caesura, Lucy would add.

They gained nothing if I was to be out of work due to the mistakes flattery exposes you to.

The tenor was solicitous with them as he never had been in our first days. In front of others, he was kind and affectionate to me. In private, we almost never spoke.

He had kept up his affair with Maxine, I knew, even as he continued his very public courtship of me. I could only understand both as compulsions—I was sure he understood neither pursuit. Maxine, for her part, did not complain, humiliated by her inability to vanquish me. Any connection to him was valuable. I could not fault her as I had done the same.

From the stage at the end, as I stood and my tiny audience applauded and shouted, I looked out through the gaslights, the brightness separating us, and for an instant they were as dim in that moment as the faces of the dead, as if I saw Doro and Lucy from on the other side of this veil.

The sensation left me then, and we went back to my apartment and they made their comments to me at home as I sat and played bezique with them and we soaked sugar cubes in gin as the tenor looked on, drinking champagne and teasing, occasionally pointing out our cards to spoil this or that hand.

I barely heard any of it.

Some final separation was coming, approaching through the dark on the other side of all these days, I was sure of it. I could not see what it would be. I only knew, whatever this was, I would welcome it all the same.

∾

I spent the next day alone, in preparation for the performance that evening. When the tenor asked to stop by, I put him off.

I didn't feel prepared. There hadn't been enough rehearsal time,

it seemed to me, and I was nervous because I felt I was still searching for her, for Carmen. I knew my music, my cues, all this was
correct and had been checked again and again, like the seams of my
dresses — the seamstress had even obliged me by pricking herself as
she sewed those foolish fishing weights into my costume, though to
do this deliberately felt like its own sort of bad luck. The director
appreciated my ability to perform Carmen's dance on the table and
smoke convincingly. He liked everything I was doing and it made
me nervous, for I did not.

My Carmen was a woman with a lover's impatience with the
whole world, a woman who feared when she did not get what she
wanted that it meant she was not loved by creation itself; her need
for success at seduction was like her need for dinner or breakfast.
When her death is foretold to her by a Gypsy near the opera's end,
she is calm. She has always imagined one day that the world would
leave her, and she is not surprised.

This much I understood.

I did not like the end, which seemed implausible to me and thus
contemptible. She is a huntress, a ruthless sorceress of desire. She
has her own knife but she does not draw it. She pleads with Don
José instead.

I tried to imagine why I would not draw my own knife. I reached
down to touch it.

She faces her murderer outside the arena, her toreador lover inside, killing a bull for her. Toreador, love awaits for you, the chorus
sings, as she dies.

Which one does she love? I asked myself. *Does she not draw her knife
because she loves him?*

I spent the day at this fruitlessly and then finally went to the theater; dressed myself; greeted the cast cordially, the director also; and
took my place backstage.

The orchestra began. The insistent back and forth of the strings
slipped over me and there was the familiar music appearing in my
mind a moment ahead of where it was in my ear. I stood. Perhaps

it was the same audience as at the opera's debut. I couldn't see these men and women as the limelights burned, only the smooth seashell walls of the Comique and the gaps where the boxes were, like the sockets in a skull, a depthless dark from the moment the curtain went up. I could still hear the chatter and clatter of the subscribers, but it was low. They were on their best behavior tonight.

She loves neither the toreador nor the killer, it came to me as I went on the stage. More than these men, she loves her freedom.

At the end, as my Don José approached, I watched the knife in his hand, watched it move across the stage toward me in the dark until it was time for me to fall.

I understood at last.

She chose herself. She chose death.

∾

From the cheering at the end, when I roused myself, I knew the voice at least had had another of its victories. I had sensed, however, during my death cry, something unfamiliar.

The voice had nearly failed.

I smiled at the director, and we gestured at each other, and the applause continued. He gestured as to the possibility of a curtain call. I nodded, and we went out onto the stage.

In the orchestra was an oboist I recognized from the Conservatoire, a round-headed young man who had been close to Bizet. The oboist turned up just the left side of his mouth in a smile as he examined the crowd and then looked down.

I looked to the oboist again. His face was still turned down. I will ask him to have a drink with me, I decided. I could ask him about his friend. And then I saw that he wept.

The conductor's eyes met mine and he bowed to me. I curtsied to him. I withdrew, walking backward through the curtains and refusing further curtain calls. The curtain smacked with flowers and shouted pleas.

I changed quickly and went outside. As the *calèche* passed in front, the oboist sat on the steps, his head in his hands, a cigarette burning. I made the driver stop and then waited a moment, undecided.

He could still hate me as all of my Conservatoire classmates did.

I got out and walked to him. He didn't recognize me until I sat down.

His eyes glittered. Really, he said. He exhaled his cigarette heavily. He poked at one of my wig's ringlet curls. The first theatergoers came outside to smoke and wait for those still talking inside. The carriages began to line up.

We waited.

They chose *you* for this role, he said, and stopped himself. He tossed his cigarette into the street and spit after it. The crowd moved down the stairs. He stood somewhat unsteadily and faced me. Did they know your secret? he asked. Did they know how well they chose?

I said nothing, only waiting.

I was never fooled, he said. He waved a finger in the air until it pointed at me. I knew you from the Bal Mabille. I played for money there; I saw you night after night after night, though it was before your transformation into La Dame Blanche.

I had not heard this name for me before.

Jou-jou, I believe, he said. Yes?

I nodded my head yes slowly, a little afraid.

We, he said. Are disgusting. But you are a disgrace.

I left him there.

My dresser the next evening told me of how the oboist had gone with some of the others, including the house manager, to splash champagne on his friend Bizet's grave. They had worked together performing at the dances where Bizet had worn himself out playing through the night.

As I left to find the oboist, my director appeared in front of me, holding the newspaper, excited. The review he thrust at me heralded the opera's return. The run is secure; she has finally seduced them, my director said, and kissed me twice in greeting.

I smiled at him, nodding my head, and continued walking across the dark stage to the orchestra pit. When the oboist saw me, he greeted me by saying, I apologize for last night; I was drunk and full of grief. I cannot blame you for the world that makes us all.

I shrugged and handed him an envelope with Aristafeo's name on it and waited as he recognized it, as I suspected he would.

The note inside was simple: *Please tell me how to return the ring.*

The oboist nodded, as if he knew of me from him, and put it in his breast pocket.

~

My answer came after a fortnight.

The envelope had the appearance of an ordinary letter left for me in the last mail of the night and now on my breakfast tray. Inside was music, written out by hand, no accompanying note of any kind, no name signed to it, no title, no lyrics.

I took it into the music room, sat down, and began to play.

I knew the melody at once.

I had mocked him for not having music, and now there was this.

Play this for me always, I heard myself say, so many years ago, in this same room.

I paused, my hands over the keys.

I had regretted my message. In retrospect, the impulse struck me as indulgent, and it endangered what I'd sacrificed to create. I had told myself I wanted to return the ring so he could give it to a woman worthy of it, but, of course, I'd only wanted to see him again. I had questions now, as well. The first among them was as to where he'd been hidden all this time. He hadn't confessed where he'd been, only that he was sorry to have stayed away.

My hands hesitated still. I pressed one finger down into the first note.

I stopped then pressed it again. The clear note rang out and I let it fade.

I pressed the first and second then, and then the third until I was repeating it and then began again when I was done. It was nearly like pressing his finger to mine—near enough. His hands, the ghost of them, making this.

When the time came for me to prepare my voice before leaving for the theater, I had spent the day this way, and so I sang the theme as my vocalize.

Wherever it is he was, wherever he had been in the last decade apart from me, he was writing for me. Ten years away from me, with this, his long dream of me. This opera that began as the theme he played to cover our conversation.

This was the one way I could keep him with me then, no matter the rest. If I learned his music, I would never lose him.

~

That night the tenor came by my dressing room. He remarked it had been published that the soprano had fainted at the end. Did you faint? he asked. If so, I didn't notice. Apologies if I left you alone in a faint.

Of course not, I said. I refused to appear in the later curtain calls.

The moment of trouble with my voice had not returned, but I decided against exposing myself to even the suggestion of an encore.

The crowds around the theater tripled at the rumor I'd fainted, however, and now the audiences came in at the beginning, seated and silent with waiting.

Each night as Carmen, I threw a rose to the soldier Don José, the one man who didn't whistle and jeer at me as I passed him by. Each night he kept the rose to show me later, to prove his devotion. Each night he murdered me.

The spell works, she tells him. *Le charme opère.* Keep it, she tells him, and he doesn't hear her, and each night it leads, circumstance by circumstance, to Carmen's death under Don José's knife. As the soldiers passed me nightly, I found I held the flower before throwing it. The gesture, as rehearsed, was meant to appear like careless coquetry. My hesitation soon deepened.

Five

REMEMBER FOR NOW Carmen's rose. See it float in the wind to
land at the feet of the young soldier. Her song to him as he turns to
her, about the rebel heart, how it obeys no rules.

This flower with the power to turn strangers into lovers, lovers
into murderers. He picks it up.

~

Félix wrote to say he had made me a gown, a gift, he said, to thank
me for a glorious season. I wasn't sure I would hear from him after
the scene with the Comtesse had so foully exposed me. He seemed
to care not at all.

I was, of course, delighted.

At his atelier, as he fitted me for it, he described a dream of Carmen, naked in the river, washing off the blood of her stab wounds,
alive again. She turned to him and smiled, and the river filled with
roses that left on the current.

Paris was under a siege of dreams.

You must wear it when you celebrate the end of *Carmen*, he said.
Perhaps another ball? And it must be thrown for you by someone in
love with you. Who is in love with you? Anyone? There must be at
least a few, or have you lost all your skill at these things?

I laughed as I swatted him.

You're in love, he said then. Or you would have thought of it already. I wouldn't even be speaking of it.

I gave him as much of a mocking glare as I dared for having struck me to the quick.

Does he love you also? Is he very rich? He should be very rich. The place should be very grand, with a staircase appropriate for your entrance.

He pushed at my waist to smooth a piece of cloth there.

He's poor, isn't he? he said, for I had said nothing, stunned into silence.

He drew a deep breath. Is he the one you're said to be marrying?

No, I said, very quickly. No, no. And I'm not marrying.

He unlaced and unhooked me, the fitting was done, and sent me behind a screen where his *femmes* stripped me bare. As they did their work, he said, over the screen, Don't marry poor. But perhaps don't fear to love poor. Better to be wise than a coward, yes? This was my mother's advice to my sisters.

I was soon in my own dress again. Are your sisters very happy? I asked.

Yes, I believe so.

When you know the room, he said, we'll go and see it and prepare accordingly. You must be stunning, a goddess. He must be very handsome, he said.

He was, I said finally.

Well, then it's better, he said. You won't love him too much.

I came from behind the screen at last, and he saw my face and everything there.

Except you do, of course, already. You already do, don't you? It's what the dress is for, isn't it?

We had never once exchanged even the slightest affection, and he gave me the very lightest kiss.

Ah, dearest one, there, there, he said. It was going to happen eventually.

Six

I SENT NO OTHER messages, received no more music. Finally, a note.

> You will receive an invitation to Rouen.
>   This will be from a friend, to her salon there. Bring the ring, and if you are still intent on returning it, you can present it to me there.

Several days later a card from the tenor waited in my hall. There was a salon, he wrote. An old friend with a new interest in opera. Would I come sing the Habanera and a few other songs for her and her friends on one of my free evenings? It would be out at her château in Rouen, and he would come for me. She had guests there for the week but we would not stay the night, only sing and return by evening on the train.

She does not normally invite women, the tenor had written underneath the rest and underlined it, and he had included her note to him.

If she has no other appointments that day, you must bring her out to Rouen.

The tenor told me of her as he waited for me to dress that day. She was a widowed baroness who had her fortune and title from a baron killed in a duel he'd fought and lost with her lover. That lover, certain of his claim, had left for South America as quickly as he could once she'd explained she could not take up with her husband's killer.

Her recent interest in opera took the form of a new lover, a young composer who lived at her house in Rouen as he struggled with his commission from the Imperial Court of Russia.

An amusement for the young Alexander. He is, the tenor said of it, trying to delight a child who can afford pet tigers.

The tenor seemed very unhappy that afternoon. I attempted to amuse him by showing him several of my new gowns as if I had not already made my decision, and he was unmoved by all of them. Lucy and Doro gave me guarded looks over my shoulders and I shrugged.

She is a spy, you know, he said, quite suddenly. A fatal sort of woman and, perhaps, fatal to other women in particular.

I went into my dressing room and returned in another dress.

I was a fatal sort of woman, too.

I had gone at once to Félix's atelier to say to him, *I know the room.* I had told him of the invitation and the salon, and he said, A duel, then, not a party at all. With a smile on his mouth, he swore he would help me be ready in time even if he had to bandage his seamstresses' hands himself.

And what is this? the tenor asked, pulling himself to his feet and walking to where I stood at the mirror.

It is the afternoon visiting costume of a diva, I said.

Félix's tribute to my time as Carmen was more costume than visiting costume. A black silk velvet gown for evening with very tight short sleeves and a square cut décolletage that pushed my breasts forward somewhat lasciviously. The waist severely corseted, the bodice trimmed in a black Spanish lace. The skirt was likewise silk velvet, but if I liked, it had some of the swift movements of a cancan dress due to panels of dyed muslin hidden at rest in the folds but visible if I danced. A court train began at my waist and went back for five full yards behind, red organza roses fastened to this black organza tail. A red brocade loop hidden there went over my wrist if I chose, in which case the train could move up like a sail if I raised my arm while I danced.

And it takes so much time to get her into it she appears finally at sunset, the tenor said. Where is your present? I want you to wear it.

His humor had returned suddenly. He turned from the mirror and drew me to him, put his face to my neck; his lips there barely grazed the skin. He pushed his face against me and his sharp whiskers bit my neck. I winced as I let out a gasp and he held me there, pushing against me as if he were going to take me there before we left. Lucy and Doro backed out of the room. When he released me, he smiled at me in the mirror. Put them on, he said.

It's rude to wear jewels of this kind in the afternoon, I said.

It's rude to be late, he said. Put them on.

I put them on.

He fell to brooding again on the train, and it lasted until we were in the coach on our way from the station. He finally said, I won't pretend anymore; it's your little friend we'll see today. He has found himself a wealthy protector in my old friend.

He looked out at the window then. Or did you know?

I said only, I guessed as much. And then, after some time, I added, Remember your promise.

He gazed at me then with something like a measuring eye and smiled. Do you remember when Cora Pearl put that little emerald on you that I gave her and made you wear it out to greet me?

I looked away from his eyes as he said this.

He leaned forward, reached out, and lifted one of the stones at my neck. How she laughed that day at my gift. She wouldn't laugh at this necklace now, I think.

He smoothed it back.

They say she's dying now, you know, he said. Very ill, very poor. Perhaps we'll go see her. Pay our respects once more. And tell her of our engagement.

As late as we were, a fierce rainstorm came and made us even later, though it left as we arrived at the estate.

The pale golden wet bricks of this baroness's château were like the scales of a dragon, and her gardens were wreathed in clouds of red roses. It was the home of a beautiful monster from myth.

In the distance I saw her stables, something else for which the tenor said she was famous, some forty horses it was said were kept in perfect condition, and I could see the deep woods beyond.

As we entered, the tenor reached with a dagger and cut a rose. He twirled it for me. Your prop, he said.

I took it. How does she have roses? I asked him. It's nearly the end of autumn.

The devil is her gardener, I'm sure, he said. But ask her. I believe the secret is the roses are Chinese. He winked.

She herself was a handsome apparition that day. She had a delicate color to her cheeks, which she'd set off well with a pale afternoon dress that looked to be a Worth, a green chiffon-and-silk confection. Her dark hair was curled and arranged prettily, an ivory comb completing the effect. She was not a young woman, but she had kept herself very carefully.

When I entered, Aristafeo stood near her, dressed in a simple dark suit. He smiled at me familiarly and saluted.

La Générale, he said, and then bowed.

I mastered my face so as not to laugh—he had seemed briefly comic—but the rose in my hand trembled. His eyes went to it as he stood.

How kind of you to come all this way, the Baroness said. I offered a grave curtsy to her.

The tenor apologized and asked as to whom else might be presenting but there was no one else; the hostess had decided it would be a private audience for the famous voice. She explained, as she brought us into the music room, how she was only recently interested in opera despite her family box and was so honored I could attend. My appearance at the ball in the Marquise de Lambert's home had so impressed her, she had wanted to attempt something like it here in her salon. She hoped the arrangements were appropriate.

She had seen, then. She had seen it all. Here she was, the woman he had been ready to leave at once for me. The woman who had kept him all this time.

I tried to remember if I'd seen her, but she was entirely unfamiliar, and in any case, I was more preoccupied with the sense of the tableau we presented, two women in front of a room full of men. Her light toilette beside my dark one.

We will be in the ballroom, she said. You are acquainted with my guests, yes? Now that you are here, we shall begin.

We passed through then into the ballroom, the men following the two of us.

A beautiful piano waited under an enormous crystal chandelier in a ballroom to rival anything I'd seen—delicately painted frescoes and friezes in an Italian style decorated dark gray walls, the windows opening out to a formal garden with a maze. The chandelier was lit with candles and blazed brightly in the light of the late afternoon rain. Around the piano in a perfect half circle were arranged delicate gilt chairs. I did know her guests, all of them, and most of them were the men who mattered most to opera in Paris. I smiled and waved at them as they took their seats. She'd made an impressive display, and it could only be the work of the Baroness he'd told me of so long ago, and this was precisely the sort of support I would have expected her to offer Aristafeo, who I then noticed had seated himself in the back.

He smiled at me and I to him.

This was not her Paris ballroom, where he had first met her; we were in Rouen. Here was at least a little of the rest of the story his expensive jacket had told me at my ball, the answer to the question as to where he had hidden all this time. These rooms, these gardens, these forests.

Since you are late, perhaps you can shorten your program, she said. Her gloved hand executed a wave.

I went to stand near the piano. I meant to begin with "*Casta diva,*" from *Norma,* "*Carlo vive?*" from *I Masnadieri,* then move to

Aida's "*O patria mia*," and then finish with the Habanera; but after her remark, I was now anxious to leave. I handed the music to just the Habanera to the accompanist there, waiting as he reviewed the pages and set them down.

In the long moment between when the pages left my hand and the first notes on the piano began, I thought of how unaccustomed I was to seeing the faces of an audience as I sang, or even sunlight. The engagement at La Scala would begin soon, Verdi's *Un Ballo in Maschera*—singing for this group was a little beneath me and another violation of my voice's need for rest. I had told myself I was behaving cautiously, that I was making sacrifices for this love of mine, but now I was in the home of his lover, about to sing for him in front of my soon-to-be fiancé, here despite his vow not to speak to me again. His ring in the waist of my gown again.

As the introit began, I prepared the breath, inhaled. Velvet curtains, the rain, *verveine*, carefully dried cigar tobacco waiting to be lit later. The scent of the Rhône wine in the glasses around the room. I wanted a glass of wine right then, though the thought was interrupted when I felt with a little surprise how the movements of the music, perfunctory to me, still moved me. Even if I did not care to feel the song's flirtatious sentiments now, the music assured me that I would be made to care against my will, the care corseted into each note. The first syllable formed in my mouth.

L'amour est un oiseau rebelle.

I looked past all of them out to the gardens visible through the windows, where branches of the roses tapped wetly on the glass. I watched the blooms wave as I pressed on, even absent-minded as I anticipated the glass of wine and, perhaps, something to eat later that I might get, and then I concentrated on the piano arrangement, admiring it as it ran under my voice, as well as the tidy playing of the accompanist, and passed out of the sadness into the realm of the music. By the end, as the tenors sing, when she passes, *Carmen, sur tes pas nous, nous pressons tous.*

Carmen, we all follow, wherever you go.

At the last notes, in the silence at the close, I whirled, the dress moving exactly as Félix had planned, and as I came to a stop, I threw the rose.

It slid over the wood floor to Aristafeo's feet. There was laughter from the men. As he picked it up, the sun came through the roses behind him, and he stood in their green-red shadows and smiled as the men in the room behind me threw me to their shoulders and ran with me out into the garden, cheering.

I ducked through the windows, thrown open, and was able to notice with a little pleasure that the train of my dress still reached to the ground behind me. The roses, beaten by the rain, had given their petals to the wind that comes constantly through Rouen and mixed with the leaves falling from the trees to make clouds of them drifting in the air around us. From that height, I could see the entrance and the garden maze that reached back into the property behind, where the forest caught at the setting sun, cutting the gold light as it fell over us.

They set me down on the ground again only when we were within the maze out of sight of the château. Aristafeo stood there in front of me, the rose I'd thrown in his hand. The men, all smiles, offered laughing apologies, stepped back, and were gone, shouting as they ran through the maze.

His friends were very loyal, I noted.

Did you know of her roses when you chose your dress? he asked.

I did not, I said. As I spoke, he offered the flower to me.

I watched it and then looked back to him. I did not reach for it.

How does she have roses so late into the fall? I asked. Is it magic? I smiled as I said this, instantly aware of how childish the question was.

No, he says. Her gardener cuts them so they never fruit, only flower.

He held it out once more. The rose always tries again, he said.

I did not take it.

Cette fleur, tu l'as gardée, I said. *Tu peux la jeter.* The line Carmen uses to tell Don José to throw the flower he has kept away.

I withdrew the ring and held it out to him.

Le charme opère, he said quietly.

The spell works.

It belongs to you, he said.

I shook my head, and yet as I let it go into his hand, I knew he was right.

He tried to meet my eyes, and when I would not let him, he went back quickly. I waited and walked slowly enough to let him arrive first.

The Baroness was standing outside her ballroom windows as the wind blew around us. I carried my dress and train as she waited and watched.

Do you ride?

I smiled and nodded.

I thought we would ride before the storm returns. I'm sorry, it was planned before. Did our friend not tell you? We thought we might discuss it over dinner but you have planned to return by then, yes? And you've no costume to ride, she said. And I've nothing that would fit you. Perhaps you will entertain yourself until we return?

Behind her, the forest looked like a legion of black-skirted widows. She their leader.

I pushed at the silk skirt of my gown suddenly, enlivened, and gestured at it. My riding costume, I said.

She laughed. You speak after all! Very well, perhaps you are also a horsewoman? I shouldn't like you, she said. But I do. Thank you for indulging me.

A horse was brought for me, a mare, as well as my cloak. I walked up to her and looked to the stable hand, who came close and offered me his clasped hands to step into. With his help, I settled the gown into place, the train at my wrist so it wouldn't catch the horse up, and sat at attention, waiting as the men emerged on their mounts.

The tenor appeared first, very handsome in a riding costume he appeared to have had ready, sheepish as he caught sight of me. From behind him, Aristafeo appeared, likewise attired. I borrowed his, the tenor said, as if he understood me. But, my God, you're beauti-

ful this way. I'll have your wedding portrait painted for you just like
this, he said.

~

If you love me, you'll run away with me to the hills, Carmen tells
her lover.

The storm returned more than restored almost as soon as the riding party set out, and the assorted nobles, industrialists, novelists,
philosophers, and foreign heads of state lost control of their horses
all at once. I was separated from them quickly or, rather, we were all
separated from one another.

I had insisted on riding as it had been so long since I'd ridden in
woods like this I couldn't have cared if I'd ridden naked.

I slid from my horse and tied its reins to a tree, prepared to
wait out the storm. I'd lost patience with the mare well before she
calmed, and soaked to my skin in this gown, I hoped the mare,
when calm, would know the way home, but I wanted to be sure. I
walked to the middle of the field to see if I could find my bearings.

The lightning's bright cracks along the sky made it look as if
Rouen's countryside were a painting thrown on a fire and burning
from underneath, the hills running with autumn color, gold and red.

I tipped my head back and drank from the rain. It was cold and
sweet.

During the haying season when I was a girl, I stalked storms, ran
to meet them. Rain at the horizon looked like grass burning. The
horses weren't any good then as well, their screams like grass cuts
along the thunder, thinning as they rose in the air. As if they felt
they could hold it back. My mother would say, *You'd let yourself die
from it*, when I returned wet. To which I always said nothing.

All thirsts are without explanations, as are all loves.

I was relieved to be lost in an open field under the retreating
storm, far from my troubles. I decided to sing to console myself,
as I had when I was young, and began softly with *Aida*, her lament
aria, where she asks for death as her lover and her father face each

other in battle, her lover sure to become her mistress's husband. I sang her part in the scene after she has seen her father dragged back alive in front of her; I sang her begging to be allowed to see her own country again, and I sang it as if it could reach to the country I was sure I'd never see again while I stood there on the grassy roof of the world. I begged to be let back, and when I was done, I sang this part again rather than go on, and then again, and once more, louder and louder, in full voice finally, until the woods rang.

People told me what my voice did to them but they did not know what I wished it could do. Could I do one thing with this voice more than be made to entertain the world's kings and their replacements, in the company of their wives, whores, and assassins? What was this gift, as my mother had called it, for? How I wished it could sing open graves, ransack Hell for my dead friends, smooth Aristafeo's crippled hands, bring my family back to life—a voice that could change the course of Fate, summoning out of my many roles a storm of Fates until they were scattered and I was free, alone with nothing less than the world shining and made whole.

That was what I wanted; it would have sufficed.

Were we done? Was it all only for this? The ring was with him, at last; were we were done? I sank to my knees in the rain.

So then let it play on, this game of ours, I decided, when I stood. Curse or no curse, that was my prayer to whatever it was that ruled me. The Comtesse and her bargains, the tenor and his games, my voice, God, the Fates. Let us play and be done. To the death and beyond.

I stood and saw he was behind me. His dark eyes still full of love despite it all.

∼

If you sang a lyric, it traveled farther than if it was shouted. Anything for any of the gods to hear was sung—for this reason the first theater was set to music. So they could hear, too.

Aristafeo had followed my voice in the distance until he came near the top of the hill behind me and then waited as I sang, unable to come any closer until I was done. This was how he'd always imagined operas, not as stages filled with women and men in wigs, but a storm, woods, a woman lost and in love singing somewhere in the dark.

He had been weaned practically on horseback and had never had any trouble riding, even in storms.

He had said nothing, waiting for me to notice him.

I brought my hand to my mouth as I turned to face him, and he put his arms around me and held me against the cold.

The rain had plastered his hair to his head, and the silver curls rose in a crown.

Leave with me, I said. I'm ready now. I'm sorry I wasn't before. We can leave through the woods and never return.

He blinked from the rain and surprise. No, he said. Not this way. For now, I cannot.

Are you so afraid to leave her now? I asked. I gathered my dress to me. If you won't, please, get me back so I may at least leave this place. I pulled away from him.

He remained standing there, looking down to his feet.

The rain fell softly again as we stood there, neither of us moving. In some way, our refusal to act or speak allowed us to be at rest with each other again.

What hold does he have over you? he asked me again, as he had at the ball.

You, I said. If I will marry him, he lets you live.

He laughed. What then?

I let my head rest on his chest.

Leave with me, I said. If not today, soon. Leave with me and I will create the role. But not here. London, Saint Petersburg, Rome. Anywhere but here. If I leave, you must also.

Are you mine, then? he asked.

Yes, I said. I knew it as soon as I gave the ring back. And you, are you mine? What of this? And her? I waved at the woods.

He took the ring from his pocket and slid it back on my hand and pulled the tenor's ring off, handing it to me.

Yes, he said. I'm yours. I will always be grateful to her, he said. Because of her, I was able to grow strong enough here to find you. But I'm yours, always yours.

❧

I saw the old friends, as the tenor had put it—he and the Baroness—emerging from the house as we approached.

She had already dressed for dinner.

I dismounted and Aristafeo ran off and returned with a black blanket warmed at a fire. Behind him came men carrying hot-water bottles. When I slid the blanket over my shoulders, I could smell his *verveine* and something else, of neither Rouen nor Paris. Him. His own blanket then? I wondered.

He looked down and to the side as I wrapped it around myself.

A pity, the Baroness said, as she walked toward me. Your dress! I will pay for it.

I shook my head, for it felt like bad luck to take any money from her in light of what I had just taken.

She relented a little and allowed me to undress in one of her apartments with the help of her maids, who clucked over the ruins of the dress and prepared a hot bath for me. When I was warm and dry, they dressed me in a muslin shift and wrapped me in hot blankets again.

Her carriage would take us home.

From inside it, as the driver's whip cracked, I did not look at her or Aristafeo as we left, or at the tenor, who prattled on as to the party and the Baroness, saying, I'm ashamed to say it was some sort of audition. I'm very sorry, I was not told, not until after, when she bragged to me of it.

The tenor was changed. He was speaking as if to someone else in the cab. Your composer apparently told her he needed to hear you without the costumes and the lights, he said. To which she said, Then she will come and sing for us, and if she must, she'll appear naked.

He laughed. Now look at you!

I laughed as well, but my thoughts were of Aristafeo now. The tenor had not noticed I was sitting there waiting for him to turn to me, to acknowledge me. He was only speaking, saying things he thought I would want to hear. Something in all of this had frightened him and now it frightened me as well.

By the time we were in Paris, he seemed himself again, but I was not. I could feel the seal of the life I had led until that afternoon press back over me, insistent, asking that I return to it, and to the little prison hidden within it, where there was no room for Aristafeo, no room even for me. Here was the door to it, the door of the apartment on the avenue de l'Opéra, the place I had thought I could keep somehow and not also keep all that had come with it. I entered the apartment to the shocked exclamations of Doro and Lucy, who undressed me and made horrified faces at the dress's condition as I unpacked it from the bundle of its ruins while they tried to set me in my own bath. I refused it, though, and asked for a fire and gin.

When they left me, I saw, as if for the first time, the dove-gray walls of the place—I had thought I was so different from the Comtesse. I had found her living crypt pitiable; I had not seen my own.

If she had buried herself alive there, I was entombed within my own life as well. She had, perhaps, taught me even this.

What was my own, though, was the plan we had begun. I would finish *Carmen* and he would finish the opera, and then he would suggest a plan.

I will take care of it, he had said. I know how long you have waited, wait just a little longer. I will send you a message next week. Wait for my word.

～

Perhaps the very last person I expected to see a week later then was the Baroness, and so I was incredulous when Doro brought me her card and I insisted she at once show her in.

May I speak to you in private? she asked, as she sat.

Of course, I said, ringing the bell and telling Doro and Lucy we would not take tea.

Monsieur Cadiz has challenged our tenor friend to a duel, pistols at dawn in Rouen the morning after *Carmen* concludes, she said.

When was this challenge issued, I asked, and for what?

When you were in Rouen, of course, she said. As we rode into the woods, he reached over and struck the tenor with his riding gloves and issued the challenge there in front of witnesses.

The strangeness of the tenor in the carriage. Aristafeo's assurance he would take care of it.

By the time he came to me in the woods, this had all happened.

It is to the death, she said.

Why are you here? I asked.

I am here . . . to beg you to end this. Yes, that is what we can call it. I am here to beg you, I who have never begged, not once. She said it coolly, levelly, her eyes averted at first.

He cannot fire a pistol quickly, she said, as she turned back to me. Not as an uninjured man would. For this reason, he never accompanies me on the hunts with weapons. He only rides. He will . . . he will die.

Does he have no second? I asked.

He will accept none. It is for your honor, she said. He is insisting, insisting he will prevail again.

Again? I asked.

Again, she said. He was the lover sent away after the duel with my late husband.

And he was also then . . .

The very same. I arranged for him to receive the Prix de Rome, she said. And so he was the lover I sent away, and the new one as well, on his return. Easy enough. No one had met him before that except the police. I couldn't introduce him before.

What would you have of me? What brings you here? I asked. For I could not understand why she was not angrier, why she had come at all—it was an insult to her.

The duel is for the honor of your hand in marriage, she said. If you accept the tenor, it will be off. Accept the tenor and spare his life.

The tenor has not proposed to me, I said.

He has not but we both know he means to, she said. Please, I beg of you. Accept the tenor and spare Aristafeo's life. I beg this of you. He will die.

She leaned forward. My husband was no match for him. *I* could have shot my husband. Your tenor friend is a former officer who has seen combat in Africa, has killed in battle. He will not hesitate the same as an aging aristocrat once did. Aristafeo will die.

She stood and pulled on her gloves. No, she said, I cannot marry again—this is true. He will never be my husband. But I do love him. I love his music. As I think you also do. And I have a hope of saving him, she said, and it begins here, asking this of you.

Good day, I said.

She left, showing herself out.

⁓

Name the hour you will accept, the tenor had asked.

So I did.

Three nights before the closing night, backstage at his dressing room, his door opened and Maxine exited angrily, coldly, as he laughed behind her.

As he came to his door to close it, he saw me standing there, having witnessed the scene, and gave me a little wave as though I were a child, as he smiled and closed the door.

I hesitated, then knocked on his closed door, and he opened it, a questioning look in his eye.

I have something important to tell you, I said. I am naming the hour. Dine with me after our final performance?

I'll reserve a private room at the Café Anglais, he said.

~

A note came at last from Aristafeo via the oboist. He mentioned nothing of the duel; he only suggested a plan: that I leave at once after my last performance in *Carmen* and wait for him in Milan, and if he was delayed, to go to visit the Verdis in Italy in Sant'Agata. Their home there had recently been finished, and they could now have visitors. We could go together and receive their blessing, he said. We should leave after my final *Carmen* performance.

I imagined myself waiting in Milan for him, thinking he might be dead or receiving news of his death. The Verdi plan sounded to me like his sending me to the place I would go to be comforted for his loss.

I wrote back to Aristafeo and agreed, placing yet another note in the oboist's hand before the curtain rose that night.

And then after the performance, I dressed in my finest new gown and waited for the tenor in the green room, wearing his emeralds.

He did not come.

His habit by now was to go with Maxine to her apartments after the performance and spend the evening. It was my guess that he would end their affair on the night of the last performance, given his instinct for cruelty. What I had not expected is that he would leave me to wait for him.

I waited just past an hour before asking one of the stagehands if he had seen the tenor leave, and when the answer was yes, I returned to my dressing room and put myself in my usual disguise and left as well.

I went first to the Café Anglais. When I held out his card, indicating I was to be brought to him, they said he was not there, so sorry, they had not expected him.

It was then I knew. He would not risk bargaining with me, not anymore. He meant to do this, to kill Aristafeo and be done. Perhaps he had guessed my reason for accepting. Perhaps he even planned to return to accept me only after killing him.

After Maxine's, he would return to his apartment and prepare for his duel in the morning.

I had done almost everything in my power to prevent the duel. There was only one thing more to do. My only path opened up in the night.

~

His own apartment was near her home, close enough that he would walk along the Seine and take the air. I waited along the passage.

I sat sitting so only my bare foot showed in the light — my old signal, though I had never used it with him. I didn't want him to know me. And in the dark, with my different silhouette, the wig, at a distance, when he smiled at me and I made for him to follow me, he did not know me and followed me down under the bridge where it was possible to sneak in an assignation.

Dark Night, Queen of Silence, protector of thieves, the sleep of the world that covers over the shame of whores, she protected me in that instant and delivered him to me. But even as she did, she put me under her spell.

I suspect it is her price.

He pulled me to him. I wrapped my arms around him, and when he came close enough to see my eyes, even as he stared now that he knew me, I did not hesitate. I sank my poisoned barb into his neck and pulled it so that it cut the vein at his throat.

The heart is a difficult target, Priscilla had said so long ago. I did not have my knife, so I used this last gift of Eugène's, a barb filled with prussic acid, the one he had asked me to use if captured.

I had been captured. But I did not want to die.

His blood sprayed wide and he stepped back, coughing, and as he did so, he gathered his hands to his neck to try to hold the blood in just as I'd been taught to expect. I'd jumped back as well. His eyes were wild with rage and despair, his breath ragged and steaming the air. He had the choice of lunging for me and choking on his blood or holding it in with his hands.

I was sure killing him was not enough to keep us safe. He needed to vanish, to never be found. And I, I had come prepared to do this. I was possessed, a daughter of the Night, a Fury—Alecto, who fans the spark.

Ere it dawns the second time, the whole game I'll shiver.

I took a breath, struck a match, and as the flame guttered alight, sipped the *pétrole* into my mouth quickly from a flask at my side and then blew gently above the match. A cloud of flame moved out from my lips, lighting the underside of the bridge. He shrank back, choking as his blood filled his throat, smoke rising on his hair.

Here we were; it was always going to be to the death between us.

With my second breath, I stepped closer; the fire blew out across to him in a sheet, and when he saw the flames, he lifted his hands to protect his face. Blood flew from his throat into the fire burning now on his shoulder. Still he struggled; he was a powerful man. He charged for me.

I stepped back, and this time he slapped at my hand. The *pétrole* splashed across us both. I leapt up onto the banks, and he slipped on the slick. As he fell, he leapt from his fall toward the Seine in a halting dive.

The river put out the fire, but the poison had stiffened his limbs finally, and he went under.

I wanted to run, but instead I had the presence of mind to pick up my flask off the ground and hide under the bridge, watching the water until I was satisfied the tenor would not return from the river.

I do not know how long I stayed staring at the dark Seine. Only when the dawn came did I make my way home past the faltering swells and *cocottes* emerging from their last assignations.

At home again, I sat in front of a fire I'd built up high. In a few hours I would begin to prepare to leave for Milan. I would give Lucy and Doro their notices. I would prepare to sell the apartment

and everything within it. But for now, I sat in front of the fire, naked, and as the flames leapt, the emeralds showed me him burning
in the night, staggering toward me, his arms raised, his voice gone.
Falling into the Seine, out of the world, away from me, again and
again.

I'd sell them, too.

It was done. Nothing of his could stay. I had defeated my curse.
I had always thought he would be my doom, and instead I'd been
his. There would be no duel in the garden. Leonora had killed the
Count. Aristafeo would wait on the hill for him and wonder. And
live to come to me, mine again at last.

Seven

In MILAN, I had accepted the invitation of a prince to make use of an apartment in his ancient Milanese palazzo. This was a gesture of thanks, he said when he offered it, for a performance of mine he'd attended in Rome, of *Aida*. He reassured me he would never intrude on me and this was true: He never did. His staff, in fact, worked according to the same instructions as my Paris staff, at Doro's impeccable direction and yet more invisibly, as if I were attended by magical servants. I had a feeling of being even more alone than I had in years.

It was there I waited to see if I would be joined.

I had left Paris without having received any further word from Aristafeo. Here was where I was to wait for him, to pretend to be surprised when he returned with word the tenor had not shown for their duel.

The quiet in the wing of the Milanese palace that I occupied was such that I spent much of that first evening following the sound of what turned out to be a wandering dove inhabiting a lonely ballroom, rising and descending in and out of a beam of light that came in through the crystal windows lining the ceiling. As it leapt, blue feathers glowed from underneath, as if from a lamp hidden under its wings.

I wondered if it had hatched there in the dark ballroom or if it had flown in and become lost. Or if, perhaps, it was some lover under a spell, doomed by a sorceress to stay there forever.

This Milanese prince had not invited me for being lonely. He asked only that I dine with him once, an invitation I accepted gladly, and there I was introduced to his wife, as stylish as a Parisienne, but more voluptuous, warmer, and more generous. She was a dark-haired beauty with the large, firm breasts of a mermaid and a dolphin's appetite. She came to dinner in a chic gown of exceptional black silk satin and velvet set off by a collar of rubies and diamonds. She seemed aware of her beauty in the manner of someone with something she is determined you should enjoy. Their two daughters and one son, also at dinner, all took after her, all beautiful and proud of their beauty.

She did not seem to my mind a conventional Milanese, but rather something more southern his line had dipped itself in.

They smiled when I thanked him, and I thought of how rare real affection was in noble families.

He stroked the bottom of his wine goblet. You're very welcome, he said. The rooms are so numerous there are inhabitants entirely unknown to me.

An odd stillness stole in when he said this, as if his family and servants watched their own secrets move in the air for that moment. The inhabitants were known to him is what this said; this his way of telling us all this was so.

All palaces of this size usually hid at least a mistress or more, perhaps even the children of the mistresses, some his, some not, all of these in apartments alongside the others'. Perhaps even one of the young footmen who'd helped me with my trunks was his bastard from some woman half remembered, who now patched his wife's linens.

I've met one, I announced. And then told the story of the dove, which made them laugh.

I returned to my apartment after the dinner by carriage, driven across to the other side of the estate. That night, as I waited, unable to sleep, I went farther in my explorations. I walked with an oil lamp through more grand rooms covered in the frescoes of nymphs, satyrs, gods, and goddesses typical to the apartments of royals of the age. The furnishings covered in muslin made the rooms seem like the ghosts of still other rooms, and here and there in the dark flashed a bit of gilt and crystal. The mirrors were shrouded.

The echoes of my footsteps in the marbled halls were all that kept me company. Only when I paused could I hear the silence return, filling in my footsteps behind me.

I found a music room, with paintings of Apollo and his lyre, of Pan and his flute. It was a contest between them for Pan's flute, made from the canes of a reed that was once a nymph whom Pan had pursued. She'd changed into a reed in order to escape, and he found her, cutting and then binding her to make what was left of her into this instrument that plays at his will.

I stood for a while, waiting, sure my hopes were lost, looking out of the nearest window.

I also had changed into a reed in order to escape a god. Was there a way to change back?

What then? I asked myself.

In the dark, the vast shapes of the palace seemed like the pieces of ancient nights remade into this place at the prince's will. Sure my vigil had finally come to some lonely end, I left for Sant'Agata after the run in Milan concluded.

There, the Verdis greeted me with great affection. They told me they'd heard the tenor had been killed in a duel and expressed their condolences. I expressed shock and grief, kissed them, and sat down to listen to Giuseppina tell me what she knew.

～

After a very long, very fine dinner, I bid the two of them good night and went back to my rooms.

I felt it before I entered, the warmth ahead of me in the dark as I walked the halls to my rooms with a lamp. I heard the fire in my apartment and moved toward it quickly, expecting Doro to appear and help me dress for bed. Doro had refused me when I gave her notice, insisting I was not well, and saying, Would you really refuse me a trip to Italy?

Instead, there in an armchair was Aristafeo, exhausted and afraid, and in his lap an envelope I had long expected, very like the one he'd sent before.

I knew it had to have been a magnificent bribe for Doro to do this; the ferocity of her loyalty had never once allowed such a thing. I'd had no shortage of admirers attempting to sneak into my rooms. I admired them both in this instant.

I shut and bolted the door before I walked behind the chair and embraced him, bending down. His head tilted back against my brow then.

I did not think I would get here, he said. He looked at his hands.

He turned the envelope over to me. I peeled open the flap, tossed the wax into the fire where it sizzled against the wood, and sat myself in the chair opposite him.

What did you tell Verdi? I asked. Or does he approve?

It was your maid I bribed, he said. The master never saw me. He does not yet know I am in his house.

He then reached and poured himself a cognac from the table beside him. He reached and handed me a cognac of my own.

It has been reported the tenor was killed in a duel, I said, of Giuseppina's news. Was it you? I asked.

At first I thought it was, he said. We had set the date for the morning after his last performance in *Carmen* so it would not disturb the run. But he never came. Even his valet was surprised. It was very sad, in its way. We waited on the lawns of the Baroness's estate in Rouen until evening, and I was declared the victor. I had the news published to shame him, he said, when he failed to show.

To first blood? I asked.

To the death, he said.

And on what terms? I asked.

Pistols. For your honor, he said. But my own as well. In truth, for many things.

When were you going to tell me?

Tonight, he said. If I had lived.

What delayed you, then? I asked.

The fire cracked and sputtered, and I could not look at it.

I was under suspicion for his murder, he said. Until they found his body in the Seine. The Baroness and her staff testified I had been in Rouen all night preparing to meet him, and I was cleared. And as I had not actually fought the duel, I could not be charged with dueling, either.

Are we free, then? I asked.

It may be we are, he said. At last.

I drew his ring out from the pocket at my waist and put it on, slid out a cigar and lit it, offering him one as well, which he took. As he did so, I saw in his eyes that he had guessed.

He was waiting for me to tell him what I could not tell him.

I must go, he said. I will spend the night nearby and arrive in the morning as a proper guest.

I reached back and undid the diamond comb holding my cadogan in place so my hair fell down around me in a dark wave past my shoulders. I stood and opened my dress swiftly at the back until it slid down before his chair. He sat forward to rest his face against my bare stomach.

Thank you, he said. And he then rose from his chair, turned me around, and brought me into the bed.

$\sim$

We lay there together afterward.

What of your curse—what will you do when you become a circus rider? he asked.

It was only a lie, I said. There is no curse.

He laughed. Then, yes, it's fine; it's clearly impossible. The rest of the opera is there, he said, indicating the manuscript. For you.

I went to the new pages after he left, finding the final scene. He had reminded me of my dissatisfaction with the ending. I was pleased he'd altered the end, at first. The circus rider found her old circus as before, but now she sang as a way to remind the angel who she was — it was the aria at the end of which she would lose her voice.

While she performs, the wizard, her former captor, and the wingless angel lost in his amnesia both sit in the audience. Her voice is the one thing that reminds him of who he is, the angel gradually remembering her, this last aria concluding on a high E-flat over high C.

This was my favorite note of my register for the imperial quality to it; a note, that if sustained, could cover the sound of the orchestra, the other singers, the crowd, all of it gone and only the E-flat remaining until it was the only thing you knew. For me, it felt like the one true thing about me, that I could produce this note.

What of your curse? I thought again, this question still in his eyes as he waited for me to admit what I would not admit. And I would not; I could not. I would never tell him, could never tell him. This now was the curse. He would never forgive me.

Let me prepare for my return to the back of a horse, then, I said to him. Good night to you.

He tried to smile at the joke as he stood and dressed. Then he kissed me good night, and was gone.

≈

Doro came red faced the next morning to set my fire and lay out my clothes.

I'm proud of you, I said. I'm sure it cost him dearly.

She nodded and held out her hand, palm up. A beautiful ruby ring, face turned in.

It's quite fine, I said. You did well.

She held out her hand, admiring the ring before turning it to face her and returning her attention to my dressing table.

≈

When Aristafeo arrived, we were still at breakfast. As he was announced, I noticed, behind my feigned surprise, the Verdis gave
each other a knowing glance.

The sun outside was so bright it seemed to roar, and it filled the
room so that when he came to a stop in front of us his face was difficult to see.

I was waiting for a sign he had possibly forgiven me for this secret
he knew I carried, the one I could never admit to or apologize for.
I wanted to know this before we began what was next, but I could
not, and so I had to content myself with that as he greeted our hosts
warmly and then came around to my side, where he took my hand.

He looked down at me and smiled, a smile of pure love, more
intimate than if he had kissed me there.

She has accepted a role in my opera, Aristafeo said. They cheered,
and next Verdi said he had received my note regarding *I Masnadieri*,
which had pleased him. I am afraid I replaced you, but I do not care
for the singer if you are still available. I hoped you would come to
your senses; I can now replace her. Then he called out for champagne to be brought despite the early hour. The bottles were opened
and we toasted the two operas.

After we had drunk our toast and the glasses were refilled, Verdi
suggested we take them into the garden. As we went out, Giuseppina
said, I wish you more luck than we had with *Il Trovatore*.

What is this? Aristafeo asked.

It was a terrific struggle to get it to the stage, but I think they all
must be, she said, before she went to examine the shrubs along the
wall. Aristafeo followed, chuckling.

This is the garden that inspired the one in the opera, Giuseppina
said. Did you never know that? She asked this of Aristafeo, who
said he did not: and he asked her questions as to which part was
which as she took us around, pointing out the plantings. Verdi followed behind.

Did you originate the role? I asked her finally, as she finished her
explanations and Verdi and his protégé walked on ahead.

Oh, no, my dear. You may remember that I retired; I wanted some respite from operas coming true. She winked. But I translated the play he took it from for him, she said. I did most of the work here. And then when he wrote the opera, he walked here quite often to think on it. It's very pleasant here. In any case, I think of it as our opera, as you two should of yours.

She came to a stop. Imagine it, if you will, and she pointed back to the villa. Here is our *trovatore* come to serenade his beloved. There she is, waiting for him. Over there, the count hidden, jealous. Sometimes he would have me stand there and sing from it to see how it sounded.

I looked back. I could not see her. I saw instead a shadow, the Leonora of the night the tenor sang at the Théatre-Italien, the night I was given back to him. I could see him bringing me to Baden-Baden, full of hope that I would learn to be his Leonora there; I could see the garden at Villa Turgenev, where I sat imagining, again and again, the reappearance of the man standing near me now, my fearing his death, fearing us all caught in some game of Fate that would lead relentlessly to the place we apparently stood now and end with the two of us dead—the tenor our killer. I saw all that I had done to keep Aristafeo and me from this garden, and so I could not help but feel as if being here this way was yet another joke between me and whatever god had chased me for so long. Despite all my efforts, we stood here, so very alive. And the one we'd feared was dead.

I laughed. It was the wrong sort of laugh, I knew—this laugh spoke to the joke, the one this god had made of my life, and not to my companions, who could tell there was something strange to it and who watched me, waiting to know more. I set the champagne down instead, pointed at my glass, my hand over my mouth, as if the wine were at fault, at which they all three smiled as I mastered myself.

Afterward, the Verdis excused themselves, and Aristafeo and I were left alone. We sat on a bench in the cold sunshine and made our next plan: He needed us to travel to the Russian empress at once to secure her approval of the commission. Only after securing that approval would he then return to Paris and officially end his ties with the Baroness. When he returned from that trip, our new life together would begin in London.

He withdrew the tiny rose, my knife, and my old route book, and set them on the bench between us.

Until then, he said. Let them remind you of me.

~

After his departure, I decided to speak with Doro about her notice again and returned to my rooms.

When I'd given Lucy her notice, she had been simplicity itself; she said she understood. She had always been sweet to me, content to do her one job well, and if she'd ever stolen from me or cheated me, I never knew it. After I provided her with a letter of reference and a reward for her long service and loyalty to me, she'd hugged me and we agreed she was to leave shortly after my return to Paris. Doro had scoffed and refused, however, insisting I would need her, and . . . I had needed her. This, in turn, had shamed me a little — my resolve looked foolish. We both knew I relied on her good humor and gossip, as well as her ways of tending my hair and clothes, and looking after the upkeep of my accommodations, were they in Paris or Milan or Saint Petersburg. But I was now what I had once pitied, the grand lady with too many gowns and jewels, and not enough friends she could trust, and Doro was the companion I saw every day who knew most of my secrets, if not all of them, and of whom I knew very little. I disliked this. I still did not know where in Italy she had come from, for example; and during our time here, she'd never spoken of it despite insisting on this return. I thought to begin there when I saw her by the dresser, a strange expression on her face.

Are you sad to leave? I asked, as she packed our things.

I am, she said. I have a presentiment that I may never see Italy again.

I would speak to you again about your next placement, I said. I am moving to London, and I would see you taken care of, placed in a new situation. Here, even. Madame Verdi might need someone with your talents or be able to help place you.

She paused—she had been smoothing my coat—and then said, That's very kind. Thank you. I will take that under consideration. I meant to ask sooner, she said. I found this empty flask on your dresser back in Paris. It smelled faintly of *pétrole*. What is it for? Will you need it again soon? Should I ask the Verdis if they have *pétrole* to refill it?

I had been so sure it was in the Seine, this frightened me; it was as if the tenor's ghost had brought it himself. How had I been so stupid to keep it? And yet I had. I remembered I had put it in my pocket and now it was here.

The flask gleamed in her hand. She held it up, turning it so the light reflected on it, as if my silence meant I didn't recognize it.

How strange, I managed to say. I don't know anything about it. Perhaps it is Lucy's?

I think not, she said. But it is safe; we will discover the rightful owner. And with that, she put it away. I did not think there had been malice or suspicion in her voice; she seemed only genuinely puzzled, but I was not sure. As she did this, I noticed the bed, where a modest black suit was laid out for me, waiting like my own shadow.

What is this? I asked.

I thought mademoiselle would wear mourning, she said.

And why?

Your fiancé is dead. This is customary.

You know he was not—

If I may, Madame Verdi did not seem to know why you were not in mourning. She asked her maid as to it. *She does not seem to mourn him. She did not even cry out at the news of his death.* Her maid told me when she asked of it to me. I said, no, you were bereft, of course, but when you left Paris, he was still alive. You are in shock.

This surprised me—she had just been so happy for Aristafeo and me. Yes, I said. Of course. But you of all people know I was not engaged, I said. Did you not tell her maid this also?

I did not say. I don't gossip about you, she said. If you wish Madame Verdi to know this, would you not tell her yourself? I feared offending you. But may I be frank?

Of course, I said.

You should not return to Paris. Not for some time.

What? Why not?

Mademoiselle should go directly to London. In Paris you will most likely be under suspicion for the murder of your tenor friend. And if you should not appear in mourning, whether here, on the train, or in London, suspicion for his death will fall on you—especially if you are seen with your new lover. The police will always look for the surviving fiancée who does not grieve—and who takes up with another man in public immediately.

And here the sunlight coming in from the window behind me seemed to flash like the sword of an angel. Michael himself swinging it down.

I stared around me at the dark wood furniture lining the elegant guest room as if it offered protection.

Are you feeling faint? she asked. I can call for the salts.

No, I said, and, finding a chair, sat, at last in shock.

We will dress you in that suit, she said, pointing at the bed. And we should leave at once. Downstairs, ask Madame Verdi about where we may go to purchase a mourning toilette in Sant'Agata. I'll enter and say there was a telegram, that you are needed back in Paris urgently, and we will leave, but we will go directly to London instead. And you should not return until the murder is solved and the killer is found.

Mademoiselle, she said, when I did not stand. We should be on our way.

Giuseppina was both sad to see me go and also, I could see, pleased to see me dressed in black. The shock of my conversation with Doro neatly masked me as someone finally beset with grief. When I asked as to where to purchase a mourning toilette in town, she began to weep as well—I had forgotten that, of course, they knew him. A bell rang, and shortly after, Doro appeared to announce there had been a telegram, and we were to leave for Paris at once. Verdi fussed, made me the present of an unwieldy ham for the journey, and both of them kissed me and conveyed condolences of such heartfelt sadness that they made me ashamed of my bringing these theatrics with me as I bid good-bye to them and the sweet golden rooms of their home.

We went in the Verdis' carriage to the train station, and on Doro's advice, I bought tickets for travel through Switzerland rather than France so as to avoid any French authorities. Once we were on the train, Doro took out her cards and dealt me into a game of piquet I was grateful for, playing in quiet nearly half the way to Zurich.

Do you truly imagine you will not need a lady's maid in London? Or do you have one there already? she asked.

I shook my head. I've not even a household yet, I said.

And will you bring nothing from Paris?

I want nothing of it, I said. I want to begin with new things. All new things.

I don't, she said. It was very kind of you to offer me help finding a new position, but I am an old woman or will be soon, and it would be hard to learn the ways of a new mademoiselle, she said.

England will be strange to you, I said.

Not as strange as a new mademoiselle, she said. Bring me with you. I can be new, too.

I studied her then, waiting for her to meet my eyes. I was, in fact, contending with a new maid—she was a stranger to me now. Who had she served before me? From where came all of this knowledge of avoiding the police? When she looked up at last, she smiled, and I returned the smile. I will have Lucy do an inventory of the house in preparation for the sale, she said. I will instruct her to put black paper over the windows, to continue ordering food as normal, and to refuse all visitors, saying you are grieving. And we will get you as thick a veil as they make. You must go in secret.

She set down her cards.

Thank you, I said to her. She withdrew the bottle of gin she kept and poured us each a glass. I had been waiting for it, afraid to ask for it, and drank deeply. She refilled my glass, clucking. I hope they have gin in London, I said, and she laughed at me, and then we played on.

Eight

I WENT TO LONDON dressed in black, like a crow, a bird of death. Even my jewels had to be black except for those emeralds, which I could wear because they were his, at least according to Doro. If anyone should ask, it will look like devotion, she said. And if anyone asks as to the ring, she added, pointing at Aristafeo's ring, tell them it was a gift from him as well.

She reasoned that this would be enough to placate Aristafeo while I was in mourning for another man. I did not believe it would, but I resolved to try.

On arrival, I checked into a lavish suite at Brown's Hotel to console myself. I gave them a name I invented on the spot, Peloux Martineau, a somewhat lugubrious name that I forgot instantly so that each time the staff used it to speak to me and deliver the newspaper I'd ordered, they would have to repeat themselves until I remembered, embarrassing them and myself both. I was out of practice.

The newspaper was my vigil, my widow's walk. I bought the *Times* each day as Aristafeo was to take out an advertisement in the paper when he arrived, saying he had lost a falcon and giving instructions for the return of the bird "if it was found." He would give an address and I would write to him there. There was no way for me to get a message to him any longer — and I was in London as we'd agreed, just earlier than we'd agreed.

It was strange to be able to speak English to everyone. I found the words difficult to remember and my accent uncertain, much the way my French had been ten years before.

The first task at hand was consuming. Doro was busy instructing me on how to shop for my mourning toilettes—I kept nearly calling them costumes—and so we began at once.

I had always liked black, but only when I chose it. Not like this. I resented the way the foyer to this new life would be decked in black. All to hide his blood. Even in death, it seemed, I would dress for him. Even in death I would make false names because of him, would deny my lover because of him. And, of course, the color would be black. The black madness I knew so well from him now poured over my whole life in a flood after his death. I had killed him hoping to free myself of it and of him, to save the little world I hoped to make without him, only to discover there was no corner of it where he did not reach. The blow I had struck rang still, the rays of it spreading, and now I would see if what was left without him could hold. But as I donned the new black dresses I would spend the year in, I knew there was every chance that destroying him was as likely to destroy me.

After several days of such shopping, I found myself in front of a window to a store that seemed to sell only Chinese things. I had been to a milliner nearby, examining black hats and toques, black-jet hair combs, and any number of veils. I was rebelling, drawn to any color, first the beautiful gold thread and then the jewel colors in the satins, and so I stepped inside.

I found myself before a case of coins, Chinese coins, curious to me because of their square centers.

You want to see how they work? the proprietress asked, and drew the case out of the vitrine. She put them in her hand and shook them so they jingled lightly. She was Chinese also, with a whiskey voice, her skin white like a mushroom, the wrinkles on her face ridged like the veins of leaves. She had spent her life before this in the sun and was, I could see, much older than I had thought at first. Her silver hair she wore tight in a bun where it sat like a tin cap.

If it's a coin, I know how it works, I said.

She laughed. I will show you, she said.

She lit a piece of incense, handed me the coins, and directed me on how to shake and throw them like dice, six times. She counted out whatever this measures, and in ink drew a character much like I could see on the coins. She looked at it long and hard, and this is what she said to me: When the earth opens up under your feet, be like a seed. Fall down; wait for the rain.

Wait for the rain, I repeated.

Yes. Rain is coming, she said. Everything you lose you get back. She folded the paper into my hand and pressed it shut.

It would be the first time, I said, as I pocketed it. I thanked her, offered to pay her, which she accepted.

Back out on the streets of London, each person passing me appeared like the shape of a Fate, and the feeling didn't leave me until I shut the door to my hotel suite, alone with Doro and the British cook she'd hired for me, there with supper ready.

I asked the new cook if she believed the fortunes of fortune-tellers when she set my plate down.

I'll show you your future, milady, she said, and then she smiled as she pointed at the plate.

$$\sim$$

When Aristafeo came at last, I nearly shouted when I read the ad; I had almost given up.

Here is your lost falcon, I wrote, and included a card from Brown's. He came the next evening to take me to dinner and met me with a cab at the hotel.

I suppose I thought he would expect me in mourning dress. His eyes lost some of their light when he saw me. I was dressed in an evening cloak trimmed in black mink over my black dinner gown, a black hat covered in black feathers, a trim little veil. I had even bought black furs, anxious to at least enjoy myself.

Must you, he said, as he took my arm and led me from the lobby.

I must, I said. Six months, a year.

Even the veil? he asked, as he sat beside me.

Yes, I said.

It's like looking at him every day, he said.

Yes it is, I said. For me as well. I took the veil off then, and as I did, I made sure he saw the ring.

That's better, he said, and then he kissed me chastely, as if we were being watched.

By the end of the first evening, we were restored to each other. Soon we were making plans for our trip to Saint Petersburg and our audience there. He spoke of how *Un Ballo in Maschera* was being performed there at the Royal Opera, and we agreed we should see it. He said he would make the arrangements so we could write to the Verdis of it as we left for Russia.

~

A single item consumed me, however, more important than any of these mourning clothes.

The flask.

I could think of nothing else other than how to get it back.

Every singer knows to be careful of her dressing table; it is its own kind of stage, an intimate one. Most of her secrets appear there. Admirers often sought to give gifts so they would be displayed and thus warn off another suitor. And if you wanted to make someone jealous, you left out something they would not recognize—you could even buy it for yourself.

This tiny bottle, it was the size of my death if I did not get it back; I knew it. But having disavowed the flask, I couldn't think of how to ask for it. Doro was never not in the room when I was there. She found London odd and a little dull, she said, when I offered to give her a day off.

How funny to think it so, she said to me, when she told me this. I had expected more of London.

I had expected more also. I'd imagined finding a house in London where Aristafeo and I would be alone at last, no reminders of our life previous except each other. I dreamt of a simpler life, one where I would sell my jewels, furnishings, gowns, all down to the last trinket. Everything would be new.

Instead, I had left nothing behind, it seemed. Or, at least, not what I had hoped to lose. As Doro wrote to Lucy to tell her to sell my things, I thought of the fortune-teller telling me I would get everything back. I only hoped she meant the flask.

Nine

As the veil had bothered Aristafeo so much, I left it off when I dressed for the opera the next evening and had even assured myself I would not be recognized. Mourning only mattered if you were known to those watching. But the London audience outside the Royal Opera, to my surprise, recognized me immediately as we exited our cab. The low mutter came: *Is it her? Is it her? It is, it is,* and then *La Générale,* and just as someone might have come forward to introduce himself, just as I felt that flush of something like pride at being recognized, Aristafeo ran to speak with an acquaintance of his, leaving me alone with the public gathering around me.

We were the guests of his friends in their box. I wore a jet silk velvet gown cinched to the waist and black velvet gloves beaded with jet, this to set off the tenor's emeralds. Their color was the rich green that is called poison green — why, I have never known.

Poison, in my experience, is always hidden; it seems to me we never know its color.

As the murmur of the crowd grew, another elegant carriage drew up to the entrance. This one adorned with the unmistakable insignia of the French Empress-in-exile, now simply known as Eugénie de Montijo.

She had come for the Royal Opera the same as we, she now a somewhat extraordinary resident of London's suburbs. Her driver leapt down, knocked out the footstool, and opened her door. I glimpsed her looking off to the side as if she waited for something more than this to summon her from the depths of the carriage.

She stood, still a regal beauty. She wore black as well, though she was no longer officially in mourning—the Prince Imperial's death had been three years before, in summer, and with him had gone the hope of a restoration. France had meanwhile shouldered on, as if the imperial return she'd hoped for were out of the question and the Empire and the excesses of it and the excesses of its fall were all the sorts of sins democratic elections could atone for in the Third Republic. The papers were still full of discussions of imperial excess, even now. And everywhere, still, was the ostentatious false piety regarding luxury.

Which is to say, it was easier to wear these emeralds in London.

I stood there, full of my old longing to run to her, to make her smile again as she had once smiled at me. It would have only frightened and confused her, though. What's more, I wanted to be sure she did not recognize me as she stood uncertainly in the cold night air and stepped down from the carriage. While I am sure there is a way to greet one's ruler in a foreign land, I did not know it, and so instead, with a suddenness that surprised me, I dropped into my old servant's curtsy and threw myself at her feet, my face pressed into my skirt.

The London crowd, momentarily stunned by my appearance and then hers—her celebrity, her air of tragedy and fallen empire, her hair white since the Emperor's death and illuminating her still-fragile beauty—reacted with shocked silence.

I'm told she paused to smile down at me with affection, as the reports all said later.

It was not the manner of this curtsy to look up.

The British newspapers reported the French singer Lilliet Berne, the famous Falcon soprano who never spoke in order to protect her voice, greeted her Empress-in-exile with the full grand curtsy that night. The grand curtsy was very different, though, performed at the balls the Empress had once thrown, done when one was presented to her. That curtsy was performed by sinking noiselessly to the floor and pressing one's face into the skirt of your gown as you held it out to the sides, so that the woman performing it resembled a bloom that had fallen on its face. You then rose up again and dipped, your face tipped down, your head, and, what's more, your hair never above the height of her eyes, before you sailed on, making room for the next lady coming in behind you.

But this was not what I had done.

The newspaper's writer also assumed her smile was a memory of having heard me sing, but I wonder if she ever had or if she remembered something else if she did, in fact, smile: her New Year's balls, the Tuileries, the dances at Compiègne. Or perhaps it was simply the pleasure of seeing the emeralds along my neck, reminding her of her own — my taste in emeralds came from handling hers. It is almost certain to me she did not recognize the girl who'd once cared for her furs and put away her jewels, the one who had packed her for Compiègne, waiting for her to ring all those times in the back stairs of her palaces, running to her at once at the sound of her bell. Until she ran away.

The girl who also had so foully betrayed her, in other words. And if she did recognize me, it may be she smiled for seeing that girl bow to her one more time. For, of course, she had seen my neck the most of all.

Afterward, as Aristafeo rejoined me, after she had moved on, we toasted our luck in avoiding recognition by ordering champagne in our box. He laughed at how something as simple as a bow or curtsy could disguise one. I felt sure the evil I'd feared coming for us had passed over us now. And that this luck of ours had come about because we were together finally.

And so we toasted a long life together, full of this luck.

We could see her in the distance. Her white halo of hair in the royal box across from ours glowed in the gaslight, she the guest of the Queen, of course, her opera glasses flashing or, mostly, turning to an unseen friend to make remarks on what was certainly not the opera.

I had not wanted to see her again in Aristafeo's company; after all that had transpired, it seemed too much. Now, though, I could think of it all more easily. Still, the moment in Aristafeo's library when I lifted the musket returned. The memory of her scent, the sight of her nightgown. Her bracelets on the table.

The ruby rose from the Emperor that I'd set down beside them.

I understood finally something I had never understood before then. The Emperor wore no ruby flowers. My ruby token, it had been from her.

The Emperor, the Comtesse, the Empress. Their loneliness had made a back passage through all their lives, and I had spent so much of my life there. It was fitting, it seemed to me, that I should see her here like this.

For theirs had been my loneliness, too.

I should have known her for the omen she had to be, there in the dark. It was fitting that I should see her right before this departure. She in her exile some sign of my own to come. The Comtesse having hunted us both here. But I did not.

Instead, I wondered if she had known the way I was used against her or if I was only a secret between the Emperor and the Comtesse, a counter in the secret battle they had waged. I would never know. Those were always the terms.

And then the opera began, and we watched as Amelia, the soprano lead, searched the execution grounds for an herb of forgetfulness, eager to rid herself of the memory of sinful passion. I had the thought I always had at this point in the opera: *How young she must be to think an herb could take something like this memory away.*

～

In the paper the next day, the item of our meeting ran with a caricature of us, THE EMPRESS AND HER GÉNÉRALE.

The item read: *At last night's performance of Verdi's* Un Ballo in Maschera, *the attendees outside were greeted to another performance, that of Paris's own La Générale, Lilliet Berne, greeting her Empress-in-exile Eugénie with that most proper French curtsy, bringing a smile to*

her face and gasps from the crowd around her. No doubt the sight of her
subject-in-exile giving her this honor warmed Eugénie's heart.

We were drawn with doll's bodies and the enormous outsized
heads of dolls. Her crown was drawn askew, of course, giving her
the appearance of being confused or drunk. And I, I appeared to
be the picture of servility, my general's coat drawn over my gown
despite my having left it at home; I wore it only when I wanted to be
recognized.

The item soon made it to Paris, where it was repeated in the
French papers with the same caricature and a great deal of public
outrage. I should not, as a patriot, have greeted her this way, to do
so was to declare oneself still her subject. Was I a monarchist? And
so on. And what's more, speculation ran as to why I was there at all,
as I was thought until then to still be in Paris, in mourning for the
tenor.

This was not the beginning of our good luck, then, but the long
shadow's first fall. It was not where we thought it would be, and so
we did not see it for what it was.

~

We left for Russia the next morning. From the Empress-in-exile we
then went for an audience with another, reigning under a near permanent midnight at the end of the Baltic Sea in her palace of crystal
and mirrors. Our trip was long but urgent—if we waited any longer
the sea ice would soon make the trip impossible.

At first, I thought the Russian Empress had sensed that the opera
was not precisely *for* her, much less her son, in the way any woman
who's become an empress can tell these things. She was a patroness
of the arts with a sapphire the size of an infant's face in her crown.
And the face of a child herself. She was a beautiful woman, Maria
Feodorovna, but with large sad eyes. She looked as if she were the
fisherman's wife whose husband had caught the magic fish and the
jewel of wishing, the one she uses to wish herself a palace—and
finds herself lonelier than she thought.

During our audience, I watched my reflection in her sapphire as I sang for her the opera's major arias in the mirrored recital room of her frightening palace. I knew not to look directly at an empress's eyes, and so I looked instead into the sapphire.

A peculiar hunger, that for sapphires. I wanted to reach out and pluck it from her brow, to press it against my cheek.

I forgot myself only once and looked down to see her terrified eyes look back. I pitied her what I saw in those eyes. My song never broke. I swept my eyes down farther as if this were only a part of the dramatic gesture.

At the conclusion, she was polite, but she rejected the opera commission, declaring it, with its cast of animals and circus freaks, too expensive to produce on the stage anywhere in Europe.

Perhaps the Prussians can afford this, she said, with a dark look at us both. With their war duties.

I tried not to laugh at this, for how clearly it was a lie. The opera had been written precisely to anticipate the extravagance of a young Russian prince's celebration. The animals alone wouldn't have cost more than the jewels on one of her slippers that day. As she pronounced against it, I listened as if I were very far away. I watched as Aristafeo accepted her decision politely, for she was an intelligent woman somewhere under the enormous gems.

I knew her sapphire, then; I was sure it had been Eugénie's. There on her brow a fortune enough to set us up for the rest of our days, though it would appear not to have been enough to rescue Eugénie after all.

We were to have stayed for a fortnight. He had expected to audition other singers, to speak to animal trainers, to meet the orchestra. Instead, we were told we could return the next day.

Who'd have thought the Russians were paupers now, he said, once we were at sea again.

She spent all their money on that sapphire, I said. I should have had you trip her and I'd have snatched it.

The Prussians, he said. Are they so rich?

They are, I said, melancholy to think of it.

It's said she's a beauty, he said, of the Empress. What did you think?

I liked the sapphire, I said. What did you think?

I liked the sapphire, too, he said.

~

An opera too expensive for the Russian Empress attracted a great deal of talk; and gossip, sometimes kind, found the composer and his soprano lover returned to Paris the more famous for their defeat in Saint Petersburg, complete with great reviews: My performance of the arias was said to have been astonishing. And wasn't this likely be the last role to which I would consent?

Aristafeo had taken rooms at Brown's on our return from Russia, down the hall from my own so as to be closer to me. I listened from within my bed as he read these reports to me, and while I tried to be as amused as he seemed to be, I wondered who had spied on us and how they had traveled back more quickly than we.

He did not wonder. Instead, as he set the papers down, he was all confidence, convincing me of the soundness of his new plan to stage the opera in London after my run in *I Masnadieri*—with the Empress's dismissal, we were free of the Baroness's last favor to him. And so we made the rounds of the British theaters for a week, giving our presentation, and I let go of my curiosity as to our enemies. Our next new future seemed possible, after all, and now our little spy in Russia wouldn't matter. There was a new lightness to that week, the one I had waited for. But these theaters all eventually rejected the opera as well, in the same spirit as the Russian Empress, complaining of the costs, of having to clean after manure, of animal smells, questions of where the animals could be stabled. All of this was published in the gossip columns with speculation that the failure of the opera to find a home was perhaps related to my voice's famous curse, and I thought again of that day in Rouen when I entered the Baroness's château, the garden covered in her deathless roses. The circle of chairs in her ballroom full of opera's most powerful men.

I knew she could turn them toward him; I knew she could turn them against him.

The wind out of the forest in Rouen that never stops, the chairs turning and turning, for and against, for and against. That wind had reached all the way to the Russian Empress, no doubt the author of her rejection before we had even arrived. And that rejection would be the least of it.

A letter came from Verdi asking me to withdraw from *I Masnadieri*. The resultant scandal in Paris over my curtsy to Eugénie meant there was an unreasonably hostile atmosphere to me there, and so the production was endangered financially, and did I understand?

At first I did not—the production was to be here in London, not in Paris, but then I did understand all too well. Aristafeo's Baroness had reached even Verdi.

I wrote back to Verdi and told him that of course I would withdraw from *I Masnadieri* and offered to withdraw from *Un Ballo in Maschera* as well. When this letter was ready to send, I called for Doro to send it, and when she did not appear, unlike her, I checked her room.

I found it empty of even her things.

Only a note waited on the empty vanity, addressed to me. The Castiglione insignia was pressed into the red wax seal.

I see you are in London, having found a way to grovel to that woman still. I am writing to say I reviewed our agreement and have taken my price. Our business is now concluded.

To be sure, never return to Paris again.

Nicchia

The curse now the least of my troubles.

Ten

I STOOD VERY STILL in Doro's room, the note in front of me.

I had wondered who Doro had worked for before the tenor hired her, but, of course, Doro could only have belonged all this time to the Comtesse, much as I had. An agent in the tenor's household, bound there as well.

All those years I had wondered as to the four hundred, the Italian assassins waiting for the Emperor to fail in his devotion to their cause—Doro could only have been one.

Doro, then, good, kind Doro, who always had the answers no matter the question, giver of cards and gin, on her way from the hotel to the train, the train to the ferry, most likely at that instant on a boat back to Paris, the little metal flask in her bags. She would soon be in that apartment on the Place Vendôme, all the windows sealed in black, watching as the Comtesse lit her candles in order to examine her newest gift. I knew how long the trip could take; I had perhaps three days at best before the Paris police would begin their hunt for me, and this was provided they had not already begun.

When the earth opens up under your feet, be like a seed. Fall down; wait for the rain.

Everything you lose you get back.

The fortune-teller's words mocked me almost as much as the Comtesse's.

I felt myself dropping, again and again, into that curtsy before the Empress, the skirt of my gown rushing up at me as I kept falling, falling all the way into the underworld, falling down into the darkness.

If only I had worn a veil that night . . . but I had not. I had wanted a night where he could look at my face in public and not first frown.

That sly pickpocket, love, who will ask you to let down your guard and make a mark of you to the world. What finds you next will take everything and leave nothing.

I resisted the urge to run down into the street, to shriek Doro's name, to try to follow her and catch her. I knew she was gone; she was surer than I. She always had been. I ran back to my rooms instead.

~

Aristafeo waited there, looking up, faintly cross as I entered. You're not ready for dinner, he said. What's wrong?

My maid has left me, I said.

Ring for one from the hotel, he said, as if that would be all of it. Maids left you, after all, all the time.

I did as he said, and a hotel maid arrived, clucking her disapproval as I explained mine had left suddenly. Did she steal from you? this new maid asked me, and I nearly laughed to think of the answer. She then asked me if I would need her to go through my things with her to be sure they were all there. I found I was afraid of maids now and told her I would do it myself.

I dressed instead, in yet another elaborate mourning costume, this one with a black feather ruff, the bodice shining with black beads, a black fur cuff for the cold, black ostrich shoes that gleamed so that my feet were like that of some even stranger bird, hoping to make myself brave; but this costume was nothing, and as I sat before Aristafeo at dinner, I still felt myself falling, the speed quickening, and the wind of that passage and its growing hush of fear were such that I could not make out what Aristafeo was saying to me, not until he asked, Are you listening? What is troubling you? And I knew I would need to speak to him.

He raised an eyebrow.

The maid still? The Italian one, Doro, the one you've had all this time?

Yes, I said. We were close.

Advertise the position at once. I am trying to speak to you of something quite serious, he said. You must write to the Paris police. The papers say they are searching for you, hoping to ask you questions.

So, I thought. *There would be less time than I'd hoped.*

Here I am, I said. Will they come to London?

The Paris papers publish stories on the murder each day. The police patrols along the Seine have doubled as they search for what is now believed to be a savage band of killers. They have questioned his mistresses, his household staff, and now they search for you. He nodded his head as he said this, as if toasting me.

His mistresses. This amused me. Of course there would be many.

You smile, he said. Why?

How do they say he was he killed? I asked. For I knew I should ask.

Someone slit his throat and then set him on fire, he said, and then they tossed him in the Seine. When the police found him, they only knew him by a letter in his coat's pocket, his address there. It was dry enough to read.

He paused here. The newspapers say it was from you.

I never wrote to him in advance, I said, but even as I said it, I knew the note was my own, accepting him, telling him to meet me that night. The meeting he had abandoned for the duel I had kept him from fighting.

Worn over his heart.

Aristafeo picked up his glass, and looked deeply into the wine inside, and then added, I would have given him a better death; I would have shot him just the once. This was what I told the police when they questioned me.

I said nothing, for there was nothing to say to this.

They told me they found his money on him—he had not been robbed. Who would kill him and take only his life?

So he was killed by a rich man, I said. Someone who wouldn't think to rob him. He had many enemies, and only a very few of them needed his money.

You must write to the police, he said.

Of course, I said. Of course.

It can perhaps wait until we return to Paris, for we must find a theater there now. But you could write in advance that you will come and answer questions.

And here it was. I could not go back to Paris. Already our little dream of a life here in London was dead.

Of course, I said, instead. I will write to them. I'm not the killer. If I'd wanted to be rid of him, I would have married him.

The joke was wrong even as I said it, as the silence after it told me. We finished the dinner this way, quietly, alone again with what I could not say and what he would not ask.

I would not go back to Paris, and I would not write this letter, and I think he knew this also.

I've upset you, Aristafeo said finally, setting his fork and knife down, and patting his mouth with his napkin.

No, I said. I came to dinner upset; I am much the same.

Do I have your word you will write the police and clear your name? he asked.

Yes, I said. I will explain how I was en route to Milan.

Any witnesses? he asked.

My maid, I said. The one who left. But perhaps they can find her.

He asked the waiter for our bill and waited for it to be brought, unable to look at me.

I was like the cat pretending it had not swallowed the bird or, really, the bird who had swallowed the cat and was now too heavy to fly away. He was tired of these lies and so was I, but still I could not tell him the truth.

~

After dinner, as we ascended the stairs, he told me he would be leaving Brown's for cheaper rooms until our return to Paris. He went down the hall, and I waited for him after I had undressed; when he did not appear at my door as was his habit, I went to him, letting myself in after he did not answer my knock.

I nearly feared he had already left, but when I let myself into his suite with the spare key he'd given me, I found him asleep, the smell of brandy sweet in the air, rising off him.

I sat in the chair beside the bed, and as my eyes adjusted to the dark, I remembered the way his music sprang up from under my fingertips that day in my own Paris music room, it was like the visit from his ghost I had never had.

All because he was alive, of course.

And yet while that ghost had never visited me over the years, his phantom had never left my side.

There had never been a place for that impossible life born all those years ago in that kiss. All those years he had worked in secret in that woman's château to prepare a glorious future for us, he had been so sure it was only waiting for us to step into it. What was increasingly clear, however, was that the ground behind us was vanishing as quickly as the ground in front of us was refusing to appear. And the sacrifice I had made to the gods out of the tenor, it would not be enough.

It seemed the gods would take this, too.

I would not be questioned, I knew. There would be no mercy. Yes, the brute who had killed the tenor was surely a monster. No clean death, no; there was no honor to it; but I had wanted to do more than kill him. I had not wanted honor. I had wanted to remove him from this world. I had made myself that monster with my long tongue of flame burning through the night to chase him from this life. Burning, it seemed, even my voice.

Or the *pétrole* was not to blame. Or I had sung too much this season. Perhaps my adventure outside my *Fach* as the Queen of the Night had truly changed my fate, if for the worse — my voice breaking on it like so many others had.

I was sure Aristafeo heard it; the voice now lacked the liquid quality it once had. He had never said if he ever wondered whether the rejections were due in part to this, but I had. There had been no cracks since the one in *Carmen*, and I could hide the loss some in vibrato, but the voice's little failures terrified me for the way they signaled this other end I knew was near, an end I knew he would hear approaching. I could pretend for a while it was due to fatigue after a heavy season, that the voice could heal with rest, but only for a while.

Without my voice, I would soon be only that hated thing, an eccentric courtesan in her twilight. I was pretty enough still; I always had been. But any true beauty I had was here in my throat — all those gentlemen admirers had taught me that, looking at me as if the one thing they could not see were right before them. Once it was gone, even if I had murdered no one, I knew what the Comtesse knew, what Eugénie knew, what Cora Pearl surely knew — what we all sought to forget.

In this world, some time long ago, far past anyone's remembering, women as a kind had done something so terrible, so awful, so fantastically cruel that they and their daughters and their daughters' daughters were forever beyond forgiveness until the end of time — unforgiven, distrusted, enslaved, made to suffer for the least offenses committed against any man. What was remembered were the terms of our survival as a class: We were to be docile, beautiful, uncomplaining, pure, and failing that, at the least useful. In return, we might be allowed something like a long life. But if we were not any of these things, by a man's reckoning, or if perchance we violated their sense of that pact, we would have no protection whatsoever and were to be treated worse than any wild dog or lame horse.

A woman murderer, she would be treated the worst of these. I could not be caught.

If the loss of my voice was the only price I paid for killing the man who had made me a singer, I might still be a fortunate woman. But it wouldn't be nearly enough to be fortunate this way at all.

I could wake him, I knew. I could ask why he had not come to me that night. He would protest, insist it was only drink and tiredness. I had been waiting for him to say he needed to go back to Paris to placate the Baroness—I had thought he would slip away, run from his failure, and mine, and return to her, beg her forgiveness. I never wanted to hear him say it and preferred, if he was to leave me, that he did so without explanation or even a good-bye. Now he had mentioned Paris tonight, and here he was, in his room and not mine. A first, tiny departure.

I forgave Aristafeo then for knowing the truth I would not tell him and for being driven to drink by it. I forgave him for not being able to make me confess. I forgave him for giving up, for his intention to leave me. I leaned down and kissed him lightly in case either he or I left before I could kiss him again. And then I returned to my own rooms for such sleep as I could find, where I stayed half a fortnight without leaving.

And so we find ourselves near the end of my tale.

Eleven

MORE LETTERS CAME. One from Verdi, saying he accepted my offer of withdrawing from both operas and that it was very kind of me. Not one but two letters from Pauline as well, desolate at the news of the tenor's death— *The papers say he was set on fire and then drowned! What monster could do this?*—and upset that I had not accepted a grieving call from her, turned away by my maid. *Why would she not tell me you were away? I have not told the men the news of the murder,* she said. *They are not well enough.*

My heart ached to think of this.

There was a note from Euphrosyne as well. *If you leave me once more without saying good-bye, never come to look for me again.*

She knew. And if they knew to find me here, the police would as well.

I wrote back with some little lies. I wrote to Euphrosyne and assured her I would be back soon. I wrote to Pauline and apologized, telling her I would see her on my return. I wrote to Verdi and asked him to forgive me—this was sincere.

I had written meanwhile to Lucy to inquire as to the sale of my things and to see to the money being sent to me. A letter came from the concierge instead to say the apartment was empty, ready for a new tenant, and would I like to let it or sell? She had my address from the letter to Lucy, which had waited unopened, arriving after she had left. It never reached her.

This pleased me somehow, despite my shock, and I laughed. I had never suspected that at the end Lucy would steal everything down to the forks. That she would put any bandit to shame. I laughed as it was what I had wanted, for every remnant of that life to vanish as if it had never been. I wanted the past to die to me, to let me go; I wanted the relief of vanishing. And with the tenor dead, I might really escape this time, unlike the others. But this was the moment to steal away.

Instead, I stayed in bed, seeing only Aristafeo when he chose to come for short visits neither of us could quite endure. Each day I thought on how I had meant to leave at once, and to my amazement, I could not bring myself to do so. There seemed to be nowhere to go. Each hour made the need for a departure more urgent, but each hour also made departure feel the more impossible.

My rooms collected dishes and dresses, unkempt without Doro's regular tidiness — the hotel's maid was unreliable. I had not opened the curtains. To see any of it repulsed me. I began to send the newest clothes back, hoping to seek refunds and discounts, afraid of needing to withdraw the money from that Prussian reward given to me by the Prince — that seemed sure to bring the tenor back from the dead — though I feared also discovering that it too was gone as well.

The Prince, if he guessed, would either never forgive me the crime or never forgive me that I had killed his beloved heldentenor first.

I had finally separated them forever.

That monster they searched the Seine for, then, in London, having made her own chains as I always did.

～

When Aristafeo called on me last, he entered with a very different air about him — circumspect, cautious, managing a tiny smile even as he grimaced at my rooms. I assumed he was there to say his good-byes, and I was about to send him away before he did.

Get out, I said.

They've asked me to come in and see if you'll let them clean. But I have news. Make yourself presentable, he said to me, looking to the mess around him. Order a bath. Perhaps two.

Why?

Le Cirque de Monde Déchu has a new suitor, he said.

Who could have more money than the Russians?

Americans, he said. Thunder broke overhead as he said this, as if to remind us we were still on stage in a drama, and so I laughed, and he did as well.

~

All the years I'd lived in Europe, the Atlantic had seemed impassable and return impossible. But as the coach sent for us drew up to the front of Brown's, as I stepped into that coach, I did so as if I were leaving on the trip itself. Thunder broke overhead and then the carriage roof became a drum for the rain. By the time we arrived, the streets soon ran with water, and so the doorman came out to offer to carry me across.

P. T. Barnum was a man who knew how coins worked.

The notorious impresario had read of our troubles in the newspapers and was intrigued. A circus opera too expensive to be staged anywhere in Europe was a cheap circus to Mr. Barnum. And a cursed soprano, a gold mine, his London agent said, as he pushed a sheaf of papers across the desk to us.

Barnum had telegraphed him after reading of our news, instructing his agent to make an offer. Contracts, he said, as he gestured to what he had put before us. He proposes a tour of America. A hippodrama, his agent said. Do you know them?

I nodded.

The agent then spread his hands in the air, and as if he read from a headline there, said, *One of Europe's most famous singers comes to America, running from a curse that might take her life. Only here, in this show, the last she has agreed to be in, can she be seen for one last time.*

He put his hands down. You'll be rich. We'll all be rich.

Bill it as a farewell tour. It would run even if you lose your voice, if you like, he said. If that happens, we can hide someone behind you and have her sing. We'll have you say good-bye until all the good-byes are said. So, a year, maybe two. He drummed his fingers on the desk, a sound like the drumroll of a circus, and then lifted his hands in the air, palms spread.

You *are* retiring, yes? To marry? This the lucky suitor? And here he glanced at Aristafeo, and I did as well. He looked at me, and I could see he was eager to leave.

Think it over, take one night, the agent said.

In the carriage Aristafeo was silent until we drew close to our hotel.

Defy your fate, he said, very quietly.

What do you mean? I asked.

Don't do this. Don't become this.

This is what I always was, I said. There is nothing to become.

I thought to compel you once, he said, to blackmail you. When you first refused, I thought I will force her to do this, I will make her free herself. But then I did not, in the end, because I knew you would never forgive it from me.

I only waited. I would not sign the contracts in front of him, but I had already decided to sign.

The curse wins after all, he said. You were right. Did you know this all along? You warned me that if you said yes you would be a circus rider again, and here you are.

Change the ending, I said. Give her back her voice, keep them together.

No, he said. She must lose her voice. It is what she traded for her soul.

I knew he was right, as did he.

And how will I know if I win it back? I asked.

You'll lose your voice, he said. Perhaps you'll lose everything. Even me. Everything but that.

He signed the contracts and left me sitting in the carriage, and as soon as the door was closed, I ordered it back the way we came.

~

Barnum's agent expected me, laughing a little when I disturbed his dinner.

I'd waited too long as it was.

I could feel a palpable relief at his smile. He knew me, much as I knew him—we were of that same peculiar family that finds itself time and again. After so much time trying to learn the ways of this place that I was leaving, it was a relief to find myself feeling at home.

As I handed the contracts over, he asked, There's no real curse, is there?

I only smiled.

We will need to hire a troupe for this show that can enact a hippodrama, the agent said, as he signed the contracts. But not one committed to the silent traditions of French pantomime. One that will permit singing.

I may know of one, I said.

Twelve

I FOUND THEM WHERE the route book said they'd be. At the edge of the rail yard in the outskirts of London. As I approached, it looked as if a group of children held ropes, struggling to hold on to the world's largest kite. They had the faces of angels and the determination of demons. As I grew closer, it was clear it was an enormous new tent and that some of the strugglers, in fact, *were* children, but others looked to be the smallest small people I'd ever seen. A few looked me over as I approached.

What is it? one asked.

What does it want? It's looking at us.

Find out what it wants!

It's a tart, so it wants what a tart wants! And at this, they laughed and yet did not stop pulling.

It's pale! It's the Ice Queen herself, come to take us away!

They were speaking several languages to one another, but they all seemed to understand, and as I listened I felt a pang of home-coming.

You there, the show isn't till much later. Go on, before we're strung up on morals charges. This was said in some very odd French with a grin by a very small man. But thanks for coming by.

I took my card from my pocket; but before I'd finished handing it to him, he said, Oh, darling, I can't read a lick of that, I'd bet. He took the card from me and passed it behind his back, holding it so someone there could read it.

It wants a job!

Ach, darling. Much, much needs doing around here. And he waved at the tent that was still rising.

He likes it! He's . . . he's flirting with it!

At this, he took off his hat, bowed to me, and then, as he stood up, backhanded the young boy who'd just said that, who sneezed in surprise, and shouted, Don't make me fall!

Darling, he said, you'll need to speak to *la maîtresse*. I don't know if she wants anyone what can read, though. That's probably more trouble to her than it might be worth.

It can't have my spot!

Ah, no one's got their eye on that.

No one's had their eye or anything else on it in years!

With that, there was again much general laughter.

What does it do? Ask, ask!

Yes, darling, my inquisitor asked. What *do* you do? That is what we need to find out for you to be useful. It's better in the circus if you can do many things. So let's see, simple yeses and nos . . . can you . . . can you sew?

I nodded.

There's not . . . well . . . we darn our own costumes here. Or we have at least.

Can it tumble!

I smiled at that and nodded again.

Can it tumble from a horse!

I nodded once more.

It's a kinker, I knew it!

Nah, it's a chava josser, isn't it?

If it is, she's like none I've ever seen. I couldn't bet on it. She's a kinker, you can tell. She's got a talent somewhere.

I'm a kinker, to be sure, I said at last. And I'm here to hire you all. But for now, I would speak with Ernesto.

At this they laughed. Ah, so it's like that, said one of them. It's coming home, is what it is.

And then Ernesto appeared from behind a corner of the tent and roared as he ran toward me; sweeping me into his arms, he lifted me to kiss my face, my feet dangling at his hips. Oh, sweet girl, thank God, he said. I've missed you so.

~

I sat together with Ernesto for a little while at the hotel tent, over mugs of beer, as we waited for Priscilla, now the new boss. When I asked after Flambeau, he only shook his head. His absence like an omen.

You're lovelier than ever, he said finally. I can't get over it. Look at you. Who'd have thought you were ever our little Settler's Daughter? He reached down and plucked at the dress I wore, which swept out around the edge of the booth. You could fit a team of you in there.

He swept his hands up. I can't fancy that you're here to come back.

I am, I said.

But you're a woman of means now, as we can see.

I explained myself.

A hippodrama? he said.

Yes, I said. And I'm paying.

~

I could not vanish as I had hoped I might. I instead needed to put myself once more at the center of the public's eye as the cursed soprano. News of the curse would be my letter to the police and my escape from the police both.

I sent a statement to the press through Barnum's agent, asking them to my rooms at Brown's and saying I would make an announcement concerning my imminent retirement.

All questions would be answered in writing.

I suppose I did not believe what I would do until the appointed hour, when, under the watchful eye of the agent and his assistants, I opened the door to my suite myself, dressed in my best widow's weeds and the tenor's emeralds, and welcomed the crowd I found there inside.

I was inside my love's opera, I knew, very near the ending. If the curse was true, and it did seem to rise up around me, as if it would become the very ship that would take me back to America, then I would sing for Aristafeo at least once more, somehow, before losing my voice forever—perhaps regaining my soul if it had ever really been lost. His opera and its fate for me even protecting what had been true so far of us, may be true once again: Aristafeo delivered to me, his steps away from me once again leading back to me in some way neither of us could imagine.

If not, I would never see him again. But the only way to know was to go away and see.

And I would accept no other role until he was at my side.

Each answer I wrote to the journalists in my room was like a signature on this contract with Fate.

When did I know of my curse? I first guessed after my debut as Amina, when my only love returned to me after I had lost all hope.

The tenor's death has left me terribly changed. I loved him dearly. But you see, the news of his death told me this curse, it was coming for me next.

In *Un Ballo in Maschera*, the husband of the soprano Amelia is murdered, his fate sealed by a fortune-teller. I knew I could not take the stage after it was reported he'd died.

In death, then, one last role for the tenor to play with me. And then a last message for Aristafeo, left here.

You may understand then why it is so important to me to per form this last role, to create the role as written for me. The worst that might happen? That I would lose my voice.

When I returned, I went to the desk to pay for Aristafeo's rooms with some of the new money from Barnum, but he was gone.

Epilogue

LE CHARME OPÈRE. The spell works.

The crowds begin at the pier the day we arrive, vast and dark, wet from the rain, like a funeral for a head of state.

On seeing the gangplank lower, they say my name as if singing in a discordant round, *Lilliet Berne, Miss Berne, Lilliet Berne, Miss Berne, vive La Générale!*

The gangplank lands on the dock and even the crew is cheered by the crowd until I emerge. At the foot of it waits one Mr. Frederick March, Mr. Barnum not in sight.

I'd know later the reason Mr. Barnum hadn't been there—there'd been one more journalist to strong-arm, one more feature story to run. The morning editions of the New York papers waited for me at my hotel, all with stories of the diva who'd fled the stages of Europe for fear of a curse, here now to perform on her final farewell tour, this circus her first official visit to America. As I stood finally in the air and the cheering crowd roared, I raised my hand to keep out the rain and waved to them.

My name, taken from the little graveyard by the East River, hadn't sounded like the stolen thing it was in years.

Mermaids and nightingales, Columbus wrote, of what he saw in the New World. *Creatures of music, monstrous and fair.* I was home.

~

The Americans favor a dark color, at least in New York, the people there colored like crows and sparrows. When I make my first entrance, on a trapeze decorated like a crescent moon, I feel them below me, the heat of them rising through the cold night air, the tobacco, the smoke, the cologne, and the perfume all together. I watch the jewels of the women flash in the dark as I descend. When I look down, the indigo silk panels to the backdrops, hung to make it look like night, are not as dark as the crowd, and so it looks, each time as I enter the ring, as if some of the real night from outside has come inside to wait below me.

My future, then: a traveling show, a hippodrama with a year-long tour featuring two stars, a beautiful young man from Paris who plays the captured angel and me. And now we are in trains, the opera about a circus now a circus opera; and the crowds move in and out, all applause and tobacco, oily smoke off the tapers; and the tents rise, fill, fall. The angel wears taxidermy wings taken from a condor and isn't, according to the posters, allowed to fly because then he might "escape." He holds me tightly instead from behind as I ride the horse with him around the tent, the wings flapping in an imitation of flight. The man himself never wants to leave, and sometimes neither do I.

Though there's only one escape I long for now.

The boy who plays the angel in our show is from Pest. He's unspeakably beautiful, taller than aerialists usually are, with pale white skin to match my own and long dark hair that flies in the air behind him like a flag. He's from a family of aerialists; his family has performed in circuses for at least a century. Perhaps since the birth of Christ. He launches himself into the air with only a rope tied to the roof of the tent. The prop master and the taxidermist used three normal condor wings each to make them. No living thing has ever used them to fly.

Of course, if there's wings that can't be trusted, I want to try them on.

At night, I go to the train's roof with him. When the cars wait patiently in the dark for some night procedure, and as the trainmen shout to one another, he hands the wings up to me, and I slide the harness on. As he ties them in place, a passing wind tugs the nets of feathers, bones, and glue, and I can feel where, if the harness wings were to grow into place, these might allow me to shrug up into the air. In the sky my eyes follow the path of the wind's gesture. I see for a moment as if from the place I would have gone to then, the distant train below me, how this boy would stare at me as I left, soaring.

I watch that spot as he comes behind me and undoes the knots, and then we return to our compartments. Alone again, I draw back the curtains and watch the sky until the vertigo and the wishing go away.

I had always imagined any return home would wait until after my death when perhaps, at my mother's Lord's command, this would be His only mercy to me, that I would have those wings. *What kind of angel would I be?* I ask myself. And yet I know. I'd ride storms like they were old ponies, sing off-key from behind the statue of Saint Mark, organize the pigeons to scald the bishop's miter with their dung. But I would obey finally, at the end, for the chance to fall from the sky's belly over the ruined farm, wings spread wide, in a gown as dark as crows, the angel face so bright the lightning dims. I'd obey for the chance to be the one who comes for her then, on the Lord's return. To open her grave, me hidden in that final storm she waits for to wash her tenderly from the ground under my direction until she is clean again. Until she should feel newborn.

~

When I make my entrance now on the trapeze swing, the tent painted to look like the sky at night, I want it then, ask for it from God. As I step to the ground, the applause sounds to me at moments like hard rain. I try not to search for the places in the sky where I would be if I could fly. And yet, the wind at my back, this new appetite awakes, and I do.

For now, it seems, the heroine is separated from her lover by the act he had hoped would bind them. I can feel the miles run under me, and I hope, by the tour's end, I will know which was greater, curse or fate. Soprano or song.

In my compartment at night, where I write this now, I draw back the curtains and see myself in flight, riding down the dome of the night sky, the stars a road descending to the composer's windows in London. Knocking on his shutters, I would be wearing the Russian Empress's sapphire crown, our ransom lifted gently from her sleeping brow. My first stop.

New ending, I would say, and press a finger to shut the lower lip of his astonished mouth. *The equestrienne steals the angel wings.* And then the wings would swing shut around us both.

And I would tell him, as we rise into the air, *The curse is not that we cannot choose our Fates.*

The curse, the curse we all live under, is that we can.

Historical Notes and Acknowledgments

This novel began one day in 1999 after a conversation with the late David Rakoff on the street in the East Village of New York City. He told me a long story about the opera singer Jenny Lind, the Swedish Nightingale, starting with her discovery as a child at her music lesson, overheard from the street, and ending with her mysterious early retirement and her subsequent two-year farewell tour of America promoted by P. T. Barnum—a tour that left her a very rich woman.

I am pretty sure David called her a nineteenth-century Cher.

By the time I got home that day, I had an image of an opera singer on a train, singing in a circus at night, and making her way across the United States, her life full of secrets.

A little research quickly showed that what I'd imagined wasn't anything like the real Jenny's life. But I liked my shadow Jenny better—and I knew she was the seed of a novel.

I still don't know why David told me that story. I just know that if he hadn't, I would never have written this novel. I cannot express how much I regret that I did not finish in time for him to read it. Any acknowledgments could only begin with him.

~

This is a work of fiction. Lilliet bears only the lightest resemblance to Jenny Lind—she is not Swedish, but American born, and sings in an era where Jenny Lind is a vivid memory, not a rival. If she is meant to resemble anyone, it is Pamina, from *The Magic Flute*—this book is meant as a reinvention of the Mozart opera as a novel.

There are many historical figures in these pages, however, and many texts proved invaluable as a resource. I have listed them in order of appearance with any credits regarding sources.

Giuseppe and Giuseppina Verdi came to life for me first in the letters of Giuseppina Verdi, translated as a part of Hans Busch's *Verdi's "Aida": The History of an Opera in Letters and Documents*; I was also aided by *Verdi: A Biography* by Mary Jane Phillips-Matz.

The scene with Cora Pearl's famous performances in *Orpheé aux Enfers* and then her party afterward is a fiction based on a fiction and derives from the description of the performance and afterparty that appeared in Zola's *Nana*—Zola based Nana partly on Cora, but had Nana sing the role in his novel. Some of those performance details were confirmed in Cora Pearl's autobiography, *The Memoirs of Cora Pearl*.

The description of Eau de Lubin was made possible by the distinguished French perfume house Lubin, who shared their ancient recipe with me; I am grateful to them, Colleen Williams, and Barbara Herman, who put me in touch with Lubin as the scent is allergenic and so isn't available now; thank you also to Brian Chambers, who helped me understand how the fragrance would wear.

The character of the Comtesse de Castiglione was drawn in large part from *"La Divine Comtesse": Photographs of the Countess de Castiglione*, the catalogue from the Metropolitan Museum of Art's show of the photographs Pierre-Louis Pierson took of the Comtesse. One of those photographs, from the series called "The Opera Ball," is used in the cover design with permission from the Metropolitan, and I'm especially grateful to them for this, and to the designer of the cover, which I love. Thank you also to all of the contributing scholars: Philippe de Montebello, Pierre Apraxine, Xavier Demange, Françoise Heilbrun, and Michele Falzone del Barbarò. As I read their catalogue essays and footnotes, a picture appeared of a woman who was often underestimated as decorative all while she wielded tremendous political influence—and who was also not without wit and an eye for revenge. Very little of the political role of the Comtesse was invented—she really was sent at nineteen by the Italian embassy to seduce the Emperor Napoleon III to Italian reunification; she was blamed partly for the assassination attempt on his life as it was thought she controlled the Italian assassins hidden in Paris; she had a Prussian prince friend who took her to the showing of her portrait by Pierson in a boat along the Seine; she was in weekly mail contact with Adolphe Thiers over the three years leading up to the destruction of the Second Empire; she befriended the Orleanists; she appears to have met with Bismarck to spare Paris from shelling; after she returned to Paris, she lived for quite some time protected by the Paris police, on orders from her correspondent Adolphe Thiers. Her apartments in this novel are imagined as much as they could be from the available descriptions in the catalogue. It is my hope that this story respects her for being the political spymaster she appears to have been, at home and abroad, even if the plot is imagined. This plot is the sort of assertion a historian can't make, but that a novelist can.

For the Tuileries Palace details and the details of the lives of the Emperor Napoleon III and Eugénie, I relied on *Life in the Tuileries Under the Second Empire, By Anna Bicknell, An Inmate of the Palace*, the autobiography of a British governess to the Duke and Duchess de Tascher. The story of the parrot who learned to swear from her maid's lovers comes from there, as well as my portrait of Pepa, the Empress's confidante, and the noble sisters who hated her, and also my description of all of the Empress's habits at the Tuileries. For the Empress at Compiègne, I used *In the Courts of Memory*, the letters of Lillie Moulton, the American soprano and wife of Charles Moulton; she was a close friend to the Emperor and Empress, and a regular guest at the imperial series at Compiègne. From her letters came the stories of the Empress sitting in war councils in the afternoons, her ladies-in-waiting angry at the snub; the schedule of the day; the hunts in a given week; the costume balls and skits and affairs. The *poupée dérangée* scene is drawn from the letters most closely, in particular the joke made by the Prince Metternich and the lyrics to the songs. That scene in her letters occurred at approximately the time Lilliet would have been in the palace, so I knew I had to put Lilliet into it. Moulton's letters are also the inspiration for the guest character the tenor tries to seduce, though there is no sign she was ever unfaithful to her husband in life. I don't use her name in the story, but I hope Moulton is enjoying one last pantomime in disguise from the beyond. I mean that character as a tribute to her.

Moulton also kept careful record of her lessons with Delsarte and Pauline Viardot-García's brother in those letters, which contributed to the novel as well.

The gossip in the Tuileries Palace comes primarily from the Bicknell but also from *Pages from the Goncourt Journals* by Jules and Edmond de Goncourt, in particular from their records of the regular complaints of the Princess Mathilde. I also drew from those diaries for the details of Lilliet's life during the Siege and the Commune. Alistair Horne's *The Fall of Paris* was especially valuable for the way it described Paris's preparations for the Franco–Prussian War and the Amazons of the Seine program. The list of furs left behind when the Empress fled was republished in Rupert Christiansen's *Paris Babylon* from a British newspaper at the time, and I altered it with the addition of the otter Lilliet steals and places in her room. I also relied on his *Tales of the New Babylon* for information, timeline, and local color during the Siege and the Commune.

The details of the intimate life of the Turgenev and Viardot-García set in Baden-Baden—and the collaboration between Turgenev and Viardot-García—come from the works of Patrick Waddington, in particular his monograph *A Probable Detente*. Most of this is available through JSTOR, along with Viardot-García's letters, translated by Waddington. These were the model for the letters by Pauline, and so thank you also to JSTOR. The portrait of Pauline's teaching methods and the teaching book of exercises come from her own published course book.

The Waddington monograph was also my source for details

about George Sand's home life at Nohant, as were her autobiography, and her published diary. The German traveling version of *Hamlet* performed at Nohant is that much shorter version, *Fratricide Punished*, the Johannes Velten text. The Queen of the Night speech Lilliet reads aloud is my own translation, but the Furies lines are taken from the 1905 translation by Horace Howard Furness, available online, which were poetically superior.

The details of the war and the flight from Baden-Baden came from Waddington again and also from Turgenev's letters, published as *Turgenev's Letters*, the edition edited and translated by Edgar H. Lehrman. The portrait of Bizet and the scandal around *Carmen* derives in large part from Winton Dean's *Georges Bizet: His Life and Work*, and the introduction to Céleste Mogador's autobiography — Mogador was believed to be Bizet's muse for *Carmen*.

I am also indebted to the following: Arthur Goldhammer's translation of Emile Zola's *The Kill* and the Penguin Classic edition of Zola's *Nana*, translated by George Holden; *Nineteenth-Century Fashion in Detail* by Lucy Johnston; *Strapless* by Deborah Davis; *My Blue Notebooks* by Liane de Pougy; *Evenings with the Orchestra* by Hector Berlioz; *The Courtesans* by Joanna Richardson; *Courtesans* by Katie Hickman; *Grandes Horizontales* by Virginia Rounding; *Napoleon III and Eugénie* by Jasper Ridley; *The Price of Genius* by April Fitzlyon; Sarah Bernhardt's memoirs, *My Double Life*; *Mitsou* by Colette, and her collected stories, also *Chéri* and *The Last of Chéri, Gigi, Julie de Carneilhan,* and *Chance Acquaintances*; *The Circus Age: Culture and Society Under the American Big Top* by Janet Davis; *The Memoirs of a Courtesan in Nineteenth-Century Paris* by Céleste Mogador; Bertrand Bonello's excellent film *House of Pleasures*, and the two-volume graphic novel *Miss Don't Touch Me* by Hubert and Kerascoet; and *Voyage in the Dark* by Jean Rhys.

The opera lyrics quoted here are from my own translations.

As characters, Euphrosyne, the tenor, and the Prince are all imaginary. Aristafeo and his dogs, the Lords of the Lower Garden, appeared to me in a dream.

~

Thank you to my partner, Dustin Schell, who read drafts, made dinners, did laundry, paid the bills, talked me down off of whatever ledge I had managed to get on, and still met me with champagne when I was done. His love changed my life, and his readings dramatically improved the novel. I will thank him for the rest of my life, but here especially.

Thank you to my beautiful family, who were so patient despite the many vacations ruined by drafts and deadlines; thank you to my late father, Choung Tai Chee, who brought me up to love Italian opera and Russian novels, and thank you to my mother, whose stories of her childhood and her family informed the creation of Lilliet.

Thank you to my agent, Jin Auh, who I cannot thank enough, and everyone at the Wylie Agency. Jin loved this novel from the first few pages I sent a very long time ago and is the only person who's read this novel anywhere near as often as I have. I am so grateful for her enduring enthusiasm and her wisdom and hard work.

Thank you to everyone at Houghton Mifflin Harcourt but especially to my editors: Webster Younce, who acquired it; Andrea Schulz, for her enthusiasm and patience despite receiving me as an orphan, and her determination to bring this novel out; and to Naomi Gibbs, who has seen it in so many forms and whose thoughtful work on its intricacies made this final version possible. I'm very grateful to them all. Thank you to Marian Ryan and David Hough, my copyeditors, on the first and second rounds, respectively—the novel is buttoned up and ready for the ball because of you.

I am very grateful for the support this novel received from fellowships from the National Endowment for the Arts; the Whiting Foundation; the Massachusetts Cultural Council; the MacDowell Colony; Ledig House; the Civitella Ranieri Foundation; the Hermitage in Englewood, Florida; and the University of Leipzig. I am also indebted to many museums and libraries: the University of Rochester Library and Special Collections; Amherst College's Frost Library and Special Collections; the Performing Arts Library of New York at Lincoln Center; the special collections of the New York Public Library; the British Library; the Butler Library at Columbia; the Museum of Fashion in Paris; the Museum of the Decorative Arts; the Musée Nissim de Camondo; the Musée Carnavalet; the Musée Cognacq-Jay; the museum of the Empress Eugénie at Compiègne; the Metropolitan Museum of Art. This novel owes a special debt to the Center for Fiction Library, where much of it was written — thank you especially to Noreen Tomassi, Kristin Henley, Christopher Messer, and Matt Nelson.

I am very grateful to the many friends who helped with this novel. Thank you to Shauna Seliy, Kirsten Bakis, Patrick Nolan, Stan Parish, Steve Chasey, Melanie Fallon, Katie Horowitz, Rhonda Pressley Veit, Patrick Merla, Maud Newton, Catherine Chung, and Anna Keesey — you all provided much needed readings, encouragement, and insights. Thank you to Lauren Cerand for your faith in me and this novel. Thank you to Madalyn Aslan, who introduced me to the Falcon soprano legends. Thank you to Scott Miller for telling me about the superstitions of seamstresses. Thank you to Kera Bolonik, Meredith Clair, and Theo Bolonik, my Camp Knotty Pines family. Thank you to Chris Offutt, Roxana Robinson, Honor Moore, Liz Harris, and Anne Greene, my Wesleyan Writers Conference cofaculty who were such good listeners to this novel over the years, for their feedback and enthusiasm. A special thank-you to Edmund White, who helped me understand courtesans best of all. Thank you to Jami Attenberg, who made a pact with me to finish this novel — it helped. Thank you to Josef Asteinza for assistance with my research in Paris. Thank you to Gerard Koskovich for your many insights and historical research assistance. Thank you to Paula Lee for your general fact-check regarding France in the nineteenth century. Thank you to my Amherst College family: Daniel Hall, Peng Yew Chin, Judy Frank, Catherine Newman, Cathy Ciepiela, Marisa Parham, John Drabinski, John Hennessy, Gabe and Nick Hennessy-Murray, John Urschel, Sydne Didier,

Ron Rosbottom. Special thanks to Anston Bosman for the night we dressed up in sheets and played at being Hamlet—this inspired the scene at Nohant. Thank you to Barry O'Connell for the loan of his writing carrel in Frost Library while I was the Visiting Writer at Amherst—it was a glorious refuge. Thank you to Sabina Murray for the long talks about writing historical fiction and research. Thank you to the Amherst coffee crew—Mukunda Feldman; his wife, Kylie Feldman; Jay Venezia; Andrew Sanni; Jeremy Browne; Marisa Eva; Martin O'Malley; Claire Kavanagh; and Nick Brown—you all kept me good company. In Paris, special thanks are due to Matthew Hicks, my consummate guide to Paris, and Pascal Touin-Stratigeas, his husband, who together told me of the zoo at the Jardin des Plantes and inspired the scene set there. In Detroit, thank you to Leon Johnson and Megan O'Connell, Marlowe and Leander Johnson, and the Salt and Cedar Press crew. In Leipzig, thank you to Jennifer Porto, Andrew Curry, Avery Jennings, and Timothy Fallon, who told me about the heldentenor. In Berlin, thank you to Bill Martin, Libby Bunn Neumann, Peer Neumann, and Daniel Schreiber.

And finally, thank you to my readers, especially those of you who checked in over the years, waiting for this book. I'm grateful to you all.

Reading Group Guide

Topics for Discussion

1. What is Lilliet's belief in Fate? How does she see it ruling over her life? Do you think she is in control of her own actions? In what ways do you see her at the will of Fate and in what ways does she make her own way in the world?

2. "Your *Fach* was your fate as a singer, as far as roles went, and so no wonder if we felt our fates came from our *Fächer* as well" (page 478). What does it mean that she is a Falcon? How did it affect Lilliet's fate? What is the tenor's *Fach* and how does it compare to Lilliet's?

3. What is Lilliet's real name? What are some of her many nicknames and why does she have so many?

4. What is Lilliet's curse (or curses)? Do you think the curse is real?

5. How is Lilliet "the Queen of the Night"? Why is the book called this?

6. Why does Lilliet allow herself to be registered when she is arrested with Euphrosyne? Why is this so surprising to everyone else? Think about how and if characters are acting ac-

cording to gender norms of the day, and how they look to subvert them.

7. Look at the various role models Lilliet had—Euphrosyne, the Comtesse, Eugénie, Cora, her mother. What did Lilliet want for herself that these women didn't have? How did she set out to achieve that?

8. Discuss the importance of clothing and appearance in the novel. What do Lilliet's cancan shoes mean to her? How do men use the gift of clothing to their advantage? How does Lilliet's change of clothing in the opening scene change people's perception of her?

9. Who were Lilliet's voice teachers and how did each shape her as a person?

10. For Lilliet, what does it mean to be free? Are there any female characters in this novel who are truly free? Discuss the idea of freedom, how it has evolved for women since the time of the setting of this novel, and what it means to you.

~

A Conversation with Alexander Chee

Q: When did you begin writing The Queen of the Night?

My friend, the late David Rakoff, struck the match. I ran into him on the street one day, and he told me a story about Jenny Lind, "the Swedish Nightingale," a Swedish opera singer who famously retired very young in 1850. She'd long had problems with her voice, but that didn't seem to be the reason for her retirement, as she then toured the U.S. for two years in a farewell tour promoted by P. T. Barnum, doing nearly a hundred concerts and becoming a very wealthy woman. In the nineteenth century, she got a six-figure advance from Barnum for that tour.

By the time I got home that day, I had a picture in my head of a woman on a swing in the middle of a circus tent, descending into the ring, prepared to sing. When I finally looked up her life, a few days after that, I found she had done the more formal concert tour—no circus. I was disappointed, but then I thought, *Oh, you've fallen in love with a mistake. If you were to write a novel, it would be there, in the mistake.*

I woke up a few days later to the narrator's voice in my head. I was coming up out of sleep, my eyes closed: *When the earth opens up under your feet, drop down—be like a seed. Drop down, wait for the rain.*

Q: How did you find this plot for this novel?

I was interested in the way Jenny Lind had kept her reasons for leaving the stage personal. And I kept reading very different writers—say, Joan Didion and Oscar Wilde—say something very similar, which is, "Be careful what you write, as it comes true." This was interesting to me, especially given how my first novel ended.

That was when I got the idea of a cursed soprano, or, really, a soprano who fears she is cursed. And retires because of it.

I was also interested in how courtesans were often said to be spies back then, but we never get the story of what they've done. In any novel about them you can point to, they are written as decorative, ridiculous, even pathetic. Their power is usually romanticized in the wrong way. And in their memoirs, they are usually either overly pious or overly vague.

The Comtesse de Castiglione was perfect for me, then. She really was a spy; she really was the Empress's rival and the Emperor's most famous lover; she really did have a photographer photograph her for ten years in her most famous clothes. She really had a friend who was a Prussian prince, who really did take her down the Seine to see her portrait at the International Exposition of 1867. And she really did correspond weekly with Adolphe Thiers, starting in her widowhood, also in 1867—the Adolphe Thiers who would become the head of the provisional government of Paris after the fall of the Empire. And he really did order police protection for her when she returned to Paris after the war's end.

That last detail seemed most telling. Did she know he would be in power after the fall of the Empire? Perhaps. Perhaps she even picked him, in which case this was how he said thank you—and protected her from whomever she had angered by choosing him. There's a story everyone tells about her, that she intervened with Bismarck and got him to stop shelling Paris. The sentimental version is that she convinced him not to destroy the Louvre. But men like him don't stop bombs for sentiment. They stop because they are checkmated.

Pretty soon, I understood she would need a very special tool to do what she did—Lilliet—and then the rest of this plot appeared.

Q: How did you get so close to a character who is so different from you?

Some parts were easy, some hard. I sang in opera choruses as a child but was never an opera singer. A close friend from school did become a mezzo, and I thought she was the most thrilling singer I ever saw.

The novel's deepest inspirations come from my parents: my mother's stories of growing up on a farm in Maine, with her 300-year-old family graveyard behind the house. She really did have a relation with the story I gave to the Settler's Daughter. And my late Korean immigrant father, who believed that you weren't really educated unless you read the Russians—he would sing songs from *La Traviata* as he mowed the lawn. He's the reason Turgenev is a character in this book, and the reason I love Italian opera.

Q: So, somehow this came from "write what you know"?

Sort of. But I prefer to think of fiction as a way to think about something, a way of thinking that is entirely unique. So it is more like *Write what you're thinking about.* Or, *Write what you want to know.*

Lilliet, for example, doesn't feel she belongs anywhere. She feels orphaned by the world, not just her parents, like she doesn't belong, and that she must hide that from the world also—before she then feels the need to make her place in it. I've felt all of that, growing up mixed race and a writer—the novel let me explore it, as well as the experience of passing, of allowing people to believe what they need to believe about you. She's a shapeshifter, like me. That's very much a mixed race experience, for example, as well as a gay one, and while it wasn't intentional, it is no surprise to me to find it there.

Koreans, it should be said, love French culture and cooking. Every legitimate Koreatown in the U.S. has a French bakery staffed by Koreans. My aunt, the translator Chee Choung-Sook, translated Proust into Korean and studied literature at the Sorbonne. So while I know some of my original readers will be surprised by my second novel, in retrospect it makes complete sense to me. Though it was a surprise to me too, at the time I began.

Q: Given the whole novel was a surprise to you, what then was the biggest surprise for you in writing this?

That I wasn't really writing about the past. My research showed me a France run by a man who was uncultured, a bad public speaker, but who had become emperor, in part, because the previous republic had forgotten to make it illegal. He put "voting helpers" at the polls, was more popular in the countryside than with the sophisticates in Paris. He got the country into a war essentially to raise morale, and having spent the country into bankruptcy with his excesses, sent his soldiers into battle with bad equipment. And as there was very little freedom of the press, the stories in the papers were all about the sex lives of women celebrities. Does any of this sound familiar yet?

So much of the way we live our lives, even something like a celebrity not repeating a dress, began at this time. And yet the reasons are lost to us. I was most horrified by the lives of women then—and newly sympathetic to those who sought celebrity. It offered them protections, at least, until whatever gave them their celebrity was gone. We still live that way. Sometime around when Britney Spears shaved her head, I noticed that once a year, without fail, the whole culture seems to turn on a woman celebrity until she's destroyed, and I don't know why. This may be the real topic of this novel, down underneath it all.